COMMON MURDER

The Second Lindsay Gordon Mystery

by

Val McDermid

Spinsters Ink

Duluth, Minnesota

First published by The Women's Press Ltd., ©Val McDermid, 1989
A member of the Namara Group
34 Great Sutton Street, London EC1V 0DX
Reprinted 1993

Second edition published in 1995 by Spinsters Ink
10-9-8-7-6-5-4-3

Spinsters Ink
32 E. First St., #330
Duluth, MN 55802-2002

Cover design by Lois Stanfield, LightSource Images
Production: Lindy Askelin   Carolyn Law
             Patty Delaney   Jami Snyder
             Helen Dooley   Jean Sramek
             Joan Drury   Liz Tufte
             Kelly Kager   Lee Ann Villella
             Claire Kirch   Nancy Walker

Library of Congress Cataloguing-in-Publication Data
McDermid, Val, 1955–
     Common murder: the second Lindsay Gordon mystery / by Val
McDermid.
     p.   cm.
ISBN 1-883523-08-7 (alk. paper)
1. Women journalists–Fiction. 2. Lesbians–Fiction. I. Title.
PR6063.C37C65   1995
823' .914–dc20   95–23565
                                                          CIP

Printed in the U.S.A. on acid-free recycled paper

Also by Val McDermid:

Report for Murder (1987, The Women's Press, London)
Final Edition (1991, The Women's Press, London)
Dead Beat (1992, Victor Gollancz, London)
Union Jack (1993, The Women's Press, London)
Kick Back (1993, Victor Gollancz, London)
Crack Down (1994, Harper Collins, London)

Forthcoming:

Clean Break (1995, Harper Collins)
A Suitable Job for a Woman (Non-Fiction, 1995, Harper Collins)
The Mermaids Singing (1995, Harper Collins)

For my father

Acknowledgments

Thanks to: Helen for keeping us laughing at Greenham; Andrew Wiatr for advice on computers (any errors are mine); Diana for all the constructive criticism; Lisanne and Jane for their hard work; John and Senga, Laura and Ewan for their hospitality at the crucial point; Sue Jackson for her inimitable skills; and Henry the lawyer for letting me pick his brains.

1

"This is murder," Lindsay Gordon complained, leaning back in her chair and putting her feet up on the desk. "I can't bear it when there's nothing doing. Look at us. Eight p.m. on the dynamic news desk of a national daily. The night news editor's phoning his daughter in Detroit. His deputy's straining his few remaining brain cells with the crossword. One reporter has escaped to the pub like a sensible soul. Another is using the office computer to write the Great English Novel . . . ."

"And the third is whingeing on as usual," joked the hopeful novelist, looking up from the screen. "Don't knock it, Lindsay, it's better than working."

"Huh," she grunted, reaching for the phone. "I sometimes wonder. I'm going to do a round of calls, see if there's anything going on in the big bad world outside."

Her colleague grinned. "What's the problem? Run out of friends to phone?"

Lindsay pulled a face. "Something like that," she replied.

As she opened her contacts book at the page with the list of police, fire, and ambulance numbers she thought of the change in her attitude to unfettered access to the office phone since she'd moved from her base in Glasgow to live with her lover Cordelia in London. She had appreciated quiet night shifts in those days for the chance they gave her to spend half the night chattering about everything and nothing with Cordelia. These days, however, it seemed that what they had to say to each other could easily be accommodated in the hours between work and sleep. Indeed, Lindsay was beginning to find it easier to open her heart to friends who weren't Cordelia. She shook herself mentally and started on her list of calls.

Cliff Gilbert, the night news editor, finished his phone conversation and started checking the computerized news desk for any fresh stories. After a few minutes, he called, "Lindsay, you clear?"

"Just doing the calls, Cliff," she answered.

"Never mind that. There's a bloody good tip just come in from one of the local paper lads in Fordham. Seems there's been some aggro at the women's peace camp at Brownlow Common. I've transferred the copy into your personal desk. Check it out, will you?" he asked.

Lindsay sat up and summoned the few paragraphs onto her screen. The story seemed straightforward enough. A local resident claimed he'd been assaulted by one of the women from the peace camp. He'd had his nose broken in the incident, and the woman was in custody. Lindsay was instantly skeptical. She found it hard to believe that one of a group pledged to campaign for peace would physically attack an opponent of the anti-nuclear protest. But she was enough of a professional to concede that her initial reaction was the sort of knee-jerk she loved to condemn when it came from the other side.

The repercussions unfolding outside Fordham police

station made the story interesting from the point of view of the *Daily Clarion* news desk. The assaulted man, a local solicitor called Rupert Crabtree, was the leader of Ratepayers Against Brownlow's Destruction, a pressure group dedicated to the removal of the peace women from the common. His accusation had provoked a spontaneous demonstration from the women, who were apparently besieging the police station. That, in its turn, had provoked a counter-demonstration from RABD members outraged at the alleged attack. There was a major confrontation in the making, it appeared.

Lindsay started making phone calls but soon hit a brick wall. The police station at Fordham was referring all calls to county headquarters. Headquarters was hiding behind the old excuse: "We can make no statement yet. Reports are still coming in." It was not an unusual frustration. She walked over to Cliff's desk and explained the problem. "It might be worth taking a run down there to see what the score is," she suggested. "I can be there in an hour at this time of night, and if it is shaping up into a nasty, we should have someone on the spot. I don't know how far we can rely on the lad that filed the original copy. I've got some good contacts at the peace camp. We could get a cracking exclusive out of it. What do you think?"

Cliff shrugged. "I don't know. It doesn't grab me."

Lindsay sighed. "On the basis of what we've got so far, we could be looking at a major civil disturbance. I'd hate the opposition to beat us to the draw when we've got a head start with my contacts."

"Give your contacts a bell, then."

"There are no phones at the camp, Cliff. British Telecom has shown an incomprehensible reluctance to install them in tents. And besides, they'll probably all be down at the copshop protesting. I might as well go. There's sod all else doing."

He grinned. "Okay, Lindsay, go and take a look. Give me a

check call when you get there. I'll see if we can get any more information over the phone. Remember your deadlines—there's no point in getting a good exclusive if we can't get it in the paper."

"What about a pic man?"

"Let me know if you need one when you get there. I seem to remember there's a local snapper we've used before."

Five minutes later, Lindsay was weaving through the London traffic in her elderly MG roadster. She drove on automatic pilot while she dredged all she knew about the peace camp to the surface of her mind.

She'd first been to the camp about nine months before. She and Cordelia had made the twenty-mile detour to Brownlow Common one sunny May Sunday after a long lunch with friends in Oxford. Lindsay had read about the camp in one of the Sunday papers and had been intrigued enough by the report to want to see it for herself. Cordelia, who shared Lindsay's commitment to opposing the nuclear threat, had been easily persuaded to come along on that initial visit, though she was never to share Lindsay's conviction that the camp was an effective form of protest. For Cordelia, the channels of dissent that came easiest were the traditional ones of letters to the *Guardian* and MPs. She had never felt comfortable with the ethos of the camp. Cordelia always felt that she was somehow being judged and found wanting by the women who had made that overwhelming commitment to the cause of peace. So she seldom accompanied Lindsay on later visits, preferring to confine her support to handing cash over to Lindsay to purchase whatever necessities the camp was short of, from lentils to toilet chemicals. But for that first visit, she suspended her instinctive distrust and tried to keep her mind open.

The peace camp had started spontaneously just over a year before. A group of women had marched from the West Country to the American airbase at Brownlow Common to protest at the sitting of US cruise missiles there. They had been so fired by anger and enthusiasm at the end of their three-week march that they decided to set up a peace camp as a permanent protest against the nuclear colonization of their green unpleasant land.

Thinking back to that early summer afternoon, Lindsay found it hard to remember what she'd expected. What she had found was enough to shatter her expectations beyond recall. They had turned off the main road on to a leafy country lane. After about a mile and a half, the trees on one side of the road suddenly stopped. There was an open clearing the size of a couple of football pitches, bisected by a tarmac track that led up to a gate about 250 yards from the road. The gate was of heavy steel bars covered with chain-link fencing and surmounted by savage angled spikes wrapped with barbed wire. The perimeter fence consisted of ten-foot tall concrete stanchions and metal-link fencing, topped by rolls of razor wire. More razor wire was laid in spirals along the base of the fence. The gate was guarded by four British soldiers on the inside and two policemen on the outside. A sign declared "USAF Brownlow Common."

In the distance, the long low humps of the missile silos broke the skyline. Three hundred yards inside the perimeter fence were buildings identifiable as servicemen's quarters—square, concrete blocks with identical curtains. From beyond the wire, they looked like a remand centre, Lindsay had thought. They provided a stark contrast to the other human habitation visible from the car. Most of the clearing outside the forbidding fence had been annexed by the peace women. All over it were clusters of tents—green, grey, orange, blue, brown. The women were sitting out in the warm sunshine, talking, drinking, cooking, eating, singing. The bright colours of their clothes mingled and formed a kaleidoscope of constantly changing patterns. Several young children were playing a hysterical game of tag round one group of tents.

Lindsay and Cordelia had been made welcome, although some of the more radical women were clearly suspicious of Lindsay's occupation and Cordelia's reputation as a writer who embodied the establishment's vision of an acceptable feminist. But after that first visit, Lindsay had maintained contact with the camp. It seemed to provide her with a focus for her flagging political energies, and besides, she enjoyed the company of the peace women. One in particular, Jane Thomas, a doctor who had given up a promising career as a surgical registrar to live at the camp, had become a close and supportive friend.

Lindsay had come to look forward to the days she spent at Brownlow Common. The move to London that had seemed to promise so much had proved to be curiously unsatisfying. She had been shocked to discover how badly she fitted in with Cordelia's circle of friends. It was an upsetting discovery for someone whose professional success often depended on that mercurial quality she possessed which enabled her to insinuate herself virtually anywhere. Cordelia, for her part, clearly felt uncomfortable with journalists who weren't part of the media arts circus. And Cordelia was no chameleon. She liked to be with people who made her feel at home in the persona she had adopted. Now she was wrapped up in a new novel, and seemed happier to discuss its progress with her friends and her agent than with Lindsay, who felt increasingly shut out as Cordelia became more absorbed in her writing. It had made Lindsay feel uncomfortable about bringing her own work problems home, for Cordelia's mind always seemed to be elsewhere. Much as she loved and needed Cordelia, Lindsay had begun to sense that her initial feeling that she had found a soulmate with whom she occasionally disagreed was turning into a struggle to find enough in common to fill the spaces between the lovemaking that still brought them together in a frighteningly intense unity. Increasingly, they had pursued their separate interests. Brownlow Common had become one of Lindsay's favourite boltholes.

But the camp had changed dramatically since those heady summer days. Harassment had sprung up from all sides. Some local residents had formed Ratepayers Against Brownlow's Destruction in an attempt to get rid of the women who created in the camp what the locals saw as an eyesore, health hazard, and public nuisance. The yobs from nearby Fordham had taken to terrorizing the camp in late-night firebomb attacks. The police were increasingly hostile and heavy-handed in dealing with demonstrations. What media coverage there was had become savage, stereotyped, and unsympathetic. And the local council had joined forces with the Ministry of Defence to fight the women's presence through the civil courts. The constant war of attrition coupled with the grim winter weather had changed the camp both physically and spiritually. Where there had been green grass, there was now a greasy, pot-holed morass of reddish-brown clay. The tents had vanished, to be replaced with benders—polythene sheeting stretched over branches and twine to make low-level teepees. They were ugly but they were also cheap, harder to burn and easier to reconstruct. Even the rainbow colours the women wore were muted now that the February cold had forced them to wrap up in drab winter plumage. But more serious, in Lindsay's eyes, was the change in atmosphere. The air of loving peace and warmth, that last hangover from the sixties, had been heavily overlaid with the pervading sense of something harder. No one was in any doubt that this was no game.

It was typically ironic, she thought, that it needed crime to persuade the *Clarion* that the camp was worth some coverage. She had made several suggestions to her news editor about a feature on the women at the peace camp, but he had treated the idea with derision. Lindsay had finally conceded with ill grace because her transfer to the job in

London was a relatively recent achievement she couldn't afford to jeopardize. The job hadn't quite turned out the way she'd expected either. From being a highly-rated writer who got her fair share of the best assignments, she had gone to being just another fish in the pool of reporters. But she remembered too well the years of hard-working, nail-biting freelancing before she'd finally recovered the security of a wage packet, and she wasn't ready to go back to that life yet.

Jane Thomas, however, encouraged her to use her talents in support of the camp. As a result, Lindsay had rung round her magazine contacts from her freelance days and sold several features abroad to salve her conscience. Thanks to her, the camp had had extensive magazine coverage in France, Italy and Germany, and had even been featured in a colour spread in an American news magazine. But somewhere deep inside, she knew that wasn't enough. She felt guilty about the way she had changed since she'd decided to commit herself to her relationship with Cordelia. She knew she'd been seduced as much by Cordelia's comfortable lifestyle as by her lover's charm. That had made it hard to sustain the political commitment that had once been so important to her. "Your bottle's gone, Gordon," she said aloud as she pulled off the motorway on to the Fordham road. Perhaps the chance for redemption was round the next corner.

As she reached the outskirts of the quiet market town of Fordham, her radiopager bleeped insistently. Sighing, she checked the dashboard clock. Nine fifteen. Forty-five minutes to edition time. She wasted five precious minutes finding a phone box and rang Cliff.

"Where are you?" he said officiously.

"I'm about five minutes away from the police station," she explained patiently. "I'd have been there by now if you hadn't bleeped me."

"Okay, fine. I've had the local lad on again. I've said you're *en route,* and I've told him to link up with you. His name's Gavin Hammill, he's waiting for you in the lounge bar of the Griffon's Head, in the market place, he says. He's wearing a Barbour jacket and brown trousers. He says it's a bit of a stalemate at present; anyway, suss it out and file copy as soon as."

"I'm on my way," Lindsay said.

Finding the pub was no problem. Finding Gavin Hammill was not so simple. Every other man in the pub was wearing a Barbour jacket and half of them seemed to be alone. After the second failure, Lindsay decided to buy a drink and try again. Before she could down her Scotch, a gangling youth with mousy brown hair and a skin problem inadequately hidden by a scrubby beard tapped her on the shoulder and said, "Lindsay Gordon? From the *Clarion?* I'm Gavin Hammill, *Fordham Weekly Bugle.*"

Far from relieved, Lindsay smiled weakly. "Pleased to meet you, Gavin. What's the score?"

"Well, both lots are still outside the police station, but the police don't seem to know quite how to play it. I mean, they can't treat the ratepayers the way they normally treat the peace women, can they? And yet they can't be seen to be treating them differently. It's kind of a stand-off. Or it was when I left."

"And when was that?"

"About ten minutes ago."

"Come on then, let's go and check it out. I've got a deadline to meet in twenty minutes."

They walked briskly through the market place and into the side street where a two-story brick building housed Fordham police station. They could hear the demonstration before they saw the demonstrators. The women from the camp were singing the songs of peace that had emerged over the last two years as their anthem. Changing voices attempted to drown them out with "Close the camp! Give us peace!"

On the steps of the police station, sat about forty women

dressed in strangely assorted layers of thick clothing, with muddy boots and peace badges fixed to their jackets, hats and scarves. The majority of them looked remarkably healthy, in spite of the hardships of their outdoor life. To one side, a group of about twenty-five people stood shouting. There were more men than women, and they all looked as if they ought to be at home watching "Mastermind" instead of causing a civil disturbance outside the police station. Between the two groups were posted about a dozen uniformed policemen who seemed unwilling to do more than keep the groups apart. Lindsay stood and watched for a few minutes. Every so often, one of the RABD group would try to push through the police lines, but not seriously enough to warrant more than the gentlest of police manhandling. These attempts were usually provoked by jibes from one or two of the women. Lindsay recognized Nicky, one of the camp's proponents of direct action, who called out, "You're brave enough when the police are in the way, aren't you? What about being brave when the Yanks drop their bombs on your doorstep?"

"Why aren't the cops breaking it up?" Lindsay asked Gavin.

"I told you, they don't seem to know what to do. I think they're waiting for the superintendent to get here. He was apparently off duty tonight, and they've been having a bit of bother getting hold of him. I imagine he'll be able to sort it out."

Even as he spoke, a tall, uniformed police officer with a face like a Medici portrait emerged from the station. He picked his way between the peace women, who jeered at him. "That him?" Lindsay demanded.

"Yeah. Jack Rigano. He's the boss here. Good bloke."

One of the junior officers handed Rigano a bullhorn. He put it to his lips and spoke. Through the distortion, Lindsay made out, "Ladies and gentlemen, you've had your fun. You have five minutes to disperse. If you fail to do so, my officers have orders to arrest everyone. Please don't think about causing any more trouble tonight. We have already called for reinforcements, and I warn you that everyone will be treated with equal severity unless you disperse at once. Thank you and goodnight."

Lindsay couldn't help grinning at his words. At once the RABD protesters, unused to the mechanics of organized dissent, began to move away, talking discontentedly among themselves. The more experienced peace women sat tight, singing defiantly. Lindsay turned to Gavin and said, "Go after the RABD lot and see if you can get a couple of quotes. I'll speak to the cops and the peace women. Meet me by that phone box on the corner in ten minutes. We'll have to get some copy over quickly."

She quickly walked over to the superintendent and dug her union Press Card out of her pocket. "Lindsay Gordon. *Daily Clarion,*" she said. "Can I have a comment on this incident?"

Rigano looked down at her and smiled grimly. "You can say that the police have had everything under control and both sets of demonstrators were dispersed peacefully."

"And the assault?"

"The alleged assault, don't you mean?"

It was Lindsay's turn for the grim smile. "Alleged assault," she said.

"A woman is in custody in connection with an alleged assault earlier this evening at Brownlow Common. We expect to charge her shortly. She will appear before Fordham magistrates tomorrow morning. That's it." He turned away from her abruptly as his men began carrying the peace women down the steps. As soon as one women was carried into the street and the police returned for the next, the first would outflank them and get back on to the steps. Lindsay knew the process of old. It would go on until police reinforcements arrived and outnumbered the protesters. It was a ritual dance that both sides had perfected.

When she saw a face she recognized being dumped on the pavement, Lindsay quickly went over and grabbed the woman's arm before she could return to the steps. "Jackie," Lindsay said urgently. "It's me, Lindsay. I'm doing a story about the protest. Can you give me a quick quote?"

The young black woman grinned. She said, "Sure. You can put in your paper that innocent women are being victimized by the police because we want a nuclear-free world to bring up our children in. Peace women don't go around beating up men. One of our friends has been framed, so we're making a peaceful protest. Okay? Now I've got to get back. See you, Lindsay."

There was no time for Lindsay to stay and watch what happened. She ran back to the phone box, passing a police van loaded with uniformed officers on the corner of the marketplace. Gavin was standing by the phone box, looking worried.

Lindsay dived into the box and dialed the office copy taker's number. She got through immediately and started dictating her story. When she had finished, she turned to Gavin and said, "I'll put you on to give your quotes in a sec, okay? Listen, what's the name of this woman who's accused of the assault? The lawyer will kill it, but I'd better put it in for reference for tomorrow."

"She comes from Yorkshire, I think," he said. "Her name's Deborah Patterson."

Lindsay's jaw dropped. "Did you say . . . Deborah Patterson?"

He nodded. Lindsay was filled with a strange sense of unreality. Deborah Patterson. It was the last name she expected to hear. Once upon a time it had been the name she scribbled idly on her notepad while she waited for strangers to answer their telephones, conjuring up the mental image of the woman she spent her nights with. But that had been a long time ago. Now her ghost had come back to haunt her. That strong, funny woman who had once made her feel secure against the world was here in Fordham.

2

Lindsay stroked the four-year-old's hair mechanically as she rocked her back and forth in her arms. "It's okay, Cara," she murmured at frequent intervals. The sobs soon subsided, and eventually the child's regular breathing provided evidence that she had fallen asleep, worn out by the storm of emotions she'd suffered. "She's dropped off at last," Lindsay observed to Dr. Jane Thomas, who had taken charge of Cara after her mother's dramatic arrest.

"I'll put her in her bunk," Jane replied. "Pass her over." Lindsay awkwardly transferred the sleeping child to Jane, who carried her up the short ladder to the berth above the cab of the camper van that was Deborah's home at the peace camp. She settled the child and tucked her in then returned to sit opposite Lindsay at the table. "What are your plans?" she asked.

"I thought I'd stay the night here. My shift finishes at midnight, and the boss seems quite happy for me to stop here tonight. Since it looks as if Debs won't be using her bed, I thought I'd take advantage of it and keep an eye on Cara at the same time, if that sounds all right to you. I'll have to go and phone Cordelia soon, though, or she'll wonder where I've got to. Can you stay with Cara while I do that?"

"No sweat," said Jane. "I was going to kip down here if you'd had to go back to London, but stay if you like. Cara's known you all her life, after all. She knows she can trust you."

Before Lindsay could reply, there was a quiet knock at the van's rear door. Jane opened it to reveal a redheaded woman in her early thirties wearing the standard Sloan Ranger outfit of green wellies, needlecord jeans, designer sweater, and the inevitable Barbour jacket.

"Judith!" Jane exclaimed, "Am I glad to see you! Now we can find out exactly what's going on. Lindsay, this is Judith Rowe, Deborah's solicitor. She does all our legal work. Judith, this is Lindsay Gordon, who's a reporter with the *Daily Clarion,* but more importantly, she's an old friend of Deborah's."

Judith sat down beside Lindsay. "So it was you who left the note for Deborah at the police station?" she asked briskly.

"That's right. As soon as I found out she'd been arrested, I thought I'd better let her know I was around in case she needed any help," Lindsay said.

"I'm glad you did," said Judith. "She was in a bit of a state about Cara until she got your message. She seemed calmer afterwards. Now, tomorrow, she's appearing before the local magistrates. She's been charged with breach of the peace and assault resulting in actual bodily harm on Rupert Crabtree. She's going to put her hand up to the breach charge, but she wants to opt for jury trial on the ABH charge. She asked me to tell you what happened before you make any decisions about what I have to ask you. Okay?"

Lindsay nodded. Judith went on. "Crabtree was walking his dog up the road, near the phone box at Brownlow Cottages. Deborah had been making a call and when she left the box, Crabtree stood in her path and was really rather insulting, both to her and about the peace women in general. She tried to get past him, but his dog started growling and snapping at her and a scuffle developed. Crabtree tripped over the dog's lead and crashed face first into the back of the phone box, breaking his nose. He claims to the police that Deborah grabbed his hair and smashed his face into the box. No witnesses. In her favour is the fact that she phoned an ambulance and stayed near by till it arrived.

"It's been normal practice for the women to refuse to pay fines and opt for going to prison for non-payment. But Deborah feels she can't take that option since it would be unfair to Cara. She'll probably be fined about twenty-five pounds on the breach and won't be given time to pay since she'll also be looking for bail on the assault charge and Fordham mags can be absolute pigs when it comes to dealing with women from the camp. She asked me to ask you if you'd lend her the money to pay the fine. That's point one."

Judith was about to continue, but Lindsay interrupted. "Of course I will. She should know that, for God's sake. Now, what's point two?"

Judith grinned. "Point two is that we believe bail will be set at a fairly high level. What I need is someone who will stand surety for Deborah."

Lindsay nodded. "That's no problem. What do I have to do?"

"You'll have to lodge the money with the court. A cheque will do. Can you be there tomorrow?"

"Provided I can get away by half past two. I'm working tomorrow night, you see. I start at four." She arranged to meet Judith at the magistrates' court in the morning, and the solicitor got up to leave. The night briefly intruded as she left, reminding them all of the freezing February gale endured by the women outside.

"She's been terrific to us," said Jane, as they watched

Judith drive away. "She just turned up one day not long after the first court appearance for obstruction. She offered her services any time we needed legal help. She's never taken a penny from us, except what she gets in legal aid. Her family farms on the other side of town, and her mother comes over about once a month with fresh vegetables for us. It's really heartening when you get support from people like that, people you'd always vaguely regarded as class enemies, you know?"

Lindsay nodded. "That sort of thing always makes me feel ashamed for writing people off as stereotypes. Anyway, I'd better go and phone Cordelia before she starts to worry about me. Will you hold the fort for ten minutes?"

Lindsay jumped into the car and drove to the phone box where the incident between Deborah and Crabtree had taken place though it was too dark to detect any signs of the scuffle. A gust of wind blew a splatter of rain against the panes of the phone box as she dialed the London number and a sleepy voice answered, "Cordelia Brown speaking."

"Cordelia? It's me. I'm down at Brownlow Common on a job that's got a bit complicated. I'm going to stay over. Okay?"

"What a drag. Why is it always you that gets stuck on the out-of-towners?"

"Strictly speaking, it's not work that's the problem." Lindsay spoke in a rush. "Listen, there's been a bit of bother between one of the peace women and a local man. There's been an arrest. In fact, the woman who's been arrested is Deborah Patterson."

Cordelia's voice registered her surprise. "Deborah from Yorkshire? That peace camp really is a small world, isn't it? Whatever happened?"

"She's been set up, as far as I can make out."

"Not very pleasant for her, I should imagine."

"You've hit the nail on the head. She's currently locked

up in a police cell, so I thought I'd keep an eye on little Cara till Debs is released tomorrow."

"No problem," Cordelia replied. "I can get some more work done tonight if you're not coming back. It's been going really well tonight, and I'm reluctant to stop till my eyes actually close."

Lindsay gave a wry smile. "I'm glad it's going so well. I'll try to come home tomorrow afternoon before I go to work."

"Okay. I'll try to get home in time."

"Oh. Where are you off to? Only, I thought you were going to be home all week."

"My mother rang this evening. She's coming up tomorrow to do the shops, and I promised I'd join her. But I'll try to be back for four."

"Look, don't rush your mother on my account. I'll see you tomorrow in bed. I should be home by one. Love you, babe."

A chill wind met her as she stepped out of the phone box and walked quickly back to the car. She pictured her lover sitting at her word processor, honing and refining her prose, relieved at the lack of distraction. Then she thought of Deborah, fretting in some uncomfortable, smelly cell. It wasn't an outcome Lindsay had anticipated all those years before when, a trainee journalist on a local paper in Cornwall, she had encountered Deborah at a party. For Lindsay, it had been lust at first sight. As the evening progressed and drink had been taken, she had contrived to make such a nuisance of herself that Deborah finally relented and agreed to meet Lindsay the following evening for a drink.

That night had been the first of many. Their often stormy relationship had lasted for nearly six months before Lindsay was transferred to another paper in the group. Neither of them could sustain the financial or emotional strain of separation, and soon mutual infidelities transformed their relationship to platonic friendship. Not long after, Lindsay left the West Country for Fleet Street, and Deborah announced her intention of having a child. Deborah bought a ruined farmhouse in North Yorkshire that she was virtually rebuilding single-handed. Even after Lindsay moved back to Scotland, she still made regular visits to Deborah and was surprised to find how much she enjoyed spending time with Deborah's small daughter. She felt comfortable there, even when they were joined for the occasional evening by Cara's father Robin, a gay man who lived nearby. But Lindsay and Deborah never felt the time was right to revive their sexual relationship.

After she had fallen for Cordelia, Lindsay's visits had tailed off, though she had once taken Cordelia to stay the night. It had not been a success. Deborah had been rebuilding the roof at the time, there was no electricity, and the water had to be pumped by hand from the well in the yard. Cordelia had not been impressed with either the accommodation or the insouciance of its owner. But Lindsay had sensed a new maturity in Deborah that she found appealing.

Deborah had clearly sensed Cordelia's discomfort, but she had not commented on it. She had a willingness to accept people for what they were and conduct her relationships with them on that basis. She never imposed her own expectations on them and regarded her reactions to people and events as entirely her responsibility. It would be nice, thought Lindsay, not to feel that she was failing to come up to scratch. Time spent with Deborah always made her feel good about herself.

Back at the van, she brought in a bottle of Scotch from the car and poured a nightcap for herself and Jane.

"Are you all right, Lindsay?" Jane asked.

Lindsay's reply was drowned out by a roar outside, louder even than the stormy weather. It was a violent sound, rising and falling angrily. Lindsay leapt to her feet and pulled back the curtain over the van's windscreen. Fear rose in her throat. The black night was scythed open by a dozen brilliant headlamps whose beams raked the benders like prison-camp searchlights. The motor bikes revved and roared in convoluted patterns round the encampment, sometimes demolishing benders as they went. As Lindsay's eyes adjusted to the night, she could make out pillion riders on several of the bikes, some wielding stout sticks, others swinging heavy chains at everything in their path. It was clearly not the first time the women had been raided in this way, for everyone had the sense to stay down inside the scant shelter the benders provided.

Lindsay and Jane stood speechless, petrified by the spectacle. The van's glow seemed to exert a magnetic effect on three of the bikers and their cyclops lamps swung round and lit it up like a follow-spot on a stage.

"Oh shit," breathed Lindsay as the bikes careered towards the van. She leaned forward desperately and groped round the unfamiliar dashboard. What felt like agonising minutes later she found the right switch and flicked the lights on to full beam. The bikes wavered in their course and two of them peeled off to either side. The third skidded helplessly in the mud and slithered into a sideways slew on the greasy ground. The rider struggled to his feet, mouthing obscenities, and dragged himself round to his top-box. Out of it he pulled a large plastic bag which he hurled at the van. The women instinctively dived for the floor as it slammed into the windscreen with a squelching thud. Lindsay raised her head and nearly threw up. The world had turned red.

All over the windscreen was a skin of congealing blood with lumps of unidentifiable material slowly slithering down on to the bonnet. Jane's head appeared beside her. "Oh God, not the pigs' blood routine again," she moaned. "I thought they'd got bored with that one."

As she spoke, the bikes revved up again, then their roar

gradually diminished into an irritated buzz as they left the camp and reached the road.

"We must call the police!" Lindsay exclaimed.

"It's a waste of time calling the police, Lindsay. They just don't want to know. The first time they threw blood over our benders, we managed to get the police to come out. But they said we'd done it ourselves, that we were sensation seekers. They said there was no evidence of our allegations. Tyre tracks in the mud don't count, you see. Nor do the statements of forty women. It doesn't really matter what crimes are perpetrated against us, because we're sub-human, you see."

"That's monstrous," Lindsay protested.

"But inevitable," Jane retorted. "What's going on here is so radical that they can't afford to treat it seriously on any level. Start accepting that we've got any rights and you end up by giving validity to the nightmares that have brought us here. Do that and you're halfway accepting that our views on disarmament are a logical position. Much easier to treat us with total contempt."

"That's intolerable," said Lindsay.

"I'd better go and check that no one's hurt." Jane said. "One of the women got quite badly burned the first time they fire-bombed the tents."

"Give me a second to check that Cara's okay, and I'll come with you," Lindsay said, getting up and climbing the ladder that led to Cara's bunk. Surprisingly, the child was still fast asleep.

"I guess she's used to it by now," Jane said, leading the way outside.

It was a sorry scene that greeted them. The headlights of several of the women's vehicles illuminated half a dozen benders now reduced to tangled heaps of wreckage, out of which women were still crawling. Jane headed for the first aid bender while Lindsay ploughed through the rain and wind to offer what help she could to two women struggling to salvage the plastic sheeting that had formed their shelter. Together all three battled against the weather and roughly re-erected the bender. But the women's sleeping bags were soaked, and they trudged off to try and find some dry blankets to get them through the night.

Lindsay looked around. Slowly the camp was regaining its normal appearance. Where work was still going on, there seemed to be plenty of helpers. She made her way to Jane's bender, fortunately undamaged, and found the doctor bandaging the arm of a woman injured by a whiplashing branch in the attack on her bender.

"Hi, Lindsay," Jane had said without pausing in her work. "Not too much damage, thank God. A few bruises and cuts, but nothing major."

"Anything I can do?"

Jane shook her head. "Thanks, but everything's under control." Feeling slightly guilty, but not wanting to leave Cara alone for too long, Lindsay returned to the van. She made up the double berth where Jane had shown her Deborah normally slept.

But sleep eluded Lindsay. When she finally dropped off, it was to fall prey to confusing and painful dreams.

Cara woke early, and was fretful while Lindsay struggled with the unfamiliar intricacies of the van to provide them both with showers and breakfast. Luckily, the night's rain had washed away all traces of the pigs' blood. Of course, the keys of the van were with Deborah's possessions at the police station, so they had to drive into town in Lindsay's car.

Fordham Magistrates Court occupied a large and elegant Georgian townhouse in a quiet cul-de-sac off the main street. Inside, the building was considerably less distinguished. The beautifully proportioned entrance hall had been partitioned to provide a waiting room and offices and comfortless plastic chairs abounded where Chippendale furniture might once have stood. The paintwork was grubby and chipped and there was a pervasive odour of stale bodies and cigarette smoke. Lindsay felt Cara's grip tighten as they encountered the usual odd mixture of people found in magistrates' courts. Uniformed policemen bustled from room to room, up and down stairs. A couple of court ushers in robes like Hammer Horror vampires stood gossiping by the WRVS tea stand from which a middle-aged woman dispensed grey coffee and orange tea. The other extras in this scene were the defeated-looking victims of the legal process, several of them in whispering huddles with their spry and well-dressed solicitors.

For once, Lindsay felt out of her element in a court. She put it down to the unfamiliar presence of a four-year-old on the end of her arm and approached the ushers. They directed her to the cafe upstairs where she had arranged to meet Judith. The solicitor was already sitting at a table, dressed for business in a black pinstripe suit and an oyster grey shirt. She fetched coffee for Lindsay and orange juice for Cara, then said, "I'd quite like it if you were in court throughout, Lindsay. How do you think Cara will cope if we ask a friendly policeman to keep an eye on her? Or has she already acquired the peace women's distrust of them?"

Lindsay shrugged. "Best to ask Cara." She turned to her and said, "We're supposed to go into court now, but I don't think you're allowed in. How would it be if we were to ask a policeman to sit and talk to you while we're away?"

"Are you going to get my mummy?" asked Cara.

"In a little while."

"Okay, then. But you won't be long, will you, Lindsay?"

"No, promise."

They walked downstairs to the corridor outside the courtroom, and Judith went in search of help. She returned quickly with a young policewoman who introduced herself to Cara.

"My name's Barbara," she said. "I'm going to sit with you till Mummy gets back. Is that all right?"

"I suppose so," said Cara grudgingly. "Do you know any good stories?"

As Lindsay and Judith entered the courtroom, they heard Cara ask one of her best questions. "My mummy says the police are there to help us. So why did the police take my mummy away?"

The courtroom itself was scarcely altered from the house's heyday. The parquet floor was highly polished, the paintwork gleaming white. Behind a table on a raised dais at one end of the room sat the three magistrates. The chairwoman, aged about forty-five, had hair so heavily lacquered that it might have been moulded in fibreglass, and her mouth, too, was set in a hard line. She was flanked by two men. One was in his late fifties, with the healthy, weatherbeaten look of a keen sailor. The other, in his middle thirties, with dark brown hair neatly cut and styled, could have been a young business executive in his spotless shirt and dark suit. His face was slightly puffy round the eyes and jowls, and he wore an air of dissatisfaction with the world.

The court wound up its summary hearing of a drunk and disorderly with a swift £40 fine and moved on to Deborah's case.

Lindsay sat down on a hard wooden chair at the back of the room as Deborah was led in looking tired and dishevelled. Her jeans and shirt looked slept in, and her hair needed washing. Lindsay reflected, not for the first time, how the law's delays inevitably made the person in police custody look like a tramp.

Deborah's eyes flicked round the courtroom as a uniformed inspector read out the charges. When she saw Lindsay she flashed a smile of relief before turning back to the magistrates and answering the court clerk's enquiry about her plea to the breach of the peace charge. "Guilty," she said in a clear, sarcastic voice. To the next charge, she replied equally clearly, "Not guilty."

It was all over in ten minutes. Deborah was fined £50 plus £15 costs on the breach charge and remanded on bail to the Crown Court for jury trial on the assault charge. The bail had been set at £2500, with the conditions that Deborah reported daily to the police station at Fordham, did not go within 200 yards of the Crabtree home, and made no approach to Mr. Crabtree. Then, the formalities took over. Lindsay wrote a cheque she fervently hoped would never have to be cashed which Judith took to the payments office. Lindsay returned to Cara, who greeted her predictably with, "Where's my mummy? You said you'd get her for me."

Lindsay picked up the child and hugged her. "She's just coming, I promise." Before she could put Cara down, the child called, "Mummy!" and struggled out of Lindsay's arms. Cara hurtled down the corridor and into the arms of Deborah who was walking towards them with Judith. Eventually, Deborah disentangled herself from Cara and came over to Lindsay. Wordlessly, they hugged each other.

Lindsay felt the old electricity surge through her and pulled back from the embrace. She held Deborah at arms' length. "Hi," she said.

Deborah smiled. "I didn't plan a reunion like this," she said ruefully.

"We'll do the champagne and roses some other time," Lindsay replied.

"Champagne and roses? My God, you've come up in the world. It used to be a half of bitter and a packet of hedgehog-flavoured crisps!"

They laughed as Judith, who had been keeping a discreet distance, approached and said, "Thanks for all your help, Lindsay. Now you'll just have to pray Deborah doesn't jump bail!"

"No chance," said Deborah. "I wouldn't dare. Lindsay's

motto used to be 'don't mess with the messer,' and I don't expect that's changed."

Lindsay smiled. "I've got even tougher," she said. "Come on, I'll drop you off at the camp on my way back to London."

They said goodbye to Judith and headed for the car park. Deborah said nonchalantly to Lindsay. "You can't stay, then?"

Lindsay shook her head. "Sorry. There's nothing I'd rather do, but I've got to get back to London. I'm on the night shift tonight."

"You'll come back soon, though, won't you, Lin?"

Lindsay nodded. "Of course. Anyway, I'm not going just yet. I expect I can fit in a quick cup of coffee back at the van."

They pushed through the doors of the courthouse and nearly crashed into two men standing immediately outside. The taller of the two had curly greying hair but his obvious good looks were ruined by a swollen and bruised nose and dark smudges beneath his eyes. He looked astonished to see Deborah, then said viciously, "So you're breaking your bail conditions already, Miss Patterson. I could have you arrested for this, you know. And you wouldn't get bail a second time."

Furious, Lindsay pushed forward as Deborah picked up her daughter protectively. "Who the hell do you think you are?" she demanded angrily.

"Ask your friend," he sneered. "I'm not a vindictive man," he added. "I won't report you to the police this time. When the Crown Court sentences you to prison, that will be enough to satisfy me."

He shouldered his way between them, followed by the other man, who had the grace to look embarrassed.

Deborah stared after him. "In case you hadn't guessed," she said, "that was Rupert Crabtree."

Lindsay nodded. "I figured as much."

"One of these days," Deborah growled, "someone is going to put a stop to that bastard."

3

The alarm clock went off at a quarter to six. Lindsay rolled on her side, grunting "Drop dead, you bastard," at the voice-activated alarm Cordelia had bought her to replace the Mickey Mouse job she'd had since university. She curled into a ball and considered going back to sleep. The early Saturday morning start to her weekend at the peace camp that had seemed such a good idea the night before now felt very unappealing.

As she hovered on the verge of dozing off, she was twitched into sudden wakefulness as Cordelia's finger ends lightly traced a wavy line up her side. Cordelia snuggled into her and kissed the nape of her neck gently. Lindsay murmured her pleasure, and the kisses quickly turned into nibbles. Lindsay felt her flesh go to goose pimples; thoroughly aroused, she twisted round and kissed her lover fiercely. Cordelia pulled away and said innocently, "I thought you had trouble waking up in the morning?"

"If they could find an alarm clock that did what you do to

me, there would be no problem," Lindsay growled softly as she started to stroke Cordelia's nipples. Her right hand moved tentatively between Cordelia's legs.

Cordelia clamped her thighs together, pinning Lindsay's hand in place. "I've started so I'll finish," she murmured, moving her own fingers unerringly to the warm, wet centre of Lindsay's pleasure.

The feeling of relaxation that flooded through Lindsay afterwards was shattered by the alarm clock again. "Oh God," she groaned. "Is that the time?"

"What's your hurry?" Cordelia asked softly.

"I promised I'd be at Brownlow really early. There's a big action planned for today," Lindsay replied sleepily.

"Oh, for Christ's sake, is that all you think about these days?" Cordelia complained, pulling away from Lindsay. "I'm going for a bloody shower." She bounced out of bed before Lindsay could stop her.

"I wasn't finished with you," Lindsay called after her plaintively.

"I'll wait till your mind's on what you're doing, if it's all the same to you," came the reply.

It was just after seven when Lindsay parked alongside the scruffy plastic benders. She had tried to make her peace with Cordelia, but it had been fruitless. Now Cordelia was on her way to spend the weekend with her parents, and Lindsay was keeping the promise she'd made to Deborah three weeks before. She parked her MG between a small but powerful Japanese motor bike and a 2CV plastered with anti-nuclear stickers. If they ever stopped making 2CVs, she mused, the anti-nuclear sticker makers would go out of business. She cut her engine and sat in silence for a moment.

It was a cool and misty March morning, and Lindsay marvelled at the quiet stillness that surrounded the encampment. The only sign of life was a thin trickle of smoke coming from the far side of the rough circle of branches and plastic. She got out of the car and strolled over to Deborah's van. The curtains were drawn, but when Lindsay tried the door, she found it unlocked. In the gloom, she made out Deborah's sleeping figure. Lindsay moved inside gingerly and crouched beside her. She kissed her ear gently and nearly fell over as Deborah instantly woke, eyes wide, starting up from the bed. "Jesus, you gave me a shock," she exploded softly.

"A pleasant one, I hope."

"I can't think of a nicer one," said Deborah, sitting up. She pulled Lindsay close and hugged her. "Put the kettle on, there's a love," she said, climbing out of bed. She disappeared into the shower and toilet cubicle in the corner of the van, leaving Lindsay to deal with the gas rings.

Lindsay thought gratefully how easy it was to be with Deborah. There was never any fuss, never any pressure. It was always the same since they had first been together. They slipped so easily into a comfortable routine, as if the time between their meetings had been a matter of hours rather than months or weeks. Lindsay always felt at home with Deborah, whether it was in a Fordham courtroom or a camper van.

Deborah reappeared, washed and dressed, towelling her wavy brown shoulder-length hair vigorously. She threw the towel aside and settled down with a mug of coffee. She glanced at Lindsay, her blue eyes sparkling wickedly.

"You picked the right weekend to be here," she remarked.

Lindsay leaned back in her seat. "Why so?" she asked, "Jane told me it was just a routine blockade of the main gate."

"We're going in. Through the wire. We think it should be possible to get to the bunkers if we go in between gates three and four. The security's not that wonderful over there. I suppose any five-mile perimeter has to have its weak spots.

The only exposed bit is the ten yards between the edge of the wood and the fence. So there will be a diversion at the main gate to keep them occupied while the others get through the wire. And it just so happens that there's a Channel 4 film crew coming down anyway today to do a documentary." Deborah grinned broadly and winked complicity at Lindsay.

"Good planning, Debs. But aren't you taking a hell of a risk with the assault case already hanging over you? Surely they'll bang you up right away if they pick you up inside the fence?"

"That's exactly why we've decided that I'm not going in. I'm a very small part of the diversion. Which is why it's good that you're here. Left to my own devices, I'd probably find myself carried along with the flow. Before I knew it, I'd be back in clink again." Deborah smiled ruefully. "So, since I presume you're also in the business of keeping a low profile, we'll have to be each other's minder. Okay?"

Lindsay lit a cigarette and inhaled deeply before she replied. "Okay. I'd love to go along with the raiding party to do an "I" piece, but given my bosses' views on peace women, I guess that's right out of the question."

"You can help me sing," said Deborah. She leaned across the table to Lindsay, grasped her hand tightly and kissed her. "My, but it's good to be with you, Sister," she said softly.

Before Lindsay could reply, Cara's dark blonde head and flushed cheeks suddenly appeared through the curtains. As soon as she realised who was there, she scrambled down the ladder to hurl herself on Lindsay, hugging her fiercely before turning to Deborah. "You didn't tell me Lindsay was coming," she reproached her.

"I didn't tell you because I wasn't sure myself, and I didn't want both of us to be disappointed if she couldn't make it. Okay?"

The child nodded. "What are we having for breakfast?

Have you brought bacon and eggs like you promised last time?"

"I managed to smuggle them past the vegetarian checkpoint on the way in," Lindsay joked. "I know you're like me, Cara, you love the things that everybody tells you are bad for you."

"You really are a reprobate, aren't you?" Deborah said, amused. "I know you like taking the piss out of all the vegetarian non-smokers, but don't forget that a lot of us are veggies from necessity as much as choice. I love the occasional fry-up, but beans are a hell of a lot cheaper than bacon. Not everyone has the same sense of humour about it as I do."

"Don't tell me," Lindsay groaned. "Cordelia never stops telling me how people like me who love red meat are causing the distortion of world agriculture. Sometimes I feel personally responsible for every starving kid in the world."

Impatient with the conversation, Cara interrupted. "Can we have breakfast, then?"

By the time they had eaten the bacon, eggs, sausages, and mushrooms that Lindsay had brought, the camp had come to life again. Women were ferrying water from the standpipe by the road in big plastic jerry cans while others cooked, repaired benders, or simply sat and talked. It was a cold, dry day with the sun struggling fitfully through a haze. Lindsay went off to see Jane and found her sitting on a crate, writing in a large exercise book. She looked tired and drawn.

"Hi, Doc. Everything fine with you?"

Jane shrugged. "So so. I think I'm getting too close to all this now. I'm getting so wrapped up in the logistics of the camp I'm forgetting why I'm here. I think I'm going to have to get away for a few days to put it back into perspective."

"There's always a bed at our place if you need a break." Jane nodded as Lindsay went on, "Debs says you can fill me in with the details of today's invasion plan."

Jane outlined the intended arrangements. Nicky was

leading a raiding party of a dozen women armed with bolt-cutters. They would be waiting in the woods for a signal from the look-out post that the diversion at the main gate was attracting enough attention from camp security to allow them to reach the fence and cut through the wire. What followed their entry into the base would be a matter for their own judgment, but it was hoped that they'd make it to the missile silos. The diversion was timed for noon, the main attraction for fifteen minutes later.

"You should keep out of the front line," she concluded. "Help Deborah with the singing. Keep an eye on her, too. We don't want her to get arrested again. It would be just like her to get carried away and do something out of order. I imagine that a few of the local coppers know perfectly well who she is and wouldn't mind the chance to pick her up and give her a hard time. Crabtree is pretty buddy-buddy with the local police hierarchy according to Judith. Understandably enough, I suppose. So do us all a favour unless you desperately want to take on Cara full-time—keep the lid on Deborah."

By late morning there was an air of suppressed excitement around the camp. The television crew had arrived and were shooting some interviews and stock background shots around the benders. It wasn't hard for Lindsay to suppress her journalistic instincts and avoid them. She was, after all, off duty. Since the *Clarion* had no Sunday edition, she felt no guilt about ignoring the story. She noticed Jane and a couple of other long-standing peace campers having a discreet word with the crew, which had included a couple of unmistakable gestures towards the long bunkers that dominated the skyline.

At about midday, Deborah came looking for her. Leaving Cara and three other children in the van with Josy, one of the other mothers living at the camp, they joined the steady surge of women making for the main gate. About forty women were gathered round. A group of half a dozen marched boldly up to the sentry boxes on either side of the gate and started to unwind the balls of wool they carried with them. They wove the wool around the impassive soldiers and their sentry boxes, swiftly creating a complex web. Other women moved to the gates themselves and began to weave wool strands in and out of the heavy steel mesh to seal them shut. Deborah climbed on top of a large concrete litter bin just outside the gates and hauled Lindsay up beside her. Together they started to sing one of the songs that had grown up with the camp, and soon all the women had joined in.

Inside the camp, the RAF police and behind them the USAF guards came running towards the gate. On the women's side, civil police started to appear at the trot to augment the pair permanently on duty at the main gate. The film crew was busy recording it all.

It looked utterly chaotic. Then, one of the women let out an excited whoop and pointed to the silos. There, silhouetted against the grey March sky, women could be seen dancing and waving. Alerted by her cries, the film crew ran off round the perimeter fence, filming all the while. Inside the wire, the military turned and raced across the scrubby grass to the bunkers constructed to house the coming missiles.

Outside the base the women calmly dispersed, to the frustration of the police who were just getting into the swing of making arrests. Lindsay, feeling as high as if she'd just smoked a couple of joints, jumped down from the litter bin and swung Deborah down into her arms. Like the other women around them they hugged each other and jumped around on the spot, then they bounced away from the fence and back towards the main road. A tall man stood at the end of the camp road. On the end of a lead was a fox-terrier. A sneer of scorn spoiled his newly healed features.

"Enjoy yourself while you can, Miss Patterson. It won't be long before I have you put some place where there won't be much to rejoice over." His threat uttered, Crabtree marched on down the main road away from the camp. Lindsay looked in dismay at Deborah's stunned face.

"Sadistic bastard. He can't resist having a go every time he sees me," said Deborah. "He seems to go out of his way to engineer these little encounters. But I'm not going to let him get the better of me. Not on a day like today."

4

The women had gathered in the big bender that they used for meeting and talking as a group. Lindsay still couldn't get used to the way they struggled to avoid hierarchies by refusing to run their meetings according to traditional structures. Instead, they sat in a big circle and each spoke in turn, supposedly without interruption. The euphoria of the day's action was tangible. The film crew was still around, and not even the news that the dozen women who had made it to the silos had been charged with criminal damage and trespass could diminish the high that had infected everyone.

But there was a change in attitude since Lindsay had first encountered the peace women. It was noticeable that far more women were advocating stronger and more direct action against what they perceived as the forces of evil. She could see that Jane and several other women who'd been with the camp for a long time were having a struggle to impress upon others, like the headstrong Nicky, the need to keep all action non-violent and to minimize the criminal element in what they did. Eventually, the meeting was adjourned without a decision till the following afternoon.

The rest of the day passed quickly for Lindsay who spent her time walking the perimeter fence and picking up on her new friendships with women like Jackie. Lindsay appreciated the different perspectives the women gave her on life in Thatcher's Britain. It was a valuable contrast with the cynical world of newspapers and the comfortably well-off life she shared with Cordelia. Jackie and her lover Willow, both from Birmingham, explained to Lindsay for the first time how good they felt at the camp because there was none of the constant pressure of racial prejudice that had made it so difficult for them to make anything of their lives at home. By the time Lindsay had eaten dinner with Cara and Deborah, she knew she had made a firm decision to stay. By unspoken consent, Deborah took Cara off to spend the rest of the night with her best friend Christy in a bender she shared with her mother Josy. When she returned, she found Lindsay curled up in a corner with a tumbler of whisky.

"Help yourself," said Lindsay.

Deborah sensed the tension in Lindsay. Carefully, she poured herself a small drink from the bottle on the table and sat down beside her. She placed a cautious hand on her thigh. "I'm really glad to be with you again," she said gently. "It's been a long time since we had a chance to talk."

Lindsay took a gulp of whisky and lit a cigarette. "I can't sleep with you," she burst out. "I thought I could, but I can't. I'm sorry."

Deborah hadn't forgotten the knowledge of Lindsay that six hectic months had given her. She smiled. "You haven't changed, have you? What makes you think I wanted to jump into bed with you again?" Her voice was teasing. "That old arrogance hasn't deserted you."

Outrage chased incredulity across Lindsay's face. Then her sense of humour caught up with her and she smiled.

"Touché. You never did let me get away with anything, did you?"

"Too bloody true I didn't. Give you an inch and you were always halfway to the next town. Listen, I didn't expect a night of mad, passionate lovemaking. I know your relationship with Cordelia is the big thing in your life. Just as Cara is the most important thing in my life now. I don't take risks with that, and I don't expect you to take risks with your life either."

Lindsay looked sheepish. "I really wanted to make love with you. I thought it would help me sort out my feelings. But when you took Cara off, I suddenly felt that I was contemplating something dishonest. You know? Something that devalued what there is between you and me."

Deborah put her arm around Lindsay's tense shoulders. "You mean, you'd have been using me to prove something to yourself about you and Cordelia?"

"Something like that. I guess I just feel confused about what's happening between me and her. It started off so well—she made me feel so special. I was happy as a pig. Okay, it was frustrating that I was living in Glasgow and she was in London. But there wasn't a week when we didn't spend at least two nights together, often more, once I'd got a job sorted out.

"We seemed to have so much in common—we liked going to the same films, loved the theatre, liked the same books, all that stuff. She even started coming hill-walking with me, though I drew the line at going jogging with her. But it was all those things that kind of underpinned the fact that I was crazy about her and the sex was just amazing.

"Then I moved to London and it seemed like everything changed. I realised how much of her life I just hadn't been a part of. All the time she spent alone in London was filled with people I've got the square root of sod all in common with.

They patronise the hell out of me because they think that being a tabloid hack is the lowest form of pond life.

"They treat me like I'm some brainless bimbo that Cordelia has picked up. And Cordelia just tells me to ignore it, they don't count. Yet she still spends great chunks of her time with them. She doesn't enjoy being with the people I work with, so she just opts out of anything I've got arranged with other hacks. And the few friends I've got outside the business go back to Oxford days; they go down well with Cordelia and her crowd, but I want more of my life than that. And it never seems the right time to talk about it.

"About once a fortnight, at the moment, I seriously feel like packing my bags and moving out. Then I remember all the good things about her and stay."

Lindsay stopped abruptly and leaned over to refill her glass. She took another long drink and shivered as the spirit hit her. Deborah slowly massaged the knotted muscles at the back of her neck. "Poor Lin," she said. "You do feel hard done by, don't you? You never did understand how compromise can be a show of strength, did you?"

Lindsay frowned. "It's not that. It just seems like me that's made all the compromises—or sacrifices, more like."

"But she has too. Suddenly, after years of living alone, doing one job where you really need your own space, she's got this iconoclast driving a coach and horses through her routines, coming in at all hours of the day and night, thanks to her wonderful shift patterns, and hating the people she has to be nice to in order to keep a nice high profile in the literary world. It can't be exactly easy for her either. It seems to me that she's got the right idea—she's doing what she needs to keep herself together."

Lindsay looked hurt. "I never thought I'd hear you taking Cordelia's side."

"I'm not taking sides. And that reaction says it all, Lin," Deborah said, a note of sharpness creeping into her voice.

"I'm trying to make you see things from her side. Listen, I saw you when the two of you had only been together for six months, and I saw you looking happier than I'd ever seen you. I love you like a sister, Lin, and I want to see you with that glow back. You're not going to get it by whingeing about Cordelia. Talk to her about it. At least you're still communicating in bed—build on that, for starters. Stop expecting her to be psychic. If she loves you, she won't throw you out just because you tell her you're not getting what you need from her."

Lindsay sighed. "Easier said than done."

"I know that. But you've got to try. It's obviously not too late. If you were diving into bed with me to prove you still have enough autonomy to do it, I'd say you were in deep shit. But at least you're not that far down the road. Now, come on, drink up and let's get to bed. You can have Cara's bunk if you can't cope with sharing a bed with me and keeping your hands to yourself."

"Now who's being arrogant?"

Lindsay stood by the kettle waiting for it to boil, gazing at Deborah who lay languidly in a shaft of morning sunlight staring into the middle distance. After a night's sleep, the clarity she had felt after the conversation with Deborah had grown fuzzy round the edges. But she knew deep down she wanted to put things right between her and Cordelia, and Deborah had helped her feel that was a possibility.

She made the coffee, and brought it over to Deborah. Lindsay sat on the top of the bed and put her arms round her friend. Lindsay felt at peace for the first time in months. "If things go wrong when it comes to court, I'd like to take care of Cara, if you'll let me," she murmured.

Deborah drew back, still holding Lindsay's shoulders.

"But how could you manage that? With work and Cordelia and everything?"

"We've got a crèche for newspaper workers' kids from nine till six every day. I can swap most of my shifts round to be on days, and I'm damn sure Cordelia will help if I need her to."

Deborah shook her head disbelievingly. "Lindsay, you're incredible. Sometimes I think you just don't listen to the words that come out of your mouth. Last night, you were busily angsting about how to get your relationship with Cordelia back on an even keel. Now today you're calmly talking about dumping your ex-lover's child on her. What a recipe for disaster that would be! Look, it's lovely of you to offer, and I know she'd be happy with you, but I hope that won't be necessary. We'll look at the possibilities nearer the time, and I'll keep it in mind. What counts is what's going to be best for her. Now, let's go and get Cara, eh? She'll be wondering where I am." They found Cara with Jane, and after a bread and cheese lunch, the four of them went for a walk along the perimeter fence. Lindsay and Cara played tig and hide-and-seek among the trees while Jane and Deborah walked slowly behind, wrangling about the business of peace and the problems of living at Brownlow.

They made their way back to the camp, where the adults settled down in the meeting bender for a long session. Three hours later, it had been agreed that the women charged the day before should, if they were willing, opt for prison for the sake of publicity and that a picket should be set up at the gate of Holloway in their support. Jane offered to organise the picket. Lindsay thought gratefully that at least that way her friend could make a small escape without offending her conscience. It had been a stormy meeting, and Lindsay was glad when it was over. Even though she had, by now, experienced many of these talking-shops, she never failed to become slightly disillusioned at the destructive way women could fight against each other in spite of their common cause.

Deborah went off to collect Cara and put her to bed, and Lindsay joined Willow and Jackie and their friends in their bender. There were a couple of guitars, and soon the women were singing an assortment of peace songs, love songs, and nostalgic pop hits. Deborah joined them, and they sat close. Lindsay felt she couldn't bear to wrench herself away from the sisterhood she felt round her. Sentimental fool, she thought to herself as she joined in the chorus of "I Only Want To Be With You."

Just after ten, the jam session began to break up. Most of the women left for their own benders. Lindsay and Deborah followed. "I'm going to have a word with Jane about the Holloway picket," said Lindsay. "You coming?"

"No, I'll see you at the van."

"Okay, I'll not be long."

Deborah vanished into the darkness beyond the ring of benders to where the van was parked near the road. Lindsay headed for Jane's makeshift surgery and found the harassed doctor sorting through a cardboard box of pharmaceutical samples that a sympathetic GP had dropped off that evening. She stopped at once, pleased to see Lindsay in spite of her tiredness and began to explain the picket plans. Although Lindsay was itching to get back to Deborah, it was after eleven when she finally set off to walk the fifty yards to the van.

The first thing that caught her eye as she moved beyond the polythene tents was bright lights. Now that the army had cleared the ground round the perimeter fence, it was possible to see the temporary arc lights from quite a distance. That in itself wasn't extraordinary as workmen occasionally sneaked in a night shift to avoid the picketing women.

She stopped dead as she caught sight of three figures approaching the camp, silhouetted against the dim glow from the barracks inside the fence. Two were uniformed policemen, no prizes for spotting that. The third was a tall, blond man she had noticed in the area a couple of times before. Her journalistic instinct had put him down as Special Branch. She was gratified to find that instinct vindicated. She glanced around, but the only other women in sight were far off by a campfire. Most of them had already gone to bed.

Lindsay had no idea what was going on, but she wanted to find out. The best way to do that was to stay out of sight, watch and listen. She crouched down against the bender nearest her and slowly worked her way round the encampment, trying to outflank the trio who were between her and the lights. When she reached the outer ring of tents, she squatted close to the ground while the three men passed her and headed for Jane's bender with its distinctive red cross. Lindsay straightened up and headed for the lights, keeping close to the fringes of woodland that surrounded the base. As she neared the lights, she was able to pick out details. There were a couple of police Landrovers pulled up on the edge of the wood. Nearby, illuminated by their headlamps and the arc lights, were a cluster of green canvas screens. Beyond the Landrovers were three unremarkable saloon cars. A handful of uniformed officers stood around. Several people in civilian clothes moved about the scene, vanishing behind the screens from time to time.

Lindsay moved out of the shelter of the trees and approached the activity. She had only gone a few yards when two uniformed constables moved to cut off her progress. Her hand automatically moved to her hip pocket and she pulled out the laminated yellow Press Card which in theory granted her their co-operation. She flashed it at the young policemen and made to put it away.

"Just a minute, miss," said one of them. "Let's have a closer look if you don't mind."

Reluctantly, she handed the card over. He scrutinised it carefully; then he showed it to his colleague who looked her up and down, noting her expensive Barbour jacket, corduroy trousers and muddy walking boots. He nodded and said, "Looks okay to me."

"I'm here writing a feature about the camp," she said. "When I saw the lights, I thought something might be doing. What's the score?"

The first constable smiled. "Sorry to be so suspicious. We get all sorts here, you know. You want to know what's happening, you best see the superintendent. He's over by the Landrover nearest to us. I'll take you across in a minute, when he's finished talking to the bloke who found the body."

"Body?" Lindsay demanded anxiously. "What is it? Accident? Murder? And who's dead?"

"That's for the super to say," the policeman replied. "But it doesn't look much like an accident at this stage."

Lindsay looked around her, taking it all in. The scene of the murder was like a three-ring circus. The outer ring took the form of the five vehicles and a thinly scattered cordon of uniformed police constables. Over by one of the Landrovers, a policewoman dispensed tea from a vacuum flask to a nervous-looking man talking to the uniformed superintendent whom Lindsay recognised from the demonstration outside the police station. She crossed her fingers and hoped the victim was no one from the camp.

The temporary arc lights the police had rigged up gave the scene the air of a film set, an impression exaggerated by the situation, part of a clear strip about fifteen yards wide between a high chain-link fence and a belt of scrubby woodland. It was far enough from any gates to be free of peace campers. The lamps shone down on the second ring, a shield of tall canvas screens hastily erected to protect the body from view. Round the screen, scene-of-crime officers buzzed in and out, communicating in their own form of macabre shorthand.

But the main attraction of the circus tonight was contained in the inner circle. Here there were more lights, smaller spotlights clipped on to the screens. A photographer moved round the periphery, his flash freezing forever the last public appearance of whoever was lying dead on the wet clay. Could it be one of the women from the camp lying there? Superintendent Rigano said a few words to the man, then moved back towards the scene of the crime. The constable escorted Lindsay across the clearing, being careful, she noted, to keep between her and the tall canvas screens. Once there, he secured the attention of the superintendent, whom Lindsay recognised from their earlier encounter outside Fordham police station. "Sir, there's a journalist here wants a word with you," the constable reported.

He turned to Lindsay, fine dark brows scowling over deep-set eyes. "You're here bloody sharpish," he said grudgingly. "Superintendent Rigano, Fordham Police."

"Lindsay Gordon, *Daily Clarion*. We met at the demonstration after Deborah Patterson's arrest. I happened to be at the camp," she replied. "We're doing a feature comparing the peace camps at Brownlow and Faslane," she lied fluently. "I saw the lights and wondered if there might be anything in it for me."

"We've got a murder on our hands," he said in a flinty voice. "You'd better take a note. It would be a pity to screw up on a scoop." Lindsay obediently pulled out her notebook and a pencil.

"The dead man is Rupert Crabtree." The familiar name shocked Lindsay. Suddenly, this wasn't some impersonal murder story she was reporting. It was much closer to home. Her surprise obviously registered with Rigano, who paused momentarily before continuing. "Aged forty-nine. Local solicitor. Lives up Brownlow Common Cottages. That's those mock-Georgian mansions half a mile from the main gate of the camp. Bludgeoned to death with a blunt instrument, to wit, a chunk of drainage pipe which shattered on impact. Perhaps more to the point, from your side of things, is the fact that he was chairman of the local ratepayers' association who were fighting against that scruffy lot down there. It looks as if there was a struggle before he was killed. Anything else you want to know?"

Lindsay hoped her relationship with "that scruffy lot down there" was not too obvious and that she was putting up a sufficiently good performance in her professional role as the single-minded news reporter in possession of a hot exclusive. "Yes. What makes you think there was a struggle?"

"The mud's churned up quite a bit. And Crabtree had drawn a gun but not had the chance to fire it."

"That suggests he knew his life was at risk, doesn't it?"

"No comment. I also don't want the gun mentioned just yet. Any other questions?"

She nodded vigorously. "Who found the body?"

"A local resident walking his dog. I'm not releasing a name, and he won't be available for interview in the foreseeable future."

"Any suspects? Is an arrest likely within the next few hours? And what was he doing on the common at this time of night?"

Rigano looked down at her shrewdly. "No arrest imminent. We are actively pursuing several lines of enquiry. He was walking the bloody dog. He usually did this time of night. Well-known fact of local life."

"Any idea of the time of death?" she asked.

Rigano shrugged expressively. "That's for the doctors to tell us. But without sticking my neck out, I can tell you it was probably some time between ten and eleven o'clock. I hope you've got an alibi," he said, a smile pulling at the corners of his mouth. "Come and have a quick look." He strode off, clearly expecting her to follow. She caught up with him at the entrance to the screens.

"I'd rather not, if you don't mind," she said quickly.

His eyebrows shot up. "Happy to dish the dirt, not so happy to see the nastiness?"

Lindsay was stung by his sardonic tone. "Okay," she said grimly. He led her through the gap in the screens.

She would not have recognised Rupert Crabtree. He lay on his front, the wet March ground soaking the elegant camel hair coat and the pinstripe trousers. His wellingtons were splashed with vivid orange mud, as were his black leather gloves. The back of his head was shattered. Blood matted his hair and had spattered over the fragments of a two-foot-long piece of earthenware water pipe which had clearly broken under the force with which it had been brought down on the skull. A few feet away, a handgun lay in the mud. Lindsay felt sick. Rigano took her arm and steered her away. "You'll be wanting to get to a phone," he said, not unkindly. "If you want to check up on our progress later on, ring Fordham nick and ask for the duty officer. He'll fill you in with any details." He turned away, dismissing her.

Slowly, Lindsay turned her back on the depressing camouflage of death. And, at once, her mind was torn away from murder. Across the clearing, the trio she had seen earlier were returning. But now there were four people in the group. She felt a physical pain in her chest as she recognised the fourth. As their eyes met, Lindsay and Deborah shared a moment of pure fear.

5

For a moment, Lindsay stood stock still, the journalist fighting the friend inside her. This was an important story. She had the edge on the pack, and she needed to call the office as soon as possible. Logically, she knew there was little she could do for Deborah as the police Landrover carried her off. That didn't stop her feeling an overwhelming rage that translated itself into the desire for action. Abruptly, she turned back to the scene of the crime and found Rigano. Forcing herself to sound casual, she elicited the information that Deborah had not been arrested but was assisting police with their enquiries. End message. Lindsay turned and started to run back to the van.

Once out of the circle of light, she was plunged into darkness. Tripping over tree roots and treacherous brambles, she stumbled on, her only guide the distant glow of the campfire and the dim light from a few of the benders. At one point, she plunged headlong over a rock and grimly picked herself up, covered in mud. Cursing, she ran on till she reached the camp. As she reached the benders, she realised that several knots of women had gathered and were talking together anxiously. Ignoring their questioning looks, she made straight for the van, where she burst in, gasping for breath, to find Jane sitting over a cup of coffee. She took one look at Lindsay and said, "So you know already?"

"How's Cara? Where is she?" Lindsay forced out.

"Fast asleep. The coppers were very quiet, very civil. But the van mustn't be moved till they've had a chance to search it." She was interrupted by a knock on the door. Lindsay leaned over and opened it to find a policewoman standing on the threshold.

"Yes?" Lindsay demanded roughly.

"I've been instructed to make sure that nothing is removed from this van until our officers arrive with a search warrant," she replied.

"Terrific," said Lindsay bitterly. "I take it you've no objection to me moving a sleeping child to where she won't be disturbed?"

The policewoman looked surprised. "I don't see why you shouldn't move the child. Where is she?"

Lindsay pointed up to the curtained-off bunk. She turned to Jane and said, "I'll take Cara to Josy's bender. She'll be all right there."

Jane nodded and added, "I'll stay here to make sure everything's done properly."

Lindsay smiled. "Thanks. I've got to get to the phone." Then, with all the firmness she could muster, she said to the police officer, "I'm a journalist. I've got the details of the story from Superintendent Rigano, and I intend to phone my office now. I'll be back shortly. Till then, Dr. Thomas is in charge here."

She climbed the ladder and folded Cara into her arms. The child murmured in her sleep but did not wake. Lindsay carried her to Josy, then ran as fast as she could to the phone box. She glanced at her watch and was amazed to see it was still only half past midnight. Her first call was to Judith Rowe. When the solicitor surfaced from sleep, she promised to get straight round to the police station and do what she could.

Next, Lindsay took a deep breath and put in a transfer charge call to the office. The call was taken by Cliff Gilbert himself. "Listen," she said. "There's been a murder at Brownlow Common. I've checked it out with the cops locally, and the strength of it is that the leader of the local opposition to the women's peace camp has been found with his head stoved in. I've got enough to file now, which I'll do if you put me on to copy. I'll also get stuck in to background for tomorrow if you think that's a good idea."

Cliff thought for a moment. Lindsay could almost hear the connections clicking into place to complete the mental circuit. "You've got good contacts among the lesbian bean-burger brigade down there, haven't you?"

"The best. The prime suspect seems to be an old pal of mine."

"What shift are you on tomorrow?"

"Day off."

"Fine. Take a look at it if you don't mind and check in first thing with Duncan. I'll leave him a note stressing that I've told you to get stuck in. And Lindsay—don't do anything daft, okay?"

"Thanks, Cliff. How much do you want now?"

"Let it run, Lindsay. All you've got."

There followed a series of clicks and buzzes as she was connected to the copytaker. She recited the story off the top of her head, adding in as much as she knew about Crabtree and his connection with the camp. "A brutal murder shocked a women's peace camp last night," she began.

Then, at nearly two o'clock, she made her final call. Cordelia's sleepy voice answered the phone. "Who the hell is it?"

Lindsay swallowed the lump that had formed in her

throat at the sound of the familiar voice. She struggled with herself and tried to sound light. "It's me, love. Sorry I woke you. I know you'll be tired after driving back from your parents', but I'm afraid I've got a major hassle on my hands. There's been a murder down here. Rupert Crabtree the guy whose face Debs is supposed to have rearranged—he's been killed. The cops have pulled Debs. I don't think they're going to charge her. I know I said I'd be home tomorrow lunchtime, but I don't know when the hell I'll make it now."

"Do you want me to come down?"

Lindsay thought for a moment. The complication seemed unnecessary. "Not just now, I think," she replied. "There's nothing either of us can really do till I know more precisely what's happening. I simply wanted to tell you myself, so you wouldn't panic when you heard the news or saw the papers. I'll ring you later today, all right?"

"All right," Cordelia sighed. "But look after yourself, please. Don't take any chances with a murderer on the loose. I love you, don't forget that."

"I love you too," Lindsay replied. She put the phone down and walked back to the camp. She opened the door to the van, forgetting momentarily about the police. The bulky presence of two uniformed men searching the van startled her.

"What the hell are you doing?" she demanded angrily.

"We'll be as quick as we can," said the older of the two, a freckle-faced, grey-haired man with broad shoulders and a paunch. "We have a warrant. Your friend said it was all right," he added, nodding towards Jane.

"I'd forgotten you'd be doing this." Lindsay sighed as she collapsed into the comfortable armchair-cum-driver's seat.

True to the constable's word, they departed in about fifteen minutes with a bundle of clothing. Lindsay poured a large whisky for Jane and herself.

"I could do without another night like this," Lindsay said.

"I don't know what it is about my friends that seems to attract murder."

Jane looked puzzled. "You mean this happens often?"

"Not exactly often. About two years ago, a friend of mine was arrested for a murder she didn't commit. Cordelia and I happened to be on the spot and got roped in to do the Sam Spade bit. That's when the two of us got together—a mutual fascination for being nosey parkers."

"Well, I hate to say it, but I'm glad you've had the experience. I think you could easily find yourself going through the same routine for Deborah."

Lindsay shook her head. "Different kettle of fish. They've not even arrested Debs, never mind charged her. I'm pretty sure they don't have much to go on. It's my guess that Debs will be back here by lunchtime tomorrow if Judith's got anything to do with it. Let's face it, we all know Debs is innocent, and I'm sure the police will find a more likely suspect before the day's out. They've just pulled her in to make it look good to anyone who's got their beady eyes on them. Now I'm going to bed, if you'll excuse me."

In spite of Lindsay's exhaustion she did not fall asleep at once. Crabtree's murder had set her thoughts racing in circles. Who had killed him? And why? Was it anything to do with the peace camp, or was Debs' connection with him purely coincidental? And what was going to happen to Debs? Lindsay hated being in a position where she didn't know enough to form reasonable theories, and she tossed and turned in Debs' bed as she tried to switch off her brain. Finally she drifted into a deep and dreamless sleep, which left her feeling neither rested nor refreshed when she awoke after nine.

After a quick shower, she emerged into a mild spring day with cotton-wool clouds scudding across the sky to find the camp apparently deserted. Puzzled, Lindsay glanced over at the big bender used for meetings; it seemed that was where the women had gathered. She decided to take advantage of the quiet spell by phoning the office and checking the current situation with the police.

Her first call was to the police HQ in Fordham. She asked for Rigano and was surprised to be put straight through to him. "Superintendent Rigano? Lindsay Gordon here, *Daily Clarion*. We met last night at Brownlow..."

"I remember. You were quick off the mark. It's been hard to get away from your colleagues this morning. Now, what can I do for you?"

"I wondered where you were up to. Any imminent arrest?"

"You mean, are we going to charge your friend? The answer is, not at the moment. Off the record, we'll be letting her go later this morning. That's not to say I'm convinced of her innocence. But I can't go any further till I've got forensics. So you can say that at present good old Superintendent Rigano is following several lines of enquiry, but that the woman we have been interviewing is being released pending the outcome of those enquiries. Okay?"

"Fine. Do you mind if I drop in on you later today?"

"Please yourself," he said. "If I'm in, I'll see you. But I don't know what my movements will be later, so if you want to take a chance on missing me, feel free."

Lindsay put the phone down, thoughtful. Her experience with the police during the Paddy Callaghan case had fueled her ingrained mistrust of their intelligence and integrity. But in her brief encounter with Rigano she had felt a certain rapport which had not been dispelled by their telephone conversation. She had surprised herself by her request to call in on him, and now she felt slightly bewildered as to what on earth she would find to discuss with him once Debs was released.

But that was for later. Right now, she had the unpleasant task of talking to Duncan Morris, the *Daily Clarion*'s news editor and the man responsible for her move to London. She put the call in and waited nervously to be connected to her boss. His voice boomed down the line at her. "Morning, Lindsay," he began. "I see from the overnight note that you're back in that nest of pipers. Still, you did a good job last night. We beat everyone else to the draw and that's the way I want to keep it. It's of interest for us in terms of the link with the peace camp, okay, so let's keep that in the front of our minds. What I want from you by noon is a good background piece about the camp, a few quotes from the loony lefties about this man Crabtree and his campaign. I don't have to spell it out to you." Lindsay fumed quickly as the venom of his prejudices ran over her. "I also want to be well up on the news angles too. Try for a chat with the widow and family or his colleagues. And try to overcome your natural prejudices and stay close to the cops. Now, what's the score on all that?"

Lindsay somehow found her tongue. She was aware that she should know better than to be surprised by Duncan's about-turn when faced with a strong news story, but she still couldn't help being a little taken aback that he was now hassling her for a background piece on the camp. She stammered, "The cops are releasing the woman they held for questioning. She's Deborah Patterson, the woman charged with assaulting him last month. I don't know what the legal implications are as yet—I should imagine that with his death the prosecution case automatically falls, but whether that releases us immediately from *sub judice* rules, I don't know.

"As far as the news feature's concerned, no problem. Also, I'm hoping to see the copper in charge of the case again this afternoon, so I can let you have whatever he says. I'll try the family but I don't hold out much hope. They're a bit too well clued-up about Her Majesty's gutter press to fall for the standard lines. But leave it with me."

"Fine. Normally on one this big, I'd send someone down to help you out, but you're the expert when it comes to the lunatic fringe, so I'll leave you to it." Patronising shit, she thought, as he carried on. "We've got a local snapper lined up, so if you've got any potential pics, speak to the picture desk. Don't fall down on this one, Lindsay. File by noon so I can see the copy before I go into morning conference. And get a good exclusive chat with this woman they're releasing. If the lawyers say we can't use it, we can always kill it. Speak to you later."

The phone went dead. "Just what I love most," Lindsay muttered. "Writing for the wastepaper bin." She walked back to the van and made herself some coffee and toast before she sat down to put her feature together. She had only written a few paragraphs when there was a knock at the van door.

"Come in," she called. Jane entered, followed by Willow and another woman whom Lindsay knew only by sight.

"The very people I wanted to see," she exclaimed. "My news desk has said I can do a piece about the camp reaction to Crabtree's campaign. So I need some quotes from you about how you are here for peace and, while you didn't have any sympathy for his organisation, you wouldn't ever have stooped to violence, etc., etc. Is that all right?"

Willow grinned. "We'll have to see about that," she replied. "But first, we've got something to ask you. We've just had a meeting to discuss this business. We've decided we need to safeguard our interests. Already there have been reporters round here, and we don't like the attitude they've been taking. That leaves us with a bit of a problem. We need someone who can help us deal with the situation. It's got to be someone who understands why none of us could have done this, but who also knows the way the system works. It looks like you're the only one who fits the bill."

The third woman chimed in. "It wasn't a unanimous decision to ask you. Not by a long chalk. But we're stuck. Personally, I don't feel entirely happy about trusting someone who works for a paper like the *Clarion*, but we don't have a lot of choice. Deborah's already been picked up, and even if she's released without charges, the mud's been slung and it will stick unless we can get our point of view across."

Lindsay shrugged. "I do know how the media works. But it sounds more like you're looking for a press spokeswoman, and that's not a job I can really do. It gives me a serious conflict of interest."

The third woman looked satisfied. "I thought you'd say that," she said triumphantly. "I knew that when the chips were down you'd know on which side your bread was buttered."

Needled, Lindsay said, "That's really unfair. You know I want to do everything I can. Deborah's been my friend for years. Look, I can help you project the right kind of image. But don't expect miracles. What I do need, if I'm going to do that, is total cooperation. Now I know there are women here who would die before they'd help a tabloid journo, but from those of you who are willing to help I need support."

Jane replied immediately. "Well, I for one am willing to trust you. The articles you've written abroad about the camp have been some of the most positive pieces I've seen about what we're doing here. You're the only person capable of doing what we need that we can any of us say that about."

"I'll go along with that," Willow added. "I'll pass the word around that you're on our side."

"Care to supply some quotes before you go?" Lindsay asked as Willow and the other woman seemed about to leave.

"Jane can do that. She's good with words." Willow said over her shoulder as they went out, closing the van door on Jane and Lindsay.

"There was something else I wanted to discuss with you," Jane said hesitantly. "I know a lot of the women would disagree with me, so I didn't raise it at the meeting. But I think we need someone to investigate this on our behalf. We are going to be the centre of suspicion over this, and while they've got us as prime candidates, I don't think the police will be looking hard for other possible murderers. Will you see what you can find out?"

For the second time that morning, Lindsay was taken aback. "Why me?" she finally asked. "I'm not any kind of detective. I'm a journalist, and there's no guarantee that my interests aren't going to clash with yours."

Jane parried quickly. "You've told me you'd cleared a friend of a murder charge. Well, I figure if you did it once, you can do it again. Those features you wrote for the German magazine seem to have a feel for the truth, even if you don't always choose to report it. You can talk to the cops, you can talk to Crabtree's family and friends. None of us can do that. And you're on our side. You can't believe Deborah's guilty. You of all people can't believe that."

Lindsay lit a cigarette and gazed out of the window. She really didn't want the hassle of being a servant of two masters. Jane sat quietly, but Lindsay could feel the pressure of her presence. "All right," she said, "I'll do what I can."

By noon Lindsay had dictated her story and spoken to Duncan who, never satisfied, started to pressurise her about an interview with Deborah. Disgruntled, she was walking back from the phone box when a car pulled up alongside. Suddenly, Lindsay found herself enveloped in a warm embrace as Deborah jumped out of the car. Nothing was said for a few moments. Judith leaned over from the driver's seat and called through the open door, "I'll see you up at the camp," before driving off.

"Oh, Lin," Deborah breathed. "I was so afraid. I didn't know what was going on. The bastards just lifted me, I couldn't even do anything about Cara. I've been so worried. I haven't slept, haven't eaten . . . Thank God you had the sense to get Judith on to it straight away. God knows what I wouldn't have confessed to otherwise, just to get out of there. There was a big blond Special Branch bloke, but he was no big deal, they're always too busy playing at being James Bond. But the superintendent is so fucking clever. Oh Lin . . ." And the tears came.

Lindsay stroked her hair. "Dry your eyes, Debs. Come on, Cara will be wanting you."

Deborah wiped her eyes and blew her nose on Lindsay's crumpled handkerchief, then they walked back to the camp, arm in arm. Behind her, to Lindsay's astonishment, came Cordelia, looking cool and unflustered in a designer jogging suit and green wellies, her black hair blowing in the breeze.

As mother and daughter staged a noisy and tearful reunion, Cordelia greeted Lindsay with a warm kiss. "I couldn't sit in London not knowing what was happening," she explained. "Even if there's nothing I can do, I had to come."

Lindsay found a smile and said, "It's good to see you. I appreciate it. How long can you stay?"

"Till Wednesday lunchtime. Jane's filled me in on what's been happening. What's the plan, now that you've been appointed official Miss Marple to the peace women? Do I have to rush off and buy you a knitting pattern and a ball of fluffy wool?"

"Very funny. I'm not entirely sure what I'm supposed to be doing. But I'll have to speak to Debs about last night. I've already warned her not to talk to anyone else. Of course, Duncan wants me to do the chat with her, but the lawyer will never let us use a line of it. I suppose I should have a crack at the family, too. I've got a good contact, the copper who's handling things at the moment, a Superintendent Rigano. I'm going to see him this afternoon. Let's go and have a pint, and I'll fill you in."

Lindsay swallowed the emotional turmoil triggered off by Cordelia's appearance and told her lover all she knew about the murder over a bowl of soup in the nearest pub that accepted peace women customers—nearly three miles away. Cordelia was fired with enthusiasm and insisted that they set off immediately in her car for Brownlow Common Cottages which, in spite of their humble name, were actually a collection of architect-designed mock-Georgian mansions.

There could be no mistaking the Crabtree residence. It was a large, double-fronted, two-storey house covered in white stucco with bow windows and imitation Georgian bottle-glass panes. A pillared portico was tacked onto the front. At the side stood a double garage, with a fifty-yard drive leading up to it. In front of the house was a neatly tended square lawn which had been underplanted with crocuses, now just past their best. The road outside was clogged on both sides by a dozen cars, the majority new. At the wrought-iron gate in the low, white-painted wall stood a gaggle of men in expensive topcoats. A few men and women stood around the cars looking bored. Every few minutes, one reporter peeled off from a group and ambled up the drive to ring the door bell. There was never any reply, not even a twitch of the curtains that hid the downstairs rooms from view.

"The ratpack's out in force," Lindsay muttered as she climbed out of the car and headed for her colleagues. She soon spotted a familiar face, Bill Bryman, the crime man from the *London Evening Sentinel*. She greeted him and asked what was happening.

"Sweet FA," he replied bitterly. "I've been here since eight o'clock and will my desk pull me off? Will they hell! The son answered the door the first time and told us nothing doing. Since then, it's a total blank. If you ask me, they've disconnected the bell. I've told the office it's a complete waste of time, but you know news editors. Soon as they get promoted, they have an operation on their brains to remove all memory of what life on the road is all about."

"What about the neighbours?"

Bill shook his head wearily. "About as much use as a choc-olate chip-pan. Too bloody 'okay yah' to communicate with the yobbos of the popular press. Now if you were to say you were from the *Tatler*—though looking at the outfit, I doubt you'd get away it." Lindsay looked ruefully at her clothes which still bore the traces of her headlong flight the night before, in spite of her efforts to clean up. "You been down the peace camp yet?" he added. "They're about as much help as this lot here."

"So I'd be wasting my time hanging around here, would I?"

"If you've got anything better to do, do it. I'd rather watch an orphanage burn," Bill answered resignedly with the cynicism affected by hard-boiled crime reporters the world over. "I'll be stuck here for the duration. If I get anything, I'll file it for you. For the usual fee."

Lindsay grinned to herself as she returned to the BMW. As they pulled away, Lindsay noticed the tall blond man she'd tagged as Special Branch when she'd seen him at the camp. He was leaning against a red Ford Fiesta on the fringes of the press corps, watching them.

"To Fordham nick," she said to Cordelia. "And stop at the first public toilet. Desperate situations need desperate remedies."

6

Lindsay emerged from the public toilet on the outskirts of Fordham a different woman. Before they left the camp she had retrieved her emergency overnight working bag from the boot of her car, and she was now wearing a smart brown dress and jacket, chosen for their ability not to crease, coupled with brown stilettos that would have caused major earth tremors at the peace camp. Cordelia wolf-whistled quietly as her lover got back into the car. "You'll get your lesbian card taken away, dressing like that," she teased.

"Fuck off, she quipped wittily," Lindsay replied. "If Duncan wants the biz doing, I will do the biz."

At the police station, Lindsay ran the gauntlet of bureaucratic obstacles and eventually found herself face to face with Superintendent Rigano. They exchanged pleasantries, then Lindsay leaned across his desk and said, "I think you and I should do a deal."

His face didn't move a muscle. He would have made a good poker player if he could have been bothered with anything so predictable, thought Lindsay. When he had finished appraising her, he simply said, "Go on."

Lindsay hesitated long enough to light a cigarette. She needed a moment to work out what came next in this sequence of unplanned declarations. "You had Deborah Patterson in here for twelve hours. I imagine she wouldn't even tell you what year it is.

"They'll all be like that," she continued. "They've gone past the 'innocents abroad' stage down there, thanks to the way the powers that be have used the police and manipulated the courts. Now, they have a stable of sharp lawyers who don't owe you anything. Several of the peace women have been in prison and think it holds no terrors for them. They all know their rights, and they're not even going to warn you if your backside is on fire.

"So if you want any information from them, you're stymied. Without me, that is. I think I can deliver what you need to know from them. I'm not crazy about the position I find myself in. But they trust me, which is not something you can say about many people who have a truce with the establishment. They've asked me to act as a sort of troubleshooter for them."

He looked suspicious. "I thought you were a reporter," he said. "How have you managed to earn their trust?"

"The women at the camp know all about me. I've been going there for months now."

He could have blustered, he could have threatened, she knew. But he just asked, quietly, "And what's the price?"

Glad that her first impression of him hadn't been shattered, Lindsay replied, "The price is a bit of sharing. I'm a good investigative reporter. I'll let you have what I get, if you'll give me a bit of help and information."

"You don't want much, do you?" he complained.

"I'm offering something you won't get any other way," Lindsay replied. She doubted she could deliver all she had promised, but she reckoned she could do enough to keep him happy. That way, she'd get what she and the women wanted.

He studied her carefully and appeared to come to a decision. "Can we go off record?" he asked. Lindsay nodded. His response, at first, appeared to be a diversion. "He was an influential man, Crabtree. Knew most of the people that are supposedly worth knowing round these parts. Didn't just know them to share a pink gin with—he knew them well enough to demand favors. Being dead seems to have set in motion the machinery for calling in the favors. I'm technically in charge of the CID boys running this at local level. But CID are avoiding this one like the plague. And other units are trying to use their muscle on it.

"Our switchboard has been busy. I'm under a lot of pressure to arrest your friend. You'll understand that, I know. But I'm old-fashioned enough to believe that you get your evidence before the arrest, not vice versa. That wouldn't have been hard in this case, if you follow me.

"I happen to think that she didn't kill him. And I'm not afraid to admit I'll need help to make that stick. You know I don't need to make deals to achieve that help. Most coppers could manage it, given time and a bit of leaning. But I don't have time. There are other people breathing down my neck. So let's see what we need for a deal."

Lindsay nodded. "I need access to the family. You'll have to introduce me to them. Suggest that I'm not just a newspaper reporter. That I'm working on a bigger piece about the Brownlow campaign for a magazine that will feature an in-depth profile of Crabtree—a sort of tribute."

"Are you?"

"I can be by teatime. Also point out to them that it will get the pack off their back and end the siege. I'll be taping the conversation and transcribing the tapes. You can have full access to the tapes and a copy of the transcripts."

"Are you trying to tell me you think it was a domestic crime?"

"Most murders are, aren't they? But I won't know who might have killed him till I've found out a lot more about his life. That means family, friends, colleagues, and the peace women will all have to open up to me. In return, any of the peace women you want to talk to, you tell me honestly what it's about, and I'll deliver the initial information you need. Obviously, you'll have to take over if it's at all significant, but that's got to be better for you than a wall of silence."

"It's completely unorthodox. I can't run an investigation according to the whim of the press."

"Without my help, I can promise you all you'll find at the camp is a brick wall. Anyway, you don't strike me as being a particularly orthodox copper."

He almost smiled. "When do you want to see the family?" he asked.

"Soon as possible. It really will get the rest of the press off the doorstep. You'll have to tell my colleagues at the gate that the family asked expressly to talk to a *Clarion* reporter, or you'll get a load of aggravation which I'm sure you could do without."

"Are you mobile?"

"The BMW cabriolet outside."

"The fruits of being a good investigative reporter seem sweeter than those of being a good copper. Wait in the car." He rose. The interview was over.

Slightly bewildered by her degree of success, Lindsay found her way through the labyrinthine corridors to the car park, feeling incongruous in her high heels after days in heavy boots, and slumped into the seat beside Cordelia, who looked at her enquiringly.

"I think perhaps I need my head examined," Lindsay said. "The way I've been behaving today, I think it buttons up the back. I've just marched into a superintendent's office and offered to do a deal with him that will keep Debs out of prison, get me some good exclusives, and might possibly, if we all get very lucky indeed, point him in the right direction for the real villain. Talk about collaborating with the class enemy. Mind you, I expected him to throw me out on my ear. But he went for it. Can you believe it?"

Lindsay outlined her conversation with Rigano. When she'd finished, Cordelia asked, "Would he be the one who looks like a refugee from a portrait in the Uffizi?"

"That's him. Why?"

"Because he's heading this way," she said drily as Rigano's hand reached for Lindsay's door. Lindsay sat bolt upright and wound down the window.

"Open the back door for me, please," said Rigano. "I believe we may be able to do a deal."

Lindsay did as she was told, and he climbed in. A shadow of distaste crossed his face as his eyes flicked round the luxurious interior. "Drive to Brownlow Common Cottages," he said. "Not too fast. There will be a police car behind you."

Cordelia started the car, put it in gear, then, almost as an afterthought, before she released the clutch, she turned round in her seat and said, "I'm Cordelia Brown, by the way. Would it be awfully unreasonable of me to ask your name?"

"Not at all," he replied courteously. His face showed the ghost of a smile. "I am Superintendent Giacomo Rigano of Fordham Police. I'm sorry I didn't introduce myself. I've grown so accustomed to knowing who everyone is that I forget this is not a two-way process. Because I knew who you were, I assumed you knew me too."

"How did you know who I was?" she demanded, full of suspicion. She never seemed to remember that, as the writer of several novels and a successful television series, she was a minor celebrity. It had often amused Lindsay.

As usual, Rigano took his time in replying. "I recognised you from your photographs." He paused, and just before

Cordelia could draw again on her stock of paranoia, he added, "You know, on your dust jackets. And, of course, from television."

Fifteen love, thought Lindsay in surprise. They drove off, and Lindsay swiveled round in her seat. "What's the deal, then?"

"I've just spoken to Mrs. Crabtree. She wasn't keen, but I've persuaded her. I'll take you there and introduce you to her. Then I'll leave you to it. On the understanding that I can listen to the tapes afterwards and that you will give me copies of the transcript as agreed. In return, I need to know who was at the peace camp last night and where each woman was between ten and eleven. If you can give me that basic information, then I know who I need to talk to further."

"Okay," Lindsay agreed. "But it'll be tomorrow before I can let you have that."

"Then tomorrow will have to do. The people who want quick results will have to be satisfied with the investigation proceeding at its own pace. Like any other investigation."

"Yes, but to people round here, he's not quite like any other corpse, is he?" Cordelia countered.

"That's true," Rigano retorted. "But while this remains my case, he will simply be a man who was unlawfully killed. To me, that is the only special thing about him."

That must endear you to your bosses, Cordelia thought. Just what is Lindsay getting into this time? Maverick coppers we don't need.

Cordelia steered carefully through the crowd of journalists and vehicles that still made the narrow road in front of Brownlow Cottages a cramped thoroughfare. Lindsay noticed the blond watcher was no longer there. At the end of the Crabtrees' drive, Rigano wound down the window and shouted to the constable on duty there, "Open the gate for us, Jamieson!"

The constable started into action, and, as they drove

inside, Lindsay could see the looks of fury on the faces of her rivals. As soon as the car stopped, Rigano got out and gestured to Lindsay to follow him. He was immediately distracted by journalists fifty yards away shouting their demands for copy. Lindsay took advantage of the opportunity to lean across and say urgently to Cordelia, "Listen, love, you can't help me here. I want us to work as a team like we did before. Would you go back to the camp and see if you can get Jane to help you sort out this alibi nonsense that Rigano wants? And make it as watertight as possible. Okay?"

"We have a deal," said Cordelia, with a smile. "As the good superintendent says."

"Great. See you later," Lindsay replied as she got out of the car and joined Rigano standing impatiently on the doorstep.

"Mrs. Crabtree's on her own," he remarked. "There were some friends round earlier but she sent them away. The son, Simon, is out. He apparently had some urgent business to see to. So you should have a chance to do something more than ask superficial questions to which we all know the answers already."

He gave five swift raps on the door knocker. Inside, a dog barked hysterically. As the door opened, Rigano insinuated himself into the gap to block the view of the photographers at the end of the drive. Using his legs like a hockey goalkeeper he prevented an agitated fox terrier taking off down the drive to attack the waiting press eager to snatch a picture of Rupert Crabtree's widow. Lindsay followed him into a long wide hallway. Rigano put his hand under Mrs. Crabtree's arm and guided her through a door at the rear of the hall. The dog sniffed suspiciously at Lindsay, gave a low growl and scampered after them.

Lindsay glanced quickly around her. The occasional tables had genuine age, the carpet was dark brown and deep, the pictures on the wall were old, dark oils. This was money, and not *arriviste* money either. Nothing matched quite well enough for taste acquired in a job lot. Half of Lindsay felt envy, the other half contempt, but she didn't have time to analyze either emotion. She reached into her bag and switched on her tape recorder, then entered the room behind the other two.

She found herself in the dining room, its centerpiece a large rosewood drum table, big enough to seat eight people comfortably. Against one wall stood a long mahogany sideboard. The end of the room was almost completely taken up by large French windows which allowed plenty of light to glint off the silver candlesticks and rosebowl on the sideboard. On the walls hung attractive modern watercolors of cottage gardens. Lindsay took all this in and turned to the woman sitting at the table. Her pose was as stiff as the straight-backed chair she sat in. At her feet now lay the dog, who opened one eye from time to time to check that no one had moved significantly.

"Mrs. Crabtree, this is Miss Lindsay Gordon. Miss Gordon's the writer I spoke to you about on the phone. She's to write a feature for *Newsday*. I give you my word, you can trust her. Don't be afraid to tell her about your husband," Rigano said.

Emma Crabtree looked up and surveyed them both. She looked as if she didn't have enough trust to go round, but she'd hand over what she had in the full expectation that it would be returned to her diminished. Her hair was carefully cut and styled, but she had not been persuaded either by husband or hairdresser to get rid of the gray that heavily streaked the original blonde. Her face showed the remnants of a beauty that had not been sustained by a strong bone structure once the skin had begun to sag and wrinkle. But the eyes were still lovely. They were large, hazel, and full of life. They didn't look as if they had shed too many tears. The grief was all being carried by the hands, which worked continuously in the lap of a tweed skirt.

She didn't try to smile a welcome. She simply said in a dry voice, "Good afternoon, Miss Gordon."

Rigano looked slightly uncomfortable and quickly said, "I'll be on my way now. Thank you for your cooperation, Mrs. Crabtree. I'll be in touch." He nodded to them both and backed out of the room.

Emma Crabtree glanced at Lindsay briefly, then turned her head slightly to stare through the windows. "I'm not altogether sure why I agreed to speak to you," she said. "But I suppose the superintendent knows best and if that's the only way to get rid of that rabble that's driving my neighbors to distraction, then so be it. At least you've not been hanging over my garden gate all day. Now, what do you want to know?"

Her words and her delivery cut the ground from under Lindsay's feet. All the standard approaches professing a spurious sympathy were rendered invalid by the widow's coolness. The journalist also sensed a degree of hostility that she would have to disarm before she could get much useful information. So she changed the tactics she had been working out in the car and settled on an equally cool approach. "How long had you been married?" she asked.

"Almost twenty-six years. We celebrated our silver wedding last May."

"You must have been looking forward to a lot more happy years, then?"

"If you say so."

"And you have two children, is that right?"

"Hardly children. Rosamund is twenty-four now and Simon is twenty-one."

"This must have come as an appalling shock to you all?" Lindsay felt clumsy and embarrassed, but the other woman's attitude was so negative that it was hard to find words that weren't leaden and awkward.

"In many ways, yes. When the police came to the door last night, I was shaken, though the last thing that I would have expected was for Rupert to be bludgeoned to death taking Rex for his bedtime stroll."

"Were you alone when the police arrived with the news?"

She shook her head. "No. Simon was in. He'd been working earlier in the evening; he rents a friend's lock-up garage in Fordham. He's got all his computing equipment there. He's got his own computer software business, you know. He commutes on his motorbike, so he can come and go as he pleases."

At last she was opening up. Lindsay gave a small sigh of relief. "So the first you knew anything was amiss was when the police came to the door?"

"Well, strictly speaking, it was just before they rang the bell. Rex started barking his head off. You see, the poor creature had obviously been frightened off by Rupert's attacker, and he'd bolted and come home. He must have been sitting on the front doorstep. Of course, when he saw the police, he started barking. He's such a good watchdog."

"Yes, I'd noticed," Lindsay replied. "Forgive me, Mrs. Crabtree, but something you said earlier seems to me to beg a lot of questions."

"Really? What was that?"

"It seemed to me that you implied that you're not entirely surprised that your husband was murdered. That someone should actively want him dead."

Mrs. Crabtree's head turned sharply towards Lindsay. She looked her up and down as if seeing her properly for the first time. Her appraisal seemed to find something in Lindsay worth confiding in.

"My husband was a man who enjoyed the exercise of power over people," she said after a pause. "He loved to be in control, even in matters of small degree. There was nothing that appealed to Rupert so much as being able to dictate to people, whether over their plea on a motoring offense or how they should live their entire lives.

"Even when shrouded in personal charm of the sort my husband had, it's not an endearing characteristic. Miss Gordon, a lot of people had good cause to resent him. Perhaps Rupert finally pushed someone too far. . ."

"Can you think of anyone in particular?" Lindsay asked coolly, suppressing the astonishment she felt at Mrs. Crabtree's open admission but determined to cash in on it.

"The women at the peace camp, of course. He was determined not to give up the battle against them till every last one was removed. He didn't just regard it as a political pressure campaign. He saw it as his personal mission to fight them as individuals and as a group and wear them down. He was especially vindictive towards the one who broke his nose. He said he'd not be satisfied till she was in prison."

"How did you feel about that mission of your husband's? How did it affect you?" Lindsay probed.

Mrs. Crabtree shrugged. "I thought he was doing the right thing to oppose the camp. Those women have no morals. They even bring their children to live in those shocking conditions. No self-respecting mother would do that. No, Rupert was right. The missiles are there for our protection, after all. And that peace camp is such an eyesore."

"Did it take up a lot of your husband's time?"

"A great deal. But it was a good cause, so I tried not to mind." Mrs. Crabtree looked away and added, "He really cared about what he was doing."

"Was there anyone else who might have had a motive?"

"Oh, I don't know. I've no idea who might hold a professional grievance. But you should probably talk to William Mallard. He's the treasurer of Ratepayers Against Brownlow's Destruction. He and Rupert were in the throes of some sort of row over the group's finances. And he'd be able to tell you more about Rupert's relations with other people in the group. There was one man that Rupert got thrown out a few weeks ago. I don't know any details, I'm afraid. Does any of this help?"

"Oh yes, I need to get as full a picture as possible. Your husband was obviously a man who was very active in the community."

Emma Crabtree nodded. Lindsay thought she detected a certain cynicism in her smile. "He was indeed," she concurred. "One could scarcely be unaware of that. And for all his faults, Rupert did a lot for this area. He was very good at getting things done. He brooked no opposition. He was a very determined man, my husband. Life will be a lot quieter without him." For the first time, a note of regret had crept into her voice.

Lindsay brooded on what had been said. It seemed to her that it was now or never for the hard questions. "And did his forcefulness extend to his family life?" she pursued.

Mrs. Crabtree flashed a shrewd glance at her. "In some ways," she replied cautiously. "He was determined the children shouldn't be spoilt, that they should prove themselves before getting any financial help from him. Rosamund had to spend three years slaving away in restaurants and hotel kitchens before he'd lend her enough to set up in business on her own. Then Simon wanted to set up this computer software company. But Rupert refused to lend him the capital he needed. Rupert insisted that he stay on at college and finish his accountancy qualifications. But Simon refused. Too like his father. He went ahead with his business idea, in spite of Rupert. But of course, without any capital, he hasn't got as far as he had hoped."

"Presumably, though, he'll inherit a share of his father's money now?" Lindsay pursued cautiously.

"More than enough for his business, yes. It'll soften the

blow for him of losing his father. He's been very withdrawn since . . . since last night. He's struggling to pretend that life goes on, but I know that deep down he's in great pain."

Her defence of her son was cut off by the opening of the dining room door. Lindsay was taken aback. She failed to see how anyone could have entered the house without the dog barking as it had when she and Rigano arrived. She half turned to weight up the new arrival.

"I'm back, mother," he said brusquely. "Who's this?"

Simon Crabtree was a very tall young man. He had his father's dark curling hair and strong build, but the impression of forcefulness was contradicted by a full, soft mouth. Lindsay suddenly understood just why Emma Crabtree was so swift to come to his defense.

"Hello, darling," she said. "This is Miss Gordon. She's a journalist. Superintendent Rigano brought her. We're hoping that now all the other journalists will leave us alone."

He smiled, and Lindsay realised that he had also inherited his slice of Rupert's charm. "That bunch? They'll go as soon as they've got another sensation to play with," he said cynically. "There was no need to invite one in, mother." He turned to Lindsay and added, "I hope you've not been hassling my mother. That's the last thing she needs after a shock like this."

"I realise that. I wanted to know a bit about your father. I'm writing a magazine feature about the camp, and your father played an important role that should be recognised. I need to talk to everyone who's involved, and your mother kindly agreed to give me some time. In return, I've promised to get rid of the mob at your gate. A few quotes should persuade them to leave," Lindsay replied, conciliatory.

"You'd be better employed talking to those women at the peace camp. That way you'd get an interview with my father's murderer, since the police don't seem to be in any hurry to arrest her."

"I'm not sure I understand what you mean," Lindsay said.

"It's obvious, isn't it? One of those so-called peace women had already assaulted my father. It doesn't take much intelligence to work it out from there, does it?" Lindsay wondered if it was grief that made him appear so brusque.

"I can understand why you feel like that," she sympathised. "I'm sure your father's death has upset you. But at least now you'll be able to afford to set up your business properly. That will be a kind of tribute in a way, won't it?"

He shot a shrewd look at Lindsay. "The business is already set up. It's going to be successful anyway. All this means is that I do things a bit quicker. That's all. My father's death means more to me than a bloody business opportunity. Mother, I don't know why you brought this up." Turning back to Lindsay he added, "I'm going to have to ask you to leave now. My mother is too tired to deal with more questioning." He looked expectantly at his mother.

The conditioned reflex built up over the years of marriage to Rupert Crabtree came into play. Simon had come into his inheritance in more ways than one. "Yes," she said, "I think I've told you all I can, Miss Gordon. If you don't mind."

Lindsay got to her feet. "I'd like to have a few words with your daughter, Mrs. Crabtree. When will she be home?"

"She doesn't live here any more. We're not expecting her till the funeral," Simon interjected abruptly. "I'll show you out now." He opened the door and held it open. Lindsay took the hint and thanked the widow routinely.

In the hall, with the door closed behind them, Lindsay tried again. "Your father's death has obviously upset you. You must have cared for him very deeply."

His face remained impassive. "Is that what you've been asking my mother about? Oh well, I suppose it's what the masses want to read with their corn flakes. You can tell your readers that anyone who knew my father will realise how deeply upset we all are and what a gap he has left in our lives. Okay?" He opened the front door and all but shoved her through it. "I'm sure you've already got enough to fabricate a good story," was his parting shot as he closed the door behind her.

She flipped open her bag, switched off the tape recorder and headed off down the drive to offer a couple of minor tit-bits to her rivals.

7

Bill Bryman had offered to drive Lindsay the mile back to the peace camp principally because he thought he might be able to prise more information from her than the bare quotes she had handed out to the pack. He was out of luck. Neither gratitude nor friendship would make Lindsay part with those pearls she had that were printable. But as she left the Crabtree's house, she noticed that the Special Branch man with the red Fiesta was back, which added indefinably to her eagerness to leave the scene. So she had frankly used Bill's car as a getaway vehicle to escape her colleagues and any watching eyes. As soon as he pulled up near the van, she was off. There was hardly a sign of life at the camp, and she realised a meeting must be in progress. Clever Cordelia, she thought.

She struggled through the mud in her high heels to Cordelia's car and retrieved her other clothes. Back at the van, she changed into jeans and a sweater then set off jogging down the road towards the phone box on the main road, in the opposite direction to Brownlow Common Cottages. She had deliberately chosen the further of the two boxes in the neighborhood to avoid being overheard by any fellow journalists hanging around waiting to talk to their offices. To her relief the box was empty. She rang the police at Fordham to check that there were no new developments, then got through to the *Clarion's* copy room. She dictated a heavily edited account of her interview with Emma and Simon Crabtree, coupled with an update on the case.

When she was transferred to the newsdesk, Duncan's voice reverberated in her ear. "Hello, Lindsay. What've you got for me?"

"An exclusive chat with the grieving widow and son," she replied. "Nobody else got near them, but I had to give a couple of quotes to the pack in exchange for the exclusive. You'll see them from the agency wire services, probably. Nothing of any importance. Any queries on the feature copy I did earlier?"

"No queries, kid. Your copy has just come up on screen, and it looks okay. Any progress on the exclusive chat with the bird who broke his nose?"

Lindsay fumed quietly. How much did the bastard want? "Hey, Duncan, did you know that women get called birds because they keep picking up worms? I doubt if I'll get anything for tonight's paper on that. The woman concerned is still a bit twitchy, you know? First thing tomorrow, though. I'll file it before conference. And I've got another possible angle for tomorrow if the lawyers won't let us use the interview. Apparently there were one or two wee problems with Crabtree's ratepayers' association. Possible financial shenanigans. I'm going to take a look at that, okay?" Lindsay couldn't believe she was taking control of the conversation and the assignment, but it was actually happening.

"Fine," Duncan acknowledged. "You're the man on the spot, that sounds all right to me. Stick with it, kid. Speak to me in the morning." The line went dead. Man on the spot, indeed. She made a face at the phone and set off at a leisurely pace to the camp.

As the benders came into sight, she saw that things were no longer quite so quiet. Outside the meeting tent were several figures. As she got closer, Lindsay could distinguish Cordelia, Jane, Deborah, Nicky, and a couple of other women. There seemed to be an argument in progress, judging by the gestures and postures of the group. Lindsay quickened her pace.

"Lindsay!" Jane exclaimed. "Thank goodness you're here. Maybe you can sort this mess out."

Cordelia interrupted angrily. "Look, Jane, I've said already, there's nothing *to* sort out. Just count me out in future."

"Look, just calm down, all of you," soothed Deborah. "Everybody's taking this all so personally. It's not any sort of personality thing. It's about the principle of trust and not reneging on the people you've entrusted something to. You know?"

"Are you saying I'm not to be trusted?" Cordelia flashed back.

"Personally, I don't think either of you are," Nicky muttered.

"It's really nothing to do with you, Cordelia," Jane replied in brisk tones. "The women find it very hard to trust people they see as outsiders and they used up all their available good-will on Lindsay."

Exasperated, Lindsay demanded, "Will someone please tell me what the hell is going on?"

The others looked at each other, uncertain. Cordelia snorted. "Typical," she muttered. "Everything by committee. Look, Lindsay, it's pretty simple. You asked me to sort out the alibis for you and your pet policeman. I figured the quickest and most logical way to do it was get everyone together. So I got Jane to call a meeting. Which eventually got itself together only to decide that I wasn't right-on enough for them to cooperate with. So I upped and left, which is where you find us now."

Lindsay sighed. Jane said with no trace of defensiveness, "I think that's a bit loaded, Cordelia. The women didn't like someone they perceive as an outsider calling a meeting and making demands. We had enough difficulties getting agreement on asking Lindsay for help. Maybe you could have been a bit less heavy. I still think they'll be okay if you both explain to them why we need the information to protect ourselves and to protect Deborah. Right now, it's seen as being simply a case of us doing the police's job for them and exposing ourselves to groundless suspicion."

Cordelia scowled. "You can do all the explaining you want, but you can leave me out of the negotiations. I've had it. I'm going back to London," she said, and stalked off towards her car.

"How childish can you get?" Nicky asked airily of no one in particular.

"Shut it," Lindsay snarled. "Why the hell did nobody help her? Debs, could you and Jane please go and talk them down in there? I want a word with Cordelia before she goes. I'll be back as soon as I can." She ran off in Cordelia's wake and caught up with her before she could reach the car.

Lindsay grabbed her arm, but Cordelia wriggled free. Lindsay caught up again and shouted desperately, "Wait a minute, will you?"

Cordelia stopped, head held high. "What for?"

"Don't take off like this," Lindsay pleaded. "I don't want you to go. I need you here. I need your help. It's perfectly bloody trying to deal with this situation alone. I've got to have a foot in both camps. Nobody really trusts me either; you know I'm just the lesser of two evils, both for the women and for the police. Don't leave me isolated like this."

Cordelia continued to stare at the ground. "You're not isolated, Lindsay. If you go into that meeting, you won't be humiliated like I was. It's not enough with these women to have your heart in the right place. You've got to have the right credentials too. And my face just doesn't fit."

"It's not like that, Cordelia. Don't leave because there was one hassle between you." Lindsay reached out impulsively and pulled Cordelia close. "Don't leave me. Not now. I feel . . . I don't know, I feel I'm not safe without you here."

"That's absurd," Cordelia replied, her voice muffled by Lindsay's jacket. "Look, I'm going back to London to get stuck into some work. I'm not mad at you at all. I simply choose not to have to deal with these women solely on their terms. All right? Now don't forget, I want to know where you are and what you're doing, okay? I'm worried about you. This deal you've done with Rigano could get really dangerous. There are so many potential conflicts of interest—the women, the police, your paper. And you should know from experience that digging the dirt on murderers can be dangerous. Don't take any chances. Look, I think it will be easier for you to deal with the peace women if I'm not around. But if you really need me, give me a call and I'll come down and book myself into a hotel or something."

Lindsay nodded, and they hugged each other. Then Cordelia disengaged herself and climbed into the car. She revved the engine a couple of times and glided off down the road, leaving a spray of mud and a puff of white exhaust behind her. Lindsay watched till she was long gone, then turned to walk slowly back to the meeting tent.

She pushed aside the flap of polythene that served as a door and stood listening to Deborah doing for her what someone with a bit of sense and sensitivity should have done for Cordelia. Deborah finally wound up, saying, "We've got nothing to hide here. We asked Lindsay to help us prove that. Well, she can't do it all by herself. When she asks us for help, or sends someone else for that help, we should forget maybe that we have some principles that can't be broken or suspicions we won't let go, or else we're as bad as the ones on the other side of that wire."

Lindsay looked round. The area was crowded with women and several small children. The assortment of clothes and hairstyles was a bewildering assault on the senses. The warm, steamy air smelled of bodies and tobacco smoke. The first woman to speak this time was an Irish woman; Lindsay thought her name was Nuala.

"I think Deborah's right," she said in her soft voice. "I think we were unfair the way we spoke before. Just because someone broke the conventions of the camp was no reason for us to be hostile, and if we can't be flexible enough to let an outsider come in and work with us, then heaven help us when we get to the real fight about the missiles. Let's not forget why we're really here. I don't mind telling Lindsay everything I know about this murder. I was in my bender with Siobhan and Marieke from about ten o'clock onwards. We were all writing letters till about twelve, then we went to sleep."

That opened the floodgates. Most of the women accepted the logic of Nuala's words, and those who didn't were shamed into a reluctant co-operation. For the next couple of hours, Lindsay was engaged in scribbling down the movements of the forty-seven women who had stayed at the camp the night before. Glancing through it superficially, it seemed that all but a handful were accounted for at the crucial time. One of that handful was Deborah, who had gone on alone to the van while Lindsay talked to Jane. No-one had seen her after she left the sing-song in Willow's bender.

Trying not to think too much about the implications of that, Lindsay made her way back to the van. She looked at her watch for the first time in hours and was shocked to see it was almost eight o'clock. She dumped the alibi information, then went down to the phone box yet again. She checked in with the office only to find there were no problems. She phoned Cordelia to find she had gone out for dinner leaving only the answering machine to talk to Lindsay. She left a message, then she checked in with Rigano.

"How is our deal progressing?" he asked at once.

"Very well. I'll have the alibi information collated by morning, and I should have a fairly interesting tape transcribed for you by then. Tomorrow, I'm going to see William Mallard. Do I need your help to get in there?"

"I shouldn't think so. He's been giving interviews all day. The standard hypocrisy—greatly admired, much missed, stalwart of the association." She could picture the expression of distaste on his mouth and thought a small risk might be worth the taking.

"Any mention of the financial shenanigans?" she enquired.

"What financial shenanigans would they be, Miss Gordon?"

"Come, come, Superintendent. You live here, I'm just a visitor, after all. There must have been talk, surely."

"I heard they had a disagreement, but that it had all been cleared up. The person you want to talk to in the first instance is not Mallard but a local farmer called Carlton Stanhope. He was thoroughly disenchanted with the pair of them."

"Do you think he'll play for an interview? That's just the sort of person I need to crack this," Lindsay said.

"I don't know. He's not as much of a stick-in-the-mud as a lot of them around here. He's been helpful to me already. He might be persuaded to talk to you off the record. Being outside his circle, he might tell you a bit more than he was prepared to tell a policeman. And, of course, you could pass that on to me, unofficially, couldn't you?"

"Any chance of you helping me persuade him?" In for a penny, thought Lindsay.

There was a silence on the other end of the phone. Lindsay crossed her fingers and prayed. Finally, Rigano spoke. "I'll ring him tonight and fix something up. I'm sure if I ask him, he'll give you all the help he can. Besides, he might even enjoy meeting a real journalist. How about half past ten tomorrow morning in the residents' lounge of the George Hotel in Fordham?"

"Superintendent Rigano, you could easily become a friend for life. That will do splendidly. I'll see you then."

"Oh, there won't be any need for me to be there. But I'll see you at ten o'clock in my office with the information you've gathered for me so far. Goodnight, Miss Gordon."

By the time she got back to the camp, Lindsay was exhausted and starving. She made her way to Jane's bender, where she found her deep in conversation with Nuala. Jane looked up, grinned at her and said, "Cara's with Josy's kids. Deborah's in the van cooking you some food. You look as if you could do with it, too. Go on, go and eat. And get a good night's sleep, for God's sake. Doctor's orders!"

Lindsay walked back to the van, realising that she was beginning to find it hard to remember life outside the peace camp with real houses and all their pleasures. But the thought was driven from her head as soon as she opened the van door. The smell that greeted her transported her back into the past. "Bacon ribs and beans," she breathed.

Deborah looked up with a smile. "I got Judith to whizz me round Sainsbury's this morning. Cooking your favorite tea's about all I can do to thank you for all you've done."

"Wonderful," said Lindsay, "I'm starving. Is it ready now?"

Deborah stirred the pot and tried a bean for tenderness. "Not quite. About fifteen minutes."

"Good, just long enough for you to tell me your version of events on the night of the murder during the crucial time for which you have no alibi. Care to tell me exactly what you did?"

Deborah left the stove and sat down at the table. She looked tired. Lindsay took pity, went to the fridge and took out a couple of coolish cans of lager. Both women opened their beer and silently toasted each other. Then Deborah said, "I'm afraid you're not going to like this very much.

"After I left you, I came back to the van and made sure Cara was sleeping quietly. I was just about to brew up when I remembered I wanted to get hold of Robin. He's staying at my place just now. We did a deal. I said he could stay rent free if he did the plumbing for me. I've never been at my best with water. It's the only building job I always try to delegate. Anyway, I'd been thinking that I wanted him to plumb in a shower independent of the hot water system.

"So I thought I'd better let him know before he went any further, and I decided to phone him."

Lindsay broke in. "But your house isn't on the phone."

"No. But if I want to get hold of Robin, I ring the Lees. They've got the farm at the end of the lane. They send a message up with the milk in the morning telling Rob to phone me at a particular time and number. It works quite well. So I went to the phone."

"Which box did you go to?"

"The wrong one, from our point of view. The one nearer Brownlow Common Cottages."

"Will the Lees remember what time it was when you phoned?"

"Hardly. No one answered. They must have been out for the evening. So I just came back and made a brew."

"Did you see anything? Hear anything?"

"Not really. It was dark by the perimeter fence anyway. I thought I might have seen Crabtree walking his dog, but it was quite a bit away, so I wasn't sure."

Lindsay sat musing. "Any cars pass you at all?"

"I don't remember any, but I doubt if I would have

noticed. It's not exactly an unusual sight. People use those back lanes late at night to avoid risking the breathalyser."

Lindsay shrugged. "Oh Debs, I don't know. I just can't seem to get a handle on this business."

Deborah smiled wanly. "You will, Lin, you will. For my sake, I hope you will."

Later, fortified by a huge bowl of bacon and beans, Lindsay settled down to work. It took her over an hour to transcribe the tape, using her portable typewriter. Next came the even more tedious task of typing up her notes of the camp women's alibis. It was after midnight before she could put her typewriter into its case and concentrate again on Deborah, who was curled up in a corner devouring a new feminist novel.

"You look like a woman who needs a hug," said Deborah, looking up with a sympathetic smile.

"I feel like a woman who needs more than a hug," Lindsay replied, sitting down beside her. Deborah put her arms round Lindsay and gently massaged the taut muscles at the back of her neck.

"You need a massage," she said. "Would you like me to give you one?"

Lindsay nodded. "Please. Nobody has ever given me back-rubs like you used to."

They made up the bed, then Lindsay stripped off and lay face down on the firm cushions. Deborah took a small bottle of massage oil from a cupboard. She rubbed the fragrant oil into her palms and started kneading Lindsay's stiff muscles.

Lindsay could feel warmth spreading through her body from head to foot as she relaxed.

"Better?" Deborah asked.

"Mmm," Lindsay replied. She had become aware of Deborah's nearness. She rolled over and lightly stroked Deborah's cheek. "Thank you," she said, moving into a half-sitting position.

Deborah slid down beside her, and their two bodies intertwined in an embrace that moved almost immediately from the platonic to the passionate, taking them both by surprise. "Are you sure about this, Lin?" Deborah whispered.

For reply, Lindsay kissed her.

8

The morning found Lindsay in good humor as she breezed into the police station at Fordham. She had dived into the local Marks and Spencer and bought a pair of smart mushroom coloured trousers and a cream and brown striped shirt that matched her brown jacket. She felt she looked her best and was on top of things professionally. The events of the night before were fresh in her memory, and for as long as she could put Cordelia out of her mind, she felt good about what had happened with Deborah too.

Her benign mood lasted for as long as it took her to reach the reception counter. At a desk at the back of the office she spotted a now familiar blond man flicking through some papers. Lindsay frowned as the SB man glanced up at her. Pressing the bell for service, she turned her back to wait. By the time the duty constable responded, the man had disappeared.

Rigano didn't keep her waiting. As soon as she sat down in his office, he attacked. "We've turned up a witness who saw Deborah Patterson walking down the road towards the camp at approximately ten forty-five."

"In that case, Deborah's statement won't come as a surprise to you," Lindsay retorted. "It's all here, Superintendent. Where she went, when, and why." She put two files on the desk. "This one: the peace women. That one: Emma and Simon Crabtree."

He smiled coldly. "Thank you. It might have made things a little simpler if Miss Patterson had chosen to make her statement when she was here, don't you think?" Lindsay shrugged. "Anyway, I've spoken to Stanhope. He's expecting you in the George."

Lindsay deliberately lit a cigarette, ignoring the implicit dismissal. "Do you know where I can get hold of Rosamund Crabtree?" she enquired. "I didn't have the chance to get that information from Mrs. Crabtree."

"Don't know why you want to see her," Rigano grumbled. "The way this case seems to be breaking, we're going to have to take another long, hard look at Miss Patterson. But if you really feel it's necessary, you'll probably be able to catch up with her at work. She and a partner run this vegetarian restaurant in London. Camden Town. Rubyfruits, it's called."

"Rubyfruits?" Lindsay exclaimed.

He looked at her uncomprehendingly. "Funny sort of name, eh?" he said.

"It isn't that, it's just the small-world syndrome striking again."

"You know of it?"

Lindsay nodded. "Fairly well. We go there quite a lot."

"You surprise me. I wouldn't have put you down as one of the nut cutlet brigade. Anyway, you're going to be late for Carlton Stanhope, and I wouldn't recommend that. I'd like to hear how you get on. If you're free at lunchtime, I'll be in the snug at the Frog and Bassett on the Brownlow road. Now run off and meet your man."

Lindsay got to her feet. "How will I recognise him?" she asked.

Rigano smiled. "Use your initiative. There won't be that many people in the residents' lounge at half past ten on a Tuesday morning, for starters. Besides, I've described you to him, so I don't imagine there will be too many problems of identification."

Lindsay scowled. "Thanks," she muttered on her way to the door. "I'll probably see you later in the pub. Oh, and by the way, do tell your Special Branch bloodhound to stop following me around. I'm not about to do a runner." She congratulated herself on her smart response. She would remember that arrogance later.

Ripe for takeover by the big boys, thought Lindsay as she entered the George Hotel. The combination of the faded fifties decor and odd touches of contemporary tatt was an unhappy one. She could imagine the prawn cocktail and fillet steak menu. A neon sign that looked like a museum piece pointed up a flight of stairs to the residents' lounge. Lindsay pushed open the creaky swing door. The chairs looked cheap and uncomfortable. The only occupant of the room was pouring himself a cup of coffee. Lindsay's heart sank. So much for Rigano's assumption that they'd have the place to themselves, for the young man sprawled leggily in an armchair by the coffee table didn't look like a farmer called Carlton Stanhope.

He wore tight blue jeans, elastic-sided riding boots, and an Aran sweater. His straight, dark blond hair was cut short at the sides, longer in the back, and had a floppy fringe that fell over his forehead from the side parting. He didn't look a day over twenty-five. He glanced over at Lindsay hesitating by the door and drawled, "Miss Gordon, do sit down and have a cup of coffee before it gets cold."

As he registered the surprise in her eyes, he smiled wickedly. "Not what you expected, eh? You thought a Fordham farmer called Carlton Stanhope who was a sidekick of Rupert Crabtree was bound to be a tweedy old foxhunter with a red face and a glass of Scotch in the fist, admit it! Sorry to disappoint you. Jack Rigano really should have warned you."

Lindsay's mouth wavered between a scowl and a smile. She sat down while Stanhope poured her a cup of coffee. "Do say something," he mocked. "Don't tell me I've taken your breath away?"

"I was surprised to see someone under fifty, I must say. Other than that, though, I can't say I'm greatly shocked and stunned. Don't all young gentlemen farmers dress like you these days?"

"Touché," he replied. "And since you're not what I expected of either a journalist or a peace woman, I'd say we're probably about quits. You see, Miss Gordon, we moderate men are just as much subject to stereotypes as you radical women."

Lindsay felt a hint of dislike in her response to him. She reckoned he knew himself to be a highly eligible young man, but she gave him credit for trying to build on his physical charm with an entertaining line of conversation. His manner irritated rather than appealed to her, but that didn't stop her acknowledging that it would normally find its admirers. "Superintendent Rigano seemed to think you might be able to fill me in on some background about Ratepayers Against Brownlow's Destruction."

"Jack says you're doing the investigative crime reporter bit over Rupert's death. He seems to think you're a useful sort of sleuth to have on his side, so I suppose I'm the quid pro quo," he observed.

"I appreciate the help," she responded. "I'm sure you've got more important things to be doing—drilling your barley or whatever it is farmers do in March."

"Lambing, actually. My pleasure, I assure you. Now, what exactly is it you want to know?"

"I'm interested in RABD. How did you come to get involved with it?" Lindsay asked. She found her cigarettes and offered Stanhope the packet. He dismissed it with a wave of his hand as he began his story.

"Let's see now . . . I got involved shortly after it was formed. That must have been about six or seven months ago, I guess. I hadn't been back in the area long. My father decided he wanted to bow out of the day-to-day hassle of running the farm, so he dragged me back from my job with the Forestry Commission to take over what will one day be mine. That is, what the bank and the taxman don't get their hands on.

"Anyway, to cut a long story short, I was appalled when I arrived back home and found these women camped on the common. I mean, Brownlow Common was always a place where people could walk their dogs, take their sprogs. But who'd actually want to take their offspring for a walk past that eyesore? All that polythene and earth-mother cooking pots and lesbians hugging each other at the drop of a hat or any other garment. Grotesque, for those of us who remember what a walk on the common used to be like.

"Also, say what you will about the Yanks, their base has brought an extraordinary degree of prosperity to Fordham. It's cushioned the local people against the worst excesses of the recession. And that's not something to be sneezed at."

He paused for breath, coffee, and thought. Lindsay dived in. "Was it actually Rupert Crabtree who recruited you, then?"

"I don't know if recruit is quite the word. You make him sound like some spymaster. I was having dinner with my parents at the Old Coach restaurant, and Rupert was there with Emma—Mrs. Crabtree, you know? Anyhow, they joined us for coffee, and Emma was complaining about how ghastly it was to have this bloody camp right on the doorstep, and Rupert was informing anyone who'd care to listen that he was going to do something about it and that anyone with any civic pride left would join this new organization to get rid of the women at the camp for good and all."

Lindsay looked speculatively at the handsome, broad-shouldered young man. It would be nice to shake that self-assurance to its roots. But not today. "That sounds a bit heavy duty," she simply said.

"Oh no, nothing like that. No, RABD was all about operating within the law. We used the local press and poster and leaflet campaigns to mobilise public opinion against the camp. And of course, Rupert and a couple of other lawyers developed ways of harassing them through the courts using the by-laws and civil actions. And whenever they staged big demos, we'd aim to mount a token counter-demonstration, making sure the media knew."

"In other words, peaceful protest within the law?"

"Absolutely."

"Just like the peace women, in fact?" Avoiding Stanhope's glance Lindsay screwed out her cigarette in the ashtray. "So, tell me about the in-fighting at RABD."

He looked suddenly cautious. "We don't want all this to become public knowledge."

Lindsay shrugged. "It already is. All sorts of rumours are flying round," she exaggerated. "It's better to be open about these things, especially when the world's press is nosing about, otherwise people start reading all sorts of things into relatively minor matters. You don't want people to think you've got something to hide, do you?"

Stanhope picked up the coffee jug and gestured towards Lindsay's cup. "More coffee?" He was buying time. When Lindsay declined the offer he poured coffee into his own cup. "It's not quite that simple, though, is it?" he demanded. "We're talking about a murder investigation. Something one would happily have gossiped about in a private sort of way last week can suddenly take on quite extraordinary connotations after a man has been murdered. I know I seem to take everything very lightly, but in fact I feel Rupert's death strongly. We didn't always see eye to eye—he could be bloody irritating, he was so arrogant at times—but he was basically an absolutely straight guy, and that's something I find I have to respect. So I'm wary of pushing something he cared about into an area where it could become the subject of public scorn."

Lindsay groaned inwardly. Scruples were the last thing she needed. She had to get something out of Stanhope to provide a fresh lead for the next day's paper, at the very least. And she needed to get it fast, before Duncan could start screaming for copy on Debs. She had foolishly thought that an interview set up by Rigano, with all the force of his authority, would be an easy answer. She set about overcoming Stanhope's objections. It took less persuasion than she anticipated, and she suspected he had simply put her through the hoops in order to salve his conscience. And she managed to elicit the useful information that he had been alone in the lambing shed at the time of the murder.

"There were two things that might interest you," he said. "One, a lot of people knew about. The other, only a handful of people. So, while I don't mind what you do about the first matter, I want to be left well out of anything to do with the second. Okay?"

Lindsay nodded. "Okay."

"I really don't want to be brought into this as your source. I mean it," he added.

He sighed. "The first concerns a man called Paul Warminster. He's local. He owns a couple of gents' outfitters in Fordham. He joined RABD shortly after I did and was always mouthing off against the women. He wasn't happy with the way our campaign was being run.

"He said we should take the fight into the enemy territory instead of simply reacting to them. He always speaks in that sort of jargon. I suspect he must have been in the Pay Corps or something like it in the war. He thought we should be actively banning them from shops, pubs, cinemas, the lot. He thought also that we should be harassing them in the town—insulting them, jostling them, generally making life hard for them.

"Rupert always managed to keep the lid on him till about a month or so ago. Paul stood against him in the election for chair and made the most scurrilous attack on him. He ended up by saying that Rupert was so wishy-washy that he was lucky the motorbike gangs weren't throwing pigs' blood on *his* house. That, I'm afraid, was his big mistake. Our group has always utterly repudiated the thugs who terrorise the women at the camp. But I'd certainly heard mutterings that perhaps Paul wasn't as quick to condemn as one would expect, if you catch my drift. As I said, this was all common knowledge.

"Well, Rupert was duly re-elected with a thumping majority, and he announced that since Paul's policies and attitudes had been so soundly defeated at the ballot box, it would seem there was no place for him within the group. It didn't actually leave Paul any option except resignation. So out he stormed, making sure we all knew he was right and Rupert was wrong. He didn't actually make any threats, but the inference was there to be taken."

"Okay, Mr. Stanhope. And the second incident?"

"Call me Carl, please. I'm not old enough yet for Mr. Stanhope." He radiated charm at her.

She felt like throwing up over his clean jeans. But she didn't even grind her teeth as she said, "Okay, Carl. The second incident?"

"Look, I really meant what I said about keeping my name out of this. If I thought you'd drop me in it I'd shut up now . . ."

"No, no," said Lindsay, "I'll forget you told me. Just give me the details."

"I was told this by someone I can't name. But I'm certain

it's true, because it's referred to in the agenda for next week's meeting, though not in any detail that would make clear what it's about. William Mallard is the treasurer of RABD. He's a local estate agent. We're quite a wealthy organization. We need to be because we try to fight civil court actions, which costs an arm and a leg. But we are a popular cause locally, and all our fund-raising is well supported by the locals. And we've had some financial donations from outside the area too."

"So at any given time, there's a few hundred in the kitty, is that what you're trying to say?" Lindsay interjected, frustrated.

"More like a few thousand," he said. "Rupert was a bit concerned that we weren't using our money properly—you know, that we should be keeping it in a high interest account instead of a current one. Mallard wouldn't agree. Now, being an awkward sort of bloke, Rupert thought his reaction was decidedly iffy. So, armed with the latest treasurer's report, he zapped off to the bank and demanded a chat with the manager. The upshot was that instead of there being about seven thou in the account, as the report stated, there was barely five hundred.

"Rupert blew a fuse. He hared off to see Mallard and confront him. They apparently had a real up and downer. Mallard claimed he'd simply been doing what he always did with large lumps of money in his care, to wit, dumping them in high interest, seven-day accounts. But he couldn't show Rupert the money then and there. Rupert accused him of speculating with the RABD's money and pocketing the profits—Mallard's known for having a taste for the stock market, you see.

"Anyway, Rupert went off breathing fire. Next thing is, the following day, Mallard came to see Rupert, with evidence that the missing six-and-a-half grand was all present and correct. But this didn't satisfy Rupert once he'd slept on it; he was baying for blood. He'd had time to think things through and realised that at some point Mallard must have forged Rupert's signature to shift the cash, since a cheque required both signatures. He told Mallard he was going to raise the matter at the next meeting and let the association decide who was in the wrong. Mallard was apparently fizzing with rage and threatening Rupert with everything from libel actions to—" he broke off, then stumbled on, "to you name it."

"Murder perhaps? Cosy little bunch, aren't you?" Lindsay remarked. "The wonder of it is that it's taken so long for someone to get murdered."

He looked puzzled. "I don't think that's quite fair," he protested.

"Life isn't fair," she retorted, getting to her feet. "At least, not for most people. Who's got the files now, by the way? I'll need to see them."

He shrugged. "Mallard, I guess."

"Could you call him and tell him Jack Rigano wants him to co-operate?" she asked.

"Look, I told you I didn't want to be connected with you on this," he protested.

"So tell him the request came from Rigano. Otherwise you've wasted your breath talking to me, haven't you?"

He nodded reluctantly, "Okay," he said.

Lindsay was at the door when he spoke again. "Jack says you'll be talking to a lot of people in Rupert's immediate circle?"

"That's right. It all helps to build up the picture."

"Will you be seeing his daughter Ros?"

Lindsay nodded. "I'm hoping to see her one evening this week," she replied.

"Will you say hello from me? Tell her I hope the business is going well, and any time she's down home, she should give me a call. We'll have a drink for old times' sake."

"Sure. I didn't realise you knew Ros Crabtree."

"Everyone knows everyone around here, you know. Ask Judith Rowe. Ros and I were sort of pals in the school holidays when we were growing up. You know the routine—horses, tennis club."

Lindsay grinned, remembering the summers of her youth fishing for prawns with her father in the thirty-foot boat that was his livelihood. "Not quite my routine, Carl, but yes, I know what you mean. Was she your girlfriend, then?"

He actually blushed. "Not really. We spent a lot of time together a few years ago, but it was never really serious. And then . . . well, Ros decided that, well, her interests lay in quite other directions, if you follow me?"

"I'm not entirely sure that I do."

"Well, it rather turned out that she seems to prefer women to men. Shame, really. I think that's partly why she moved away from home."

"You mean her parents were hostile about it?"

"Good God, no! They knew nothing about it. Rupert Crabtree would never have put up the money for her restaurant if he'd thought for one minute she was gay. He'd have killed her!"

9

"No, Duncan, I can't write anything about the RABD yet. I've only got one guy's word for it, and half of that's second-hand," Lindsay said in exasperation. "I should be able to harden up the ratepayers' routine by tomorrow lunchtime."

"That'll have to do then, I suppose," Duncan barked. "But see if you can tie it up today, okay? And keep close to the cops. Any sign of an arrest, I want to be the first to know. And don't forget that interview with the suspect woman. Keep ahead of the game, Lindsay."

The line went dead. Lindsay was grateful. The interview with Stanhope had produced more than she'd anticipated, and she'd spent the rest of the morning trying to set up meetings with Mallard and Warminster. But neither could fit her in till the next day which left her with a hole in the news editor's schedule to fill and nothing to fill it with except for the one interview she didn't want to capitalise on. The fact that she was no stranger to living on her wits didn't mean she had to enjoy it. The one thing she wasn't prepared to admit to herself yet was that the job was increasingly turning into something she couldn't square either with her conscience or her principles. After all, once she had acknowledged the tackiness of the world she loved working in, how could she justify her continued determination to take the money and run?

It was half past one by the time she reached the Frog and Basset, a real ale pub about two miles out of the town in the opposite direction to Brownlow. She pushed her way through the crowd of lunchtime drinkers into the tiny snug, which had a hand-lettered sign saying "Private Meeting" on the door. The only inhabitant was Rigano, sitting at a converted sewing-machine table with the remains of a pint in front of him. He looked up at her. "Glad you could make it," he said. "I've got to be back at the station for two. Ring the bell on the bar if you want a drink. Mine's a pint of Basset Bitter."

Lindsay's eyebrows rose, but nevertheless she did as he said. The barman who emerged in response to her ring scuttled off and returned moments later with two crystal-clear pints. Lindsay paid and brought the drinks over in silence. Rigano picked up his and took a deep swallow. "So was Carlton Stanhope a help?"

Lindsay shrugged. "Interesting. There seems to have been something going on between Crabtree and the treasurer, Mallard."

Rigano shook his head. "Don't get too excited about that. It's only in bad detective novels that people get bumped off to avoid financial scandal and ruin."

Stung, Lindsay replied, "Don't get too excited about that. There are plenty of cases that make the papers where people have been murdered for next to nothing. It all depends how much the murderer feels they can bear to lose."

"And did Carlton Stanhope come up with anyone else that you think might have something to lose?"

Lindsay shrugged. "He mentioned someone called Warminster."

"A crank. Not really dangerous. All mouth and no action."

"Thanks. And have you got anything for me? I could do with a bone to throw to my boss."

Rigano took another deep swig of his beer. "There's not much I can say. We're not about to make an arrest, and we're pursuing various lines of enquiry."

"Oh come on, surely you can do better than that. What about CID? What are they doing? Who's in charge of that end of things?"

Rigano scowled, and Lindsay felt suddenly threatened. "I'm in charge," he answered grimly. "I'll keep my end of the deal, don't worry. I've set you up with Stanhope, haven't I? I gave you the whereabouts of the daughter, didn't I? So don't push your luck."

Frustrated, she drank her drink and smoked a cigarette in the silence between them. Then, abruptly, Rigano got to his feet, finishing his drink as he rose. "I've got to get back," he said. "The sooner I do, the nearer we'll be to sorting this business out. Keep me informed about how you're getting on." He slipped out of the snug. Lindsay left the remains of her drink and drove back to the camp.

She parked the car and went to the van, which was empty. She put the kettle on, but before it boiled, the driver's door opened and Deborah's head appeared. "Busy?" she asked.

Lindsay shook her head. "Not at all," she replied. "Actually, I was about to come looking for you. I need your help again."

Deborah made herself comfortable. "All you have to do is ask. Been on a shopping spree? I can't believe all these frightfully chic outfits came out of that little overnight bag."

"I had to find something to wear that makes me look like an efficient journo. Your average punter isn't too impressed with decrepit Levi's and sweatshirts. Anything doing that I've missed?"

"Judith is coming to see me at three o'clock."

Lindsay poured out their coffee and said, "Is it about the assault case?"

"That's right," Deborah confirmed. "She wants to explain exactly what the situation is. I think she's had some news today. Or an opinion or something. Now, what was it you wanted from me? Nothing too shocking, I hope."

"I need you to have dinner with me tonight. In London."

Deborah looked surprised. "I thought Cordelia was in London? Doesn't she eat dinner any more?"

"For this particular dinner, I need you. We are going to a bijou vegetarian restaurant called Rubyfruits."

"You're taking me to a dykey-sounding place like that? On your own patch? And you're not worried about who you might run into? Whatever happened to keeping it light between us?"

Lindsay grimaced. "This is business, not pleasure. Rubyfruits is run by Ros Crabtree, our Rupert's daughter. The dyke that Daddy didn't know about, apparently. And I need you there to tell me if you saw anything of Ros or her partner around Brownlow recently. Okay?"

As Deborah agreed, Judith's car drew up outside.

She looked every inch the solicitor in a dark green tweed-mixture suit and a cream open-necked shirt. But behind the facade she was clearly bursting with a nugget of gossip that threatened to make her explode, and she was quite shrewd enough to realise that dumping it in Lindsay's lap was guaranteed to provide it with the most fertile ground possible.

"You look like the cat that's had the cream," Lindsay remarked.

"Sorry, terribly unprofessional of me. We solicitors are not supposed to show any emotion about anything, you know. But this is such a wonderful tale of dirty linen washing itself in public, I can't be all cool and collected about it. A wonderful piece of gossip, and the best of it is that it's twenty-four carat truth. Now Lindsay, if you're going to use this, you certainly didn't get it from me, all right?"

Lindsay nodded, bored with yet another demand for anonymity. When she was a young trainee reporter, it had always made the adrenalin surge when people required to be Deep Throats. But cynical experience of the insignificance of ninety per cent of people's revelations had ended that excitement years ago. Whatever Judith had to say might merit a few paragraphs, but she would wait and hear it before she let her pulse race.

"Rupert Crabtree's will is with one of the partners in the building next to ours. Anyway, the junior partner is by way of being a pal of mine, and he's managed to cast an eye over the will. And you'll never guess who gets ten thousand pounds?"

Lindsay sighed. "Ros Crabtree? Simon?"

Judith shook her head impatiently. "No, no. They each get one third of the residue, about fifty thousand each. No, the ten thousand goes to Alexandra Phillips. Now isn't that extraordinary?" She was clearly disappointed by the blank stares from her audience. "Oh Lindsay, you must know about Alexandra. You're supposed to be looking into Rupert Crabtree. Has no one told you about Alexandra? Lindsay, she was his mistress."

That last word won Judith all the reaction she could have wished. Lindsay sat bolt upright and spilt the remains of her coffee over the table. "His mistress?" she demanded. "Why the hell did nobody tell me he had a mistress?"

Judith shrugged. "I assumed you knew. It wasn't exactly common knowledge, but I guess most of us lawyers had a notion it was going on. Anyway, I rather think it was cooling off, at least on Alexandra's side."

Lindsay counted to ten in her head. Then she said slowly

and clearly, "Tell me everything you know about the affair, Judith. Tell me now."

Judith looked surprised and hurt at the intensity of Lindsay's tone. "Alexandra Phillips is about twenty-five. She's a solicitor with Hampson, Humphrey and Brundage in Fordham. She does all the dogsbody work, being the practice baby. She's a local girl, used to be friendly with Ros Crabtree, in fact. I know her through the job also because she and Ros used to kick around with my younger sister Antonia. Anyway, Alexandra came back to Fordham about eighteen months ago and almost as soon as she got back, Rupert pounced. He asked her out to dinner at some intimate little *Good Food Guide* bistro that none of his cronies would be seen dead patronizing. He spun the line that he wanted to give her the benefit of his experience and all that blah. And being more than a little impressionable, dear Alexandra fell for his line like an absolute mug. This much I know, because she confided in me right at the start. I warned her not to be a bloody fool and to see him off sharpish, which earned me the cold shoulder and no more confidences.

"But I saw his car outside her flat on a few occasions, and the will obviously indicates an ongoing situation. However, there's been a whisper of a rumour going round Antonia's crowd that Alexandra was looking for a way out. There was a very definite suggestion that she rather fancied another fish to fry. Sorry, no names. I did ask Antonia, but she's pretty sure that Alexandra hasn't spilled that to anyone."

"Great," said Lindsay, getting to her feet and pulling on her jacket. "Come on then, Judith."

Judith looked bewildered. "Where?"

"To wherever Alexandra hangs out. I want to talk to her, and the sooner the better before the rest of the world gets the same idea."

"But we can't just barge in on her without an appointment. And besides, I came here to talk to Deborah about her pending court case."

"Oh God," said Lindsay in exasperation. "Yes, of course. But after that we've just got to see Alexandra Phillips as soon as possible."

Judith, looking startled and apprehensive, rattled machine-gun sentences at Deborah. Following the demise of the sole prosecution witness, she told her, the police could offer no evidence against Deborah in the Crown Court, and the case would therefore fall since she had made no admissions of guilt. It was unlikely that the police would be able to find an eye-witness at that late stage, particularly since they were pursuing that line of enquiry with something less than breathtaking vigour.

"Except in so far as it overlaps with the murder enquiry," Lindsay muttered nonchalantly.

"Thanks for the reassurance," Deborah remarked. "Why don't you two run off now and prevent the police from making too many mistakes about me?"

Judith rose hesitantly. "Are you sure this is a good idea? I mean, Alexandra is something of a friend, or at least a friend of the family. I can't imagine she's going to take too kindly to us barging in and demanding answers about Rupert . . ."

"Look at it this way," said Lindsay. "Events are conspiring to force Debs into Rigano's arms as the obvious and easy villain. Debs is your client. Therefore you'd be failing in your professional duty if you didn't explore every possible avenue to establish her innocence. Isn't that so?"

Judith nodded dubiously. "I suppose so," she conceded. "But it doesn't mean I feel any better about going through with it." Lindsay treated Judith to a hard stare. The solicitor pursed her lips and said, "Oh, come on then. If we go now, we'll probably catch her at the office. I think it would be easier from every point of view if we saw her there."

It took them nearly twenty minutes to reach Alexandra's

office thanks to Judith's driving, rendered doubly appalling by her apprehensions about the approaching interview. Her nervousness grew in the fifteen minutes they spent in the waiting room of Hampson, Humphrey and Brundage while Alexandra dealt with her last client of the day. When they were eventually summoned by buzzer, Judith bolted into the office with Lindsay behind her. Barely bigger than a boxroom, Alexandra Philips's office was dominated by filing cabinets and a standard-sized desk which looked enormous in the confined space.

Yet the surroundings did not diminish its occupant. Alexandra was stunning. Lindsay instantly envied Rupert Crabtree and despised herself for the reaction. The woman who rose to greet them, was, Lindsay estimated, about five-foot-nine tall. Her hair was a glossy blue-black, cut close to a fine-boned head dominated by almond-shaped, luminous brown eyes. Her skin was a healthy glowing golden. Hardly the typical English rose, thought Lindsay. The clothes weren't what she expected either. Alexandra wore a black velvet dress, fitting across the bust, then flaring out to a full swirling skirt. She should have had all the assurance in the world, but it was painfully obvious that self-possession wasn't her long suit. There were black smudges under the eyes, and she looked as if tears would be a relief. The exchange of greetings had been on the formal side, and Judith threw a pleading look at Lindsay, expecting her to take over from there.

Lindsay took pity and launched in on a explanation. "Judith has a client called Deborah Patterson." Alexandra's eyebrows flickered. "I can see the name means something to you. Debs is one of my oldest and closest friends, and the way things are going at the moment it looks as if she's likely to stand accused of Rupert Crabtree's murder, which I can assure you she did not do. Judith and I are determined to see that the charge won't stick, which is why I'm sticking my nose in where it's not wanted."

Alexandra looked puzzled. "I don't actually understand either your status or what you want with me."

"I'm sorry," said Lindsay, "you do deserve a better explanation than that. I've no official status," she went on. "I'm a journalist. But as it happens my first concern with this business is not to get good stories but to make sure Debs stays free. I'm also cooperating, to some degree, with the police on behalf of the women at the peace camp. I find that people don't always want to tell things to the police in case too much emphasis gets placed on the wrong things and innocent people start to appear in a bad light. All I'm trying to do, if you like, is to act as a sort of filter. Anything you want kept within these four walls stays that way until I get the whole picture sorted out, and I can be fairly sure of what's important and what isn't."

"It's called withholding evidence from the police in the circles I move in," Alexandra countered. "I still don't understand what brings you to me."

The last thing Lindsay wanted was to start putting pressure on the young solicitor, but it appeared that in spite of Alexandra's seeming vulnerability, that was what she was going to have to do. "Rupert Crabtree's will is going to be public knowledge soon. If the police haven't already been here, they will be. And so will reporters from every paper in the land. You can bet your bottom dollar they aren't going to be as polite as me. Now, you can try to stall everyone with this disingenuous routine, but eventually you'll get so sick of it you'll feel like murder.

"Or you can short-circuit a lot of the hassle by talking to me. I'll write a story that doesn't make you look like the Scarlet Woman of Fordham. You can go away for a few days till the fuss dies down. You'll be yesterday's news by then, if you've already talked once. And by talking frankly to me, you can maybe prevent a miscarriage of justice. Now, I know you had been having an affair with Rupert Crabtree for over a year, and I know you were trying to get out of that situation. Suppose you tell me the rest?"

Alexandra buried her head in her hands. When she lifted her face her eyes were glistening. "Nice to know who your friends are, Judith," she said bitterly.

"Judith has done the best thing she could for you by bringing me. She could have thrown you to the wolves for the sake of her client, but she did it decently." Lindsay said with a gentleness that was sharp contrast to her previous aggression.

"You're not one of the wolves?"

"No way. I'm the pussycat. Don't think Judith has betrayed you. There will be plenty of others happy to do that over the next few days."

Alexandra gave a shuddering sigh. "All right. Yes, I was Rupert's mistress. I'm not in the least ashamed of that."

"Tell me about him," Lindsay prompted.

Alexandra looked down at her desk top and spoke softly. "He was wonderful company, very witty, very warm. He was also a very generous lover. I know you might find it hard to believe that he was a gentle man if all you've heard is the popular mythology. But he was very different when he was with me. I think he found it refreshing to be with a woman who understood the intricacies of the job."

Lindsay prodded tentatively. "But still you wanted to end it. Why was that?"

Alexandra shrugged. "There seemed to be no future in it. He always made it clear that he would never leave his wife, that his domestic life was one he was not unhappy with. Well, I guess I felt that I wanted more from a long-term relationship than dinners in obscure restaurants and illicit meetings when he could fit them in. I loved him, no getting away from that, but I found I needed more from life. And just when I was at that low ebb, I fell in with someone I knew years ago, someone very different from Rupert, and I realised that with him I could have a relationship that held out a bit more hope for permanence."

"And you told Rupert it was all over?"

Alexandra smiled wryly. "It's easy to see you didn't know Rupert. He had a phenomenal temper. When he raged, he did it in style. No, I didn't tell him it was all over. What I did say was that I was going to have to start thinking about my long-term future. That one of these days I was going to want children, a full-time husband and father for them, and since Rupert wasn't able to fit the bill, we'd better face the fact that sooner or later I was going to need more."

"And what was his reaction to that?" Lindsay asked gently.

"He seemed really devastated. I was taken aback. I hadn't realised how deep I went with him. He asked me—he didn't beg or plead, he'd never forget himself that much—he asked me to reconsider my options. He said that recently everything he had put his trust in seemed to have failed him, and he didn't want that to happen to us. He said he wanted time to reconsider his future in the light of what I'd said. That was on Saturday. Time's the one thing he never expected not to have. You know how I found out he was dead? I read it in the papers. I'd been sitting watching television while he was being murdered." Her voice cracked, and she turned away from them.

Lindsay found it easy to summon up the set of emotions she'd feel if she read of Cordelia's death in her morning paper. She swallowed, then said, "I'm sorry to go on pushing you. But I need to know some more. Do you know what he meant when he said everything he'd trusted had failed him? What was he referring to?"

Alexandra blew her nose and wiped her eyes before she turned back towards them. "He said Simon had let him down. That he wasn't the son he wanted. He sounded very bitter, but wouldn't say what had provoked it. He seldom discussed family matters with me, though he did say a couple of weeks ago that he'd found something out about Ros that had upset him so much he was seriously considering taking his investment out of her restaurant. I asked him what it was because I've known Ros since we were kids, and I suspected he'd finally found out that she's a lesbian."

"You knew about that?"

"Of course. I was one of the first people she told. I've not seen much of her since then, because I felt really uncomfortable about it. But I'd never have uttered a word to Rupert about it. I knew what it would do to him. But I suspect that that was at the root of his anger against Ros.

"And he was terribly upset about the Ratepayers' Association. He'd discovered that the treasurer was up to something fishy with the money. Instead of there being a large amount, about seven thousand in the current account, there was barely five hundred pounds. Rupert confronted the treasurer with his discovery, and he couldn't account for the difference satisfactorily. Rupert was convinced he'd been using it to speculate in stocks and shares and line his own pockets. So he was bringing it up at the next meeting which I'm told would have been stormy, with Rupert baying for blood."

Suddenly her words tripped a connection lurking at the back of Lindsay's brain. The combination of a repeated phrase and a coincidence of figures clicked into place. "Carlton Stanhope," she said.

Alexandra looked horrified. "Who told you?" she demanded. "No one knew. I made sure no one knew. I wouldn't hurt Rupert like that. Who told you?"

Lindsay smiled ruefully. "You just did. You were unlucky, that's all. I had a talk with Carlton this morning. He told me the William Mallard story. The figures he gave me were identical to those you gave me, and figures are an area where people are notoriously inaccurate. Also, you used a couple of identical phrases. It had to be you who told him. And the only person you'd be likely to tell would be someone very close to you. By the way, I wouldn't bother trying to hide it from the police. I suspect they already know; it was they who pointed me in his direction as a source of good information on Rupert."

"If they question me, I'll tell them the truth," Alexandra said, in control of herself again. "But I don't want to discuss it with you. I've said more than enough to someone who has no business interfering."

Lindsay shrugged. "That's your decision. But there's one more thing I have to ask. It's really important. Was Rupert in the habit of carrying a gun?"

Alexandra looked bewildered. "A gun?" she demanded incredulously.

"I'm told, a high-standard double-nine point two two revolver, whatever that is. He was carrying it when he was killed."

Alexandra looked stunned. "But why? I don't understand. Do you mean he knew he was at risk?"

"It looks like it. Did you know he had a gun? I'm told it was registered to him. Perfectly in order."

Alexandra shook her head slowly. "I never saw him with a gun. My God, that's awful. He must have been so afraid. And yet he said nothing about it. Oh, poor, poor, Rupert."

"I'm sorry you had to know," said Lindsay. "Look, if you change your mind and want to talk a bit more, you can always reach me through Judith," she added, moving towards the door.

"Oh, and by the way," she added as Judith rose to follow her, "when did you tell Carlton what Rupert had said about rethinking the future? Was it on Saturday night? Or was it Sunday morning?" She didn't wait for the answer she suspected would be a lie. The look of fear in Alexandra's eyes was answer enough.

10

Lindsay drove down the motorway at a speed that would have seemed tame in a modern high-performance car. In the soft-top sports car it was terrifying. Deborah was relieved that Lindsay's lecture on the current state of play was absorbing enough to occupy her brain. "So you see," Lindsay complained, "Alexandra has opened a completely new vista of possibilities. But the more I find out, the less I know. I don't think I'm really cut out for this sort of thing. I can't seem to make sense of any of it."

"That doesn't sound like you, Lin," Deborah said with a smile. "Just be logical about it. We now know there were a fair few people less than fond of Rupert. Let's run through them. Think out loud."

"Okay," Lindsay replied. "One: his son Simon. For reasons unknown, he was in bad odour. It sounds like more than his assertion of the right to independence by opening up his computer firm. But how much more, we don't know. Yet.

"Two: his daughter Ros. For some unspecified reason,

Rupert was seriously considering disinvestment. Now that may or may not be an effective weapon in the war against apartheid, but it sure as hell must be a serious threat to a small restaurant just finding its feet. Hopefully tonight will answer our questions about Ros. But the middle classes being what they are, five will get you ten that Daddy's disenchantment with daughter was deviance of the dykey variety.

"Three: Emma Crabtree. Our Rupert marched off on Saturday to think about his future. What we don't know is whether he told Emma about Alexandra; whether he'd decided he wanted a divorce and whether that prospect would have delighted or dismayed a woman who isn't the most obviously grieving widow I've ever encountered. A lot of questions there.

"Four: Alexandra. She's scared of his temper, she's afraid that he's not going to let her go without a very unpleasant fight. And she's had enough of him, she wants Stanhope. Personally, I'm disinclined to suspect her, though she seems to have no alibi. She did genuinely seem too taken aback by the gun to be a real candidate." She paused to gather her thoughts.

"Go on," Deborah prompted.

"Five: Carlton Stanhope. Alexandra undoubtedly told him of Crabtree's reaction. He may have figured that making an enemy of as powerful a bastard as Crabtree was not a good move and that murder might even have been preferable. Or it may have been that he felt the one sure way of keeping Alexandra was to get rid of the opposition. Depends how badly he wants Alexandra. I have to say that the bias I feel in her favour operates in the opposite direction as far as he's concerned. I took a real dislike to him, and he's got no alibi either.

"And finally, our two prize beauties from RABD. Mallard might have thought, knowing what a fair man Crabtree was, that his peculations would die with his chairman. And Warminster sounds dotty enough to opt for violence as a means of securing his takeover of RABD. What do you think, Debs?"

Deborah thought for a moment. "You realise you haven't established opportunity for any of them?"

"That is a bit of a problem. I know the police have been pursuing their own enquiries. Maybe I can persuade Rigano that it's in the best interests of his investigation to swap that info for what I've got. Such as it is. Mind you, by the time I've flammed it up a bit, maybe he'll buy it as a fair exchange."

"You also left me off the list of suspects. I should be on it."

Lindsay laughed. "Even though you didn't do it?"

"You don't know that because of facts. You only know it because of history and because we're lovers again. Don't discount the theory that I might have seduced you in order to allay your suspicions and get you on the side of my defense. So I should be on that list till you prove I didn't do it."

Lindsay looked horrified. "You wouldn't!"

"I might have. If I were a different person."

"Okay," Lindsay conceded with a smile. "But I don't reckon that you had put Rupert Crabtree into such a state of fear that he was carrying a gun to protect himself. He must have been armed because he feared a murderous attack."

"Or because he intended to kill the person he was meeting."

Lindsay threw a quick glance at Deborah, caught off guard by this flash of bright logic. She forced herself to examine Deborah's fresh insight.

Eventually, she countered it, tentatively at first and then more assuredly as she reached the end of the motorway and followed the route to Camden Town. "You see," she concluded, "he didn't need to kill you. He was going to get all the revenge he needed in court."

Deborah pondered, then blew Lindsay's hypothesis into smithereens as they approached Rubyfruits. "Not necessarily," she said thoughtfully. "Everyone says he was a fair man. He also had a degree of respect for the law, being a solicitor. Now, supposing in the aftermath of the shock of the accident, he genuinely thought I had attacked him, and on the basis of that genuine belief he gave the statement to the police that triggered the whole thing off. In the interim, however, as time has passed, his recollection has become clearer, and he's realized that he actually tripped over the dog's lead, and I had nothing to do with it. Now, what are his options? He either withdraws his evidence and becomes a laughing-stock as well as exposing himself to all sorts of reprisals from a libel suit—"

"Slander," Lindsay interrupted absently.

"Okay, okay, slander suit, to being accused of wasting police time, all thanks to me. Or he perjures himself, probably an equally unthinkable option for a man like him. His self-esteem is so wounded by this dilemma that he becomes unhinged and decides to kill me in such a way that he can claim self-defense. So he starts carrying the gun, biding his time till he gets me alone. Think on that one, Lin. Now, we're here. Let's go eat." And so saying, she jumped out of the car.

Lindsay caught up with her on the cobbled road outside the restaurant which occupied the ground floor of a narrow, three storey brick building in a dimly lit side street near the trendy Camden Lock complex of boutiques, restaurants and market stalls. It stood between a typesetting company and a warehouse. A red Ford Fiesta turned into the street, and they both stepped back to avoid it as it cruised past the restaurant. Lindsay grabbed Deborah's arm. "As a theory, it's brilliant," she blurted out. "But in human terms, it stinks. You didn't do it, Debs."

Deborah smiled broadly and said, "Just testing." She pushed open the door and moved quickly into the restaurant to avoid Lindsay's grasp. They were greeted by a young woman with short blonde hair cut in a spiky crest.

"Hello Lindsay," she said cheerfully. "I kept you a nice table over in the corner."

"Thanks Meg." They followed her, Lindsay saying, "This is Debs, Meg. She's an old friend of mine."

"Hi Debs. Nice to meet you. Okay. Here's the menu, wine list. Today's specials are on the blackboard, okay?" And she was gone, moving swiftly from table to table, clearing and chatting all the way to the swing doors leading into the kitchen.

Deborah looked around, taking in the stripped pine, the moss green walls and ceiling, and the high photographs ranging predictably from Virginia Woolf to Virginia Wade. She noticed that the cutlery and crockery on each table was different and appeared to have come from junk shops and flea markets. The background music was Rickie Lee Jones turned low. The other tables were also occupied by women. "I can just see you and Cordelia here," Deborah commented. "Very designer dyke."

"Cut the crap and choose your grub," Lindsay ordered.

"Get you," muttered Deborah. They studied the menus and settled for Avocado Rubyfruits. (Slices of ripe avocado interleaved with slices of succulent Sharon fruit, garnished with watercress, bathed in a raspberry vinaigrette) followed by Butter Beanfeast. (Butter beans braised with organically grown onions, green peppers and chives, smothered in a rich cheese sauce, topped with a *gratinée* of stoneground wholemeal breadcrumbs and traditional farm cheddar cheese) with choose-your-own salads from a wide range of the homely and the exotic colorfully displayed on a long narrow table at the rear of the room. To drink, Lindsay selected a bottle of gooseberry champagne.

"My God," Deborah exploded quietly when Meg departed with the order, "I hadn't realized how far pretentiousness had penetrated the world of healthy eating. This is so over the top, Lin. Are there really enough right-on vegetarian women around to make this place a going concern?"

"Don't be too ready to slag it off. The food is actually terrific. Just relax and enjoy it," Lindsay pleaded.

Deborah shook her head in affectionate acceptance and sat back in her chair. "Now tell me," she demanded, "since you hang out so much in this bijou dinette, how come you don't have the same intimate relationship with Ros Crabtree that you have with Meg?"

"It's very simple. Meg runs around serving at table. Meg answers the phone when you book. Meg stands and natters over your coffee. Ros, on the other hand, must be grafting away in the kitchen five nights a week. She's too busy cooking to socialize, even with people she knows. And by the end of the evening, I'd guess she's too exhausted to be bothered making polite social chit-chat with the customers. It's hard work cooking for vegetarians. There's so much more preparation in Butter Beanfeast than in Steak au Poivre."

Before Deborah could reply, their avocados appeared. Deborah tried her food suspiciously, then her face lit up. "Hey, this is really good," she exclaimed.

When Meg returned to clear their plates and serve the champagne, Lindsay made her move.

"That was terrific, Meg. Listen, we'd like to have a word with Ros. Not right now, obviously, but when she's through in the kitchen. Do you think that'll be okay?"

Meg looked surprised. "I suppose so. But . . . what's it all about, Lindsay? Oh, wait a minute . . . you're a reporter, aren't you?" Her voice had developed a hostile edge. "It's about her father, isn't it?"

"It's not what you think," Deborah protested. "She's not some cheap hack out to do a hatchet job on you and Ros. You know her, for God's sake, she's one of us."

"So what *is* it all about then?" The anger in her voice

transmitted itself to nearby tables, where a few faces looked up and studied them curiously.

Deborah took a deep breath. "I'm their number one suspect. I've already had one night in the police cells, and I don't fancy another. Lindsay's trying her damnedest to get me off the hook and that means discovering the real killer. I'd have thought you and Ros would be interested in finding out who killed her father."

"Him? The only reason I'd want to know who killed him is so that I could shake them by the hand. Look, I'm not too impressed with what you've got to say for yourselves, but I will go ask Ros if she'll talk to you." She marched off and returned a few minutes later with their main courses, which she placed meticulously before them without a word.

They ate in virtual silence, their enjoyment dulled. Meg silently removed their plates and took their order for biscuits, cheese, and coffee.

By half past ten and the third cup of coffee, Lindsay was beginning to despair of any further communication from the kitchen. The tension had dried up conversation between her and Deborah. The evening she'd been looking forward to had somehow become awkward and difficult. Then, a tall, broad woman emerged from the kitchen and exchanged a few words with Meg, who nodded in their direction. The woman crossed the room towards them. She was bulky, but she looked strong and sturdy rather than flabby. Her hair was short and curly, her face pink from the heat of the kitchen. Like her brother, Ros Crabtree strongly resembled their father. She wore a pair of chef's trousers and a navy blue polo shirt. In her hand was a brandy bowl with a large slug of spirit sobbing up the sides of the glass.

She pulled a chair up and said without preamble, "So this is the sleuth. The famous Cordelia Brown's girlfriend. Accompanied, unless I am mistaken, by the brutal peace woman who goes around beating up helpless men." She smiled gener-ously. "Enjoy your dinner?"

"As always," Lindsay answered, stung by being defined as an adjunct to Cordelia.

"But tonight you came for more than three courses and a bottle of country wine."

"We hoped you would help us," Deborah stated baldly. "Lindsay's trying to clear my name. I'm afraid that if there isn't an arrest soon, I'll be charged, just so they can be seen to be achieving something."

"We also thought you would have an interest in seeing your father's killer arrested," Lindsay added.

Ros laughed. "Look, I have no feelings about my father one way or the other. I neither loved him nor hated him, but I'm sorry about the way he died. I was glad to be out of his house but frankly, the notion of getting some atavistic revenge on the person who killed him leaves me unmoved. You're wasting your time here."

Lindsay shrugged. "So if it matters that little to you, why not talk to me, answer my questions? It could make a lot of difference to Debs."

"I can't think of anything I could tell you that would be of the slightest use. But I suppose I owe something to the woman who cost my father his precious dignity and a broken nose. Oh, the hell with it, ask what you want. If I feel like answering, I will." She swallowed a generous mouthful of brandy, seemingly relaxed.

"I'll ask the obvious question first. Where were you on Sunday night between ten p.m. and midnight?" Lindsay asked.

"Oh dear, oh dear, we have been reading all the snobbery with violence detective novels, haven't we?" The mockery in Ros's voice was still good-natured, but it was obvious that the veneer was wearing thin. "I was here on Sunday night. We have a flat above the restaurant. I think I was reading till about eleven. Then I went to bed, and I was woken up just after midnight when my mother phoned to tell me about my father's death."

"I suppose Meg can back you up?"

"As it happens, no. Meg was on her way back from Southampton. She'd been visiting her parents. She didn't get home till about half past midnight. So I don't have much of an alibi, do I? No one phoned till mother. I phoned no one. You'll just have to take my word for it." She grinned broadly.

"I'm surprised you didn't go down to Brownlow as soon as you heard the news. I mean, with your mother to comfort and all that . . . ?" Lindsay sounded off-hand.

"Acting nonchalant cuts no ice with me, darling. I can spot the heavy questions without you signposting them. Why didn't I dash off home to Mummy? For one thing, I have a business to run. On Mondays, I go to the market and see what's looking good. On that basis, I plan the special dishes for the week. We also do all the book-keeping and paperwork on Mondays. I simply couldn't just vanish for the day. It'll be hard enough fitting the funeral in. That's not as callous as it sounds. My father cared about this business too. But more importantly than all of that, I'm not at all sure I'd be the person to comfort my mother."

"Why's that?"

"Because I'm not the weepy, sentimental sort. I'm far too bloody brisk to be much of a shoulder to cry on. I'm afraid I'd be more inclined to tell her to pull herself together than to provide tea and sympathy."

"So, it's nothing to do with her attitudes to you being a lesbian? Oh, but of course, they didn't know, did they? Or so Carlton Stanhope reckons. Mind you, I always figure that parents know a lot more than they let on," said Lindsay, her eyes on a distant corner of the room.

"You've talked to Carl?" Suddenly Ros had become guarded.

"He sends his best wishes. He's seeing Alexandra Phillips these days, you know," Lindsay replied.

"How nice for him. She used to be a lovely girl when I knew her. I hope she treats him better than I did. Poor Carl," she said ruefully. "But to go back to what he said to you. He was right, as far as he was aware. They really didn't know. I'd kept it well under wraps. Let me explain the history. After I'd decided my career lay in the catering trade, my father was always keen that I should set up in business on my own when I'd done the training and got the experience. Meg and I did a proper business plan based on the costings for this place, and I presented it to him as a good investment. He lent me twenty thousand pounds at a nominal rate of interest so we could get the project off the ground. He'd never have done that much if he'd even suspected. I suppose my cover was never blown because I'd spent so much time studying and working away from home, and when I was home, there were always old friends like Carl around to provide protective coloring. It was really funny when we launched Rubyfruits—we had to have two opening nights. One with lots of straight friends that we could invite the parents to and another with the real clientele."

Lindsay lit a cigarette. "It sounds like you had a lot to be grateful to him for?"

Ros shrugged. "In some ways. But we were never really close. He was always at arms' length, somehow. With all of us. As if his real life happened somewhere else. The office, I suppose. Or one of his causes." The edge of bitterness in her voice was apparent even to Ros herself. She softened her tone and added, "But I guess I owe this place to him. I'm sorry he's dead."

"Then he didn't carry out his threat to take his money back?" Lindsay's casual words dropped into a sudden well of silence. Ros's face wouldn't have looked out of place on Easter Island.

"I have no idea what you're talking about," she declared. "No idea at all."

"I'm told that he'd recently become disillusioned with you, that he was minded to take his money out of this business as a token of his disappointment. You really should tell me about it in case I go away with the wrong idea. And you not having much of an alibi. My news editor would like that story a lot."

Ros stared hard at Lindsay. "Well, well," she muttered bitterly. "So much for lesbian solidarity. You're not the pushover I took you for, are you? Fancy me thinking that anyone who tagged along on Cordelia's coat-tails could be toothless. All right. Since you obviously know enough to make a bloody nuisance of yourself, I'd better tell you the rest.

"Ten days ago I had a phone call from my father. He informed me that he was instructing his bankers to recover the twenty thousand he'd loaned me. He refused to say why, or even to say anything else. So I rang my mother to see if she knew what the hell was going on. And she wouldn't say either.

"So I jumped on the bike and bombed down to the old homestead where I squeezed out of Mamma what it was all about. To cut a long story short, it was all down to my perfectly bloody little brother. You know he's got this business in computer software? Well, he had to start it on a shoestring, against my father's advice. Father wanted different things for Simon, and that was the end of the story as far as he was concerned. He wouldn't even listen when one of Simon's teachers came to see him and told us that Simon was the best computer programmer he'd ever encountered. Apparently, he was hacking into other people's systems by the time he was in the third form. Anyway, Simon got off the ground somehow and he's at the stage now where it's make or break, expand or fold, and he needs an injection of cash. God knows where he got the money to get this far, but he was determined that the next chunk of capital should come from Father, on the basis that he'd lent me money for the business, and it was only right that he should do the same for Simon.

"Dad refused absolutely. He said I'd proved myself, which Simon still had to do before he could come chasing around for hard-earned handouts. Mum said they were going at it hammer and tongs, then Simon blew a fuse and said something along the lines of how appalling it was that Father was prepared to finance a pair of lesbians running a restaurant for queers, and he wouldn't finance his only son in a legitimate business. Mum says there was a ghastly silence, then Simon walked out. Father apparently wouldn't say a thing, just went off in the car. She thinks he came up here to see for himself. And the next day—bombshell."

"I thought it must have been something like that," Lindsay said. "So I suppose that put you right in the cart."

"Until the death of my father, that's what you're getting at, isn't it? Not quite that easy, I'm afraid. You see, we've been doing better than we projected. It knocked some of our personal plans on the head, like new furniture for the flat, but we've simply transferred to a bank loan. We can just afford the extra interest. Any money from my father's will, unless he's cut me out of that too, will be an absolute godsend, there's no getting away from that. But we could have managed without it. I had no need to kill him. Now, you've got what you came for. Is there anything else before I get you the bill?"

"Just one thing. Any idea why your father was carrying a gun?"

"Carrying a gun? I knew nothing about that. No one said anything to me about a gun!"

"The police are trying to keep it fairly quiet. A point two two revolver."

"I can't begin to think why he had his gun with him. He

used to be a member of a small-arms shooting club at Middle Walberley. But he hadn't been for . . . oh God, it must be eight years. He gave it up because he didn't have time enough for practising, and he could never bear to do anything unless he did it to perfection. I didn't even know he'd kept his gun. I can't believe he had enemies—I mean, not the sort you'd have to arm yourself against. Wow, that really is weird." For the first time, she looked upset. "Somebody must have really got to him. That's horrible." She swallowed the remains of her brandy and got to her feet. "I'll get Meg to bring your bill." She vanished through the swing door at the back of the restaurant followed by Meg, whose eyes had never left them during the interview.

Lindsay rubbed her forehead with her fingertips. Deborah reached out and took her hand. Before they could speak, Meg re-emerged from the kitchen and strode over to them. By now, they were the centre of attention for the few diners remaining. "Have this meal on me," Meg said angrily. "Just so long as you don't come back here again. Now go. I mean it, Lindsay. Just get out!"

11

The head office of Mallard and Martin, Estate Agents, Auctioneers and Valuers, was at the far end of the main street in Fordham. The retail developers who have turned every British high street into undistinguished and indistinguishable shopping malls had not yet penetrated that far down the street, and the double-fronted office looked old-fashioned enough to appeal to the most conservative in the district. Lindsay, dressed to match the office in her new outfit, studied the properties in the window with curiosity. She noticed several houses in the vicinity of Brownlow Common were up for sale. But their prices didn't seem to be significantly lower than comparable houses in other areas. She pushed open the door, and as she entered, a sleek young woman in a fashionably sharp suit rose and came over to the high wooden counter.

"Can I help you?" she enquired.

"I'm due to see Mr. Mallard," Lindsay explained. "My name's Lindsay Gordon."

"Oh yes, he's expecting you. Do come through." The woman raised a flap in the counter and showed Lindsay through into Mallard's own office. He got up as Lindsay was ushered in and genially indicated a chair. Mallard was a short, chubby man in his fifties, almost completely bald. He wore large, gold-rimmed spectacles and tufts of grey hair stuck out above his ears, making him look like a rather cherubic owl. He smiled winningly at Lindsay. "Now, young lady," he said cheerfully, "you're a reporter, I think you said?"

"That's right. But I'm not just looking for stories. I believe Carlton Stanhope rang to pass on Superintendent Rigano's request?"

"He did indeed." He smiled. "Always delighted to help an attractive young lady like yourself. Mr. Stanhope tells me you've been able to give the police some assistance concerning dear Rupert's death? A dreadful tragedy, quite, quite dreadful."

Lindsay decided she did not care for this bouncing chauvinist piglet. But his seeming garrulity might be something she could turn to her advantage. She smiled at him. "Absolutely. I have been able to come up with some quite useful information so far. And of course, not all of it is passed directly to the police. I mean, a lot emerges in these affairs that has no bearing on the main issue. It would be a pity to cloud matters with irrelevant information, wouldn't it? So if people are open with me, I can often get to the bottom of things that would otherwise cause a lot of wasted police time. If you see what I mean?" She let the question hang in the air.

"So you want to find out how well I knew Rupert, who his friends were, if he made enemies through RABD, that sort of thing? That's what Mr. Stanhope said," Mallard replied hastily.

"Not exactly," Lindsay replied. "Though I would like to look through the RABD records. I think Mr. Stanhope arranged that with you?"

Mallard nodded vigorously. "They're all upstairs in a little office I put at the disposal of the organisation. You can take as long as you want, you'll have the place to yourself. We've got nothing to hide, you know, though obviously we don't want our future plans made public. That would put an end to our strategies against those . . . those harpies down there," he said, geniality slipping as he referred to the peace women.

"I rather thought there were one or two matters you'd prefer to keep to yourself, Mr. Mallard," Lindsay remarked idly.

"No, no we're not at all secretive. We're perfectly open, no conspiracies here."

An odd thing to say, Lindsay thought. "No conspiracies, perhaps, but one or two disagreements."

"Disagreements?" He looked apprehensive.

"Paul Warminster?"

"Oh, that," he muttered, looking uncomfortable. "Yes, that was a little unfortunate. But then, it only supports what I was saying to you about being open. We're not extremists in RABD, just people concerned about our local community and the environment our families live in. We don't want to be involved in anything at all violent. That's what Paul Warminster felt we should be doing. He wanted us to be some kind of vigilante band, driving these awful women away by force. We were glad Rupert had the strength to stand up to him. That sort of woman isn't going to go away because you throw them out physically. If we'd gone ahead and taken violent action, the next day there would have been twice as many of them. No, Rupert was right."

"And do you think Paul Warminster resented what he did?"

"No question about that, young lady. He was furious."

"Furious enough for murder?"

Mallard's smile this time was sickly. "I'm sure nobody in our circle, not even someone with Paul Warminster's views, would resort to murder." He made it sound like a social solecism.

"But someone in Rupert Crabtree's circle did just that."

Mallard shook his head. "No. Those women are to blame. It certainly wasn't Paul Warminster. He had nothing to gain. Even with Rupert out of the way, he'll never win control of RABD and its membership. He must know that. He's not a fool."

"I'm happy to take your word for it," Lindsay flattered. "Now, if I might see those papers?" She got to her feet.

"Of course, of course," he said, rising and bustling her out of the room. They climbed two flights of stairs, Mallard chatting continuously about the property market and the deplorable effect the peace camp was having on house prices in the neighborhood of the common.

"But houses at Brownlow seem about the same price as similar houses near by," Lindsay commented.

"Oh yes, but they used to be the most highly sought after in the area, and the most expensive. Now it takes a lot of persuasion to shift them. Well, here we are."

They entered a small office containing a battered desk, several upright chairs and a filing cabinet. "Here you are, m'dear," Mallard waved vaguely around him. He unlocked the filing cabinet. "Chairman's files and my files in the top drawers. Minutes in the second. Correspondence in the third and stationery in the bottom drawer. Look at anything you please, we've no guilty secrets."

"Will you be in your office for a while? I might come across some things I want to clarify."

"Of course, of course. I shall be there till half past twelve. I'm sure you'll be finished by then. I'm at your disposal." He twinkled another seemingly sincere smile at her and vanished downstairs.

Lindsay sighed deeply and extracted two bulging manila folders from the top drawer of the filing cabinet. They were both labelled "Ratepayers Against Brownlow's Destruction. Chairman's File." In red pen, the same hand had written "1" and "2" on them. She sat down at the desk and opened her briefcase. She took out a large notepad, pen and her Walkman. She slotted in a Django Reinhardt tape and started to plough through the papers.

The first file yielded nothing that Lindsay could see. She stuffed the papers back into it and opened the second file. As she pulled the documents out, a cassette tape clattered on to the desk. Curious, she picked it up. The handwritten label, not in Crabtree's by now familiar script, said, "Sting: *The Dream of The Blue Turtles*". Surprised, Lindsay put it to one side and carried on working. When her own tape reached the end, she decided to have a change and inserted the Sting tape. But instead of the familiar opening chords she heard an alien sequence of hisses, bleeps, and sounds like radio interference. Lindsay knew very little about information technology. But she knew enough to realize that although this tape was mislabelled, it was actually a computer program on tape. And fed into the right computer, it might explain precisely what it was doing in Rupert Crabtree's RABD file. She remembered the computers she had seen downstairs and wondered if that was where Mallard stored the real information about RABD's finances.

She worked her way quickly through the financial records, making a few notes as she went. It seemed to be in order, though the book-keeping system seemed unnecessarily complex. Finally she skimmed through the minutes and correspondence. "Waste of bloody time," she muttered to herself as she neatly replaced everything. The cassette tape caught her eye, and she wondered again if it might hold the key to the questions Crabtree had been asking about money. She threw the computer tape into her briefcase along with her own bits and pieces and headed downstairs for the confrontation she'd been geared up to since breakfast. As she rounded the corner of the stairs, she noticed a man coming out of Mallard's office. From above, she could see little except the top of his head of greying, gingery hair and the shoulders of his tweed jacket. By the time she reached the bottom of the stairs, he had gone.

Mallard's office door was ajar and she stuck her head round. "Can I come in?" she asked.

"Of course, of course, m'dear," he answered her, beaming. "I expect you've had a very boring morning with our papers."

"It has been hard work," Lindsay admitted. "I'm surprised you haven't got the lot on computer, with Simon Crabtree being in that line of business."

Mallard nodded. "Couldn't agree more, m'dear. But Rupert wouldn't hear of it. Lawyers, you see. Very conservative in their methods. Not like us. Our front office may look very traditional. But all the work gets done in the big office at the back—where our computers are. The latest thing—IBM-compatible hard-disk drives. I actually bought them on Simon's advice. But Rupert didn't trust them. He said you could lose all your work at the touch of a button, and he felt happier with bits of paper that didn't vanish into thin air. Typical lawyer—wanted everything in black and white."

"There was one other thing I wanted to ask you about."

"Ask away, m'dear, ask away."

"Why was Rupert Crabtree going to raise your handling of RABD funds at the next meeting?"

Mallard flushed but managed to freeze his smile in place as he replied, "Was he?"

"You know he was. The two of you had a row about it, and he said the association should decide."

"I don't know where you've got your information from, young lady, but I can assure you nothing of the sort took place." Mallard attempted to stand on his dignity. "We had a very harmonious relationship."

"Not according to my sources. Two separate people have told me the whole story, and I believe the police are aware of it. I already have enough to write a story. It's obviously doing the rounds locally. Hadn't you better put the record straight, and give me your version of events before your reputation gets shredded beyond repair?"

He dropped the geniality and looked shrewdly at Lindsay. "Young lady, even if *you* seem blissfully unaware, I'm sure your newspaper has lawyers who understand all about libel. If you are thinking of printing any sort of story about me, you had better be extremely careful."

"We don't have to print a story about you, for your reputation to be destroyed. Local gossip will see to that. All I have to write is that police are investigating alleged misappropriation of funds by one of the officials of a local organization in connection with Rupert Crabtree's death," Lindsay replied.

Mallard paused, sizing her up. Then, after a long enough pause to render himself unconvincing, he smiled again and said, "Really, there's no need for all of this. I've told you that we've got nothing to hide in RABD. That goes for me personally, too. Now, you've obviously heard some grossly distorted version of a conversation between Rupert and me. There's no reason on earth why I should attempt to explain to you, but because I'm concerned there should be no misunderstanding, I'll tell you all about it.

"We hold a substantial amount of money on behalf of our members. Most of it is for legal expenses and printing costs. As treasurer, I'm responsible for the money, and I know how important it is these days to make money work. Obviously, the more money we have, the better able we are to fight the good fight. Now, Rupert was checking something on the bank statements, and he realized there was far less in the account than he thought there should be. He was always prone to jump to conclusions, so he came round here in a great taking-on, demanding to know where the money was. I explained that I had moved it into the currency markets, an area I know rather a lot about. I was simply maximizing our returns. Rupert was perfectly satisfied with my explanation. And so he should have been, since I had succeeded in making a substantial profit."

"Then why was he raising the matter at the next meeting?"

"Why? So that I could pass on the good news to the membership, of course. Rupert felt it was a matter for congratulation, m'dear."

His glibness lowered his credibility still further in Lindsay's eyes. She was determined to get him on the run, and she racked her brains to find some leverage in what Stanhope or Alexandra had said. "But how did you move the money without Crabtree's knowledge? Surely that needed his signature?"

A momentary gleam of hatred flashed at Lindsay. "Of course, of course, my dear girl. But Rupert had actually signed it among a pile of other papers for his signature and had simply not registered what it was. Easy to do that when you're signing several bits of paper."

"I wouldn't have thought that was the action of a conscientious lawyer. But you seem to have an answer for everything, Mr. Mallard."

His smile was genuine this time. "That's because I have nothing to hide, m'dear. Now, if that is all, I do have work to do . . ."

"One more thing. Since you've nothing to hide, perhaps you could tell me where you were on Sunday night from about ten?"

This time, Mallard couldn't keep the smile in place. "That's none of your business," he snapped.

"You're right. But I expect you've told the police already? No? Oh well, I'm sure they'll be round soon to ask. Superintendent Rigano's very interested in who I've been talking to . . ."

Lindsay felt she was doing battle. Mallard gave in. "I was at home all evening."

"Which is where, exactly?"

He shifted in his seat. "Brownlow Common Cottages. Four doors away from the Crabtrees actually."

Lindsay smiled. "Convenient. Alone, were you?"

He shook his head. "My wife was in. She . . . she almost always *is* in. She has MS, you see, confined to a wheelchair."

Nothing's ever simple, thought Lindsay. Poor woman, stuck in a wheelchair with him. She waited, then he went on. He was clearly a man who felt uncomfortable with silence.

"I put her to bed about ten. So her evidence after that could only be negative—that she didn't hear me go out or come in, that she didn't hear my car. I have no idea why I'm telling you all this," he added petulantly.

"Haven't you, Mr. Mallard?" Lindsay inquired. "Thanks very much for your time." She abruptly rose and walked out. The woman in the front office looked up in surprise as she swept through. Lindsay marched down the main street to the car park where she'd left the MG, irritated that she hadn't broken Mallard's self-possession. She hadn't even thought to ask him who he thought the murderer was. But she knew deep down that the only answer she would have received was the utterly predictable one: "those peace women." And that would have made no difference to her own gut reaction to Mallard, namely that of all the people she'd spoken to so far, he was her favorite suspect. He had opportunity, she'd established that. He looked sturdy enough to cope with the means. And he had motive aplenty. A rumor with Rupert Crabtree behind it would be enough to terminate a man's career in a small town like Fordham when that career depended on trust. And Mallard clearly couldn't afford that, especially not with a wife whose disability gave him another pressing reason for maintaining a comfortable lifestyle.

She drove off, checking her mirrors for Rigano's blond SB

man. There was no sign of the red Fiesta. She pulled into the traffic to keep the appointment she'd made with Paul Warminster and following his directions, left Fordham in the opposite direction to Brownlow. Surburban streets gave way to more rural surroundings. Chocolate-box countryside, thought Lindsay, struck as she was occasionally with a sharp pang of longing for the sea lochs and mountains of her native landscape. A couple of miles out of the town, she pulled off the main road into a narrow country lane. Soon she came to a thatched cottage attached to a converted cruck barn. The garden was a mass of daffodils and crocuses with occasional patches of bright blue scilla. A powerful motorbike was parked incongruously by the side of the barn. Lindsay got out of the car and walked up a path made of old weathered brick.

The door was opened by a tall spare man in his late forties. His gingery hair was lank and greying, his face weather-beaten to an unattractive turkey red and a network of fine lines radiated from the corners of his lively blue eyes. In his tweed jacket with the leather patches he looked more like a gamekeeper than a shopkeeper. With a sudden shock, Lindsay realized this was the man she had seen leaving Mallard's office a short time earlier. Covering her confusion, she quickly introduced herself and established her bona fides with her Press card. Warminster ushered her into a chintzy, low-ceilinged living room with bowls of sweet-smelling freesias scattered around.

"So, you're writing about what local people are doing to put a stop to that so-called peace camp," he said, settling himself in a large armchair.

Lindsay nodded. "I understand you've been quite actively involved in the opposition."

Warminster lit a small cigar as he replied. "Used to be. Probably will be again soon."

"Why is that?" Lindsay asked.

"Had a bit of a run-in with that chap, Crabtree, the fellow

who was murdered at the weekend, so I hadn't been doing too much lately. Blighter thought he ran Fordham. Perhaps now we'll get to grips with those left-wing lesbians," he said.

"You weren't happy with the policies of Ratepayers Against Brownlow's Destruction, then?" Lindsay probed.

He snorted. "Could say that. Policies? Appeasement, that's what they were about. And look where that got us in the thirties. We should have been taking the war into their territory, getting them out of their entrenched positions instead of pussyfooting around being nicey-nicey to those bloody communists harridans." Warminster was off and running in what were clearly not fresh fields. As she listened to the tirade, trying to control her feelings of disgust and anger, Lindsay gradually began to understand why violence so often seems a solution.

She pretended to take extensive notes of his speech. There was no need to interrogate Warminster. The only difficulty was getting him to stop. Eventually, he ended up with a rabble-rousing peroration. "Very stirring, sir," Lindsay muttered.

"You think so? That's exactly what I told them on Sunday night in Berksbury. I was speaking there, you know, at the instigation of the local Conservative Party. They staged one of those debates about the issues. Had some woolly vicar in a woolly pullover from CND, the local candidate and me. Well worth the trip, I can tell you."

Lindsay's mind had leapt to attention as soon as Sunday was mentioned. "That was Sunday night just past?" she asked. "The night Crabtree was killed, you mean?"

"That's right. Round about when he bought it, we were having a celebratory drink in the Conservative Club. An excellent night. Didn't get home till the small hours. I must say the hospitality was excellent. Good job I'd taken my wife along to drive me home or I'd never have made it. Sorry she's not in, by the way, gone to visit her sister in Fordham. Now, anything else you want to know."

It all seemed so innocent. And the alibi appeared sound. But Lindsay didn't like what her instincts told her about Paul Warminster. "I see you've got a motorbike outside. Have you ever come across any of those yobs that have been attacking the peace camp?"

He looked startled. "Of course not," he said. "Why should I have?"

Lindsay shrugged. "I just wondered. I thought since you were into direct action they might have made contact with you."

Warminster shook his head violently. "Absolutely not. Ill-disciplined rabble."

"How do you know that?" Lindsay demanded, pouncing on the inconsistency.

"How do I know what?"

"That they're ill-disciplined. If you've got nothing to do with them, how do you know that?"

He looked angry and flustered. "Heard about it, didn't I? Small place, Fordham, you hear things. Absurd of you to think I'd have anything to do with them. Nearly as incompetent as the RABD softies."

"But you obviously maintain contact with some of your friends in RABD," Lindsay probed.

"What d'you mean by that?" He was now deeply suspicious. His hostility was tipping him over the borderline of rudeness.

"I thought I saw you this morning coming out of William Mallard's office," she said.

"So? The man runs a business. I do business in Fordham. Hardly surprising that we do business together, is it? I can't turn my back on every liberal I meet just because I don't agree with their way of going about things."

Lindsay shook her head. "There's no need to get so het

up, Mr. Warminster. I just wondered if the business you were doing with Mr. Mallard was anything to do with the funding of your direct action group."

Her barb hit home to Warminster, leaving high spots of colour in his checks. "Rubbish," he blustered, "absolute rubbish. Now, if you've nothing more to ask me, I'd be obliged if you'd let me get on. I'm a very busy man." He got to his feet, leaving Lindsay little choice but to follow suit. Standing in the doorway he watched her into her car then turned into the house as she drove away.

An interesting encounter, thought Lindsay. Warminster might have a rock-solid alibi for Sunday night but a tie-in between himself, Mallard, and the bikers looked suspiciously probable. It seemed likely to Lindsay that someone had put those bikers up to their attacks on the camp. If it had been only a single incident, it could have been written off as drunken hooliganism. But the concerted attacks of fire-bombing, blood-throwing, and damage to the benders looked like something more sinister. And youths like that wouldn't take those chances without some kind of incentive. Money was the obvious choice. The destination of Mallard's funny money now seemed clear too. Driving thoughtfully back to Brownlow Common, Lindsay wondered just how much it would cost to persuade a bloodthirsty biker to make the escalation from fire-bombing to murder.

12

As Lindsay joined the tight group round the smoky fire, the conversation faltered. Nicky glowered at her and turned away, but Willow moved to one side of the crate she was sitting on and offered Lindsay a place. "We were just sorting out an action for tonight," Deborah said, rather too brightly.

"So you'd better rush off and tell your tame policeman," Nicky muttered loudly.

Lindsay ignored the hostility with difficulty, since it triggered her own qualms of conscience about dealing with Rigano, and asked what was planned. Willow explained. "A few of the women were in court yesterday for non-payment of fines, and they've been sent to Holloway as per usual. So we're having a candle-lit procession and silent vigil round the wire tonight. There's a couple of coachloads coming down from London. It might be quite a big action—we've tipped off the TV and radio news, so we'll get some publicity."

"And with all you journalists kicking round looking for titbits about that creep Crabtree, we might even get some decent newspaper publicity for a change," added Nicky bitterly.

"I shouldn't think so," Lindsay replied acidly. "Why should a candle-lit procession alter all our preconceived notions? You don't still believe in Santa Claus, do you, Nicky?"

"Oh, stop it, you two," protested Deborah. "You're like a pair of kids. If you've nothing constructive to say to each other, then don't waste your breath and our time."

Lindsay got to her feet. "I've got to do some work now, but I'll be back for the demo. What time's it all starting?"

"About seven," Deborah answered. "Meet me at Gate Six, near Brownlow Common Cottages. Will you pass the word on to the other reporters if you see them?"

"Sure," Lindsay said. "If that's not too much like consorting with the enemy."

Deborah gave her a warning look, and she grinned back at her as she set off for the van. Lindsay dumped her notebook on the table that dropped down and slotted into the long L-shaped bench at night to form the base of the bed. She opened the tiny fridge set next to the two-ring gas cooker and grill, and took out a pint of milk. She swigged a couple of mouthfuls, then sat down to work. She felt comfortable in the van, a big Ford Transit conversion with enough room to stand up and move around in.

She started to scribble down the outline of her story about the in-fighting in RABD with a sneaking feeling that she'd be lucky to get it into the paper. At the end of the day, it was just a rather silly story about a bunch of grown men behaving like schoolboys, and she suspected that Duncan's sharp news sense would come to the same conclusion. Her growing suspicion that William Mallard was somehow implicated in the murder of Rupert Crabtree was not something she could commit to paper yet. Till then, the RABD story was all she had. At least it was exclusive.

She set off for Fordham, in the MG, on a search for a phone box from which to file her copy. As she drove, she remembered the computer tape she'd thrust into her brief-case. It occurred to her that she'd have to find out what computer system Simon Crabtree worked with so she could unravel the contents of the tape, since he'd sorted out Mallard's computers in the first place. The obvious way to find out was to pay a visit to his lockup garage. But that meant another fencing session with Rigano first.

Finding an empty phone box on the outskirts of the town, she read her copy laboriously, silently wishing for the next phase in computer technology that would reduce the trans-mission of stories to a few seconds of telephone time, thanks to portable remote terminals. The copy transmitted, she spoke to Duncan, telling him about the evening's procession at the base and squeezing from him agreement that she should file copy on it later.

She rang Rigano. After a long delay that involved explaining her identity to the switchboard, the duty officer, and Rigano's sergeant, she was finally connected to her contact. He was abrupt to the point of rudeness. "What is it?" he demanded.

"I need some help," Lindsay replied.

"So what's new? What do you need?"

"Just an address. Simon Crabtree's computer workshop. I want to talk to him on his own territory."

"Try the phone book. I thought you were supposed to be full of initiative."

"I can't try the phone book if I don't know what the company's called, can I?"

There was a brief pause. "Okay. I'll leave a note for you at the front counter. I want to talk to you about what you've been up to. I suspect there's a lot you could tell me that you haven't been passing on. Ring me tomorrow morning before ten," he said and put the phone down.

Puzzled and irritated at having to make a detour to the police station, Lindsay set off. Why didn't Rigano just give her the address over the phone? Why go to all the bother of leaving a note for her to pick up? It surely couldn't be an excuse to get her into the station so he could interview her, or he wouldn't have made the arrangement for the next day's phone call. Unless that was a red herring . . . there seemed to be no easy answer.

The envelope she collected from the reception desk in Fordham police station fifteen minutes later, contained the address neatly hand written: Megamenu Software, Unit 23, Harrison Mews, Fordham. Lindsay checked the index on the street map she'd bought. No Harrison Mews, but a Harrison Street on the seedier side of town, near the industrial estate. The mews would probably be an alley round the back, she speculated.

She put the car into gear and routinely checked her rear mirror. What she saw nearly caused an accident. The red Ford Fiesta, driven by the man whom she had labelled Special Branch, was right behind. Lindsay shot into the traffic without signalling and cursed her lack of familiarity with the terrain. While she concentrated on finding her route across the town centre, she was aware of the Fiesta two cars behind her, and an explanation for Rigano's perplexing telephone manner dawned on her. The man now on her tail might have been with Rigano when she called, which begged the more disturbing question: had Rigano lured her into the station just so that the Special Branch man could follow her? And if so, why was the SB interested in a routine murder? And more importantly, why the hell were they so interested in her?

The heaviness of the traffic and the search for her destination forced her to shelve the question. But as she pulled into a back alley with a roughly painted signboard saying "Harrison Mews: Megamenu Software This Way," she noticed the red hatchback drive slowly past the narrow entrance. She parked the car up against the wall opposite Unit 23 and pondered. If the blond man was SB, then it went a long way towards explaining why a uniformed copper like Rigano had been left in charge of a major murder investigation instead of a plain-clothes CID officer. But since the powers that be were so firmly convinced that Brownlow Common women's peace camp was a nest of subversives with sufficient resources to undermine the whole of western democracy, Lindsay supposed it wasn't really so amazing that the SB were taking such a keen interest in a murder that seemed to have some of its origins in the camp.

Lindsay got out of the car and surveyed Megamenu Software's premises. They scarcely inspired confidence. The double doors had been given a cheap and cheerful coat of pale green paint which was already beginning to flake off. There was a large sign in the same style as the one at the mouth of the alley, proclaiming "Megamenu Software: We Turn your Needs into Realities." Plenty of scope for a good PR officer, thought Lindsay cynically, when the budget eventually ran to it. But as she rang the bell beside the small door set in one of the larger pair, she noted with some surprise that no expense had been spared on security. The several locks all looked substantial and in spite of the peeling paint, the doors were solid. She didn't have time to speculate further, for the door was opened abruptly by Simon Crabtree.

He frowned and demanded, "What do you want?"

"A few words," Lindsay replied. "Won't take long, I promise."

"I've got nothing to say to the press," he retorted angrily. "You've had enough mileage out of my mother. Bloody vultures."

Lindsay smiled wryly. "Fair enough. But I'm not really here in my role as bloody vulture. Think of me as a seeker after truth. Your father has been murdered and the police seem keen to put one of my oldest friends in the frame for it.

I know she didn't do it, and I'm trying to prove that. All I want is a bit of information."

"Why should I help you? You and your bloody friends are no business of mine." He started to close the door, but Lindsay leaned gently against it.

"You don't owe me anything; but I'd have thought you owe your sister," she replied.

He was clearly taken aback. "Ros? What's she got to do with it?"

"I spent yesterday evening at Rubyfruits. She understood the importance of what I'm trying to do. If you rang her, I'm sure she'd tell you to help. And from what I hear, you've got a few debts to pay in that area."

His frown deepened. "You'd better come in, I suppose."

She followed him inside. It was her turn to be taken aback. Inside the shabby lock-up was a complete high-tech environment. The walls were painted matt grey. There was sound-absorbent carpet tile on the floor and the ceiling was covered with acoustic tiling, relieved only by discreet, low-level lighting. One wall was lined with filing drawers. There were four desks, each with a different type of computer terminal on it, including a small portable one, and two expensive-looking, ergonomically designed desk chairs. Several other pieces of equipment, including a standard cassette player and three printers, were sitting on the desks. In the background, baroque music played softly. Simon stood looking truculently at her as she walked round, desperately trying to memorize the names on the computers.

"Quite a set-up you've got here," she said admiringly. "You must be doing well to afford all this."

"I'm good with computers," he said.

"What sort of software do you produce, then?"

"Mainly programs for managers. So they can interpret

what's going on in the business. Now, what did you mean about my sister?"

"People like me and Ros live our lives on the edges of society. That makes it that little bit harder to achieve things. Ros has managed to get something together. And you blew it out of the water for her by telling your father what the score was. In my book, that means you owe her. And because she perceives herself as being part of a group, that means you owe the women she identifies with. Like my friend Deborah. If you don't agree with that analysis, ring up Ros and ask her yourself." Lindsay stopped abruptly, challenging him to make the phone call she knew would have her thrown out instantly.

Her gamble on his sense of guilt paid off. His scowl didn't lift, but he said grudgingly, "And what would you want to know?"

Lindsay hastily searched for a question that would justify her presence. "I wanted to know about his routine with the dog—was it something he always did at around the same time? Would someone have been able to rely on him being on the common with the dog at that time?"

Simon shrugged. "Not really. Rex always gets a walk any time between ten and midnight, depending on all sorts of things like the weather, what's on the box, who's at home. It wasn't always my father who took him out. I did sometimes, too. So if someone had been lying in wait, they might have had to hang around for hours on more than one occasion. If I'd been home earlier on Sunday, it could just as well have been me that walked him."

"So you think it's more likely that he met someone by arrangement?"

"Not necessarily. It might have been a chance meeting that turned nasty."

Lindsay recalled Crabtree's distinctive figure. "Your father would have been easy to recognize at a distance and chase after if you were looking for a chance encounter. After all, Deborah thought she spotted him from quite a way off on the night he died, when he was walking the dog," she added. "And she wasn't even on the common. She was walking back from the phone box." Simon shrugged. "But he was carrying a gun, Simon," Lindsay continued. "Surely that suggests he was expecting trouble?"

Simon paused to think. "Yes, but maybe he was just expecting trouble in a general way and had started carrying the gun when he took Rex out last thing."

Lindsay shook her head in disbelief. "This is rural England, not the New York subway. People don't wander round with guns just because they think someone might give them a hard time. If he was genuinely afraid of being attacked, if he'd been threatened in any serious way, surely he'd have gone to the police?"

Simon shrugged. "Don't ask me. It would probably have given him a buzz to confront someone with his gun and then turn them over to the cops. And I think he was genuinely frightened by those peace women. Especially after that one attacked him."

Lindsay shook her head. "I can't believe he thought the peace women were coming after him," she said. "It must have been something else. He said nothing?"

"No. And if you've no more questions, I'd appreciate the chance to get back to work," he replied.

"Okay. Thanks for the time. I'm sure Ros will appreciate your solidarity," she threw over her shoulder as she left.

Back in the car, she scribbled down the names of the computers she had seen and drove off, keeping an eye out for the red Fiesta. But her rear-view mirror was clear, so she stopped at the first phone box she came to. Typically, it was prepared to allow 999 calls only. Three boxes later, she found one that would accept her money, and she dialed an Oxford number. She was quickly connected with a friend from her student days, Annie Norton, a whiz kid in computer research.

After an exhaustive exchange of gossipy updates while she pumped coins into the box, Lindsay wound her way round to the point of the call. "Annie, I need your help on an investigation I've got tangled up with," she tossed into a gap in the conversation.

"If it's anything to do with Caroline Redfern's much publicized love-life, my lips are sealed," Annie replied.

"No, this is serious, not chit-chat. It's about computers. I've acquired a cassette tape that I think is a computer program. It could have been made on any one of four computers, and I need to know what it says. Can you help?"

"A cassette tape? How extraordinary. We're talking real computers here, are we, not video games?"

"I think so, yes."

"Hmm. No indication of what language it's in?" Annie asked.

"English, I suppose."

"No, no, what computer language—BASIC, FORTRAN, ALGOL, etc., etc."

"Oh," said Lindsay, bewildered. "No, nothing at all, unless there's a computer language called 'Sting: *The Dream Of The Blue Turtles*'."

"What? Are you serious?"

Lindsay laughed. "No, that's what's written on the cassette, that's all."

"And what computers are we talking about?"

"An Apple Macintosh, an IBM, an Apricot, an Amstrad, and a Tandy."

"A Tandy? Little lap-top job, would fit in a briefcase? With a flip-up screen?"

"Yes, that's right."

Annie sighed in relief. "That explains the tape. It's probably been transferred from one of the other machines," she mused. "It should be fairly simple to run it through our Univac and read it for you. When can you get it to me?"

"I could drop it off in an hour or so—I'm only down the road in Fordham."

"Tremendous. We could have dinner together if you fancy it."

Lindsay was tempted. She had reached the point where she wanted more than anything to walk away from the conflict of interests with the peace camp, the police, and the job. She felt guilty about two-timing Cordelia and was unsure how she felt about Debs. But she had promised to be at the vigil, and she had to keep that promise. She could just fit in the round trip to Oxford if she didn't hang about too long with Annie. "Sorry," she said. "But I'm working tonight. Maybe when I pick it up again, yeah? How long will it take you?"

"Hard to say. A day? Two, maybe, if it's not something obvious. If the person who's made it is a real computer buff, which he or she presumably is, if they really use those four systems to their full potential, then it could be a bit subtle. Still, a nice bit of hacking makes a pleasant change. I'll see you again in about an hour, then. You know where to find me?"

"Sure, I remember. I'll be with you soon as possible." Lindsay rang off and was about to leave the box when she realized she hadn't spoken to Cordelia since her angry departure on Monday. Her mind had been too occupied with Crabtree and Debs for her to pay attention to her lover's needs. It wouldn't be an easy call, for Lindsay knew she'd have to lie about what had happened with Debs. The phone wasn't the place for confessions. And Cordelia would be quite justifiably hurt that Lindsay hadn't made time for her. Especially with Deborah Patterson back on the scene. The stab of guilt made her rake through her pockets for more change, and she hastily dialed their number. On the fourth ring, the answering machine picked up the call. "Oh shit," she muttered as she listened to her own voice instructing her to leave a message. After the tone, she forced a smile into her voice and said, feeling foolish as she always did on their own machine, "Hello, darling, it's me. Wednesday afternoon. Just a check call to let you know I'm okay. Duncan's leaving me here on the murder story because of my peace camp contacts, so God knows when I'll be home. Probably not till after the funeral, or an arrest, whichever comes first. I'll try to ring tonight. Love you. Bye." She put the phone down with relief and set off for Oxford.

13

Deborah was waiting impatiently by the Gate Six encampment for Lindsay. Already, most of the women taking part in the vigil were in place. The traffic on the main road back from Oxford and the need to change into more suitable clothes had delayed Lindsay enough for her to have missed the procession, but she could see that there were not sufficient numbers there to encircle the base holding hands. They had spread out along as much of the perimeter as they could cover, with gaps of about fifty yards between them. The flicker of candles, feeble against the cloudy winter night, was gradually spreading.

Deborah hustled Lindsay along the muddy clearing by the fence for half a mile till they reached their agreed station, a corner of the fence near a deep drainage ditch. They kissed goodbye, then Lindsay walked on round the corner to her position.

She turned facing the base, where the buildings and bunkers were floodlit against the enemy—not the red menace, but the monstrous regiment, she thought. She turned back and peered towards the nearest flame. She could just make out the silhouette of the next woman in the vigil and in the distance she could hear the faint sound of singing. She knew from experience that it would soon work its way round to her like Chinese whispers. She had been pleasantly surprised to see, for once, the police and military presence were fairly low key. She hadn't seen any journalists, but assumed they would all be down by the main gates, reluctant to stagger through the mud unless it became absolutely necessary. She smiled wryly. At least her story would have the unmistakable air of verisimilitude.

She took her Zippo lighter from her jacket pocket and flicked the flame into life. She hadn't remembered to ask Debs for a candle, so the lighter would have to do. She stamped her feet to keep the circulation going and started mentally planning her story.

Her thoughts were interrupted by a short scream, which was cut off by a squelching thud and the sound of crashing in the undergrowth. It came from Deborah's direction. Before she had time to think, she was charging back round the corner in the fence towards her. In her panic, she forgot about the drainage ditch and plunged headlong into it, twisting her ankle in an explosion of pain as she fell. Instead of landing in muddy water, she fell on something soft and yielding. Lindsay pushed herself away and fumbled with the lighter which she'd somehow managed to hang on to. The little flare of light was enough to show her a sight that made her heart lurch.

Deborah lay face down in the ditch, blood flowing from a gaping wound in the left side of her head. "Oh my God," she cried, fighting back tears of panic as she grabbed her by the shoulders. She remembered all the rules of first aid that instruct not to move victims with head wounds. But Deborah would drown if left lying face down in the mud. So she pulled at her left shoulder till she managed to turn her on her side. Lindsay pulled her scarf off and gently wiped the mud from Deborah's face. She gritted her teeth and cleared the silt from her nose and mouth and checked if she was still breathing by putting her ear to Deborah's mouth. She could feel nothing. "Debs, Debs, breathe, you bastard, breathe," she muttered desperately, pummeling Deborah's chest. After a few moments that felt like an eternity, she was rewarded by a sputtering cough as Deborah retched. Lindsay, herself facing nausea, then stood upright, yelling for help at the top of her voice.

It seemed hours before another couple of women appeared with a torch, looking bewildered.

"Get help, get help!" Lindsay almost screamed. "Debs has been attacked. Get the bloody police. We need an ambulance."

The next half hour was a blur of action as first police and then ambulance drivers arrived and rushed Deborah to hospital. Lindsay realised how serious the situation was when a young constable helped her into the ambulance, and she found herself racing through the lanes with flashing lights and siren.

At Fordham General, Deborah was immediately hurried away on a trolley with the policeman still in attendance. Lindsay sat, exhausted, wet, and filthy on the steps of the casualty unit, smoking a battered cigarette. She was numb with fear for Deborah. One of the ambulance drivers stopped to speak to her on the way back to his vehicle. "You did well, back there," he said. "Your friend might have died if you hadn't got her head out of the mud. Just as well you kept your head."

Lindsay shook her head. "I didn't keep my head. I panicked. I just acted on pure instinct. I was so afraid I'd lost her. How is she? Do you know?"

He shrugged. "Not out of the woods yet. But they're good

in there. You should go inside in the warm, you'll get a chill out here. Get yourself a cuppa."

Lindsay nodded wearily. "Yeah." She got to her feet as he climbed back into the ambulance. As she turned to go, a heavy hand clapped her on the shoulder. It belonged to a reporter she recognised by sight.

"What's the score?" he demanded. "We heard someone had been attacked, but the cops are saying nothing." Lindsay stared at him uncomprehendingly. "Come on, Lindsay," he pressed. "Don't be selfish. I've only got half an hour to close copy time on the next edition. You've had every bloody other exclusive on this job. Give us a break."

She wanted more than anything to put a fist in his face. Instead, she simply said, "Fuck off," and turned on her heel, shaking his hand loose. But the incident had reminded her that there was something she could do to put a bit of distance between the attack and her emotions. She walked like a zombie into the hospital, asked a passing nurse where the nearest phone was, and transferred the charges to the *Clarion* newsdesk. Luckily, Cliff Gilbert took the call himself.

"Lindsay here, Cliff," she said, speaking very slowly. "Listen, I'm in no fit state to write copy, but there's a very good story going on here, and I've got chapter and verse on it. If I give you all the facts, can someone knock it into shape?"

"What?" he exclaimed. "What the hell's the matter with you? Are you pissed?"

"Look, someone's just tried to kill one of my best friends. I'm exhausted, I'm wet, I'm probably in shock, and I'm at the end of my rope. I need help."

He realised from her voice as much as her words that Lindsay was serious. "Okay, Lindsay," he said. "I'm sorry. I'll put you on to Tony, and you tell him what he needs for the story. No problem. Do you need back-up? I can get someone down there in an hour. Or a local freelance–"

"I don't want anyone else, Cliff. Maybe you should get

some more cover down here, though. I'm through for tonight. Now give me Tony." A series of clicks followed, and Lindsay found herself talking to Tony Martin, one of her reporting colleagues. Cliff had obviously warned him what to expect, for his voice was quiet and coaxing. Lindsay forced the lid on her emotions and stumbled through the events of the evening. At the end of her recital, he asked for the number of the police station and the hospital. Her mind was a blank.

"Never mind," he said. "Listen, I'll make sure they put your by-line on this. It's a helluva story. I hope your mate pulls through. But you go and get yourself a stiff drink. You sound as if you need one. Okay?"

"Yeah, okay," she sighed, and put the phone down. Through the door of the booth, she could see other reporters arriving. She knew she couldn't cope with them now, so she turned back to the call box and dialed home. Cordelia picked up the phone on the third ring. Lindsay's voice shook as she said, "It's me. Can you come down?"

"What?" Cordelia demanded. "Now? Whatever's the matter? You sound terrible. What's going on?"

"It's Debs. She's . . . she's been attacked. Someone tried to kill her. I'm at the hospital now. I found her. I really could do with you being here."

There was incredulity in Cordelia's voice. "Someone tried to kill Deborah? How? What happened?"

"There was a candle-lit vigil. We were by the fence, about fifty yards from each other. Someone hit her on the head and left her drowning in a ditch," Lindsay said, on the verge of tears.

"That's awful! Are you okay?"

"Physically, yes. But I'm absolutely drained. I thought she was dead, Cordelia," Lindsay wailed, tears finally coursing down her face. She sobbed helplessly, oblivious to Cordelia's words.

When she managed to control herself again, she could hear her lover's voice soothing her, saying, "Calm down it'll be okay. Why don't you come home now? There's nothing more you can do there tonight. I'd come down and get you, but I've had too much wine."

"I can't," Lindsay said numbly.

"Why ever not?" Cordelia asked. "Look, you'd be better off here. You can have a nice hot bath and a drink and try to get a decent night's sleep. Come home, Lindsay. I'll only worry about you otherwise."

"I just can't," Lindsay replied. "There's too much going on here for me to walk away from it all. I'm sorry. I'll ring you in the morning, okay? Thanks for listening. Goodnight, love."

"I'll come down first thing, how's that?"

"No, it's okay, leave it. I'm not sure what I'll be doing or where I'll be. I'll speak to you soon."

"Be careful, Lindsay, please. Ring me in the morning."

Bleakness descended on Lindsay. She stared across the busy casualty department in time to see Rigano shoulder his way through the flapping celluloid doors and head for the desk. He was immediately surrounded by reporters. She became aware that the phone was squawking.

"Lindsay? Are you there?"

"Yes, I'm here. Bye."

She put the phone down, feeling utterly defeated. She left the phone booth but could not face the melee round the information desk. She leaned against the wall, shivering slightly in spite of the airless warmth of the hospital. Rigano, whose eyes had been sweeping the room for her, picked her up almost immediately.

"That's it for now," he said brusquely to the crowd of reporters and strode over to her, followed at a few paces by her colleagues. He took her by the elbow and piloted her into a corridor. He stopped briefly and said firmly to their followers. "Go away. Now. Or I'll have the lot of you removed from the hospital altogether." Reluctantly, they backed off, and he steered Lindsay into an alcove with a couple of chairs. They sat down.

"She's going to be all right," he said. "There's a hairline fracture of the skull and a big superficial wound. She's lost quite a bit of blood and had stitches, but they say there's no brain damage."

The relief was like a physical glow that spread through Lindsay. "When can I see her?" she asked.

"Tomorrow morning. Come round about nine, and they'll let you in. She'll still be heavily sedated, so they tell me, but she should be awake. It'll be a while before we can get any sense out of her, though, so I need to know anything you can tell me about the attack."

Lindsay shrugged. "I don't know anything. I don't even know what she was hit with. What was it?"

"A brick," he replied. "There's any number of them lying around. You use them to pin down the corners of your benders."

"That's ironic," said Lindsay, stifling the hysterical giggle she felt bubbling inside her. "I really can't tell you anything. I heard a short scream—not a long-drawn-out one, quite brief—and a squelch that must have been Debs falling into the ditch. Then I heard what sounded like someone trying to run off through the woodland."

"Can you say in what direction?"

"Not really. It seemed to be more or less dead ahead of me as I ran towards the ditch, but that's the vaguest of impressions, and I wouldn't swear to it. I wish I could tell you that I'd seen someone, but even if he'd still been there, I doubt if I would have seen him. There was really no light to speak of."

"Him?"

"Well, it wouldn't have been one of us, would it?"

It was Jane who woke Lindsay at eight the next morning with a pot of hot coffee. Settling herself down on the end of the bunk, she waited patiently for Lindsay to surface. Brought back to the camp by one of Rigano's men, Lindsay had needed several large whiskies before sleep had even seemed like a possibility. Now she was reaping the whirlwind.

Jane smiled at her efforts to shake off the stupor and said, "I thought I'd better make sure you were up in time to get to the hospital. I've already rung them—Deborah is out of danger and responding well, they said. Translation—she's been sedated to sleep, but her vital signs are looking good. They say it's okay for you to go in, but they don't think Cara should visit yet."

"How is Cara?" asked Lindsay, who felt as if her limbs were wooden and her head filled with cotton wool.

"A bit edgy, but she's with Josy and the other kids, so she'll be more or less all right," Jane replied. "She wants her mummy, but at least she's old enough to understand when you say that Deborah's in the hospital, but she's going to be all right."

"Do you think we can keep her here and look after her okay, or are we going to have to get something else sorted out?" Lindsay asked anxiously.

Jane smiled. "Don't worry about Cara. She's used to the routine here now. It's better that she's somewhere she can see Deborah as much as possible."

"I'm just worried in case social services find out about her and take her into care," Lindsay said.

"If anyone comes looking for her from the council, we'll deny all knowledge of her and say she's with her father. By the time they sort that little one out, Deborah will be convalescent," Jane reassured her. "Now, drink this coffee and get yourself over to the hospital."

"Five minutes," warned the nurse as she showed Lindsay into a small side room.

Deborah lay still, her head swathed in bandages. There was a tube in her nose and another in her arm. Her face was chalky white and dark bruises surrounded her closed eyelids. Lindsay was choked with a mixture of pity, love, and anger. As she moved towards the bed, she sensed another presence in the room and half turned. Behind the door, a uniformed constable sat, notebook poised. He smiled tentatively at her and said, "Morning, miss."

Lindsay nodded at him and sat down by the bed. Reaching out cautiously, she took hold of Deborah's hand. Her eyelids flickered momentarily, then opened. The pupils were so dilated that her eyes no longer appeared blue. Frowning slightly, as she tried to focus, she registered Lindsay's presence and her face cleared.

"Lin," she said in a voice that lacked all resonance. "It's really you?"

"Yes, love, it's me."

"Cara?"

"She's okay. Josy's in charge. Everything's under control."

"Good. I'm so tired, Lin. I can't think. What happened?"

"Somebody hit you. Did you see anyone, Debs?"

"I'm so glad it's really you, Lin. I think I'm seeing ghosts. I think Rupert Crabtree's haunting me."

"I'm no ghost, Debs. And he can't hurt you. He's out of your life for good."

"I know, but listen, Lin. It's crazy, I know, but I have this weird impression that it was Rupert Crabtree who attacked me. I must be going mad."

"You're not mad, you're just concussed and sedated up to the eyeballs. It'll all be clear soon, I promise."

"Yes, but I'm sure it was him that I saw. But it couldn't be, could it? Just like it couldn't have been him I saw walking his dog on Sunday night. Because he was already dead by then, wasn't he?"

"What?" Lindsay suddenly stiffened. "You saw him after he was dead?"

"I told you before that I saw him. But he was walking towards his house. And he'd already been killed up by the fence. It's his ghost, Lin, it's haunting me." Her voice was becoming agitated.

Lindsay stroked her arm. "It's okay, Debs. There's no ghost, I promise you. You've got to go to sleep now, and when you wake up, I swear you'll be much clearer. Now close your eyes, go back to sleep. I'll be back tonight, I promise. No ghosts, just good old Lindsay."

Her soothing voice lulled the panic from Deborah's face, and soon she was sleeping again. Lindsay rose to go, and the policeman followed her. Outside he said, "Could you make head or tail of that, miss? All that stuff about being attacked by a ghost?"

Lindsay shook her head. "She's delirious, at a guess. It made no sense to me, officer," she said.

But she knew, as she walked away from the ward that she lied. The echo of her words seemed to pursue her. Deborah's words had triggered off a chain of thought in Lindsay, making a strange kind of sense. At last, vague suspicions were crystallising into certainties. Lindsay felt a growing conviction that Oxford was where the answers lay.

14

Lindsay cursed the one-way system that had turned a city she knew like the back of her hand into a convoluted maze. Wryly she remembered the April Fool's Day joke that had been played by a bunch of math students when she'd been an undergraduate. They'd worked out that if they reversed just one sign in the traffic system, vehicles would be able to enter but not to leave it. The city had ground to an infuriated, hooting halt by eight in the morning, a problem it had taken the traffic experts till noon to solve. The memory kept Lindsay mildly amused until she finally pulled into the car park at the Computer Sciences Laboratory at eleven. She had stopped only to plead with Duncan for a day off, a request he reluctantly granted after she had delivered a short, first-person piece about her visit to the hospital. Since the *Clarion* had changed the front page to accommodate her story from the night before, the pugnacious news editor was determined to milk their exclusive line for all it was worth. Lindsay had deliberately left out all references to ghosts and stressed Deborah's ignorance of her attacker's identity. Then, with great satisfaction, she switched off her radio pager for the day.

"Lindsay!" exclaimed Annie as she emerged into the reception area looking more like an earth mother than a computer scientist, dressed as she was in a Laura Ashley print. "I thought you were going to phone." She escorted Lindsay through the security doors and down an air-conditioned corridor.

"Sorry," said Lindsay. "It's just that . . . well, I needed to be doing something and I can't get any further till I know what's on that tape."

Annie stopped in her tracks and studied her friend carefully. "What's happened, Lindsay? You look completely out of it. Getting involved with murders doesn't seem to agree with you."

Lindsay sighed. "Can we sit down somewhere? I don't even know where to begin." Annie ushered Lindsay into her office, a tiny cubby hole with a remote terminal dominating it. Lindsay slumped into a low, easy chair while Annie sat at her desk. Lindsay lit a cigarette then stubbed it out almost immediately, remembering that it was forbidden in the computer areas.

"Last night, somebody tried to kill Deborah and nearly succeeded. It was me who found her. I thought . . . I thought she was going to die. It was terrible, Annie. Made me realise . . . I don't know . . . how dangerous all of this is. Unless someone equally screwy is out to avenge Crabtree's death, it's got to be Crabtree's murderer. But it's too much a coincidence to believe there are two different killers on the loose. And that means, as far as I'm concerned, that it's a race against time to prove who really did it before he has another go and succeeds." Annie nodded encouragingly.

"I thought I could rely on the police to get their fingers out," Lindsay went on. "But I don't know, it all seems very strange to me. For some reason it's a uniformed copper who's running the show, not the CID, and there's some guy who's always around who's either Special Branch or something odd. And somehow there doesn't seem to be any urgency about what's going on. This cop, Rigano, *seems* dead straight, but even he's not getting the action going. To begin with, he was keen enough to enlist my help and stay abreast of what I was up to. But now, it's almost as if he doesn't want me to get any closer to the truth.

"I think I'm beginning to have just an inkling of an idea about who did it, but I haven't a clue why. I think the answer, or part of it, is that tape."

Annie grimaced. "Well, add that to the murderer's assumption that Debs will have told you all she knows, and you could be the next target. And knowing you, I suppose all this is upfront in the *Daily Clarion*?"

"Sort of. I mean, I've done a couple of exclusives."

Annie thought for a moment. "And?" she prompted.

"And what? Isn't that enough? That I could be next on a killer's hit list?"

"I know you. There's something else. Something personal."

Lindsay gave a tired smile. "I'd forgotten how sharp you can be," she said. "Yes, there is something more. But it seems hellish trivial beside the real problems of people getting hurt and killed. I'm having a difficult time with Cordelia just now. She seems jealous of the time I spend at the camp, especially now Debs is there."

"Hmm," Annie murmured. "She does have a point, though, doesn't she?"

Lindsay looked astonished. "I didn't—"

"You didn't have to, lovey. It's not what you say, Lindsay, it's how you say it. 'Twas ever thus with you. And if it's that obvious to me, who hasn't seen you for months, then it must stick out like a sore thumb to Cordelia. She must be feeling very threatened. If I were you, I'd make a point of going home tonight, no matter what other calls you think there are on your time."

Lindsay smiled. "I'd love to do just that. But a lot depends on what you've got to tell me about that tape. I'm convinced that that's where the answers lie."

Annie frowned. "I hope not," she said. She unlocked her desk and took out a pile of print-out paper and the tape. "I'm sorry to disappoint you," she said. "I don't think you'll find many answers here."

"You mean you haven't been able to crack it?" Lindsay asked, her voice full of disappointment.

"Oh no, it's not that," said Annie cheerfully. "I won't bore you with the details, but I must thank you for a really challenging task. It took me a lot longer that I thought. I didn't get to bed till three, you know, I was so caught up in this. Whoever constructed that programme knew exactly what he was doing. But it was one of those thorny problems that I can't bear to give up till I've solved it.

"So I stuck with it. And this is what I came up with." She handed Lindsay a sheaf of print-outs, consisting of pages of letters and numbers in groups.

"Is this it?" asked Lindsay. "I'm sorry, it's completely meaningless to me. What does it represent?"

"That's what I don't know for sure," Annie admitted. "It may be some encoded information, or that in itself could be the information. But unless you know what it is you're looking for, it doesn't take you any further forward in itself. I've never seen anything quite like it, if that's any help."

Lindsay shook her head. "I hoped that this would solve everything. I think I was looking for a motive for murder. But I seem to have ended up with another complication. Annie, do you know anybody who might be able to explain this print-out?"

Annie picked up her own copy of the printed message and studied it again. "It's not my field, and I'm not sure whose it is until I know what it is, if you see what I mean." She sighed. "The only thing that occurs to me, and it's the vaguest echo from a seminar I went to months ago, is that it might possibly be some kind of signals traffic. I don't know for sure, and I can't even put my finger on why I believe that. But that's all I can go on. And I can't put you in touch with anyone who might help because, if it is signals intelligence, then the ninety-nine per cent probability is that it's Official Secrets Act stuff. I'm bound by that, and so is anyone else who might help. And if I put you in touch, they'll have to report the contact in both directions. Just what have you got yourself into this time, Lindsay?"

Lindsay sighed again. "Deep waters, Annie."

"You should be talking to the police about this."

"I can't, not yet. I don't trust what's going on, I told you."

"Where did this come from, Lindsay? For my own protection, I think you need to tell me a bit more about the provenance of this tape. It all looks extremely dodgy to me."

"I found it in a collection of papers belonging to Rupert Crabtree, the man who was murdered. His son owns a small software house in Fordham. It was in such a strange place, I figured it might be significant. And now, from what you tell me, it could be more than just a clue in a murder mystery. Have you made a copy of the tape?"

Annie nodded. "I always do, as a precaution."

"Then I'd suggest you disguise it as Beethoven string quartets or something and hide it in your tape collection. I'd like there to be a spare, in case anything happens to my copy. Or to me."

Annie's eyebrows rose. "A little over the top, surely?"

Lindsay smiled. "I hope so."

"You can make a copy yourself on a decent tape-to-tape hi-fi, you know," Annie remarked in an offhand way. "And you will be going home tonight, won't you?"

Lindsay grinned. "Yes, Annie, I'll be going home. But I've

got a couple of things to do first." She stood up. "Thanks for all your work. Soon as all of this is over, we'll have a night out on me, I promise."

"Let's hope those aren't famous last words. Be careful, Lindsay, if this is what I think it might be, it's not kid's stuff you're into." Suddenly she stood up and embraced Lindsay. "Watch your back," she cautioned, as the journalist detached herself and made for the door.

Lindsay turned and winked solemnly at Annie. "Just you watch me," she said.

As she wrestled with the twin horrors of the one-way system and the pay phones of Oxford, Lindsay decided that she was going to invest in a mobile phone, whatever the cost. In frustration, she headed out towards the motorway and finally found a working box in Headington. Once installed, she flipped through her contacts book until she found the number of *Socialism Today*, a small radical monthly magazine where Dick McAndrew worked.

She dialed the number and waited to be connected. Dick was a crony from the Glasgow Labour Party who had made his name as a radical journalist a few years earlier with an exposé of the genetic damage sustained by the descendants of British Army veterans of the 1950s atom bomb tests. He was a tenacious Glaswegian whose image as a bewildered ex-boxer hid a sharp brain and a dogged appetite for the truth. Lindsay knew he'd recently become deeply interested in the intelligence community and GCHQ at Cheltenham. If this was a record of signals traffic, he'd know.

Her luck was still with her. Dick was at his desk, and she arranged to meet him for lunch in a little pub in Clerkenwell. That gave her just enough time to go home and swap her bag of dirty washing for a selection of clean clothes. She made good time on the motorway, which compensated for the time she lost in heavy West London traffic. Being behind the wheel of her MG relaxed her, and in spite of the congested streets, she was almost sorry when she turned off by Highbury Fields and parked outside the house.

She checked her watch as she walked through the front door and decided to make time for herself for a change. She stripped off and dived into a blessedly hot shower. Emerging, she carefully chose a crisp cotton shirt and a pair of lined woollen trousers still in the dry cleaners' bag. She dressed quickly, finishing the outfit off with an elderly Harris Tweed jacket she'd liberated from her father's wardrobe. In the kitchen, Lindsay scrawled a note on the memo board: "12:45. Thurs. I intend to be back by eight tonight. If emergency crops up, I'll leave a message on the machine. Love you."

She pulled on a pair of soft grey moccasins, light relief after her boots, and ran downstairs to the street. There she picked up a passing cab which deposited her outside the pub. She shouldered her way through the lunchtime crowds till she found Dick sitting in a corner staring morosely at a pint of Guinness. "You're late," he accused her.

"Only ten minutes, for Chrissake," she protested.

"It's the job," he replied testily. "You get paranoid. What you drinking?" In spite of Lindsay's attempts to buy the drinks, he was adamant that he should pay, and equally adamant that she had to have a pint. "I'm no' buying bloody half pints for an operator as sharp as you," he explained. "If I'm on pints, so are you. That way I'm less likely to get conned."

He returned with the drinks and immediately scrounged a cigarette from Lindsay. "So," he said, "how's tricks? You look dog rough."

"Flattery will get you nowhere, McAndrew. If you must know, I'm in the middle of a murder investigation, my ex-girlfriend is recovering from a homicidal attack, Cordelia's in a huff, and Duncan Morris expects the moon yesterday. Apart from that, life's the berries. Howsabout you?" she snarled.

"Oh well, you know?" He sighed expansively.

"That good, eh?"

"So what have you got for me, Lindsay? What's behind this meet? Must be good or you'd have given me some clue on the phone and chanced the phone-tap guy not being sharp enough to pick it up. Hell mend them."

"It's not so much what I've got for you as what you can do for me."

"I've told you before, Lindsay, I'm not that kind of boy."

"You should be so lucky, McAndrew. Listen, this is serious. Forget the Simon Dupree of the gay repartee routine. I've got a computer print-out that I'm told might be coded signals traffic. Could you identify it if it was?"

Dick looked alert and intent. "Where d'you get this from, Lindsay?"

"I can't tell you yet, Dick, but I promise you that as soon as it's all sorted, I'll give you chapter and verse."

He shook his head. "You're asking a lot, Lindsay."

"That's why I came to you," she said. "Want to see it?" He nodded and she handed him the print-out. He helped himself to another cigarette and studied the paper. Ten minutes later, he carefully folded it up and stuffed it back in her handbag. "Well?" she asked cautiously.

"I'm not an expert," he said warily, "but I've been looking at intelligence communication leaks for a wee while now. As you well know. And that looks to me like a typical pattern for a US military base. Somewhere like Upper Heyford, Mildenhall."

"Or Brownlow Common?"

"Or Brownlow Common."

"And what does it mean?"

"Oh Christ, Lindsay. I don't know. I'm not a bloody expert in codes. I've got a source who might be able to unscramble it if you want to know that badly. But I'd have thought it was enough for you to know that you're walking around with a print-out of top secret intelligence material in your handbag. Just possessing that would be enough for them to put you away for a long time."

"It's that sensitive?"

"Lindsay, the eastern bloc spend hundreds of thousands of roubles trying to get their hands on material like that. Quite honestly, I don't even want to know where you got that stuff. I want to forget I've ever seen it."

"But if you know what it is, you must have seen other stuff like it."

Dick nodded and took a long draught of his pint. "I've seen similar stuff, yes. But nothing approaching that level of security. There's a system of security codes at the top of each set of groups. And I've never encountered anything with a code rated that high before. It's the difference between the official report in Hansard and what the PM tells herself in the mirror in the morning. You are playing with the big boys, Lindsay." He rose abruptly and went to the bar, returning with two large whiskies.

"I don't drink spirits at lunchtime," she protested.

"You do today," he said. "You want my advice? Go home, burn that print-out, go to bed with Cordelia, forget you ever saw it. That's trouble, Lindsay."

"I thought you were a tough-shit investigative journo, the sort that isn't happy unless you're taking the lid off the Establishment and kicking the Official Secrets Act into touch?"

"It's not like pulling the wings off flies, Lindsay. You don't just do it for the hell of it. You do it when you think there's something nasty in the woodpile. I'm not one of those knee-jerk lefties who publishes every bit of secret material that comes my way, like Little Jack Horner saying, 'See what a good boy am I.' Some things should stay secret; it's when that's abused to protect crime and pettiness and sloppiness and injustice and self-seeking that people like me get stuck in," he replied passionately.

"Okay," she said mildly. "Cut the lecture. But take it from

me, Dick, something very nasty has been going on, and I've got to get to the bottom of it before it costs any more lives. If I have to use my terrifying bit of paper to get there, I'll do it. There's nothing wrong with my bottle."

"I never said there was. That's the trouble with you, Lindsay—you don't know when it's sensible to get scared."

By silent consent, they changed the subject and spent half an hour gossiping about mutual friends in the business. Then Lindsay felt she could reasonably make her excuses and leave. She got back to the three-storey house in Highbury at half past two, with no recollection of the journey through North London streets. The answering machine was flashing, but she ignored it and went through to the kitchen to brew a pot of coffee. She had the frustrating feeling that she had all the pieces of the jigsaw but couldn't quite arrange them in a way that made sense. While the coffee dripped through the filter, she decided to call Rigano.

For once, she was put straight through. As soon as she identified herself, he demanded, "Where are you? And what have you been up to?"

Puzzled, she said, "Nothing. I'm at home in London. I visited Deborah this morning and since then I've seen a couple of friends. Why?"

"I want to know what you make of your friend's remark when you saw her in the hospital. My constable thought it might be significant."

"I told him then I didn't understand it," she replied cautiously.

"I know what you told him. I don't believe you," he retorted.

"That's not my problem," she replied huffily.

"It could be," he threatened. "I thought we were co-operating, Lindsay?"

"If I had any proof of who attacked Deborah, do you think

I'd be stupid enough to sit on it? I don't want to be the next one with a remodelled skull, Jack."

There was a heavy silence. Then he said in a tired voice, "Got anything for me at all?"

"These bikers who have been terrorising the camp—I think Warminster and Mallard are paying them."

"Have you any evidence of that?"

Briefly, Lindsay outlined what she had learned the day before. "It's worth taking a look at, don't you think? I mean, Warminster and Mallard both wanted Crabtree out of the way. Maybe they used the yobs they'd already primed for the vandalism."

"It's a bit far-fetched, Lindsay," he complained. "But I'll get one of my lads to take a look at it."

Having got that off her chest, Lindsay got to the point of the call. "Has it occurred to you that there might be a political dimension to this situation?"

His voice became cautious in its turn. "You mean that RABD is only a front for something else? That's nonsense."

"I mean real politics, Jack. Superpowers and spies. The person you're looking for didn't really kill for personal reasons; I think we're looking at a wider motive altogether. Somebody doesn't want us to do that. And that's why I think this investigation has got bogged down in trivial details about peace women's alibis."

"That's an interesting point of view, but that sort of thing is all out of my hands. I'm just a simple policeman, Lindsay. Conspiracy theories don't do much for me. I leave all that to the experts. And you'd be well advised to do the same."

Simple policeman, my foot, thought Lindsay. "Is that a warning, Jack?" she asked innocently.

"Not at all, Lindsay. I'm just telling you as simply as I know how that this case isn't about James Bond, it's about savage responses to petty situations. It's about people carrying offensive weapons for mistaken notions of self-defence. Anything else is out of my hands. Do I make myself clear?"

"So who is that blond man who keeps following me? Special Branch? MI5?"

"If you mean Mr. Stone, he's not Special Branch. There's no SB man around here, Lindsay. And no one is following you. I'd know about it if they were. If anyone's being followed, it's not you. You should stop being so paranoid."

Lindsay almost smiled. "Haven't you heard, Jack? Just because you stop being paranoid doesn't mean they're not out to get you."

15

Lindsay raked around in her desk drawer until she found a blank cassette. Going through to the large L-shaped living room where the stereo system with the twin tape decks occupied a corner, she set it up to make a copy of the computer tape and sprawled on one of the elegant grey leather chesterfields while she waited for the recording to finish. It was wonderful to lie back on the comfortable sofa surrounded by the restful atmosphere created by Cordelia's unerring talent for interior design, though she felt a pang of guilt when she remembered the squalid conditions back at Brownlow. Lindsay ruefully recalled her feelings when she had first entered Cordelia's domain two years before. She had been overwhelmed with the luxurious interior of the tall house by the park, and it had been months before she got out of the habit of pricing everything around her with a sense of puritanical outrage. Now, it was her home, far more than her Glasgow flat which she rented out to students at a rent that covered her overheads.

She turned over again what Rigano had said. As far as the blond man was concerned, it seemed plain to Lindsay that he was something to do with intelligence, since Rigano had denied so vehemently that he was SB while pointedly ignoring her MI5 allegation. And if Stone wasn't following her, that didn't leave many options for the focus of his interests. And that in turn meant she wasn't barking up the wrong tree as far as the existence of wider political implications was concerned. What she couldn't understand was why Rigano was just sitting back and letting it happen without pursuing the same person that she was interested in.

Unless, of course, she was completely wrong, and the two strands were unrelated, leaving the murder as a purely personal matter. That would leave the ball firmly in the court of Warminster, Mallard and the putative biker, or Alexandra/Carlton. The interest of the security forces could then be explained away as concern about police action jeopardizing some operation of theirs. Since Lindsay was still far from clear about the point of killing Rupert Crabtree, either option seemed possible. However, the attempt on Deborah's life seemed logical only if one assumed that it had been made to silence her. And if that was the case, Lindsay argued to herself, how did the murderer know that Debs hadn't already spilled whatever beans she possessed? And if she hadn't, then was she likely to do so now, especially since her silence must have come not from fear but from a failure to recognize what she knew or its importance? Lindsay shook her head vigorously. She was going round in circles.

She mentally replayed her conversation with Rigano again. Something he had said as a throwaway line came back into sharp focus. "It's about people carrying offensive weapons for mistaken notions of self-defense," he had remarked bitterly. Suddenly the jigsaw fell into place. Lindsay jumped to her feet and went to the phone. If Cordelia had been accessible, she would have outlined her theory then and there and waited for the holes to be picked in it. Failing that, she punched in the number of Fordham police station and drummed her fingers impatiently till the connection was made.

"Hello . . . Can I speak to Superintendent Rigano?" she demanded. The usual sequence of clicks and hollow silences followed. Then the switchboard operator came back to her and reported that Rigano was out of the building. But Lindsay was not to be deflected.

"Can you get a message to him, please? Will you tell him that Lindsay Gordon rang and needs to talk to him urgently? I'm just setting off to drive to Fordham now, and I'll be at the police station in about an hour and a half; say five o'clock. If he's not back by then, I'll hang on. Got that?"

The woman on the switchboard seemed slightly bemused by Lindsay's bulldozer tactics, but she dutifully repeated the message and promised it would be passed on over the radio. Taking the original cassette tape out of the machine and stuffing it in her pocket, Lindsay left the house, completely forgetting the flashing answering machine and her promise to Cordelia.

She walked round to the mews garage where she kept the car and was soon weaving through the traffic, seeing every gap in the cars ahead as a potential opportunity for queue jumping. Excited as she was by the new shape her thoughts had taken, she forced herself not to think about murder and its motives while she negotiated the busy roads leading to the M4.

She arrived at Fordham police station ten minutes ahead of schedule. The elderly constable on reception desk duty told her Rigano was due back within the next half hour and that he was expecting her. She was taken through to a small anteroom near his office and a matronly policewoman brought her a cup of tea, freshly brewed but strong. Lindsay found it hard to sit still and chain-smoked through the twenty minutes she was kept waiting. She looked at one cigarette ruefully as she blew smoke at the ceiling. No matter how hard she tried to give up or cut down, at the first crisis she leapt for the nicotine with the desperate fixation of the alcoholic for the bottle.

Rigano himself came to escort her to his room. More cheerful now, there was no sign that he resented her demand to see him. But he seemed determined to keep a distance between them. In his office, there was no sign of his sergeant or any of the other officers to take notes of the interview. Lindsay was disconcerted by that, but nevertheless relieved. What she had to say didn't need a big audience. And if some hard things were going to be said on both sides, it was probably just as well that they should go unrecorded.

"Well," he said, indicating a chair to her as he walked round his desk to sit down. "You seem in a big rush to talk to me now, when you could barely spare me a sentence earlier on. What's caused the big thaw? Surely not my overwhelming charm."

"Partly it's fear," she replied. "I said to you earlier that I'd be a fool if I knew who had killed Crabtree and tried to kill Deborah and persisted in keeping my mouth shut. Well, I think that now I know, and I'm ready to talk."

If she expected him to show signs of amazement or shock, she was disappointed. His eyebrows twitched slightly and he simply said, "That's assuming the two incidents are directly related."

Lindsay was puzzled. "But of course they are. You can't seriously expect anyone to believe that there are two homicidal maniacs running around out there? Deborah was connected to Crabtree while he was alive; in my book, that makes a strong case for a connection when they're both involved in murderous attacks in the same place within days of each other."

"The attack on Deborah Patterson could have been a

random attack on one of the peace women by someone who's got a grudge against the camp," he argued mildly.

Lindsay shook her head. "No way. If anyone was going to do that, they'd pick a spot much nearer the road, where they could make a quick getaway. The woods are really dense around where Debs was attacked. That was someone watching and waiting and biding his time, someone who knows enough about the way things work round here to know where to keep his eyes open."

Rigano smiled. He almost seemed to be enjoying their sparring. "All right," he conceded. "I'll grant you the assumption for now that the incidents were connected. Where do we go from there?"

"Do you want the hypothesis or the evidence?"

"I'll have the evidence, then you can give me the theory."

"Item one. A cassette tape. It was among Rupert Crabtree's papers in the RABD files. It's not what it says on the label—it's a recording of signals traffic on computer that would be of interest both to this country's allies and our enemies." She put the tape on his desk. He picked it up, studied it, and put it down again. He nodded encouragingly.

"Item two. Debs thinks she's being haunted by the ghost of Rupert Crabtree. She thinks she saw him walking the dog after he was dead, and she's convinced it was Crabtree who attacked her.

"Item three. There is someone around, the guy you called Mr. Stone, who is taking an interest in what's going on. He's not CID. You tell me he's not SB. That means, given the contents of this tape, that he's MI5 or 6. I imagine from what little I know about intelligence that he's MI6 K Branch. They're the ones who keep track of Soviet and satellite state agents, aren't they?"

A trace of the lighter side of his personality flickered across Rigano's face as he smiled and said, "You seem to know what you're talking about."

Lindsay immediately bristled. She was determined not to grant him any rights where she was concerned. "Please don't patronize me. I'm not a little woman who needs patting on the head because she can play the big boys' game."

The shutters came down over his eyes again. "That wasn't my intention," he replied coolly. "Is that the extent of your evidence?"

"There's one more thing. But it's conjecture rather than hard fact. What if Rupert Crabtree's gun was being carried not for defense but for attack?"

For the first time, Rigano looked truly alert, as if she was telling him something he did not know, or something he did not want her to know. "Why should he?" he demanded.

"If I can explain my idea about what really happened, you'll see why he should," Lindsay replied. "Are you prepared to hear me out?"

He glanced at his watch. It was almost half past five. "I've got half an hour," he said. "Will it take longer that that?"

Lindsay shook her head. "It's not a long story. It's not a very edifying one either. Treachery and greed, that's what we're into here, Jack." He nodded and sat back, attentive.

"Simon Crabtree is a computer prodigy. He's one of those people who reads a program like you or I read a page in the newspaper. And he's a hacker. Even when he was at school, they commented on his rare skill at busting into other people's private programs. No one had any doubt that he should be looking at a future in computers. No one, that is, except his father, who was conservative enough to be determined that his only son should be properly qualified in something. So he refused to help Simon set up his software business.

"I've seen inside that lock-up, and, while I don't know too much about computers, I'd say that the equipment in there must run into several thousands of pounds, easily. Maybe even five figures. Now, he wouldn't have got that kind of money from a bank, so where did it come from?

"It's my belief that it came from a foreign power. Almost inevitably the Soviets or an East European Soviet satellite. That cassette you've got there contains a recording of signals traffic from a U.S. military base. I don't know enough about these things to swear that it comes from Brownlow, but the chances are that it does, given that I found it among Rupert Crabtree's papers. What I think happened was this. I think that either Simon was scouted by the Soviets, who learned about his hacking skills and his need for capital, or he approached them with the revelation that he had the key to hack into the base's signals computer. I don't think it's been going on too long, if that's any consolation, because he's only had the business up and running for a few months.

"I'm a bit hazy about what happened to put Rupert Crabtree on to the trail. I'd guess that maybe he saw his son behaving suspiciously or saw him with someone he shouldn't have been with. Either way, he got hold of this tape. I'm still guessing here, but I think he probably did what I did—took it to someone who knows how to crack computer codes and discovered just what I did—that it's top-secret signals traffic. Only, for him, the discovery must have been utterly devastating. Here he is, a pillar of the community, a man in the vanguard of an anti-left-wing campaign, and his son's spying for the Ruskies. Also, to be fair, I think from what I've learned about him that it wouldn't just have been the personal disgrace that would have upset him.

"I think he was a patriotic man who genuinely loved his country. I could never have agreed with his politics, but I don't think he was your stereotype fascist on a power trip. I believe that the discovery of what Simon was doing must have shattered him. And something had really got to him, according to Alexandra Phillips. Are you with me so far?"

Rigano said seriously, "It's a very interesting hypothesis. I think your analysis of Crabtree's character is pretty much on the ball. But do go on. I'm fascinated. You've obviously done a lot of digging that you haven't told me about."

Lindsay smiled. "Isn't that what journalists are supposed to do?"

He frowned. "In theory. But not when they've struck deals with me. Anyway, carry on."

"Crabtree's options, once he had discovered Simon's treason, were fairly limited. He'd realized at once he couldn't ignore it and carry on as if nothing had changed. He couldn't come to your lot because that would completely destroy his life. It would bring his world crashing down about him, and once the press started digging, it would expose all sorts, like his relationship with Alexandra, like RABD's connections with the violent right. It would make it almost impossible for him to go on practising locally. The shame for him and his wife would have been too much, and he was too old to think about starting elsewhere.

"He could have confronted Simon with his knowledge and ordered him to stop, with the blackmail that if he didn't he would go to the authorities. But there's no way that could have been done effectively—Rupert had no way of checking that Simon had really stopped. And Simon probably knew his father well enough to realize that he wouldn't have carried through his bluff. So there would have been a stalemate. And it wouldn't have taken much imagination on Crabtree's part to work out what his fate would probably be, once Simon reported back to his control that his father knew he was spying.

"The only other option was to dispose of the son whose treachery was putting his family and his country at risk."

Rigano picked up a pencil and started doodling on a sheet of paper by his phone. He looked up. "Tell me more," he said.

"Not much more to tell, is there? Crabtree had a gun. He was licensed for it. He knew how to shoot. But I'd guess that he probably didn't intend to use it unless he had to. He'd have tried to divert suspicion to the peace women, so he'd likely have used the gun as a threat and then killed Simon some other way. He arranged to meet Simon on the common to have a private talk. When he pulled the gun, Simon panicked and overpowered him. Then, realizing there was nothing else for it, he killed him.

"Then that cool young man went home, bringing the bemused and terrified family dog, which of course explains why the dog was on the doorstep and not howling over the corpse of his master as one would expect. Then Simon stripped off his muddy bike leathers and put up a good show for when the police arrived. That, by the way, is when Deborah saw him. You must have noticed that he's physically, if not facially, very like his father. Deborah knew Crabtree but not Simon, and she thought it was the father and not the son she saw outlined against the night sky. It was only much later that she realized he must already have been dead by then.

"And appallingly, it was I who tipped Simon off that Deborah had seen him. I said she'd seen his father, but he was quicker to the point than me and immediately knew who Deborah had really got a glimpse of. He understood the significance and decided Deborah was too high a risk to leave unattended. Hence the attack on her, and hence her conviction that Rupert Crabtree was haunting her. She must have caught a brief, peripheral glimpse of Simon and subconsciously identified him wrongly. I hope you've still got a guard on her."

Rigano put his pencil down and sighed. "Very plausible," he muttered. "Fits all the facts in your possession."

"It's the only theory that does," Lindsay replied sharply. "Anything else relies on a string of completely implausible coincidences."

"I tend to agree with you," he replied in an offhand way.

"So what are you going to do about it? You've got the evidence there," Lindsay said, pointing at the tape. "You can get your forensic people to examine the clothes Simon was wearing that night. There must be traces."

"I'm going to do precisely nothing about it, except to say, well done, Lindsay. Now forget it," he said coldly.

Lindsay looked at him in stunned amazement. "What?" she demanded, outraged. "How can you ignore what I've just told you? How can you ignore the evidence I've given you? You've got to bring him in for questioning, at least!"

He shook his head. "No," he said. "Don't you understand?"

"No, I bloody don't," she protested bitterly. "You're a policeman. You're supposed to solve crimes, arrest the culprits, bring them to trial. You're quick enough to do people for speeding—suddenly murder is a no-go area?"

"This murder is," he replied. "Why else do you think a uniform is in charge instead of the CID? Why else am I working with two men, a dog and a national newspaper hack? I am supposed to fail."

Lindsay was dumbstruck. It didn't make any sense to her. "I . . . I don't get it," she stuttered.

Rigano sighed deeply. He spoke quietly but firmly. "I shouldn't tell you this, but I feel I owe it to you after the way you've worked through this. Simon Crabtree is part of a much bigger operation that's out of my hands and way over my head. I am not allowed to touch him. If he ran amok in Fordham High Street with a Kalashnikov, I'd have a job arresting him. Now do you understand?"

Lindsay's fury suddenly erupted. "Oh yes, I bloody understand all right. Some bunch of adolescent spymasters think they can get to some tuppenny-ha'penny KGB thug via Simon Crabtree. So it's hands off Simon. And that means it's open season on Deborah. She can't be kept under police guard forever. Simon doesn't know he's sacrosanct. He'll have another go. And next time, Deborah might not be so lucky. You expect me to stand by while an innocent woman is put at risk from that homicidal traitor? Forget it!"

"So what are you going to do about it?"

"I'm a journalist, Jack," she replied angrily. "I'm going to write the story. The whole bloody, dirty story." She got to her feet and made for the door. As she opened it, she said, "But first of all, I'm going to talk to Simon Crabtree."

16

The roar of the MG's engine was magnified by the high walls of Harrison Mews as Lindsay drew up for her showdown with Simon Crabtree. It was a cold, clear night with an edge of frost in the air, and she wound down the car window to take a few deep breaths. The alleyway was gloomy, lit only by a few dim bulbs outside some of the lock-ups. The immediacy of her anger had subsided far enough for her to be apprehensive about what she intended to do. She cursed her lack of foresight in failing to bring along her pocket tape recorder. Although she was desperate for the confrontation, she was enough of a professional to realize that the difficulties she would encounter in getting this story into the paper would only be compounded by an unwitnessed, unrecorded interview with Simon. She could try to find the *Clarion's* backup team and enlist their help, but she knew she could only expect the most reluctant cooperation from them unless specifically ordered by Duncan. After her string of exclusives, the poor bastard who'd been sent down as backup was not going to be too inclined to help her out.

She lit a cigarette and contemplated her options. Behind her apprehension lay the deep conviction of all journalists, that somehow they were immune from the risks faced by the rest of the world. It was that same conviction that had made her face a killer alone once before. She could dive in now, feet first; the chances were that Simon would deny everything. Even if he admitted it, she'd have no proof. Then he'd tip off his masters, she'd be in the firing line, and as sure as the sun rises in the morning, Duncan would send her back anyway with a photographer to get pictures and a witnessed interview. It wouldn't matter so much then if he denied it; the office lawyer would be satisfied that he'd been given a fair crack of the whip. The other alternative was to leave it for now, go and visit Debs in hospital, go home and talk it over with Cordelia, and discuss the best approach with Duncan in the morning. Then everyone would be happy. Everyone except Lindsay herself, in whom patience had never been a highly developed character trait.

Sighing, she decided to be sensible. She wound up the window, but before she could start the engine, she saw a Transit van turn into the alleyway and drive towards her. Only its sidelights were on, and it was being driven up the middle of the roadway, making it impossible for Lindsay to pass. Instinctively, she glanced in the rear-view mirror. In the dim glow of her tail lights, she saw a red Fiesta, parked diagonally across her rear, preventing any escape by that route. The Transit stopped a few feet from her shiny front bumper and both doors opened. There was nothing accidental about this, she thought.

Two men emerged. One was around the six-foot mark, with the broad shoulders and narrow hips of a body builder. He had thinning dark hair cut close to his head, and his sharp features with their five o'clock shadow were exaggerated by the limited lighting. He looked like a tough Mephistopheles. The other was smaller and more wiry, with a mop of dark hair contorted into a curly perm. Both wore leather bomber jackets and training shoes. All this Lindsay absorbed as they moved towards her, understanding at once that something unpleasant was going to happen to her. She discovered that she couldn't swallow. Her stomach felt as if she'd been punched in the middle of a period pain. Almost without thinking, Lindsay locked the driver's door as Curly Perm tried the passenger door, and Mephistopheles reached her side of the car. He tried the handle, then said clearly and coldly, "Open it."

Lindsay shook her head. "No way," she croaked through dry lips. She was too scared even to demand to be told what was going on.

She saw him sigh. His breath was a white puff in the night air. "Look," he said reasonably. "Open it now. Or else it's a brick through the window. Or, since you've done us the favor of bringing the soft-top, the Stanley knife across this very expensive hood. You choose."

He looked completely capable of carrying out his threat without turning a hair. Unlocking the door, Lindsay suddenly ached for a life with such certainties, without qualms. Immediately, he wrenched the door open and gestured with his thumb for her to get out. Numbly, she shook her head. Then, behind her, another voice chimed in.

"I should do as he asks if I were you." Lindsay twisted in her seat and saw Stone leaning against the car. Somehow it came as no surprise. She even felt a slight sense of relief. At least she could be sure which side had her. You bastard, Jack Rigano, she thought.

Stone smiled encouragingly. "I assure you, you'll be out of that car one way or another within the next few minutes. It's up to you how painless the experience will be. And don't get carried away with the notion of extracting a price in pain from us. I promise you that your suffering will be immeasurably greater. Now, why don't you just get out of the car?" His voice was all the more chilling for having a warm West Country drawl.

Lindsay turned back to Mephistopheles. If he'd stripped naked in the interval, she wouldn't have noticed. What grabbed her attention was the short-barrelled pistol which was pointing unwaveringly at her right leg. The last flickering of defiance penetrated her fear, and she said abruptly, "Because I don't want to get out of the bloody car."

Curly Perm marched round the back of the car, past Stone. He took something from his pocket, and suddenly a gleaming blade leapt forward from his fist. He leaned into the car as Lindsay flinched away from him. He looked like a malevolent monkey. He waved the knife in front of her, then, in one swift movement, he sliced her seat belt through the middle, leaving the ends dangling uselessly over her. He moved back, looking speculatively at the soft black vinyl roof.

"The first cut is the deepest," said Stone conversationally. "He's very good with the knife. He knows how to cause serious scars without endangering your life. I wonder if Deborah Patterson would be quite so keen then? Or indeed, that foxy lady you live with. Don't be a hero, Lindsay. Get out of the car."

His matter-of-fact air and the use of her first name were far more frightening than the flick-knife or the gun. The quiet menace Stone gave off was another matter. Lindsay knew enough about herself to realize that he was the one whose threats had the power to invest her life with paranoid nightmares. Co-operation seemed the best way to fight her fear now. So she got out of the car. "Leave the keys," said Mephistopheles as she reached automatically for them on the way out.

As she stood up, Stone moved forward and grasped her right arm above the elbow. Swiftly, he fastened one end of a pair of handcuffs round her wrist. "Am I under arrest or what?" she demanded. He ignored the question.

"Over to the van, please," he said politely, betraying his words by twisting her arm up her back. Stone steered her round to the back of the Transit. Curly Perm opened the doors and illuminated the interior with a small torch. Lindsay glimpsed two benches fixed to the van's sides, then she was bundled inside and the other shackle of the cuffs was fixed to one of the solid steel struts that formed the interior ribs of the van. The doors were hastily slammed behind her, casting her into complete darkness, as she asked again, "What's going on? Eh?" There were no windows. If she stretched out her leg as far as she could reach, she could just touch the doors. She could stand almost upright but couldn't quite reach the opposite side of the van with her arm. It was clear that any escape attempt would be futile. She felt thankful that she'd never suffered from claustrophobia.

Lindsay heard the sound of her MG's engine starting, familiar enough to be recognizable even inside the Transit. Then it was drowned as the van's engine revved up, and she was driven off. She had to hold on to the bench to keep her balance as the van lurched. At first, she tried to memorize turnings but realized very quickly that it was impossible; the darkness was disorientating. With her one free hand, she checked through the contents of her pockets to see if she had anything that might conceivably be useful. A handkerchief, some money (she guessed at £30.57), a packet of cigarettes, and her Zippo. Not exactly the Count of Monte Cristo escape kit, she thought bitterly. Why did reality never provide the fillips of fiction? Where was her Swiss army knife and her portable office with the scissors, stapler, adhesive tape, and flexible metal tape measure? In her handbag, she remembered, on the floor of the MG. Oh well, if she'd tried to bring it, they would have taken it from her, she decided.

The journey lasted for over an hour and a half. Debs

would be wondering why she hadn't appeared, thought Lindsay worriedly. And Cordelia would soon start getting cross that she wasn't home when she said she'd be. They'd probably each assume she was with the other and feel betrayed rather than anxious; no hope of either of them giving the alarm. She was beginning to wonder exactly where she was being taken. If it was central London, they should have been there by now, given the traffic at that time of night. But there were none of the stops and starts of city traffic, just the uninterrupted run of a motorway or major road. If it wasn't London, it must be the other direction. Bristol? Bath? Then it dawned. Cheltenham. General Communications Headquarters. It made a kind of sense.

The van was behaving more erratically now, turning and slowing down at frequent intervals. At 8:12 p.m., according to the luminous dial on Lindsay's watch, it stopped, and the engine was turned off. She could hear indeterminate, muffled sounds outside, then the doors opened. Her eyes adjusted to the surge of light and she saw they were in an underground car park. The MG was parked opposite them, the red Fiesta next to it. Stone climbed into the van and unlocked the handcuff linking Lindsay to the van. He snapped it round his left wrist and led her out into the car park.

The four of them moved in ill-assorted convoy to a bank of lifts. Stone took a credit-card-sized piece of black plastic from his pocket and inserted it in a slot, which swallowed it. Above the slot was a grey rubber pad. He pressed his right thumb to the pad, then punched a number into a console. The slot spat the black plastic oblong out, and the lift doors opened for them. Curly Perm hit the button marked 5, and they shot upwards silently. They emerged in an empty corridor, brightly lit with fluorescent tubes. Lindsay could see half a dozen closed doors. Stone opened one marked K57 and ushered Lindsay in. The other two remained outside.

The room was almost exactly what Lindsay expected. The

walls were painted white. The floor was covered with grey vinyl tiles, pitted with cigarette burns. A couple of bare fluorescent strips illuminated a large metal table in the middle of the room. The table held a telephone and a couple of adjustable study lamps clamped to it. Behind the table stood three comfortable-looking office chairs. Facing it, a metal-framed chair with a vinyl-padded seat and back was fixed to the floor. "My God, what a cliché this room is," said Lindsay.

"What makes you think you deserve anything else?" Stone asked mildly. "Sit in the chair facing the table," he instructed. There seemed no point in argument, so she did as she was told. He unlocked the cuffs again, and this time fastened her to the solid-looking arm of the chair.

A couple of hours had passed since she had been really frightened, and she was beginning to feel a little confidence seeping back into her bones. "Look," she said. "Who are you, Stone? What's going on? What am I here for?"

He smiled and shook his head. "Too late for those questions, Lindsay. Those are the first things an innocent person would have asked back in that alley in Fordham. You knew too much. So why ask questions now when you know the answers already?"

"Jesus Christ," she muttered. "You people have got minds so devious you think everyone's part of some plot. When you hemmed me in that alleyway, I was too bloody stunned to come up with the questions that would have made you happy. Why have I been brought here? What's going to happen to me?"

"That rather depends on you," he replied grimly. "Don't go away, now," he added as he left the room.

She was left alone for nearly half an hour, by which time, all her determined efforts to be brave had gone up in the smoke of her third cigarette. She was scared, and she had to acknowledge the fact, although her fear was tempered with relief that it was Rigano's masters rather than Simon Crabtree's who were holding her. She wouldn't give much for her chances if it had been the other way round.

Lindsay had just lit her fourth cigarette when the door opened. She forced herself not to look round. Stone walked in front of her and sat down at one corner of the desk, facing her. He was followed by a woman, all shoulders and sharp haircut, who stood behind the desk scrutinizing Lindsay before she, too, sat down. The woman was severely elegant, in looks as well as dress. Her beautifully groomed pepper-and-salt hair was cut close at the sides, then swept upwards in an extravagant swirl of waves. Extra strong hold mousse, thought Lindsay inconsequentially; if I saw her in a bar, I'd fancy her until I thought about running my fingers through that. The woman had almost transparently pale skin, her eyes glittered greenish blue in her fine-boned face. She looked about forty. She wore a fashionably cut trouser suit in natural linen over a chocolate brown silk shirt with mother-of-pearl buttons. As she studied Lindsay, she took out a packet of Gitanes and lit one.

The pungent blue smoke played its usual trick on Lindsay, flashing into her mind's eye a night in a café in southern France with Cordelia—playing pinball, smoking, and drinking coffee, and listening to Elton John on the jukebox. The contrast was enough to bring back her fear so strongly she could almost taste it.

Perhaps the woman sensed the change in Lindsay, for she spoke then. "Mr. Stone tells me you are a problem," she said. "If that's the case, we have to find a solution." Her voice had a cool edge, with traces of a northern accent. Lindsay suspected that anger or disappointment would make it gratingly plaintive.

"As far as I'm concerned, the problems are all on your side. I've been abducted at gunpoint, threatened with a knife, the victim of an act of criminal damage, and nobody has bothered to tell me by whom or why. Don't you think it's a little unreasonable to expect me to bend over backwards to solve anything you might be considering a problem?" Lindsay demanded through clenched teeth, trying to hide her fear behind a show of righteous aggression.

The woman's eyebrows rose. "Come, come, Miss Gordon. Let's not play games. You know perfectly well who we are and why you're here."

"I know he's MI6 division, or at least I've been assuming he is. But I don't know why the hell I've been brought here like a criminal, or who you are. And until I do, all you get from me is my name."

The woman crushed out her half-smoked cigarette and smiled humourlessly at Lindsay. "Your bravado does you credit. If it helps matters any, my name is Barber. Harriet Barber. The reason you've been brought here, in your words, like a criminal, is that, according to the laws of the land, that's just what you are.

"You are, or have been in unauthorized possession of classified information. That on its own would be enough to ensure a lengthy prison sentence, believe me, particularly given your contacts on the left. You were apprehended while in the process of jeopardizing an operation of Her Majesty's security forces, another matter on which the courts take an understandably strong line. Superintendent Rigano really should have arrested you as soon as you tossed that tape on his desk."

Thanks a million, Jack, Lindsay thought bitterly. But she recognized that she had begun marginally to relax. This authoritarian routine was one she felt better able to handle. "So am I under arrest now?" she asked.

Again came the cold smile. "Oh no," said Harriet Barber. "If you'd been arrested, there would have had to be a record of it, wouldn't there?"

The fear was back. But the moment's respite had given

Lindsay fresh strength. "So if I'm not under arrest, I must be free to go, surely?" she demanded.

"In due course," said Stone.

"Don't be too optimistic, Mr. Stone," said Barber. "That depends on how sensible Miss Gordon is. People who can't behave sensibly often suffer unfortunate accidents due to their carelessness. And someone who drives an elderly sports car like Miss Gordon's clearly has moments when impulse overcomes good sense. Let's hope we don't have too many moments like that tonight."

There was a silence. Lindsay's nerve was the first to go, and she said, struggling to sound nonchalant, "Let's take the posturing as read and come to the deal. What's the score?"

"There's that unfortunate bravado again," sighed Barber. "We are not offering any deal, Miss Gordon. That's not the way we do things here. You will sign the Official Secrets Act and will be bound by its provisions. You will also sign a transcript of your conversation with Superintendent Rigano this evening, as an insurance policy. You will hand over any copies of that tape still in your possession. And then you will leave here. You will not refer to the events of this evening or to your theories about the murder of Rupert Crabtree to anyone. On pain of prosecution. Or worse."

"And if I don't?"

"The answer to that question is not one that will appeal, believe me. What have you to lose by co-operating with what are, after all, your own country's national interests?"

Lindsay shook her head. "If we started to debate where the national interest really lies, we'd be here a long time, Ms. Barber. I've got a more immediate concern than that. I understand that you're not going to let Simon Crabtree be charged with the murder of his father?"

"Superintendent Rigano's indiscretions were quite accurate."

"So that means he stays free until you're ready?"

The woman nodded. "You have a good grasp of the realities Miss Gordon."

"Then what?"

"Then he will be dealt with, believe me. By one side or the other."

"But not immediately?"

"That seems unlikely. He has—certain uses, shall we say?"

Lindsay lit another cigarette. "That's my problem, you see, Ms. Barber. Simon Crabtree is a murderer, and I want him out of circulation."

"I'm surprised that the Protestant ethic is still so firmly rooted in you, given how the rest of your lifestyle has rejected it. I didn't expect a radical lesbian feminist to be so adamant for justice," Barber replied sarcastically.

"It's not some abstract notion of justice that bothers me," Lindsay retorted. "It's life and death. The life and death of someone I care about. You see, no one's told Simon Crabtree that he's immune from prosecution. And he thinks that Deborah Patterson has information that will tie him to his father's murder and put him away. For as long as he's on the streets, Deborah Patterson is at risk, and I can't go along with any deal that means there's a chance that she's going to die. So I'm sorry, it's no deal. I've got to tell my story. I've got to put a stop to Simon Crabtree."

"That's a very short-sighted view," Barber responded quietly. "If you don't accept the deal, Deborah will be in exactly the same position of risk that you have outlined."

Lindsay shook her head. "No. Even if I can't get the paper to use the story, I can get her out of the firing line. I can take her away somewhere he'll never find us."

Harriet Barber laughed softly. "I don't think you quite understand, Miss Gordon. If you don't accept our offer, you'll be in no position to take Deborah anywhere. Because you won't be going anywhere. Accidents, Miss Gordon, can happen to anyone."

17

The phone was ringing when Cordelia let herself in, but before she could reach the nearest extension, the answering machine picked up the call. No hurry, she thought, climbing the stairs. She took off her sheepskin, went into their bedroom, and swapped her boots for a pair of slippers. She carried her briefcase through to her study, then headed for the kitchen. She put on some coffee to brew and, with a degree of anticipation, went to read the note from Lindsay she'd spotted on her way past the memo board. She wished she'd been able to dash down to Brownlow to be with Lindsay when she'd needed her and was gratified when she found that her presumed errant lover was due home within the half hour. Only then did she play back the messages stored on the machine.

All were for Lindsay, and all were from Duncan, increasingly angry as one succeeded another. There were four, the earliest timed at noon, the latest the one she'd nearly picked up when she came in. It was all to do with some urgent query from the office lawyer about her copy, and Duncan was clearly furious at Lindsay's failure to keep in touch. Cordelia sighed. It was really none of her business, but she toyed with the idea of calling Duncan and making soothing noises while explaining that Lindsay was due back at any minute. She got as far as dialing the number of the newsdesk but thought better of it at the last minute and replaced the receiver. Lindsay wouldn't thank her if she had the effect of irritating Duncan still further, which, knowing him, was entirely possible.

Cordelia poured herself a mug of coffee, picked up the morning paper, and ambled through to the living room. She sat down to read the paper but decided she needed some soothing music and went over to the record and tape collection to select her current favorite, a tape Lindsay had compiled of Renata Tebaldi singing Mozart and Puccini arias. She slotted the tape into the stereo, noting with annoyance that the power was still switched on and that there was an unidentified tape in the other deck. It aroused her curiosity, so she rewound the tape and played it back. The series of hisses and whines puzzled her, but she shrugged and put it down to some bizarre exercise of Lindsay's. She stopped the tape and went back to her coffee and paper to the strains of "Un Bel Di Vedremo."

She was immersed in the book reviews when the phone rang again. She picked it up, checking her watch, surprised to see it was already ten past eight. "Cordelia Brown here," she said.

"Thank Christ somebody answers this phone occasionally!" It was Duncan, sufficiently self-confident not to bother announcing his identity. "Where the hell is she, Cordelia? I've been trying to get hold of her all bloody day. She's got her bloody radio pager switched off, too, the silly bitch. I mean, I told her she could have the day off, but she knows better than to do a body-swerve when she's got a story on the go. Where is she, then?"

"I really don't know, Duncan," Cordelia replied. "But I'm expecting her back any minute. She left a note saying she'd be back by eight, and she's usually very good about punctuality. I'll get her to call as soon as she gets in, okay?"

"No, it's not okay," he retorted with ill-grace. "But it'll have to do. I'll have her on the dog watch for a month for this. Makes me look a bloody idiot, you know?"

"I'm sorry Duncan. You know it's not like her to let you down."

"She's got some bloody bee in her bonnet about this peace camp. It was the same over that bloody murder in Derbyshire but at least she was freelance then. She owes me some loyalty for giving her a job. I'll get no proper work out of her till this is cleared up," he complained.

"You don't have to tell me, Duncan," Cordelia sympathized. "I'll get her to call you, okay?"

Cordelia sat for a moment, the first stirrings of worry beginning. Lindsay was pathologically punctual. If her note said "home by eight," then home by eight she'd be, or else she'd have phoned a message through. She always managed it; in the past, she'd bribed passing motorists or British Rail porters to make the phone calls on her behalf. Presumably, Lindsay was visiting Deborah, since she'd been so worried about her condition. And there was no point in fretting about that. She was only twenty-five minutes late, after all.

On an impulse, Cordelia went through to Lindsay's desk and checked her card-index file to see if there was any contact number for the peace camp. The only number that seemed to suit her purpose was that of the pub the women used regularly. She keyed in the nine digits and when a man answered, she asked if Jane was in. She was told to hang on and, after a few minutes, a cautious woman's voice said, "Hello? Who is this?"

"Is that Jane?" asked Cordelia. "This is Cordelia."

"No, it's not Jane. She's not here. Do you need to get a message to her?"

"Yes, I do. It's really urgent. Would you ask her to call Lindsay Gordon's home number as soon as possible, please?"

"No problem. Lindsay Gordon's home number," the voice said. "A couple of the women are going back in five minutes, so they can tell Jane then. She'll get your message in about quarter of an hour."

Fifteen minutes stretched into twenty for Cordelia. She poured herself a glass of wine, though what she craved was a large Scotch. But she wasn't taking the chance of being over the limit if she had to drive anywhere to rescue Lindsay from some mess or other. After twenty-five minutes, she raked around the house till she found a packet with a couple of Lindsay's cigarettes left in it and lit one.

The phone had barely rung when Cordelia snatched it up, praying for Lindsay's familiar voice. She was unreasonably disappointed to find Jane on the other end of the line.

"Hi, Cordelia. I got this urgent message to phone Lindsay. Is she there?"

"No," Cordelia sighed. "The message was from me. I'm trying to track her down. She seems to have dropped out of sight, and, given the events of the last few days, I'm a bit worried. I don't suppose you know where she's gone to?"

"I'm sorry, love. I was hoping this message was from her, to be honest. She was supposed to come to the hospital to see Deborah tonight, but she hasn't shown up. I took Cara in for five minutes to see her mum, and I deliberately left it till towards the end of visiting time to give Lindsay a chance to spend a bit of time with Deborah if she was up to it, but the policeman on duty said Lindsay hadn't been at all. I was pretty amazed because the last thing she said this morning was that she'd see me there tonight," Jane said.

"So, when was the last time you saw Lindsay?" Cordelia asked.

"This morning. Not long after nine. She'd been in to see Deborah, and I went along for moral support. She came out from seeing Deborah and asked if I could make my own way back to the camp because she'd got to go to Oxford urgently. Look, Cordelia, I wouldn't worry about her. She's probably been held up on something to do with work," Jane reassured her.

"No," Cordelia replied. "Her office is going nutso because she hasn't been in touch with them either. It's odd—she's been back here and left a note since then. God knows where she's gone now. She didn't say why she was going to Oxford, did she? Or who she was going to see?"

"She didn't mention any names, but she did say it was something to do with a computer," said Jane. "I'm sorry I can't be more help."

"No, you've been great," said Cordelia. "Look, if by any remote chance she turns up, will you tell her to phone the office as soon as possible, on pain of death? And me too?"

"Of course I will," said Jane. "I hope you get hold of her soon. She'll probably be chasing some story that's the most important thing in the world to her right now. I'm sure she's okay, Cordelia."

"Yeah, thanks. See you." Cordelia put the phone down. Oxford and computers. That could only mean Annie Norton. She trailed back to Lindsay's desk to try and find a number for Annie. There was nothing in the card-index, and Lindsay's address book listed Annie without a phone number. Cordelia tried directory enquiries, but wasn't surprised, given the way her luck was running, to find that Annie was ex-directory. A trawl through Lindsay's address book produced three other mutual friends who might be able to supply a number for Annie. Predictably, it took her three attempts to get what she wanted.

"Annie? I'm sorry to interrupt you. It's Cordelia Brown here," she apologised. "I was wondering if by any chance you know where Lindsay is? Did she come to see you this morning? The thing is, she's disappeared, and her office are desperate to contact her."

"I'm sorry, Cordelia, I really have no idea where she might be. Yes, she was here, but she left my office about half past ten, I guess. She gave me no indication of where she was heading then." Annie sounded reluctant to continue the conversation.

"I'm sorry if this is an awkward time . . ." Cordelia trailed off.

"I have some people for dinner, that's all," said Annie.

"I'm just really worried about her, Annie. She never goes walkabout like this. Not when she's got work on. She's far too conscientious. Do you mind me asking, what was it she wanted to know about?"

Annie relented, touched by the concern in Cordelia's voice. "She had left a computer tape with me for analysis, and she came round to collect the results. She did say that she intended to get back to London tonight. This attack on Deborah has taken a lot out of her. I think it frightened her badly."

"I know that," Cordelia replied, "but what was this tape all about? What kind of tape was it?"

"It was an ordinary cassette tape." That made sense, thought Cordelia, remembering the tape in the stereo. "But I think you'd better ask Lindsay what it was about. I'm not in a position to discuss it, Cordelia. I'm sorry, I'm not being obstructive, just cautious. I think there are too many people involved already."

"What do you mean, Annie? You can't leave it at that!"

"I'm sorry. I shouldn't have said as much as I have. Lindsay's mixed up in something that could cause a lot of hassle. I told her she should be talking to the police about it, not me. Maybe she took my advice."

"Jesus, Annie, what the hell's going on? Are you saying she's in danger?"

"Don't worry, Cordelia. I don't imagine for one minute that she's in any danger. She'll be in touch. She could be trying to phone now, for all we know. Take it easy and don't worry. Lindsay's a born survivor. Look, I'd better go now. Tell her to give me a call in the morning, okay?" Annie's tone was final.

"Okay," said Cordelia coldly. "Goodbye." Her anger at Annie's nonchalance had the salutory effect of making her do something to fight her own growing anxiety. She collected the mystery tape, pulled on her boots and sheepskin and ran downstairs. She climbed into the BMW and joined the night traffic. When she reached the motorway, she put her foot down and blasted down the fast lane. "Please God," she said aloud as she drove. "Please let her be all right." But the appalling fantasy of Lindsay's death would not be kept at bay by words. Cordelia was near to tears when she pulled up in the car park of Fordham police station just before ten o'clock. She marched inside, determined to find out what had happened to Lindsay.

She marched up to the duty officer. "I need to see Superintendent Rigano," she said. "It's a matter of great urgency."

The officer looked sceptical. "I don't know if he's still here, miss," he stalled. "Perhaps if you could tell me what it's all about we'll see if we can sort it out."

"Why don't you check and see if he is here? You can tell him that I need to speak to him about the Deborah Patterson attack," she responded crisply.

He compressed his lips in irritation and vanished behind a frosted-glass partition. Five minutes later he reappeared to say grudgingly, "If you follow me, I'll take you to the Super."

She found Rigano sitting alone at his desk going through a

stack of files. The lines on his face seemed to be etched more deeply, and there were dark shadows under his eyes. "So what is it now, Miss Brown? Can't Miss Gordon run her own errands? Or is she just keeping out of my way?"

"I was hoping you might be able to tell me where she is," Cordelia enunciated carefully. "She appears to have vanished, and I rather thought that was police business."

"Vanished? If she's vanished, she's done it very recently. She was here till about six o'clock. And that's only four hours ago."

Suddenly, Cordelia felt foolish. "She was due home at eight o'clock. She hadn't phoned by nine. I know that probably sounds nothing to you, but Lindsay's got a real fetish about punctuality. She never fails to let me know if she's not going to make it at a time she's prearranged. Especially when we've not seen each other for a day or two." Don't dismiss me as a hysterical female, she pleaded mentally.

"You don't think that you might be overreacting?"

"No. I believe she had some information concerning Rupert Crabtree's death and the attack on Deborah that might have put her in danger. I'm scared, Superintendent. I've got a right to be."

A spasm of emotion crossed his face. But his voice was cool. "Do you know what that information was?"

"Not in detail. But something to do with a computer tape, I believe."

He nodded. "Okay. I think we may be a little premature here, but let's make a few enquiries anyway."

She expected him to dismiss her or summon a subordinate, but he picked up his phone and dialed an outside number. "Mrs. Crabtree?" He said. "Superintendent Rigano here. I'm sorry to trouble you. Is Simon there by any chance? . . . In London? When did he go, do you know? . . . Yesterday? I see. And you expect him back Saturday. Yes, a computer exhibition. I see. Do you know the number of his stand? You don't? Never mind. No, it's not urgent. Has anyone else been trying to contact him? . . . No? Fine, thanks very much. Sorry to have disturbed you. Good night."

He clicked a pen against his teeth. Then he dialed an internal number. "Davis? Get in here, lad," he demanded. A moment later the door opened, and a plain clothes officer in shirtsleeves entered. "Where's Stone?" Rigano asked him abruptly.

"I don't know, sir. He rushed off about six, just before you went out. He's not been back since."

"What do you mean, he rushed off?"

"He came out of his room like a bat out of hell, sir, and ran out to the car park. He took off in that souped-up Fiesta of his."

"Jesus," Rigano swore softly. "I don't believe this. Is his room locked, Davis?"

"I suppose so, sir. He always locks up after himself."

"Okay. Get me the master key from the duty officer. I'm bloody tired of not knowing what's going on in my own station." The young officer looked startled. "Go on, lad, get it." He departed on the double.

"What's going on?" Cordelia asked.

"Sorry, can't say," he replied with an air of such finality that Cordelia couldn't find the energy to challenge him. There was silence till Davis returned. Then the two men left the room together. Five interminable minutes passed before Rigano stormed back into the room. His fury was frightening, his face flushed a dark crimson. Ignoring Cordelia, he grabbed the phone, dialed a number and exploded into the phone, "Rigano here. I'm letting you know that I intend to lodge a formal complaint about Stone. Do you know he's been bugging my office? Not only has he destroyed this force's credibility over this whole investigation, but now he's taking the law into his own hands.

"Listen, I have good reason to believe that someone

could be in a situation of extreme prejudice thanks to this, and I'm not going to lie down and die any longer. You'll be hearing from me formally in the morning." He slammed the receiver down. His hands were trembling with the force of his rage.

The storm had done nothing to ease Cordelia's growing fear. Rigano turned to face her and said carefully, "I'm not happy about it." He sighed. "I wish to hell she'd listened to me. Is she always so damned headstrong?"

"Never mind the bloody character analysis. Where is she? Who is she with? She's in some kind of trouble, isn't she? What's going on?" Cordelia almost shouted.

"Yes, she's in trouble. Deep trouble."

"Well, why are we sitting here? Why aren't we doing something about it?"

"I'm going to get her," he said decisively. "It's going to cause all sorts of bloody aggravation. But I can't leave her to stew. I can't walk away from it. Miss Brown . . . I suggest you go home and try not to worry. She should be home by morning. If not, I'll let you know."

Cordelia could not believe her ears. "Oh no!" she exploded. "You don't get rid of me like that. If you're going to get Lindsay, I'm coming too. I will not be fobbed off with all this static. Either you take me along or I'm going to get on the phone to Lindsay's boss and tell him she's been kidnapped by one of your sidekicks. And everything else I know."

"I can't take you with me," he said.

"I'll follow you."

"I'll have you arrested if you try it."

It seemed like stalemate. "I know about the tape," said Cordelia. "I know where there's a copy of the analysis of it, too," she said, guessing wildly about Annie's involvement. "Take me with you or the lot goes to Lindsay's paper. Even if you arrest me, I get to make a phone call eventually. That's all it'll take. And just think what a story it'll make—famous writer sues police for wrongful imprisonment."

He shook his head. "There's no point in all this blackmail, believe me. I give you my word, I'll get her back to you."

"That's not good enough. Something's going on here. And I can't leave it in anyone else's hands. It's too important."

He finally conceded, too worn out to carry on the fight. "All right. You can follow me. But you won't be allowed to come in."

"Why? Where the hell are you going? Where is she?"

"GCHQ Cheltenham, I think."

"What?"

It was nearly midnight when they reached the main gates of the intelligence complex. As Rigano instructed, Cordelia parked as unobtrusively as possible about quarter of a mile from the brightly lit gate. She watched as Rigano drove up and, after five minutes, was admitted. Tearing irritably at the cellophane on the packet of cigarettes she'd bought at a petrol station *en route,* Cordelia prepared herself for a long vigil. Rigano wasn't exactly her idea of the knight in shining armour. But he was all she'd got.

18

The chirrup of the telephone broke the stalemate in the smoky room. Lindsay was grateful for the note of normality it injected into what had become a completely disorientating experience. Harriet Barber frowned and picked it up. "Barber here," she said coolly. A puzzled look crossed her face and she turned to Stone, handing him the phone. "You'd better deal with this," she ordered.

"Yes? Stone speaking," he said. He listened for a few moments then said, "I'll be right down." He replaced the phone and got to his feet. "I don't understand this, I'm afraid. Are you staying here?" he asked.

"The situation down there is your problem, Stone," she replied icily. "Deal with it. Deal with it quickly."

He left the room.

"I suppose a visit to the loo would be out of the question?" Lindsay asked.

"Not at all."

"You surprise me."

"Provided you don't mind my company."

"What?" Lindsay demanded, outraged.

"We don't take chances with valuable government property," Barber replied easily. "Besides, I thought it might rather appeal to you. Given your . . . inclinations."

Lindsay's face revealed her contempt. "I'd rather eat razor blades," she spat.

"That could be arranged," Barber replied with a faint smile. She pulled a small black notebook from her jacket pocket and made a few notes. Lindsay glowered at her in silence. Long minutes passed before the phone rang again. "Barber here," the woman said again. She listened, then said abruptly, "Out of the question. No . . ." She listened again. "He says what?" Anger clouded her eyes. "Well, in that case, you'd better bring him up. I'm not going to forget this whole episode, Stone." She slammed the phone down and stared at Lindsay. She lit another fragrant French cigarette, then got up and offered one to Lindsay who accepted gratefully. "We have a visitor, Miss Gordon," Barber said, her voice clipped and taut.

"Who?" the journalist asked wearily.

"You'll see soon enough," was the reply before Barber lapsed into silence again.

Lindsay heard the door open and swivelled uncomfortably round in her chair. A surge of relief flooded through her when she saw an obviously disgruntled Stone hustling Rigano into the room. He stopped on the threshold, his face the stony mask that Lindsay had come to recognize as normal. But when he spoke, the concern in his voice was a distinct novelty. "Are you all right?" he asked, moving slowly towards her. Before she could reply, he spotted the handcuffs and rounded angrily on Stone. "For Christ's sake," he thundered. "She's not one of the bloody Great Train Robbers. What's all this crap?"

Stone looked helplessly at Harriet Barber, who responded

immediately. "Mr. Stone is not in charge here, Superintendent. I am, and I have no intention of releasing Miss Gordon until we have the assurances from her that we require. I am under no obligation towards you, and you are here out of courtesy only."

The tension between the two of them crackled in the air. "We'll see about that," Rigano replied grimly before turning back to Lindsay. "Are you all right?"

"Considering that I've been kidnapped at gunpoint, threatened with a knife, transported in conditions that would be illegal if I was a sheep, and interrogated by assholes, I'm okay," she answered bitterly. "You got me into this mess, Jack. You shopped me. Now call off the dogs and get me out of it."

"He doesn't have the authority," Barber said.

"We'll see about that as well," Rigano retorted. "But I didn't shop you, Lindsay. That bastard Stone had my office bugged. I have proof of that, and it's already in the hands of my senior officers. Your people, madam," he said, turning towards Harriet Barber, "had my men's full co-operation, but that wasn't good enough for you, was it?"

"As things have turned out, it looks as if that was a wise precaution. We haven't had your full co-operation, after all."

"You don't get away with bugging a senior police officer's room, whoever you are, madam."

"Your intervention at this juncture is tedious and utterly pointless, Superintendent. You have satisfied yourself as to the well-being of Miss Gordon, and I suggest that you leave now." Barber's tone suggested that she was not accustomed to being thwarted.

But Rigano refused to be intimidated. "Where are we up to, Lindsay? What's the deal?"

"I would advise you not to reply, Miss Gordon. Superintendent, you have no standing here. I strongly advise you to leave."

"You might not think I have any standing here, madam, but I'd have thought you'd welcome any intervention that might sort this business out. Now, will someone please tell me what the offer is?"

"It's simple, Jack," said Lindsay. "I sign away all my rights, promise to forget everything I know, and Simon Crabtree gets to kill Debs."

Exasperated by the situation spiralling out of her control, Harriet Barber got to her feet and said angrily, "Don't be absurd. Superintendent, we expect Miss Gordon to sign the Official Secrets Act and to be bound by it. We expect the return of any secret material still in her possession. She will not refer to the events of this evening or to her theories about what has happened at Brownlow to anyone, on pain of prosecution. Not unreasonable, I submit."

"That's the sanitised version," interrupted Lindsay. "What she misses out is that Crabtree stays free to take whatever steps he wants against Debs and that if I write the story, I'll be silenced. Permanently."

"No one has threatened your life," Barber snapped.

"Not in so many words," Lindsay agreed. "But we both know that's what we've been talking about."

Rigano shook his head. "This is bloody silly. This is not the Soviet Union. People don't get bumped off because they possess inconvenient knowledge. You're both making a melodrama out of a molehill. Do you really think that any newspaper's going to print her story? For a kick-off, no one would believe her. And besides, you can easily shut up any attempts at publication.

"There's no need to threaten Miss Gordon with dire consequences, because she'd never get any editor to take the chance of using this stuff. She's got no evidence, except the computer tape and that means bugger all at the end of the day. All you need from her is her signature on the OSA and the return of the tape. You don't need threats."

"But what about Deborah?" Lindsay interrupted. "Crabtree's going to walk away from all this believing she knows something that can put him away. You can't protect her twenty-four hours a day forever."

Rigano looked puzzled. "I still don't bloody see why you people want Crabtree free. He's a bloody spy as well as a murderer."

Barber frowned. "He has uses at present. He will eventually pay the price for his activities. That I can guarantee."

Rigano jumped on her words. "So surely until that happens, you people can put Deborah Patterson into a safe house."

Lindsay shook her head. "I can't trust them to look after her. Their organization's probably penetrated at every level already without Simon Crabtree hacking his way in. Besides, this lot would do a double-cross tomorrow if it fitted their notion of national security."

"And there's the impasse, Superintendent," Barber said. "She doesn't trust us, and we don't trust her."

Rigano thought for a moment, then said slowly, "There is one way."

Cordelia counted the cigarettes left in the packet. She fiddled with the radio tuner, trying to find a station that would take her mind off the terrifying possibilities that kept running through her head. She looked at her watch, comparing the time with the dashboard clock. He'd been in there for more than an hour. She lit another cigarette that she knew she wouldn't enjoy and stared back at the dark cluster of buildings in deep shadow under the severe overhead lights that led from the road. As she watched, a tall man came out of the main gate and started walking in her direction. She paid little attention until he stopped by her car, expectantly. Wary, she pressed the switch that lowered the window until a two-inch gap appeared. She could see a blond head of hair above a windproof jacket. His eyes glittered as he asked brusquely, "Cordelia Brown?"

"Yes," she answered. An edginess in his manner urged her to caution.

"I have a message for you." He handed her a note.

Cordelia recognized her lover's familiar handwriting, and her stomach contracted with relief. She forced herself to focus on the words and read, "Give the copy of the computer tape to the man who delivers this if you've got it. It's all right. L." She looked up at the man's impassive face. "What's going on? Am I going to see her soon?" she pleaded.

"Looks like it," he said. His voice was without warmth. "The tape?"

She fumbled in her bag and handed him the unlabelled cassette.

"The note as well, please."

"What?" she asked, puzzled.

"I need the note back." Reluctantly, she handed him the scrap of paper.

Cordelia watched him walk towards the gate and gain admission. Unnerved by the brevity of the encounter she lit another cigarette and searched the radio wavebands again.

The digital clock on the dashboard showed 2:01 when the barrier at the gate rose. Cordelia stared so hard into the pool of light by the gate that she feared the sight of Rigano's car followed by Lindsay's MG was a mirage. She sat bolt upright in her seat, then hurriedly got out of the BMW. When the other two cars reached her, they stopped, and their drivers emerged. Lindsay and Cordelia fell into each other's arms. For once, no words came between them as they clung desperately to each other. Rigano cleared his throat noisily and said, "You promised them I'd have the print-out by ten. We'd better get a move on, hadn't we?"

Lindsay disengaged herself from Cordelia's arms and rubbed her brimming eyes. "Okay, okay," she said. "And we have to work out the details of how you keep your end of the bargain. We'd better go back to London in convoy. I hope you're going to give us the benefit of the blue flashing light."

"Is someone going to explain what's been going on?" Cordelia demanded. "I've been sitting here like a lemon half the night going out of my mind with worry."

"Later," said Lindsay.

"No," said Rigano. "No explanations. That's the deal, remember."

Dawn was fading the streetlights into insignificance by the time they reached Highbury. Cordelia drove off to garage her car while Lindsay went indoors to collect the printout. When she returned, Rigano took the papers, saying, "What arrangements do you want me to make?"

Lindsay spoke abruptly. "I need to make some phone calls. If the hospital says it's okay, then I'll act tonight. Unless you hear from me to the contrary, I'll expect your men to be gone by seven. And I don't want anyone following us."

He smiled grimly. "There won't be." Rigano raised his hand in mock salute then turned and walked back to his car as Cordelia arrived at the door. After watching him accelerate out of sight, Lindsay buried her head in Cordelia's shoulder and burst into tears. "I've been so bloody scared," she sobbed. "I thought I'd never see you again."

Cordelia led her indoors and helped her upstairs. Lindsay's muscles felt like jelly, and she was shivering. "Tell me about it later," Cordelia said as she undressed her and got her into bed. "Sleep now and we'll talk later." Lindsay fell back on the pillows and fell asleep almost immediately, sprawled across the bed like a starfish. Cordelia looked down at her exhausted face with pity and decided to sleep in the spare room to avoid disturbing her.

Lindsay woke at noon to the sound of the phone ringing. She grabbed the receiver and was immediately deafened by a raging Duncan. She lay back and let him rant till he finally ran out of steam. "So what've you got to say for yourself?" he yelled for the third time.

"I was in police custody till six this morning, Duncan," she explained. "I wasn't allowed to make a phone call. They had got it into their heads that I was withholding information concerning the Rupert Crabtree murder, and they were giving me the third degree."

The phone crackled into life again as Duncan's rage transferred itself to Fordham police. Again, Lindsay let the storm blow itself out. As he threatened for the fourth time to sue the police and have questions raised in Parliament, Lindsay butted in. "Look, it's all over now, Duncan. It won't serve any purpose to jump up and down about it. Anyway, I'm on the trail of a cracking good exclusive connected to the murder. But I'm going to have to drop out of sight for a couple of days while I get some info undercover and look up a few dodgy contacts. Is that okay?"

"No, it's not bloody okay. What is this exclusive? You don't decide to fuck off chasing whatever rainbows you fancy just because you've had a lucky run with a few stories. Tell me what you're following up, and I'll let you know if it's worthwhile."

Lindsay could feel a headache starting somewhere behind her eyes. "I don't exactly know where it's going to lead me, Duncan, but I've discovered that there's an MI5 man involved somehow in the fringes of the murder. I want to dig around a bit and see if I can find out what the intelligence angle is, see what it's all about. I think it could be a belter, Duncan. I've got that feeling about it. One of the coppers has hinted to me that there could be a security angle. But I'll have to keep a low profile. I might be out of touch for a day or two." She kept her fingers crossed that the gamble would pay off. There was a pause.

"Till Monday, then," he said grudgingly. "I want a progress report by morning conference. This is your last chance, though, Lindsay. Piss me about like yesterday again and no excuses will do." The phone crashing down at the other end nearly deafened Lindsay, but she didn't mind. She had got her own way, and Duncan was only indulging in office bravado in order to terrorize her colleagues.

Sighing, she got out of bed and quickly pulled on a pair of jeans and a thick sweater. She pushed her head round the spare room door to see Cordelia apparently sound asleep. It was good to be home again. The events of the last twenty-four hours had convinced her that in spite of her frequent absorption in her own concerns, Cordelia was still totally committed to her. Grabbing a pocketful of change on her way out, Lindsay headed across Highbury Fields. She was going to have to be careful. It was at times like this she could use Cordelia's help, but it was so risky to involve anyone else unnecessarily. Lindsay couldn't justify to herself the act of confiding in Cordelia for her own selfish reasons. She put these thoughts to the back of her mind as she reached the phone box. She wanted to be sure these calls weren't going to end up on one of Harriet Barber's phone taps. She called Fordham General Hospital where, under the guise of a close relative, she eventually found a doctor who was prepared to admit that it would now be possible to move Deborah without untoward risk, though he personally would accept no responsibility for this.

There followed a series of phone calls including one to her parents in Argyllshire. She made the necessary arrangements with the minimum of fuss, then headed back home.

She put some coffee on, then stripped off, and dived under the shower. She spent a long time luxuriating in the hot water, putting off the moment when she would have to waken Cordelia and tell her she was about to go missing without a trace again. It wasn't something she relished, particularly since the business of Deborah still lay unresolved between them.

She emerged from the shower and wrapped the towel around herself. In the kitchen, Cordelia was staring moodily into a mug of coffee. Lindsay squeezed past and poured out her own. She reached across the table for a discarded packet of cigarettes and nervously lit up.

Cordelia picked up the morning paper and began to read the front page. Lindsay cleared her throat and said awkwardly, "Thanks for last night. If it hadn't been for you, I don't know what would have happened."

Cordelia shrugged. "Least I could do. I do worry about you, you know. Ready to tell me about it yet?"

"I'd rather wait till it's all sorted, if that's okay. I've got to go away again for a couple of days." Cordelia said nothing and turned the page of the paper. "We're taking Debs somewhere she'll be safe. Once that's done, I'll be able to tell you the whole story. It's not that I don't trust you—but after last night, knowing how heavy these people can get, I just don't want to expose you to any risks. I don't enjoy being secretive."

"You could have fooled me," Cordelia said with a wry smile. "Okay, Lindsay, you play it your way. When will you be back?"

"I'm not sure. I'll call you when I know."

Lindsay swallowed the remains of her coffee and went back to the bedroom. She dressed quickly; then she threw knickers, socks, shirts, and jeans into a holdall, grimacing as she noticed how few clean clothes were left in her wardrobe. Everything else she needed was in the car or Deborah's van already. She finished packing and turned to find Cordelia standing inside the room, leaning on the door jamb.

"You are coming back?"

Lindsay dropped her bag and hauled Cordelia into her arms. "Of course I'm coming back."

19

Closing the front door behind her, Lindsay felt weariness creep over her at the thought of the day ahead. She got into the MG, noticing how badly she'd parked only seven hours before. The memory of her ordeal threatened to overwhelm her, so she quickly started the car and shot off. Driving, as usual, restored some of her equanimity, and she was fairly calm by the time she reached Brownlow. She went straight to the Red Cross bender and found Jane lying on a pallet reading a novel. Lindsay marvelled, once again, at the ability of the peace women to indulge in perfectly normal activities in such an outlandish situation. Guiltily breaking in to Jane's much-needed relaxation, Lindsay sketched out what she needed and why. Her sense of urgency transmitted itself to Jane, who agreed to the plan.

Lindsay waited until dusk, then borrowed a 2CV from one of the peace women. Going first to the hospital, she made a brief reconnaissance before heading back to the camp. She linked up with Jane as arranged and hastily they loaded the van with their own bags. Then Lindsay made up the double berth and got Cara ready for bed.

At twenty past seven, Lindsay got into the MG and shot off down the winding lane away from the camp, heading in the opposite direction from the hospital. A quarter of a mile down the road she spotted a set of headlamps in her rear-view mirror. Once she hit the outskirts of the town, she figured, her pursuer, this time in a green Ford Escort, would have to close up or risk losing her. Her calculations proved right. Thanks to her earlier homework, she shook off the pursuit by doubling back down an alley and taking a short cut up a one-way in the wrong direction. Then, driving in a leisurely fashion to a small industrial estate near the motorway, she tucked the MG into a car park behind one of the factory units. Jane was waiting for her in the van. Together they made straight for Fordham General. Lindsay directed Jane into a small loading area at the back of the main hospital building.

Lindsay crouched down beside Cara, who was lying in bed, drifting in and out of sleep. "I want you to promise me you'll stay here very quiet till we get back. We won't be long. We're going to fetch your mummy, but she'll still be very poorly, so you've got to be very gentle and quiet with her. Okay?" Cara nodded. "I promise we won't be long. Try to go back to sleep." She stroked Cara's hair, then joined Jane outside.

They had no difficulty in reaching Deborah's side ward without arousing untoward interest since it was still during visiting hours. Lindsay quickly scouted round to make sure the area was not under surveillance before the pair of them ducked into Deborah's room. In the thirty-six hours since Lindsay had last seen her, Deborah had made a noticeable improvement. She was propped up on her pillows watching television, the deathly white pallor had left her skin, and she looked like a woman in recovery mode. Even the drips had been taken out. When they entered, she grinned delightedly. "At last," she said. "I thought you'd all forgotten me."

"Far from it," said Lindsay, going to her and kissing her warmly. "Listen, there's no time to explain everything now. But we've got to get you out of here. The doctors say you can be moved safely, and Jane's promised to take care of you."

Jane nodded, picking up the chart on the end of the bed. "It looks as if your condition is quite stable now," she remarked. "Don't worry, Deborah, you'll be okay with me."

"I don't doubt it, Jane. But what's all this about, Lin? Why can't I stay here? Surely I must be safe enough or the police wouldn't have left me unguarded?"

Lindsay sighed. "I know it looks like I'm being really high-handed about this, but it's because I'm scared for you. You were attacked because Rupert Crabtree's murderer thinks you know something that can compromise him. I'll explain all the details later, I promise, but take it from me that the police won't arrest the person who attacked you. He doesn't know that, though. So you've got to get out of the firing line or he'll have another go.

"I've managed to arrange somewhere for you and Cara to stay for a while till the heat dies down, somewhere no one will find you. I don't trust the police to take care of you, so we're doing it all off our own bat, without their help. Will you trust me?"

"I don't seem to have a lot of choice, do I?" Deborah replied. "But I don't know how you're going to get me out of here. I tried getting out of bed this afternoon. It turned out to be a seriously bad idea."

It was a problem that hadn't occurred to Lindsay. But Jane had already found a solution. "A wheelchair, Lindsay," she said, smiling at the look of dismay on the other's face. "We passed a couple outside the main ward, in an alcove. Can you fetch one while I get Deborah ready?"

Lindsay strolled down the corridor, trying to look nonchalant till she reached the wheelchairs Jane had spotted. With all the subtlety of Inspector Clousseau, she wrestled one out of the alcove, struggled to release the brake, then shot off back to the side ward. Luckily no one saw her, for she would have aroused suspicion in the most naïve student nurse. Between them, Lindsay and Jane got Deborah into the wheelchair and wrapped a couple of hospital blankets round her. After checking that the coast was clear, they left the room. Jane started to push the wheelchair back the way they'd come, but Lindsay hissed, "No, this way," leading them in the opposite direction. During her earlier visit, she had reconnoitered an alternative route that was quicker and less public. Back at the van, it was a matter of moments for Lindsay and Jane to lift Deborah in. Jane settled her into the double berth beside an overjoyed Cara.

Even so short a move had clearly taken its toll on Debs, who looked more tired and pinched than she had done a few moments ago. Jane carefully arranged the pillows under her to give her maximum support, but Deborah could not stifle a low moan as she tried to find a comfortable position for her head. Cara looked scared, but Jane soothed her and persuaded her to lie down quietly at the far side of the bed. Leaving the wheelchair where it stood Lindsay climbed into the driver's seat.

With perfect timing, they left the hospital grounds in the middle of the stream of visitor's cars departing from the scene of duty done. Lindsay stayed in the flow of traffic for half a mile or so, then turned off to make a circuitous tour of the back streets of Fordham town centre, keeping a constant check on her mirrors. She trusted Rigano to keep his word, but she felt no confidence that Harriet Barber would do the same. After ten minutes of ducking and diving, Lindsay felt satisfied that no one was on their trail and headed back to the MG. She drew up beside the car and turned round to confer.

"We've got a long drive ahead. I anticipate about twelve hours, given the van. We need to take both vehicles, so I can leave you the MG. Where you're going you'll need wheels, and I think I need to borrow the van for a while. I suggest that we swap at the half-way stage, Jane, around Carlisle?"

"Okay, but we'll have to stop at every service area, so I can check on Deborah's condition," Jane replied.

"Just where are we going, Lin?" Deborah asked in a tired voice.

"An old school friend of mine has a cottage about ten miles from Invercross, where I grew up. She's a teacher, and she's away in Australia at the moment, on a six-month exchange scheme, so I fixed up for you to use the cottage. It's lovely there, ten minutes from the sea. Electricity, bottled gas for cooking, telly, peat fires—all you could ask for. And no one will come looking for you there. Cara can even go to the village school if she wants. It's a small community, but they'll keep their mouths shut about you being there if my mother explains that you're convalescing after an attack, and you're scared the man who attacked you is still looking for you."

"My God," said Deborah faintly.

"I'm sorry," said Lindsay. "I had to act quickly. I couldn't just sit back. There was no one else I could trust to make sure you were protected."

"And how long do I have to hide in the heather?"

"That depends. Until Simon Crabtree is dealt with. It could be months, I'm afraid."

"I'll stay as long as you need me," Jane chipped in.

"I can't take all of this in. What has Simon Crabtree to do with me?" Deborah demanded, hugging Cara close. "One minute I'm recuperating in the hospital, the next I'm thrust into a remake of *The Three Musketeers* crossed with *The Thirty-nine Steps*."

"I'll explain in the morning when I'm driving you, I

promise," Lindsay replied. "But right now, we should get a move on."

"I'll take the van as far as Carlisle, then," Jane decided.

Lindsay nodded. "That'll be best. And don't push yourself too hard. Any time you need a rest or a coffee, just pull off at the services. I'm used to driving half the night, working shifts like I do, but I don't expect you to do the same."

"Cheeky so-and-so!" muttered Jane. "Have you forgotten the hours junior hospital doctors work? You'll be flaked out long before I will, Lindsay."

"Sorry, I forgot," Lindsay apologized.

The journey seemed endless. Deborah and Cara managed to sleep most of the way, only really waking during the last couple of hours. Lindsay explained the reasons for their flight to Deborah as she drove the last sixty miles down the familiar narrow roads with their spectacular views of the Argyllshire mountains and sea lochs on all sides. Cara was spellbound by the changing scenery and seemed not to be listening to the adult conversation.

Lindsay reached the end of her tale as they arrived in the tiny fishing village of Invercross. A cluster of brightly painted houses and cottages crowded along the harbour. "So here we are," Lindsay concluded. "Right back where I started all those years ago. Only this time, on the run like Bonnie Prince Charlie and Flora Macdonald." She pulled up outside a small, two-storey house on the harbour front. "Wait here a minute. I've got to get the keys."

The woman who opened the door before Lindsay reached it was small and wiry with curly grey hair and eyes that matched Lindsay's. She swept her daughter into her arms, saying, "It's grand to see you. It's been a long time since the New Year. Now, come in and have some breakfast. Bring your friends in. Is Cordelia up with you?"

Lindsay disengaged herself and followed her mother indoors. "No, she's busy. Listen, Mum, I want to get the others settled in at the cottage first, then I'll come back for a meal and a sleep before I get back to London."

"You're not stopping, then?" Her mother's obvious disappointment stabbed Lindsay. "You'll miss your father. He's at the fishing, he'll not be back before the morn's morning."

"I'm sorry, Mum, I'm in the middle of something big. This was a kind of emergency. Have you got Catriona's keys?"

Her mother produced a bunch of keys from her apron pocket. "I got them from Mrs. Campbell last night when you phoned. I went up this morning with a few essentials and lit the fire, so they should be comfortable."

Lindsay kissed her. "You're a wee gem, Mum. I'll be back in a couple of hours."

Her mother shook her head, an affectionate smile on her face. "You never stop, do you, lassie?"

Ten hours later, Lindsay was back on the road south. Jane, Deborah, and Cara were settled comfortably in the cottage, amply supplied with Mrs. Gordon's idea of essentials—bread, butter, milk, eggs, bacon, fish, onions, potatoes, and tea. Mrs. Gordon had promised to take Jane to sign on the following Monday. If she lied about paying rent, they could fiddle enough to live on. So there would be no need for any part of the official world to know Deborah's whereabouts. Jane thought Lindsay's precautions extreme, but she would not be moved.

Lindsay spent the night less comfortably than the three refugees. Her eyes were gritty and sore, her body ached from the jolting of the van's elderly suspension. She finally gave in when even the volume of the stereo couldn't keep her awake and alert. She parked in a lay-by off the motorway where she slept fitfully for five hours before hammering back down to London.

Somewhere around Birmingham, she realized that she'd felt no desire whatsoever to stay in Invercross with Deborah. That realization forced her to examine what she had been steadfastly ignoring during the traumatic events of the last few days. It was time to think about Cordelia and herself. Why had she felt such an overwhelming need to sleep with Deborah? Did she subconsciously want to end her relationship with Cordelia, and was Deborah just a tool she'd used? Until her kidnapping by the security forces, Lindsay had been confused and frightened about her emotions.

But there was no denying the fact that Cordelia had come to her rescue in spite of the problems there had been between them. Driving on, Lindsay gradually came to understand that her relief at seeing Cordelia outside GCHQ had been more than just gratitude. Her own behaviour had been negative in the extreme, and if she wanted to heal the breach between them, she would have to act fast. As that thought flickered across her mind, Lindsay realized there was no "if" about it. She knew she wanted to try again with Cordelia. Full of good resolutions, she parked the van outside the house just before noon and rushed in. The house was empty.

Stiff and exhausted and having lost track of time almost completely, Lindsay ran a sweet-smelling foam bath, put Monteverdi's 1610 Vespers on at high volume, and soaked for half an hour. Then, in sweat pants and dressing gown, she sat down at the word processor. Now that Deborah was safe, she had settled her obligations. There was even less honour among the Harriet Barbers of this world than among thieves and journalists, she had now realized. The promises they had made about leaving her alone had been shattered. They had tried their damndest to follow her. There was only one real insurance left. So she wrote the whole story of Rupert Crabtree's murder and its repercussions, leaving nothing out.

She had barely finished it when she heard the front door slam. Alerted by the music, Cordelia superfluously called, "I'm home." Pink-cheeked from the cold outside, she stopped in the doorway. "Welcome back," she said. Lindsay picked up the sheaf of paper on the desk and proffered it.

"I promised you an explanation," she said. "Here it is. The uncensored version. It's probably quicker if you read it rather than listen to me explaining it."

Cordelia took the papers. "I missed you," she said.

"I know," Lindsay replied. "And I've missed you, constantly. I'm not very good at being on my own. I tend to get overtaken by events, if you see what I mean."

Cordelia gave a sardonic smile. "I've heard it called a lot of things, but that's a new one on me." There was a silence, as they met in a wary and tentative embrace. Cordelia disengaged herself, saying, "Let me read this. Then we'll talk. Okay?"

"Okay. I'll be in the kitchen when you've finished. The idea of cooking dinner in a real kitchen is strangely appealing after the last few days."

It took Cordelia half an hour to work through Lindsay's account of her investigations. When she had finished, she sat staring out of the window. She could barely imagine the stress that Lindsay had been operating under. Now she could understand, even if she could not yet forgive, what she instinctively knew had happened between Lindsay and Deborah. But the most important thing now was to make sure Lindsay's natural inclination to the defence of principle was subdued for the sake of her own safety.

Cordelia found Lindsay putting the finishing touches to an Indian meal. "I had no idea," she said.

Lindsay shrugged. "I wanted so much to tell you," she said. "Not just at the end, but all through. I missed sharing my ideas with you."

"What about Deborah?"

"It's not something you should be worried about, truly."

"So what happens now? I don't mean with you and me, I

mean with Deborah. Do we wait till Simon Crabtree is dealt with and then everything returns to normal?"

Lindsay shook her head. "No. Those bastards didn't keep their word. They tried to follow me—you read that, didn't you? So as far as I'm concerned, I'm not just sitting back till I get the all-clear from Rigano. The best way to make sure they deal with Crabtree is to force the whole thing into the open. Otherwise it could be months, years till one side or the other decides Crabtree has outlived his usefulness. I don't see why we should all live under a shadow till then. Besides, the guy is a murderer. He'll do it again the next time someone gets close to the truth. And next time it could be me. Or someone else I care about."

"So what are you going to do?"

"I'm going to give the whole story to Duncan. And if he won't use it, I'll give it to Dick McAndrew. Either way, it's going to be published."

"You're crazy," Cordelia protested. "They'll come after you instead of Crabtree. They've got your signature on the Official Secrets Act. And the first journo that fronts Crabtree with your story points the finger straight at you. If our lot don't get you, the Soviets will."

"Don't be so melodramatic," Lindsay replied crossly. "I know what I'm doing."

"And did you know what you were doing when you ended up in Harriet Barber's clutches the other night? I'd have thought you'd have learned more sense by now," said Cordelia bitterly.

"Point taken," Lindsay replied. "But there's no use in arguing, is there? We're starting from different premises. I'm operating on a point of principle as well as self-defence. All you care about is making sure nothing happens to me. That's very commendable, and I'd feel the same if our positions were reversed. But I think the fact that people who have committed no crime are hounded into hiding to protect a spy and a killer is too important to ignore simply because revealing it is going to make life difficult for me. I wish I could make you understand."

Cordelia turned away. "Oh, I understand all right. Rigano set you up to do his dirty work, and you fell for it."

Lindsay shook her head. "It's not that simple. But I do feel utterly demoralized and betrayed. And I've got to do something to get rid of these feelings, as well as all the other stuff."

Cordelia put her arms round Lindsay. "I just don't want you to get hurt. When you get wound up about something, you completely disregard your own safety."

"Well, I've learned my lesson. This time, I'm going to make sure my public profile is too high for them to come after me," Lindsay retorted. "Trust me, please."

Cordelia kissed her. "Oh, I trust you. It's the other nutters I worry about."

Lindsay smiled. "Let's eat, eh? And then, maybe an early night?"

In the morning, Lindsay smiled reminiscently about their rapprochement the night before as she gathered all her papers together and prepared to set off for an early briefing with Duncan at the office. Before she left, Cordelia hugged her, saying, "Good luck and take care. I'm really proud of you, you know."

"Yes, I know. I'll see you later."

"I'm afraid I'll be back quite late. I'm sorry, I didn't know you'd be home. I promised William we could work on the script rewrites for the new series tonight," Cordelia apologized.

Lindsay smiled. "No problem. I'll probably be late myself, given the importance of the story. I might even wait for the first edition to drop. I'll see you whenever."

Outside the house, Lindsay hailed a cab and headed for

the office. She had barely stepped into the newsroom when Duncan's deputy told her to go straight to the editor's office. His secretary had obviously been briefed to expect her, for Lindsay was shown straight in, instead of being left to cool her heels indefinitely with a cup of cold coffee.

Three men were waiting for her—Duncan, Bill Armitage, the editor, and Douglas Browne, the *Clarion* group's legal manager. No one said a word of greeting. Lindsay sensed the intention was to intimidate her, and she steeled herself against whatever was to come. "I've brought my copy in," she said, to break the silence. She handed the sheaf of paper to Duncan, who barely glanced at it.

Bill Armitage ran his hands through his thick grey hair in a familiar gesture. "You've wasted your time, Lindsay," he said. "We'll not be using a line of that copy."

"What?" Her surprise was genuine. She had expected cuts and rewrites, but not a blanket of silence.

Duncan replied gruffly, "You heard, kid. We've had more aggravation over you this weekend than over every other dodgy story we've ever done. The bottom line is that we've been made to understand that if we fight on this one it will be the paper's death knell. You're a union hack—you know the paper's financial situation. We can't afford a big legal battle. And I take the view that if we can't protect our staff, we don't put them in the firing line."

Armitage cut across Duncan's self-justification. "We've got responsibilities to the public. And that means we don't make our living out of stirring up needless unrest. To be quite blunt about it, we're not in the business of printing unsubstantiated allegations against the security services. All that does is destroy people's confidence in the agencies that look after our safety."

Lindsay was appalled. "You mean the security people have been on to you already?"

The editor shook his head patronisingly. "Did you really

think the mayhem you've been causing wouldn't bring them down about our ears like a ton of bricks? Jesus Christ, Lindsay, you've been in this game long enough not to be so naïve. You can't possibly have the sort of cast-iron proof we'd need to run this story."

Lindsay looked doubtful. "I think I have, Bill. Most of it can be backed up by other people, and I can get hold of a copy of the computer tape that clinches it all. The cops can't deny what has been going on, either. Superintendent Rigano should be able to back it up."

"Rigano was one of the people who was here yesterday," Browne said heavily. "There will be no help from that quarter. The story must be killed, Lindsay."

"I'm sorry," said Duncan. "I know you worked hard for it."

"Worked hard? I nearly got myself killed for it." Lindsay shook her head disbelievingly. "This story is dynamite," she protested. "We're talking about murder, spying, security breaches, GBH, and kidnapping, all going on with the consent of the people on our side who are supposed to be responsible for law and order. And you're telling me you haven't got the bottle to use it because those bastards are going to make life a little bit awkward for you? Don't you care about what they've done to me, one of your own?"

"It's not that we don't care. But there's nothing we can legitimately do," the editor replied. "Look, Lindsay, forget the whole thing. Take a week off, get it into perspective."

Lindsay stood up. "No," she said. "No way. I can't accept this. I never thought I'd be ashamed of this paper. But I am now. And I can't go on working here feeling like that. I'm sorry, Duncan, but I quit. I resign. As of now, I don't work for you any more." She stopped abruptly, feeling tears beginning to choke her. She snatched up the sheaf of copy from the table where Duncan had laid it, turned, and walked out of the office. No one tried to stop her.

In the ladies' toilet, she was comprehensively sick. She splashed cold water on her face and took several deep breaths before heading for the offices of *Socialism Today*.

Here there were no security men on the door to challenge her, no secretaries to vet her. She walked straight up to the big room on the second floor where the journalists worked. Dick was perched on the corner of his desk, his back to her, a phone jammed to his ear. "Yeah, okay. . ." he said resignedly. "Yeah, okay. Tomorrow it is then. See you." He slammed the phone down. "Fucking Trots. Who needs them?" he muttered, turning round to reach for his mug of coffee. Catching sight of Lindsay, he actually paled. "Christ! What the hell are you doing here?"

"I've got a story for you," she said, opening her bag and taking out another copy of her manuscript.

"Is it to do with the computer print-out?" he demanded.

"Sort of. Among other things. Like murder, kidnapping, GBH, and spying. Interested?"

He shook his head reluctantly. "Sorry, Lindsay. No can do. Listen, I had the heavies round at my place last night about you. It's a no-no, darling. It may be the best story of the decade, but I'm not touching it."

A sneer of contempt flickered at the corner of Lindsay's mouth. "I expected the big boys at the *Clarion* to wet themselves at the thought of prosecution. But I expected you to take that sort of thing in your stride. I thought you were supposed to be the fearless guardian of the public's right to know?"

Dick looked ashamed and sighed deeply. "It wasn't prosecution they threatened me with, Lindsay. These are not people who play by the rules. These are not pussycats. These are people who know how to hurt you where you live. They were talking nasty accidents. And they knew all about Marianne and the kiddy. I'll take risks on my own account, Lindsay, but I'm not having on my conscience anything that might happen to my wife and child. You wouldn't take chances with Cordelia, would you?"

Lindsay shook her head. Exhaustion surged over her in a wave. "I suppose not, Dick. Okay, I'll be seeing you."

It took her more than an hour to walk back to the empty house. She was gripped by a sense of utter desolation and frustration that she sensed would take a long time to dissipate. There had been too many betrayals in the last week. She turned into their street, just as a red Fiesta vanished round the corner at the far end of the mews behind. That unremarkable event was enough on a day like this to make her break into a run. She fumbled with her keys, clumsy in her haste, then ran upstairs. At first glance, everything seemed normal. But when she went into the living room, she realized that every cassette had been removed from the shelves above the stereo. In the study it was the same story. Lindsay crouched down on the floor against the wall, hands over her face, and shivered as the sense of insecurity overwhelmed her.

She had no idea how long she crouched there feeling utterly defenseless. Eventually the shaking stopped, and she got unsteadily to her feet. In the kitchen, she put some coffee on, then noticed there was a message on the answering machine. She lit a cigarette and played the tape back.

The voice sounded scared. "Lindsay. This is Annie Norton. I've been burgled. My car has been broken into, and my office has also been turned over. I suspect this may have something to do with you since all that has been stolen are cassettes. Whoever was responsible has probably got your phone bugged, so for their benefit as well as yours, for the record, they have now got the only data I had relating to that bloody tape you brought me. I wish you'd bloody warned me you didn't have the sense to leave this alone, Lindsay. You'd better stay away from me till this is all over—I need my security clearance so I can work. Look, take care of yourself. This isn't a game. Be careful. Goodbye."

It was the last straw. Lindsay sat down at the table, dropped her head in her hands and wept till her eyes stung and her sinuses ached. Then she sat, staring at the wall, reviewing what had happened, trying to find a way forward for herself. As the afternoon wore on, she smoked steadily and worked her way down the best bottle of Burgundy she could find in the house.

By teatime she knew exactly what she had to do. She set off across the park for the phone box and started setting wheels in motion.

20

Lindsay waited patiently on hold to be connected, praying that the object of her call would still be at his desk. Even on cheap rate, the phone box was eating £1 coins at an alarming rate. While she hung on, she mentally congratulated Jane for forcing her to examine her conscience about doing something positive to support the peace camp all those months before. If it hadn't been for those features she'd sold abroad then, she wouldn't have built up the contracts she needed now. Her musing was cut short by a voice on the end of the phone.

"*Ja?*"

"Gunter Binden?" Lindsay asked.

"*Ja. Wer ist?*"

"It's Lindsay Gordon, Gunter. From London."

Immediately the bass voice on the other end of the phone switched to immaculate English. "Lindsay! How good to hear from you. How goes it with you?"

"A bit hectic. That's what I wanted to talk to you about.

I've got a wonderful story for you. I'm having problems getting anyone over here to print it because of the national security angle, but it's too important a tale to ignore. So I thought of you."

"Is it another story about the peace camp?"

"Indirectly, yes. But it's really to do with spying and murder."

"Sounds good. Do you want to tell me some more?"

Lindsay started to tell the too-familiar story of recent events. Gunter listened carefully, only stopping her to seek clarification when her journalistic idioms became too obscure for him to follow. Lindsay was glad she'd trusted her instincts about approaching him. As well as being the features editor of a large circulation left-wing weekly magazine that actively supported the Green Party, he had spent two years working in London and understood the British political scene as well as having a first-class command of English. When she reached her kidnapping by the security forces, he exploded.

"My God, Lindsay, why isn't your own paper publishing this? It's dynamite."

"That's precisely why they're backing off. They don't want a legal battle right now for business reasons—the publisher wants to float the company on the stock market later this year, and he wants to present a healthy balance sheet and a good reputation. Also, they've got no stomach for a real fight against the Establishment. If I was offering them a largely unsubstantiated tale about a soap-opera star having a gay affair, they'd go for it and to hell with the risks. But this is too much like the real thing. But let me finish the tale. It gets better, I promise."

Gunter held his tongue till Lindsay had finished her recital. Then there was a silence. "What sort of price are you looking for?"

"If I hadn't jacked my job in today, I'd let you have it for free. But I'm going to have to feed myself somehow, and I can't imagine I'm going to find much work in national news-papers. Can you stretch to five thousand Deutschmarks?" Lindsay asked.

"Do you have pictures of this man Crabtree? And of Deborah Patterson?"

"I've got pics of Deborah, and you can get pics of both Simon and Rupert Crabtree through the local paper. I've got a good contact there. And you can do pics of me. What do you say, Gunter?"

"How soon can I see copy?"

"I can fax it to you tonight. Have we got a deal?"

"Four thousand. That's as high as I can go. Don't forget, I've got translation to pay for, too."

Lindsay paused, pretending to think. "Okay," she said. "Four thousand it is. I'll get the copy on the fax tonight, and I'll bring the pix over myself."

"You're coming over?"

Lindsay nodded. "You bet. I want to be well out of the way when the shit hits the fan. And besides, I won't believe it till I actually hold the first copy off the presses in my own hands."

"So how soon can you get here?"

"I can get a night crossing and be with you by tomorrow afternoon. Does that leave you enough time?"

They arranged the rest of the details, then Lindsay hung up gratefully. Returning home, she picked up the bundle of copy she'd wasted her time writing for Duncan and left the house. She made for the tube station, not caring if she was being followed or not. It was already seven o'clock, and the rush hour press of bodies had dissipated. Emerging from Chancery Lane station she walked to the *Clarion* building. Her gamble that word of her departure wouldn't have yet got round paid off: she walked unchallenged into the building and made her way to the busy wire room on the third floor. After a quiet word with the wire room manager, he left her with the fax machine for the price of a few pints. An hour later, she left the building and headed back to Highbury. When she emerged from the tube station, she realized she wasn't able to face the empty house again just yet, so she walked slowly down Upper Street to the King's Head pub. Over a glass of the house red, she turned the situation over in her mind.

The chain reaction she had set in motion would blow Simon Crabtree's cover completely. She wished she could be a fly on the wall when it dropped on Harriet Barber's desk. The only question mark that remained in her mind was which side would get to him first. She suspected the Soviets would be the ones to terminate him; *glasnost* only extended so far. And it would be expedient for MI6 to keep their hands clean for once. But she knew she'd have to keep her head down till she was sure that Simon Crabtree had met the fate he deserved. And that might take a few weeks. A fatal accident following too closely on the heels of her revelations might seem a little too convenient even for the unscrupulous intelligence community.

The only problem that remained was how to find out when Crabtree was removed from circulation. Her first thought was to enlist Jack Rigano's help. He owed her one. As Cordelia had so forcefully reminded her, he had brought her into the frame when forces beyond his control prevented him from doing his job. But he had already stuck his neck out once for her, and the fact that it was he who had been dispatched to put the frighteners on the *Clarion* demonstrated where his allegiance lay in the final analysis.

There was one other person Lindsay could ask. It would avoid the danger of providing an interested party with too much information. And provided the storm that the story was inevitably going to raise didn't make him lose his bottle, he'd also be happy to supply information when there was something in it for him. Lindsay searched through the pages of her notebook till she found the page where she'd scribbled Gavin Hammill's number. The pub phone was mercifully situated in a quiet corner, granting her some privacy.

She was in luck. The Fordham reporter was at home for the evening. After the formalities, Lindsay explained what she wanted. "I'm going to be out of the country for a while," she said. "But I need someone to keep an eye on Simon Crabtree for me. I just want to know what he's up to, and if anything untoward happens to any member of the family. If you hear anything at all, especially if he drops out of sight for a few days, you can get in touch with me via a guy in Cologne called Gunter Binden."

She gave him Gunter's office and home numbers and explained that Gunter's magazine would pay him a generous credit for any material he supplied. "They're very generous payers, Gavin," she added. "And they never forget a good source. If you do the biz for them, they'll put work your way. Oh, and if anybody asks why you're interested, don't mention my name."

"Of course not, Lindsay. Thanks for thinking of me."

"Don't mention it. See you around."

The final phone call she made was to reserve a ticket for herself and the van on the midnight crossing to Zeebrugge. The train or the plane would have been more comfortable, but she wanted to be self-sufficient and mobile once she was out of the country.

She wished she could take Cordelia with her, turn the trip into a break for both of them. But she knew it wouldn't work out like that, even supposing Cordelia was able and willing to get to Dover for the midnight ferry. Lindsay knew that the divisions between them needed time and energy from both sides before they could be healed. A mad dash across Europe followed by all the hassles of getting this story on to the streets was no basis for a major reconciliation. Besides,

Lindsay didn't know how long she would have to stay away, and Cordelia had other commitments.

It was a quarter past eight when she reached home. She would have to leave in three quarters of an hour. The clothes she had thrown into the washing machine earlier would be dry in half an hour, and it would take her only ten minutes to pack. She had half an hour to write an explanation of her absence for Cordelia. The word processor would be quicker, if more impersonal. But getting the words right was the most important thing.

She started by explaining where she was going and why. That was the easy bit. Now came the part where years of working with words were no help at all.

"I'm going to have to keep my head down after this piece is published. The security services will want to bring charges, and I don't think it will be safe for me to come home till after Simon Crabtree is no longer a threat. I'm going to stay abroad for a while, but I don't know yet where I'll be. I'll let you know as soon as I've sorted things out and maybe you can join me for a while. I'm sorry—I really wanted to spend some time with you. I love you. Lindsay."

She scowled at the screen, deeply dissatisfied with what she had written. But there was no time now for more. She got up and stretched while the letter printed out, then left it by the answering machine. The next fifteen minutes were a whirlwind of throwing clothes, books, papers, and maps into a couple of holdalls. She went through to the lounge to pick up some tapes for the journey, forgetting the raid that had left the shelves empty. When she saw the spaces where her music had been, she swore fluently. The shock gave her the extra kick of energy she needed to get out into the night and off to the ferryport.

Three nights later, Lindsay stood in the press hall in Cologne watching the massive presses flickering her image past her eyes at hundreds of copies a minute. Gunter approached, clutching a handful of early copies from the run and an opened bottle of champagne. He thrust a magazine at Lindsay, who stared disbelievingly at the cover. Her own picture was superimposed on a wide-angled shot of the base at Brownlow Common with the peace camp in the foreground. A slow smile spread across her face, and she took a long, choking swig from the offered bottle of champagne. "We did it," she almost crowed. "We beat the bastards."

Epilogue

Excerpts from the *Daily Clarion*, 11 May 198-.

MISSILES TO GO

The Pentagon announced last night that the phased withdrawal of cruise missiles from Brownlow Common will begin in November . . .

DOUBLE TRAGEDY FOR SPY MURDER FAMILY

The man at the centre of a German magazine's revelations about Russian spies at American bases in the UK died in a freak road accident last night.

His death was the second tragedy within two months for his family. His father, solicitor Rupert Crabtree, was brutally murdered eight weeks ago.

Simon Crabtree, who had been officially cleared by British security forces of any involvement in espionage, died instantly when his motorbike skidded on a sharp bend and ploughed into the back of a tractor.

Val McDermid grew up in a Scottish mining community. After reading English at Oxford, she became an award-winning journalist and active trade unionist, ending up as Northern Bureau Chief of a national newspaper and Chair of the Union's Equality Council. She now writes full-time and lives in the north of England with her partner and four cats.

Spinsters Ink was founded in 1978 to produce vital books for diverse women's communities. In 1986 we merged with Aunt Lute Books to become Spinsters/Aunt Lute. In 1990, the Aunt Lute Foundation became an independent nonprofit publishing program. In 1992, Spinsters moved to Minnesota.

Spinsters Ink is committed to publishing novels and nonfiction works by women that deal with significant issues from a feminist perspective: books that not only name crucial issues in women's lives, but more importantly encourage change and growth; books that help make the best in our lives more possible.

McDermid, Val.
Common murder :

Overcoming Relationship Regret

Dick Purnell

with Christina Holder

HARVEST HOUSE PUBLISHERS

EUGENE, OREGON

Cover by Left Coast Design, Portland, Oregon

Cover photo © Ghislain & Marie David de Lossy/The Image Bank/Getty Images

Disclaimer: All of the interviews in this book are true stories but details have been changed to protect the privacy of those who shared their experiences with us.

OVERCOMING RELATIONSHIP REGRET

Copyright © 2005 by Dick Purnell
Published by Harvest House Publishers
Eugene, Oregon 97402
www.harvesthousepublishers.com

Library of Congress Cataloging-in-Publication Data

Purnell, Dick.
   Overcoming relationship regret / Dick Purnell with Christina Holder.
      p. cm.
   Includes bibliographical references.
   ISBN-13: 978-0-7369-1508-3
   ISBN-10: 0-7369-1508-7
   1. Single people—Religious life. 2. Dating (Social customs)—Religious aspects—Christianity.
   I. Holder, Christina. II. Title.
   BV4596.S5P88 2005
   248.8'4—dc22   2005009654

As I was writing this book, hundreds of single adults and married couples from around the world shared with me their struggles and victories in overcoming regret in their relationships. This book can contain only a few of their stories. I have changed their names and some details of their situations to protect their identities, but their stories are real.

To each of them I dedicate this book. Their openness and honesty will enlighten all who desire an enjoyable love relationship.

Dick Purnell

To the single man or woman living with a broken heart right now:

The Lord had me work on this book during the first heartbreak of my life. (What a sense of humor He has!) Sometimes I couldn't pick up the manuscript for a week. But the Lord worked on me, and soon I learned how tenderly He cares for those with broken spirits. I've learned that He wants to use our pain to help us trust Him more, to understand His love more deeply, and to live more fully in relationships with others and in the most important relationship we have in this life—the one we have with Him. I hope this book will be an encouragement to you. God knows your desires, your heart, and your pain. He is ready to use your experience and move you from your past. You can be confident that the Chief Shepherd doesn't leave His flock.

"And the God of all grace, who called you to his eternal glory in Christ, after you have suffered a little while, will himself restore you and make you strong, firm and steadfast. To him be the power for ever and ever. Amen" (1 Peter 5:10-11).

And to the Purnell family. Your love and wisdom have been overflowing gifts to me since we first met in 1998. Thank you for loving me and for giving me the opportunity to be a part of your family and your ministry.

Christina Holder

About the Authors
Dick Purnell

Dick Purnell is an internationally known speaker and author. He is the Executive Director of Single Life Resources, a division of Campus Crusade for Christ.

He has authored 13 books, including *Finding a Lasting Love, Becoming a Friend and Lover, Free to Love Again, Building a Strong Family, Making a Good Marriage Even Better, Discovering God's Unique Purposes for You, Knowing God By His Names,* and *Growing Closer to God.*

A graduate of Wheaton College, Dick holds a master of divinity degree from Trinity International University, as well as a master's in education, specializing in counseling, from Indiana University.

Dick has been featured on many national television shows, including *The Coral Ridge Hour, The 700 Club,* and *The Nashville Hour.* He has been the main guest on many radio programs, such as *FamilyLife Today, Moody Broadcasting,* and *America's Family Counselors.*

Bring Dick Purnell to Your Area

Dick Purnell speaks to audiences throughout the United States, Canada, and in many other countries. For information about the wide variety of topics he presents, contact him at:

Dick Purnell

P.O. Box 1166

Cary, NC 27512 USA

Phone (919) 363-8000

Web site: www.DickPurnell.com

Christina Holder

Christina Holder works as a researcher and reporter for a nationally syndicated newspaper columnist in Washington, D.C. Prior to coming to the nation's capital, she worked as a newspaper reporter for the *Naples Daily News* and *Bonita Banner* in Florida. She is a 2002 graduate of Meredith College in Raleigh, N.C., where she earned a bachelor's degree in English and political studies. Combining her training as a reporter and her experience as a twentysomething single, Holder enjoys following dating trends, analyzing their impact on culture and writing about a topic often overlooked as one of the most important to prioritize today—relationships.

Contents

Introduction

Do you have regrets about your love life? Or your *lack* of a love life?

Each of us has made mistakes we deeply regret. Are you asking yourself one or more of these relationship questions?

- Why are relationships so difficult?
- How can I start a quality relationship and avoid my past mistakes?
- How can I keep a new relationship healthy, growing, and strong?
- Why do I keep repeating the same mistakes with different people?
- How can I begin another relationship when I feel so tired of the dating game?
- How can I avoid the mistakes I see my parents and other couples make?
- Why is getting over a lost love so difficult?
- Why didn't the relationship work when I thought I had found the right person?
- How can I say goodbye to someone I'm dating but who is not the right one?

If you have asked yourself some of these questions, you're not alone. Others have faced—or are facing—similar situations as you. My hope is that you can learn from their experiences as you read this book and come up with the right answers to all your questions.

As for the regrets, these are the ones I hear most often in my ministry with singles. See how many of these you can relate to.

- If only I hadn't given my heart away. It hurts.
- If only we had avoided having sex.
- If only I had seen what was coming. I was blindsided.
- If only I had taken more initiative, showed my love better, listened more, or spent more time…
- If only I had changed my habits, argued less, chosen better, or broken it off sooner.
- If only I hadn't been so fearful, lonely, or emotional …so distant, insensitive, pushy, or serious…

Do some of these sound familiar? The longer you dwell on these and other regrets, the more you will struggle to build a healthy, dynamic love relationship in the future. What do you really want? Do you want to stay where you are, or are you ready to overcome your regrets and move on so that you can develop an enjoyable, quality relationship with a loving partner?

Someone has defined a fool as a person who keeps doing the same thing over and over but expects different results. In contrast, wise people learn from their past mistakes so they can obtain what they really want.

My prayer is that this book will help you to be counted among the wise.

Part 1
Why People Struggle with Relationships

Do you think you might have some blind spots that may hinder your ability to enjoy lasting relationships with others?

You do, you know. We all do.

Your friends do, your ex certainly did, and your relatives do.

Have you ever had friends who complained to you that they just couldn't seem to enter into lasting relationships, and they didn't know why? But *you* knew. You saw a couple of huge negatives that were blind spots to them. You didn't tell them, of course, because that would be too confrontational.

Have you ever been on a first date with a potential Miss Right or Mr. Right, but soon you became annoyed by how they seemed to interrupt you and insist on talking about their interests? Or maybe it was the way they picked at their food. Or how they dressed, or any number of other subtle negatives that put a dagger in your dreams. Second date? No way! Certain descriptive words come to mind: obnoxious, motormouth, egotistical, stuck up, bad attitude, flighty, too smooth…

In summary, *loser.*

But what about you? Might the people you have dated describe you with similar adjectives? Do *you* have blind spots that may be preventing you from getting a second date? From finding an enjoyable relationship? Perhaps even from marriage?

Even your best friends won't tell you. They are afraid to. They don't want to hurt your feelings or lose your friendship. So you are bewildered—*Why am I still single?* Nobody will tell you.

I was single until I was 42—for some good reasons. I had some serious blind spots that I couldn't see. For instance, I grew up with two brothers and played lots of sports. As a result, I was rough, boisterous, and hardheaded; I got into fights and mocked people. I thought girls were catty and always looking in a mirror. Did I have feelings? Yes, but I wouldn't admit them. Those were for girls. I played football, and when I got hurt on the field, I learned to suck it up.

Did I have some good qualities? Yes, but at that point in my life, my blind spots outweighed my charm. The result was that I repeatedly failed in my relationships with the opposite sex. This continued until I learned how to turn my blind spots into *bright spots*.

What are your blind spots? If you know what they are, you can change those negatives into positives. Blind spots can become bright spots. And failure in relationships can be turned into success. Maybe you will begin to get second dates...or become engaged.

That's why I've written this book. If it helps you, send me a wedding invitation.

Talking Without Communicating

If I speak in the tongues of men and of angels,
but have not love, I am only a resounding
gong or a clanging cymbal.
—1 CORINTHIANS 13:1

It was impossible to get a conversation going.
Everybody was talking too much.
—YOGI BERRA

Whoever thought that one little chromosome could make such a difference? Oh, but it does. Genetics experts have recently discovered some startling things about our chromosomes:

> As many as 300 of the genes on the X chromosome may be activated differently among women than among men. All told, men and women may differ by as much as 2 percent of their entire genetic inheritance. That degree of difference is greater than the hereditary gap between humankind and its closest relative—the chimpanzee.[1]

Maybe that's why you considered your last date as a visitor from another planet.

Another report found that men produce double the amount of

saliva than women do, but women are the talkers. They speak earlier, know more words, and get through tongue twisters with ease.[2]

Some of the gender differences are quirky. Some are obvious. Most of the contrasts are easy to recognize.

Because we often fail to take inherent gender differences into account, we may think the opposite sex is supposed to be just like us—so why don't they get it? Why are they acting so different from us?

This is one of our blind spots. Making assumptions about the opposite sex is dangerous. But for some reason, when we start interacting with them, we assume more than we should about their behavior, their motives, their expectations. The result? Confusion, bewilderment, cold shoulder, shut down, anger, escape, rejection.

For instance, guys, do you feel as if you're always apologizing, but you don't know why she's scowling? (Like the time you happened to be watching SportsCenter while you were talking to her on the phone.)

Or, ladies, do you wonder how he can be attracted to nearly any woman in a bikini?

Now, no one can tell you how to communicate perfectly with your boyfriend or girlfriend. No book can do it either. But we all can learn some tips to help us communicate more effectively with people—skills you can take with you throughout your single life to build authentic, enjoyable relationships with all your friends and especially with potential love interests.

Good communication is one of the most critical components of strong relationships. I have asked hundreds of singles, "What is the biggest reason for difficulties in your relationships?" The most frequent answer has been "Lack of good communication." I have also asked the same question to married couples. Their answers are very similar: "Poor communication."

We *talk,* but somehow we are not *communicating.* Talking and communicating are completely different. Talking is giving infor-mation. But communicating is giving information so that the other person understands you. Just because you say something does not mean the other person has understood it.

So why is relating clearly to one another so difficult, and how can we improve our communication? I could fill an entire book with answers to those questions, but I would like to focus on three critical areas that relate to this blind spot. Each can be a stubborn barrier to quality communication.

The Great Assumption

I call the first barrier the Great Assumption. I'll summarize it in two sentences. First, men really believe that women think like men (they don't!). Second, women really believe that men think like women (they don't!).

Every rule has its exceptions, but men typically have compartmentalized thinking. Our little compartments are like mental mailboxes. One might be labeled "girlfriend" or "wife"; another, "football"; another, "job"; and so on. We men have the ability to flip constantly from one compartment to another, so women seldom know which compartment we're in at any given time.

Women, let's say you're in the car talking with your boyfriend, who is sitting behind the steering wheel. You want to share something that's very personal, so you say, "Can I share something important that has been on my heart lately?"

"Sure," he says. But as you're pouring out your heart, he periodically says, "Uh-huh…yep…okay." You sense that he's tuned you out, and you become upset. That's to be expected. But, ladies, trust me, he never intended to hurt you. His mind easily switches gears—and usually ends up somewhere between ESPN and…well, "What's for dinner?"

Or let's say you're walking hand in hand with your boyfriend. You're thinking, *I like this guy. I love holding his hand and showing everyone around us that he is with me.*

But what's he thinking about? Downloading his favorite new song.

A man may spend much of his time in his job compartment and in his sports compartment. Do you know why men often spend a lot of their time in these two compartments? Our culture has convinced most men that if we can gain respectability in our job or in sports, then the ladies will love us. Of course, it usually doesn't work that way.

Let's say you are attending a fun party on Saturday night. A guy pulls up in a sleek sports car with the radio booming. He swaggers around the room, bragging to everyone about his hot car and his important job. He's checking out the scene—including you.

He really wants to impress you, so he smoothly approaches you with a beaming smile. He makes small talk for a while and then tells you how successful he is. As he exudes his credentials, he thinks that you're impressed with his resume and that he has earned your respect.

You think he's a fool.

After more than 30 years as a world renowned psychoanalyst, Sigmund Freud asked the famous question, "What do women really want?" That's still a good question. Each woman is different, but women seem to appreciate conflicting qualities. Men should be strong but sensitive, aggressive but patient, competitive but gracious, self-confident but self-deprecating, independent but dependent. Men are supposed to open their hearts to women but be strong enough to take any rejection.

We can easily see how wrong assumptions and poor communication can develop. Men are often confused about what a woman really wants.

Unfortunately, many men have reached the top rung on their ladder of success in business or sports but have lost their relationships with the people they love. Men have a great, internal need to communicate with a woman about the deep, personal issues in their hearts. Fear of rejection or being misunderstood hinders their ability to share these issues with someone they also want to impress. As a result, we often fail to express who we really are in significant relationships.

A man may get to the end of his life with all the money he desires but have nothing else to hold on to. And yet, most men would really prefer to develop relationships with close friends and family that are significant, loving, and long-lasting.

On the other hand, women usually think in global terms. That means everything fits together in their lives rather than being all compartmentalized. Their minds are like magnets that draw all the details together.

Let's look at an example. Guys, let's say you're dating this great woman, and you tell her you will call her before you head off to work one day. But you wake up late, and calling her slips your mind until you're heading out the door. As you're driving through the city, you call her cell phone in a panic. You're getting close to your destination, so you offer a quick "Hi, how are you doing? I gotta go. I'm late!" And you park your car.

On the other end of the phone, she's furiously murmuring to herself. *He didn't say "hi" the right way. And by the way he said "hi", I know something must be wrong. Where was he last night when I tried to get ahold of him? I know he's trying to tell me something…I'm going to get to the bottom of this today!*

Guys, all day long you're thinking, *Man, I can't wait for our date tonight!* But while you anticipate the date, she seethes and smolders. This I call the Volcano Effect. And believe me; the top will blow sooner or later.

That night you go to her place to pick her up for your date. You knock on the door, and when she opens it, there stands Miss Refrigerator.

"Hi, did you have a good day?" you ask.

"Yes." Cold shoulder.

"Are you okay?"

"Yes." Frozen shoulder.

And then you ask the world's dumbest question: "Is something wrong?"

Yes, Cement Brain, she thinks to herself, *something is definitely wrong.*

But she says no.

"No, really…is something wrong?" You continue probing.

"No. Let's go." Sigh.

Now the guessing game begins. You ask, "Well…did I say something that upset you?"

"No."

"Did I do something wrong?"

"No."

By now you're totally confused.

While all of this is going on, the woman is thinking, *If he* really *loved me, he would* know *what he's done wrong.*

I have news for you, women. He may love you, but he really doesn't know what's wrong. If you forget everything I say in this chapter, don't forget this: Don't assume that men will understand your hints.

You can't just assume that your date will get the message. You have to verbalize your thoughts. Relating takes hard work, and lots of good old-fashioned talking.

Beyond Waving the White Flag

Befuddled and beginning to fume? Follow these tips to better communicate with your sweetie and stop a fight before it starts.

1. Accept the fact that the opposite sex often communicates in opposite ways. You won't get very far in any relationship if you don't try to look at a situation from the perspective of the opposite sex. Before getting mad, take a moment to determine whether you are overanalyzing the situation.

2. Ask God for patience. Thinking from the perspective of the opposite sex isn't easy. But God calls us to be patient with one another. Check out 1 Timothy 1:15-17 to see how patient God has been with us and how much He wants to use us to show His great gift of life to others. Because of His sacrifice that gives us life, we can show patience to others. Refusing to be patient reveals your selfishness, and the vicious cycle often results in fights and ultimately in an unhealthy relationship.

3. *Don't just say, "I'm sorry."* Men, we're often guilty of this. But even if you are perplexed, waving the white flag without understanding why you are doing it isn't going to help you learn how to better communicate with your girlfriend. Instead, it becomes an easy out for the next time you two don't see eye to eye. Make an effort to get to the bottom of your girlfriend's frustrations. Women like to be pursued. You don't have to coddle her, but speak to her with gentleness and affection. Instead of saying, "What's your problem?" try, "Listen, I really care about you. You're smart and beautiful, and I'm so thankful that you're my girlfriend. Would you tell me how I've offended you so I can apologize and be more aware of this for next time?"

4. *Don't drag it out.* Ladies, now it's your turn. Once your man apologizes, then *let it go.* Men naturally want to fix things, and if he feels like you are constantly unhappy, he's going to feel defeated. The Bible has a lot to say about nagging (Proverbs 21:9,19; 25:24; 27:15-16). Remember that God commands us all to build each other up with our words. Ephesians 4:29 tells us, "Do not let any unwholesome talk come out of your mouths, but only what is helpful for building others up according to their needs, that it may benefit those who listen."

5. *Pray together.* Honestly, who can be mad when you are praying with someone you really care about? God can really humble us in this way. Let go of your pride, get on your knees, and pray for the ability and insight to communicate better and for God's guidance in helping you to treat each other as Christ treats us.

Stress

Another barrier to good communication is stress. In our fast-paced society, we're constantly under the pressure of deadlines and appointments. You rush, and then you wait in line. Your boss asks you to get the work done today, but it takes three days. Your professor schedules his final exam on the same day as two of your other finals. Your guests are coming to dinner in ten minutes, and you just put the baked potatoes in the oven.

Stress hits us from every direction and makes us anxious. The result? We focus more time on our activities and responsibilities and less time relating with the people we really care about.

Picture this scenario: Mark rolls out of bed at 6 AM. After showering and shaving, he hurriedly dresses and gulps down some orange juice. He gets caught in the morning rush hour traffic (again). His desperate weaving in and out of traffic not only gives him a few close calls but also a headache. Mark's boss wants to know why Mark's report is incomplete. The evening traffic is even worse than in the morning. Mark is late (again). He grabs a burger and a drink at a drive-through window and inhales it as he pulls into the driveway. He flies through the shower and puts on a new shirt that he finds is wrinkled. He disgustedly looks for another one. He's late for his date, which will mean arriving late for the movie. Mark picks up his girlfriend, Emily, and they say a few words on the way. But when he takes her home around midnight, neither Mark nor Emily has had much opportunity to share any significant personal thoughts.

This kind of schedule can undermine good communication and a strong relationship, but many of us live out a similar scene every day. We are students, single adults, or professionals who are all trying to get everything done in a day. But in the end, the pressure to produce severely cuts short our quality communication time.

When you add to that our tremendous interest in sports, a TV or sound system in practically every room at home, and our ready access to transportation, we can easily see how we can isolate ourselves and lessen our quality time with others. Bottom line? *Real communication takes effort and time.*

Pride

The third barrier to good communication is one we don't always admit—pride.

We all like to run our own lives. I know I do. No one can escape it. We humans naturally tend to take control, almost proving that no one can tell us what to do.

Sometimes we become control freaks without even realizing it. Wanting our way is so much a part of our nature that we barely recognize that part of our personality.

What's more, if you've been through a relationship and were bruised or scarred by either the person or the situation, you may want to be in control of future relationships even more. Moving forward and being honest and vulnerable with someone new is difficult when you've been hurt. It's never easy, and it takes trust—sometimes lots of trust.

But get this. Whether you are widowed or divorced or you've been dumped or your last romantic kiss was light years ago, you must know that we are all battling the pride barrier in some way or another.

Lasting, effective communication requires everything that our nature is not. Pride and jealousy aren't signs of love. The standard for communicating in love is not your parents, your friends' parents, couples on TV, or anyone else. Our model is God and His heart of love. In fact, He describes love plainly: "Love is patient, love is kind. It does not envy, it does not boast, it is not proud" (1 Corinthians 13:4-7).

In-depth, satisfying, enjoyable communication requires vulnerability and honesty. It requires developing oneness in a relationship even as you increase the potential for pain and rejection. Closeness and friendship are worth the risks because of the personal satisfaction true love brings.

BLIND SPOT 2:

"Poor Me" Attitude

No one can make you feel inferior without your consent.
—ELEANOR ROOSEVELT

People ask whether the newspaper stories
about Ted and girls hurt my feelings.
Of course they hurt my feelings.
They went to the core of my self esteem.
—JOAN KENNEDY,
WIFE OF U.S. SENATOR TED KENNEDY,
AFTER REPORTS OF HIS ALLEGED AFFAIRS

We all carry images in our heads of who we are and who we want to be. Regardless of how strong our positive images are, they can become fragile when threatened by people and situations in this world.

Our past, in part, determines who we are today. All of us are the results of things that have happened to us. Although some psychologists overemphasize the effects our childhoods and life experiences have had on our lives, I believe we can better understand ourselves by looking at our pasts.

For example, those who have had a high incidence of parental or family conflict are more likely to show low self-esteem, even when this conflict occurred long ago.

If you have grown up in an encouraging family and your parents always told you they believed in you, you are likely to be a fairly confident person. But a Miss Heartbreaker or Mr. Heart-breaker may come along and suddenly crush your self-esteem. Maybe you haven't always been a confident person, tormented by the thought of having to take the initiative to ask out a woman you like. When you finally get the courage, she turns you down, or worse yet, avoids you like a foul smell.

If you are a woman, you may have had difficulty exerting the effort to get the kind of men you would like to date to notice you. Mr. Heartbreaker acts like you're invisible or makes you feel like a wallflower. He might even give you a token pity date and leave you hanging with "I'll call you." But he never does.

This is enough to cause us to make the mistake most people do under these circumstances. We start looking inward and trying to find what is wrong with us.

Consider Joan Kennedy's story. As the wife of U.S. Senator Ted Kennedy she had to deal with an alleged wandering husband and several abortions and miscarriages. As a result, she turned to alcoholism to dull her pain.

"When one grows up, feeling that maybe one is sort of special and hoping that one's husband thinks so, and then suddenly thinking maybe he doesn't…and I began thinking, well, maybe I'm just not attractive enough, or attractive anymore, or whatever, and it was awfully easy to say…if that's the way it is, I might as well have a drink."[1]

Sometimes other people's offenses can't help but hurt—and hurt deeply. That's understandable. But when we let the circumstances and the other people take control, we get into trouble.

Why do we give other people that kind of power? God never intended for our relationships to determine how we feel about ourselves. When people base their identity on what others might think, their image will always be changing because people's attitudes and opinions are constantly changing. If today we value ourselves based on what others determine is important, then tomorrow we may find our self-esteem damaged.

Dr. James Dobson, writing in *Hide or Seek,* tells about Dr. Maxwell Maltz, a famous plastic surgeon.[2] Women used to come to him for breast reduction surgery—today they ask him to pump them up with silicone. In King Solomon's biblical love song, his future bride is ashamed because the sun had darkened her skin. Back then, a suntan was degrading, but now the brown bride would be the beauty of the beach.

Women today are ashamed to admit that they carry an extra 10 pounds of weight, yet Rembrandt, the famous Dutch painter, loved to paint plump, round bodies. Dr. Maltz continues, "Don't you see that your personal worth is not really dependent on the opinions of others and the temporal, fluctuating values they represent? The sooner you can accept the transcending worth of your humanness, the sooner you can come to terms with yourself."

We must never let our past circumstances or other people dictate how we think about ourselves. Release from our burdens is one of the major principles that Jesus taught. He talked about turning pressure and pain into peace. "Come to Me," He said, "all you who are weary and burdened, and I will give you rest" (Matthew 11:28). We don't have to be victims of our pasts—we can be victors *over* our pasts.

Many factors contribute to low self-image, but identifying what they are, where they come from, and the consequences they create can help you build a healthy self-esteem and healthy relationships.

So where does a negative self-image come from, and what are the effects?

We often let others determine our value in three areas of life: beauty, performance, and status. Let's take a brief look at each.

Beauty: How Do I Look?

The competition for dates and relationships is fierce. When you look around, you may think that the good-looking, athletic types are the ones busy on Friday and Saturday nights. The hourglass figure wins out over the pear shape. The six-pack abs trump the one-pack-over-the-belt belly.

In reality, that's not true. But our society places a tremendous emphasis and value on beauty, and we live in an age of sensory overload where we can't escape the messages. You can't read a magazine or turn on the TV or even check your email without some advertisement prompting you to invent the "new you"— referring to *physical* transformation, of course.

Such words as *sexy, sensual,* and *erotic* in huge letters jump off the covers of magazines. Women buy the latest magazines to discover all about sexy new haircuts and clothing that will help them get men to notice them. You can "satisfy your soul" with diet and makeup tips. Even an ad for something as mundane as a man's electric shaver takes on sex appeal to attract women to a man's clean-shaven face. The advertisers know that sex sells, and they flaunt it to the max.

Your friends and family may even pass along the false beauty message. Your friend exudes, "Don't Tom and Susan make a good-looking couple?" Your boyfriend mentions, "Bob's girlfriend is gorgeous, isn't she?" The woman you secretly like comments, "I've always been attracted to athletic types." But, if you don't fit these preferred ideals, such messages, regardless of how they slip in, are usually destructive.

These messages carry unrealistic expectations, causing discouragement and low self-esteem. Eventually this discouragement can lead to simply giving up all hope.

When I met Kim, she was sitting up in a hospital bed. As we talked, I noticed how feeble and weak her movements were. She obviously had a low self-image because she kept mentioning how people didn't like her. "What's the use of trying?" she finally asked.

Kim—single and in her mid-twenties—was in the last stages of an emotional disease that is increasing in our country today: anorexia nervosa. She had convinced herself that she was fat compared to her friends and the celebrities she watched on TV and read about. She also believed that because of her weight, men and her friends rejected her. She gave up trying to reach out to others and began punishing herself by going from 140 pounds to below 100. She starved herself, and when she did eat, she forced herself to vomit. She listened to counseling but would not act upon it. Nothing and nobody seemed to help. She had given up on herself. And she was dying of malnutrition.

Even though few of us go to the extent Kim did, once we surrender to negative thinking, we become less capable of developing and maintaining happy relationships. We push people away. In addition, we allow others to use and abuse us. (Sometimes we abuse ourselves too through drugs, or alcohol, or in even more severe ways as did Kim.) Most people don't enjoy spending time around negative, complaining, depressed people. Surrendering to hopelessness never has a happy ending.

You may think you haven't been fooled by the beauty lie. *Other people's opinions of how I look really don't matter,* you may think. But let me ask you this question: How do you feel when someone either compliments or criticizes the way you look? Don't their compliments send you flying and their criticisms cut you deep? Your reaction to their comments will tell you a lot about how much you are allowing others to determine how you feel about yourself.

Performance: How Am I Doing?

If we feel our achievements approach or meet the expectations of our employer, friends, or family, we have higher self-esteem. But if we feel we aren't achieving as much as others think we should, we can really feel down about ourselves. We notice messages like these:

> Employer: "You can do better than that."
> Friend: "I can't believe you're still not married!"
> Parent: "When are you going to get a real job?"

Since childhood, many of us have been encouraged to excel in all we do. Others of us have felt discouraged because we lacked our family's support. But regardless of how much we accomplish, we often think we should do better. And if we feel as if we never have achieved quite enough, we can get discouraged easily, bringing on a deep sense of inadequacy.

Here's one way to determine if you're putting too much emphasis on your own expectations or others' expectations of your performance. Ask yourself, *If I didn't have the job, income, or material possessions I have, would I still feel the same about myself?*

Insecurity in your accomplishments can translate into destructive habits in your relationships.

If you dislike something about yourself, your fear of letting someone see your weaknesses may block your ability to express the real you. But when you are yourself, you and your girlfriend or boyfriend can enjoy each other more. Sooner or later you will have to break down the walls if the relationship is to have any chance to grow.

Or you may want to give your heart to someone you care about, but you fear rejection. Feeling inadequate with the person God made you to be only leads to isolating yourself from a girlfriend or boyfriend who really wants to know you and care about you.

If this is true of you, my suggestion is to *relax.*

As long as you keep your love bottled inside (and the other person's love outside), your relationship cannot grow. Loving someone honestly requires openness and transparency. We have to be vulnerable, allowing someone to know us in the deep recesses of our hearts and to know our weaknesses as well as our strengths. Love and fear just don't grow together.

Status: How Significant Am I?

We often allow others to determine our value and worth. Have you ever heard these statements?

Employer: "We've decided to give the promotion to someone else."

Friend: "We had a party but forgot to invite you."

Family: "We are so busy, we can't attend your special occasion."

Date: "I think we should be just friends."

Almost everyone has the unspoken desire to be respected, wanted, and admired. And usually, we feel badly if people ignore us, forget our names, or make us feel unimportant. But our *true* value and importance is *never* determined by what others think.

Instead of rising above these external messages, we internalize them and accept them as legitimate indicators of our worth. That puts us on the losing side of life and affects how we think about ourselves and others.

What's more, believing these false reports can tear apart our relationships by creating destructive actions and reactions. Feeling inferior often leads to jealousy. A person who is jealous is afraid of losing love, and in the process, usually does. Our fear of failure drives other people away. "Jealousy," says psychologist Abraham Maslow, "practically always breeds further rejection and *deeper* insecurity."

Feeling insignificant can also lead us to criticize the very people we are supposed to love. We attempt to make ourselves look better by being more critical and by refusing to see the best in others. But being critical and picky all the time either drives the other person away or makes the relationship very unsatisfying.

Being critical of ourselves works in a similar way.

Craig was starting to like Beth. They had several fun dates. Although she was dating other guys, Beth asked Craig to come to a party she was having. He had a good time, but he felt inferior to her friends. They were all popular people, and he didn't feel like he belonged with Beth's kind of crowd. As he compared himself with other guys Beth was dating, Craig became discouraged. *What does she see in me? I'm not her type. How can I compete?* So he never called her back, although he wanted to many times.

A short time later, Beth married one of Craig's best friends. One evening when the three of them were having dinner together, they started talking about old times.

"Remember that party, when I invited you to be my date?" Beth asked. "We had fun, but you never asked me out again. How come? I really liked you!"

Craig was surprised that what he assumed to be true about himself wasn't the way Beth (and others) actually thought of him. Many dating relationships have failed because one of the pair felt inferior to the other. When difficulties and differences developed— as they will in any relationship—the person took a look at the competition and accepted defeat. That happened to me many times. I gave up without a fight, or I never started in the first place. I concluded, *She would never be interested in me.* And sure enough, when I stopped pursuing the relationship, the woman generally would lose interest.

How God Sees You

Remember that God is the one who gives you value, not you or anyone else. If we let others determine how we feel about ourselves, our opinions will change constantly. God has given you the greatest compliment you could ever receive in this life—better than any woman or man could give you in words. He calls you His masterpiece, His work of art that He wants to put on display and show off to everyone (Ephesians 2:10).

When you find yourself becoming depressed, insecure or doubtful, turn to God's Word. Psalms is a great place to look for encouragement. You'll read over and over again about God's everlasting love for you, His nearness to those who cry out to Him, and His great ability to hold up those who are struggling and to put their feet on solid ground.

Don't dwell on negative thinking. We all have things about ourselves that we don't like. God can help us to change some of these traits. For example, if you struggle with anger, God can work in you to make you a peacemaker.

But other things you may secretly dislike about yourself are just the unique attributes that God gave specifically to you. He loves you just the way you are. So process constructive criticism from others, but don't dwell on negative comments. Not everyone will like everything about you, but God loves you completely because He sees Jesus in you. When someone attacks you, remember 1 John 4:13,16: "We know that we live in him and he in us, because he has given us of his Spirit...And so we know and rely on the love God has for us." Ask God for help to see His true vision of who He created you to be.

Don't worry. Don't get frustrated or worried about your struggles with self-esteem. God is working on you bit by bit, and as you turn to Him, you will begin to feel His calm and peace. In Luke 12, Jesus told us not to worry about our lives. Look how He takes care of a mere bird—and how much more precious you are to Him than a bird!

Remember, it takes work. Turning to God daily for our value and self-esteem takes work plus faith. You've got to make a conscious effort to reject the false testimony of this world and to embrace God's true words for your life. James 1:22 tells us "Do not merely listen to the word, and so deceive yourselves. Do what it says." God will honor you for your efforts to study His Word and put it into practice.

(You can find many more ideas about building your self-esteem in my book *Discovering God's Unique Purpose for You*[3].)

Struggle for Control

All our acts, reasoned and unreasoned, are selfish.
—MARK TWAIN

*A me-first, satisfy-all-my-desires attitude leads to relationships
that are superficial, transitory and ultimately unsatisfying.*
—DANIEL YANKELOVICH, RESEARCHER

Take a quick look at the newspapers, and you'll find real stories about how we live, work and somehow build relationships in a self-centered world.

The *Virginian-Pilot* newspaper columnist known only as "Road Warrior" recently wrote about drivers who try to evade a sign prohibiting turns on a red light from 4:00 to 6:00 PM. She compares them to ants in her daughter's bedroom. "The ants are going to find the pinhole crack that provides access to the forgotten juice box under the bed. Motorists, likewise, will devise a me-first method of getting to Interstate 264 as creative as it is self-centered."

Signs of selfishness are everywhere in our society, sometimes blaringly obvious but often quite subtle. But with so much self-ishness in our world, we shouldn't be surprised that it pops up in our relationships just as subtly as it does elsewhere.

I'm into antiques in a big way. I admire the beauty and crafts-manship of a well-built piece of furniture, especially pieces made of oak. When I was single, I put a lot of my savings into antique furniture and knickknacks. I spent money on something that might have looked like junk to others because I could see the potential in it, and I knew that once I had it repaired and refinished, it would be restored into a beautiful piece of furniture.

Most of the time I rationalized spending money on the furniture. After all, each year the value of a nice antique increases. When I married Paula, however, my hobby became a real obstacle in our relationship. When we had a little extra money in the budget, my first tendency was to run out and look for more antiques.

Soon after we were married, I saw an antique lamp that was like one I'd wanted for years. The auctioneer started the bidding, and several people were anxious to purchase it. I didn't know how much it would be sold for, but I guessed it would be expensive. I turned to Paula and asked, "Would you like to bid on this lamp?"

"No," she answered quickly. She felt the lamp would be too expensive. She could go to a department store and buy a very nice modern lamp for much less. Besides, she didn't think our home needed another lamp.

But I wanted it.

As the frenzied bidding for the lamp grew more intense, I became more frustrated. Finally I decided I was going to bid on it regardless of Paula's wishes. I convinced myself that an opportunity like this doesn't come along very often. The auctioneer motioned toward me for a bid…my excitement intensified…I couldn't hold back. I raised my hand—"Going once, twice, sold."

Paula looked at me with horror in her eyes. "What in the world did you just do?" she erupted. It made absolutely no sense to her.

On the way home with my prized purchase in the trunk of my car, I realized my selfish decision definitely created division between Paula and me.

As you may imagine, that incident precipitated a lengthy discussion about our financial decisions. My new wife's values were radically different from mine. As a consequence, I made a decision never to buy another antique until we agreed on it. As far as I am concerned, no antique on the face of the earth is more important than my relationship with my wife. Even the most rare piece simply is not worth the conflicts that disharmony brings.

Financial conflicts are one of the leading causes of broken relationships and divorce. If we are selfish, we will end up destroying relationships that may have progressed with great promise.

Being Happy

We don't date to become unhappy. No guy has told me, "I can't wait to spend time with my latest girlfriend because she is so boring." I've never heard any woman say, "I love to date this hot guy because he makes me so miserable!" Yet misery is the state we find ourselves in *many* a time. Let's look at why.

Have you ever caught yourself wondering, *Does the person I'm dating really make me happy?* What's our purpose in finding a good relationship with someone of the opposite sex? Happiness. We all want to be happy in life. And God has so designed us that a part of our happiness can be found in an enduring relationship with a loving partner of the opposite sex.

But when you think about that question more seriously, it seems quite self-centered. *Does this person make* me *happy?* That focuses on another person meeting *our* needs, on our receiving rather than giving. We're all self-centered in many ways, and this human trait can make our relationships miserable.

Selfish? Me? You? We all have the same problem. One of the funniest ways I've seen this portrayed is through photography. Suppose you're in a group photo. When you see the picture, who is the first person you look for in the photo? Number one, that's who. You try to find yourself!

But did you ever notice that the more you look, the more you notice things you don't like about yourself in the picture? You say to your friend, "It's a terrible picture. I don't like it."

None of us like to appear less than our very best. Even if everyone in the photo is smiling and looking great, we look at our own image and decide our bad appearance far outweighs how good everyone else looks.

Here's a way to illustrate how being self-centered can affect our relationships: You begin to date a guy, and he really has it together. He's a leader, confident, and certain that some day he will have a high-paying job. He could provide you with the type of lifestyle you "would like to grow accustomed to." You might think *What a catch! He'll give me a secure future.*

But what if he were to lose his job or become crippled from an auto accident? Would you still love him?

Men are caught in this too. They have a tendency to think, *Boy, she's hot!* But they're really feeling, *Because you turn me on, I'll love you.* But what if she gets a terminal illness, or becomes depressed, or is disfigured? Will you still love her? If not, you probably don't really *love* her at all.

Selfishness says, "If you do good things for me and make me happy, I will love you." But that attitude doesn't make for a truly lasting relationship. Many relationship experts and authors advocate a 50/50 partnership that promotes the "you do your part and I'll do mine" philosophy. I've sat in on enough human sexuality and psychology classes to realize how prominent this philosophy is. It all sounds so plausible, but it contains a fatal flaw.

Don and Sally Meredith deal with this issue in their book *Two Becoming One.*

> Why, when it seems to make so much sense, is the meet-me-halfway concept dangerous? It draws the couples' eyes to each other's *performance,* and no one is perfect, or performs correctly all the time. Further, it actually promotes *independence.* You do your job; I'll do mine.

Once we start focusing on one another's performance, we begin to feel rejection and hurt.[1]

In light of all the counseling I've done with dating couples, I am convinced this kind of bargaining will never work. The reason is that you can never be sure the other person is doing as much as you think they should. "Hey, look at what I do for you, and then look at what I get in return. It's not enough! I deserve a lot more." The 50/50 relationship produces insecurity and confusion. "Does he love me enough?" "Is she giving as much as I am to this relationship?" "If I stop doing my part, will he stop loving me?" The 50/50 turns into the 80/20—you believe you are doing more than your fair share. So you complain, gripe, or badger to get the other person to meet your needs your way. The death of that kind of relationship is not far off.

Comparisons

Focusing on ourselves and our own desires for happiness produces another attitude that often splits couples apart. We find ourselves comparing our girlfriend or boyfriend against an unmerited standard. We begin to selfishly desire what someone else has.

Someone of the opposite sex may be attractive to you, and dating around can be fun—and even healthy. But the comparison I'm talking about occurs after you have been dating someone for a while. So how do you react when, after being in a relationship a while, you are attracted to someone else?

Let's say you're at a party with your boyfriend. You're standing there talking and munching on snacks when in walks Jamie with her boyfriend. You look at her boyfriend, then at yours, and you think, *How did she ever get him? What does she have that I don't have?*

We guys do the same thing. But the problem is that what initially attracts us to another person is the external or the positive side of that person. We forget that everyone has a negative side too…and that nobody can make us totally happy either.

Friends encourage you to "look your best" or "be your best" when you are in public or on a date. "You never know when Miss or Mr. Right will come along," they say. We hide our inadequacies. Thus, many couples use artificial standards when they compare their own relationships with others'. If we are all putting on masks, we are only comparing the masks. We see other people at their best and compare ourselves and relationships with that. No wonder so many relationships are superficial and temporary.

When you're not happy within yourself, you may look for that "someone out there" to make you happy. Very soon, you will discover that each new dating partner has weaknesses, though they may be in different areas. No one is perfect, including you. *Satisfaction comes when two imperfect people work together to build a realistic relationship.*

After you're married, you may still selfishly desire what doesn't belong to you. One of my college professors was a psychiatrist whom I really respected. But even he had his own struggles—and paid severely for them. He counseled a woman for several months and began comparing her to his wife. Eventually, he became involved with this woman who seemed to understand him and added "electricity" to his life.

I knew his family well. I ached terribly when I saw that slowly but surely this man, who knew how to counsel others brilliantly, could no longer counsel himself. He ended up destroying his marriage and devastating his wife and two children.

He was looking for someone else to make him happy. Unfortunately, he is still unhappy today. Pursuing selfish interests ultimately leaves us feeling miserable and empty.

Even if we do finally find one person to love and settle down with, we soon discover that our desire to have more is very much alive. The more deeply involved we become with someone, the more our selfishness is exposed. We want our own way. To get it, we argue, pout, demand, manipulate and scheme. Yet after we get what we want, the happiness is fleeting. We've clutched a fistful of sand, only to have the sand slide between our fingers and fall to the ground.

Margaret, a friend of mine, recently shared that when she was seven years old, she noticed that the nice old lady living in the big house next door was preparing to move away. In the process of packing up all the belongings of her long-time home, she decided to give many things away. This included several children's games and toys. But Margaret had her eye on something else.

Some time earlier, as she was playing in the yard, she saw a beautiful, fragile vase sitting outside a basement window. Every time she passed that window, her desire for the vase grew. One day, she could resist no longer, and she took the vase and hid it so it would be hers after the old lady moved away.

But Margaret remembers that after taking the vase, she never went to visit the lady again. She was frightened and ashamed. She felt bad about what she had done.

Probably all of us have had a similar experience about which we felt terribly guilty and ashamed.

When Adam and Eve sinned in the garden, guilt and fear made them want to hide. Both knew they had done wrong and they feared the consequences. Their "I'm in control" behavior separated them not only from God but also from each other. They hid. They realized they were naked. They were ashamed.

Selfishness always brings separation between people as well as estrangement from God.

The Ten-Second Pride Check

Second 1: Do I have a difficult time apologizing?

Second 2: If I lost my job or my health, would I still feel as good about myself as I do now?

Second 3: Do I always think I'm right?

Second 4: Do I listen to others before offering my opinion?

Second 5: Am I easily angered, or do I get upset when others criticize me, my actions, or my words?

Second 6: Do I spend more time on my appearance or developing my interests than I do on seeking God and His plan for my life?

Second 7: Do I insist on doing things my way? Am I willing to compromise?

Second 8: Do I value others' flattery more than God's stamp of approval on my life?

Second 9: Are my actions motivated by a desire to be approved by others?

Second 10: Do I have peace and satisfaction with God alone?

Desires That Become Demands

*If you accept the expectations of others,
especially negative ones,
then you never will change the outcome.*
—MICHAEL JORDAN

Those who play with cats must expect to be scratched.
—CERVANTES

Seldom in life does something good or bad happen for only *one* reason. When a relationship breaks up, usually many factors come into play. But one of the most common problems in relationships today is that many people have unrealistic expectations. They increasingly expect more than a girlfriend or boyfriend is able to provide. Their idea of what the relationship should be is more like a fantasy rather than something from the real world.

We've all heard the phrase "Love is blind." In fact, I'm sure most of us have been blinded once or twice. We see only what we *want* to see in the other person, and we believe that being with that person will make everything else in life turn up roses.

This one-liner exposes the reality of relationships: "Love is blind, but marriage is an eye-opener!"

I had unrealistic expectations of my college girlfriend, Amy, making me happy. As long as I was with her, I was the envy of all my friends. I believed she would fulfill all my fantasies. At times I felt shy or friendless, but I thought being with her would make me different. I would become more outgoing and popular because that's the way she was. I would become a better *man* because she was such an attractive *woman*.

I had the Great Expectation—that my college career would conclude with two pieces of paper. In one hand I would hold my college diploma, and in the other I would hold my marriage license. But my dream turned into a nightmare. It all came crashing down.

I'm sure that my relationship with Amy ended for several reasons. However, years later, I came to the conclusion that if we had eventually married, our relationship would have been a disaster. When I was able to see Amy with both eyes open, I realized I had overlooked many things. She was extremely immature and unsettled, churning through one dating relationship after another during her college years. The fact that she had dropped so many other guys hadn't registered with me then.

Later, after seeing the direction her life took after she graduated, I saw how our lives had been going in two different directions all along. I had made her a goddess simply because this fantastic woman had shown me some attention. The problem was that she fit better into my dream world than into my real world. I was a lovesick and unrealistic guy back then, no doubt—and my unrealistic expectations created a blind spot I can see in hindsight.

Are you ever guilty of wanting to find the fulfillment of all of your deepest desires and needs in someone else? You may desire a deep love relationship. But do you attempt to make the person more than he or she really is? If so, your attitude sets you up for disillusionment, disappointment, and bitterness.

What's your reaction when a painful breakup occurs? You may do one of two things. You search again for the right one—the person who fits your dreams—or you try to change and manipulate someone into becoming your ideal.

Of course, we can all stand a bit of improvement. In fact, we should change and grow throughout our lives. But one of the fastest ways to create tension and distance in a relationship is to continually try to make changes in the person you are dating. Our deepest desire is to be loved for who we are, to be accepted, faults and all. To attempt major changes in your girlfriend or boyfriend is to say, "I'll love you if…" And that is really not love at all.

When an engaged couple wants me to counsel them about their engagement and pending marriage, I try to help them discover each other's important character traits and personality so that they will build their relationship on friendship and mutual respect. Near the end of the counseling session, I love to ask each of them, "What don't you like about each other?"

You should hear their responses! "What we don't like about each other? Nothing." "We are in love and can't see anything we don't like." "We are perfect for each other." These couples are horrified that I would even ask such a question.

But if I were to ask that same question after they had been married five years, they would have a long list of gripes. The battle to change each other can become an all-out war.

Avoid demanding, *If you love me, you will change for me.* Instead, appreciate people for who they are underneath the surface.

The hard part is recognizing exactly what makes an expectation unrealistic.

Filling Other People's Shoes

You may naturally expect a girlfriend or boyfriend to behave in a manner similar to the people who have influenced you the most. If your mother is organized, conscientious in her life's pursuits, and an excellent cook, you may be expecting your girlfriend to live up to those expectations—without even realizing it. Ladies, if you had a father who provided well for you, pampered the girl in you, and always encouraged you to excel, then you may be expecting your boyfriend to display comparable attributes.

We sometimes forget that our significant other has a different set of parents and influences in life, and, more importantly, that that person is a unique creation, unlike anyone else in the world. I learned this the hard way soon after Paula and I were married. For six weeks we traveled, speaking at conferences and meetings in several states. We finally arrived at our apartment in California, glad to be "home" and ready to begin the process of settling in. That Wednesday, Carol, a friend of Paula's, came to stay with us for a while. When I got up Sunday morning, I couldn't wait for *a big* breakfast before going to church. After getting ready, I waited for my meal. But though I was all ready to go—and hungry—Paula was in the bathroom, fixing her hair. I looked at the clock again, getting more upset as each second ticked by. Finally she came into the kitchen. "Where is my breakfast?" I asked sternly.

"There's plenty of food in the refrigerator and cabinets for you to eat," she replied. Then, noticing my irritation, she asked, "Have you been waiting for me to fix breakfast for you? You're all ready to go, and I have a lot to do. Besides, Carol and I don't plan to eat any breakfast."

Still boiling underneath but working hard to keep my cool, I persisted, "It's too late now for any eggs and toast. But how about at least getting me a grapefruit?" Now we *both* were irritated.

"Here!" she angrily replied as she plopped a grapefruit on the plate in front of me.

"But it's not cut up!" I—a mature, newly married man—was losing my composure in front of our first houseguest. What a great way to start a Sunday. I doubt that I even heard a word during the Sunday morning worship service. I was too busy smoldering.

That afternoon, we discussed our tensions while Carol was visiting some other friends. Why did we have such a difficult time at breakfast? Paula asked me an insightful question, "What does Sunday breakfast mean to you?"

"It means family," I blurted. In my home, Sunday breakfast was always special. Mom would get up long before my two brothers and me to fix a delicious breakfast. Our Sunday morning family tradition was to have special waffles or pancakes or eggs, unlike any other morning of the week. Mom probably did that at least in part to motivate us to get up and get ready for church. But it was also a special family time in our home.

That was a tradition in my New Jersey home, many miles away from where Paula grew up in North Carolina. In her family, her mom made breakfast for her family every other morning, but on Sundays everyone made their own breakfast. Sometimes her dad would make the breakfast for everyone, but most of the time each person fixed whatever they wanted.

I expected Paula to act like my mom and serve a big family style meal. She expected me to act like her dad and simply fix my own food. After discovering our hidden expectations, we laughed. After we discussed the situation, we developed a plan that would satisfy each of our unique needs and desires to solve the Sunday morning breakfast problem.

Filling Up the Holes

Second, it's unrealistic to assume your girlfriend or boyfriend will fill up the holes in your life, especially where you feel you are personally inadequate. That was exactly what I had expected from Amy.

Our desire to unite our life with someone else in a love relationship is wonderful, but it must be founded on a mutual respect and commitment to oneness. Taking responsibility for your own actions and well-being is crucial.

That's hard to do. It's much easier to passively expect the other person to be responsible to take care of your happiness. But you can never find real satisfaction and fulfillment in relationships if that's your approach. So if you find yourself looking to someone else to meet all of (or most of) your needs, know that you are developing unrealistic expectations. You're also putting an unfair burden on another person.

Easy Answers

Third, we expect easy solutions to the difficulties we encounter. We live in a fast-food world, where everything from dinner to divorce is supposed to work out immediately with few complications. Advertising often reinforces this attitude. Need better skin? Get a Botox injection. Need a better body? Get a tummy tuck. Need love? Go to a bar and hook up with someone. If you want to marry, check out the latest online dating service.

I think we are all aware of the profound influence TV programs, movies, and magazines have in our lives. They are the background influences of the kind of people we want to date and the kind of people we are supposed to be to attract them.

Did you know that typical high school graduates have watched an average of 18,000 hours of TV? (That's 5000 more hours than they have spent in school.) On nearly every program, actors who seem to have it all together define problems and solve them—within 30 or 60 minutes.

During those thousands of hours of TV watching, those typical high school graduates have also seen approximately 250,000 commercials, each one proclaiming in 30 seconds that the advertiser's product will solve their problems and bring them happiness.

But real life doesn't work that way. (Not for anyone I know, anyway.) Sometimes working through a relationship problem can take weeks or even months of understanding, patience, prayer, forgiveness, and tender care. Sometimes the kind of solution we are wanting may not even exist. Because you are unique and your potential spouse is unique, harmonizing yourselves together calls for mutual compromise and commitment to the goal of oneness.

If you expect to be able to work through difficulties in your relationships easily and quickly, then you are in for a shock. You must first learn to resolve problems together to achieve true intimacy. You may even find that a few of your differences are extremely hard to resolve, but you both can choose to agree to disagree because the goal is oneness, not winning an argument. This takes time, hard work, determination, and commitment. But the result can be a happier, more satisfying relationship.

A Fantasy World

Fourth, we desire fantasy above reality. The quick-fix culture in TV, movies, and other media also shape the expectations of the way the ideal girlfriend or boyfriend should look. The media may have developed in us a false standard for desirable qualities in a spouse. We compare a real person with a fantasy person—and we want the fantasy. Reality pales in comparison.

Much of the time, the media portrays other people as happy and fulfilled just because they are beautiful, own the hottest car, drink the right beer, wear the right clothes, win a major athletic event, know people of influence, or star in hit movies. They are (to be brutally honest) sexy.

Sex attracts us. Good-looking models star in advertisements selling a wide variety of things for us to buy, such as toothpaste, hamburgers, vacation trips, automobile tires, and beer. I was watching a TV commercial for a minivan recently. The announcer was listing the benefits of the vehicle and proudly said, "This is a sexy minivan." Now I must ask, have you seen a sexy minivan? Have you ever looked at a minivan and exclaimed, "Wow, that turns me on"? If you do feel that way, please find a professional counselor. You have a problem.

Many men have developed their expectations from beautiful women featured in magazines, movies, or Internet sites. But let me ask you men something. The last time you were gazing bug-eyed at one of those lovely ladies, did you see a pimple on her nose? You say you weren't looking at her nose? Well, if you had been, you would have found no blemishes—on her nose or anywhere else. She was perfect. And that's the problem. *Nobody's* perfect.

If you know anything about photographers, you know they'll take hundreds of photos before they find one good enough to use on the cover of a magazine or in an ad. The movie studios pay millions of dollars to makeup artists, clothing designers, and camera professionals to get the perfect look for their star. These methods express the exceptional fake rather than a normal human being.

Reality is totally different. In everyday life, women sometimes have pimples, blemishes, messed up hair, smudged mascara, or spots on their dresses. They haven't spent five hours just getting ready for a date with you. Sex is not always on their minds. But the temptation is to compare your date with the fantasy woman and think, *What a letdown!*

Women have their fantasies also. Romance novels, the soaps, women's magazines, and chick flicks appeal to women's imaginations. These emotionally touching stories and movie-star photos attract females with their stories of how the rich and famous live and behave. The writers of the superselling romance novels exquisitely describe dreamy scenes in which the woman, aching with desire, is ecstatic as her strong, passionate lover sweeps her off her feet. It's all so mysterious and thrilling. It's a dream world, yet they sell millions of books. Does it have any basis in reality? Are these real men? Could real dates be like this? Hardly.

Romance is a mood, a feeling that the writers want you to experience as you watch the movies or read the magazine articles and books. But when you try to experience it in real life, it's not the same. In reality, the man is awkward, and the telephone rings while you're kissing. The feelings never seem to last long enough, and he doesn't quite understand all your needs, unlike the hero in the romance novel.

Even the creators of such fantasies know what an unrealistic view of romance can do to a relationship. Just read what Janet

Dailey, one of the world's bestselling romance writers, said when she was asked what sort of male behavior or attitude is romantic:

> On the whole, I think it's thoughtfulness. In courtship, a man can't do enough for a woman. He tells her she looks nice, gives her flowers, kisses her hand, is attentive to everything she does and says. Disillusionment with marriage sets in at the point when he stops acting that way, and the woman feels a tremendous loss. She has lost that wonderful part of courtship when she felt important because he treated her as if she were the most important person in the world.[1]

Certainly, all of us should bend over backward to be thoughtful and considerate with each other. But what man can cater totally to a woman's every desire and need? A man has weaknesses and faults, just as a woman does. Obviously these prevent him from being the perfect lover.

So we move from person to person, hoping to find that dreamlike love. No wonder we have so many broken relationships in the real world. When compared with fantasy, reality will be disappointing in some ways. But fantasy never satisfies—only real relationships with real people working together in harmony really satisfy for a lifetime.

Evaluating Your Expectations

We all want that dream girl or guy. But what can you *really* expect to get?

1. *Say no to the composite.* These days, you could easily form a composite in your head of the woman or man of your dreams. Don't do that! Remember that the man God has for you may not possess all the idealistic attributes you had envisioned.

2. *Pray for specific qualities you know you need.* If you are an encourager, pray for someone who will be able to speak to you and connect to you with their words. If you are easygoing and don't dwell on fights, then don't

pursue relationships with a woman who can't let a fight go. The old saying is true: The only person you can change is yourself. A quality you need in a future mate is not going to magically appear. God can help that person work on their weaknesses, but ultimately that's for Him and that person to work out.

3. *Be open to accepting dates with people you aren't immediately attracted to.* The writer of Proverbs 31 had it right. Charm is deceptive and beauty is fleeting. Attraction and chemistry are signs that you could make a good pair, but they are the weakest. If you are first willing to look for someone's heart at work, you may find more attraction and chemistry than you thought possible at first glance.

4. *Be strategic.* Make a list of the qualities you are looking for in a mate. Mark those qualities that are nonnegotiable. (A good example would be "Must be a Christian." A bad example would be "Must be a supermodel.") Finally, pray and ask God to reveal those qualities that best fit with you and can help you and your future mate serve Him together.

Sexual Fireworks That Fizzle

The hottest love has the coldest end.
—SOCRATES

Don't flunk your chemistry test.
Love is more than one set of glands calling to another.
—ANN LANDERS

The first four blind spots all alone could send a relationship reeling off course. But the fifth blind spot, sexual fireworks that fizzle, is the most damaging.

There's a reason. God reserves sexual intimacies for marriage and only marriage—never before the wedding and never with a person who is not your spouse. I know this goes against the bombardment of messages we have received from our society, our friends, and our cravings. But sex outside marriage brings unwanted, unexpected, and long-lasting consequences.

The apostle Paul was a single adult all his life. He knew the temptations of illicit sexual activity. He sent these instructions to his recent converts:

> It is God's will that you should be sanctified: that you should avoid sexual immorality; that each of you should learn to control his own body in a way that is holy and honorable, not in passionate lust like the heathen, who do not know God; and that in this matter no one should

49

wrong his brother or take advantage of him. The Lord will punish men for all such sins, as we have already told you and warned you. For God did not call us to be impure, but to live a holy life. Therefore, he who rejects this instruction does not reject man but God, who gives you his Holy Spirit (1 Thessalonians 4:3-8).

Christy met Carl in a Dallas bar one summer night. Carl was the handsome man of Christy's dreams. She quickly fell madly in love with him. They dated the entire summer. He took her to expensive restaurants and trendy dance clubs. He prepared romantic dinners for her in his apartment and generously gave her money to spend on anything she pleased. Carl smothered Christy with attention.

Christy was so smitten by Carl's advances that she couldn't resist his romantic invitations to bed. By the end of summer Christy was hopelessly hooked on Carl. But she was also becoming disillusioned with his approach to romance. Sex with Carl was exciting at first, like forbidden fruit, but it wasn't everything that the movies and magazines made it out to be. Carl was aggressive and possessive.

Sometimes Christy felt he was forcing sex on her. Sex became increasingly distasteful to her, and she felt a growing, subtle bitterness toward Carl within her heart. She secretly dreaded being alone with him, yet she desperately needed to belong to him.

Carl and Christy attended universities in different states that fall. Though Christy dated other men, Carl was her major heartthrob. She wrote him long, romantic letters, and they spent several stolen weekends together during the school year. In their hotel hideaways, Christy got the closeness she wanted, and in exchange, she gave Carl the sex he craved.

Finally Carl gave Christy every indication that he was considering marrying her. Christy was ecstatic. She felt she was one step away from being engaged. Her friends listened intently to her romantic stories of their encounters. She had given her heart to him and vowed not to date anyone but Carl.

At graduation, though, instead of proposing, Carl announced his plans to move to Washington, D.C., to work for a senator and attend law school—and he clearly did not invite Christy to come with him.

She was crushed. Carl had always talked about his thirst for power and his desire to become an influential politician. Christy suddenly realized that she had been little more to Carl than a pawn that he pushed around at will to gratify his quest for power over people. She had been used, abused, and now tossed aside.

After Carl left, Christy entered a period of severe depression that lasted more than two years. Her hurts and scars were deep. She thought she had been damaged beyond repair.

Sex Without Commitment

Christy suffered from the sexual regret raging inside many individuals today. Sex is desirable because it makes us feel accepted and loved, even if only for a short moment. It often appears to be the doorway to a deep, meaningful closeness with someone. Individuals assume that going to bed will automatically result in instant intimacy and will fulfill their deepest desires for happiness.

A popular notion is that women give sex to get love, and men give love to get sex. I used to say that some individuals wanted sex without the commitment of marriage. But it seems that nowadays people want sex without attachment of any kind. As one computer programmer said, "I work 60 to 70 hours per week and don't have much time for long-term relationships. All I want is a few minutes to take care of my sexual needs."

I know a woman who used to work at a well-known theme park. Most of the staff were single, and she said the nightlife behind the apartment doors included one sexual orgy after another. Yet this kind of behavior leaves deep regrets, broken hearts, and seared consciences. People who flaunt their bodies to get sex with strangers may well receive lifelong regrets. They use others to gratify their selfish desires and trash the beauty of a marriage commitment for a lifetime. Could you trust a person involved in that behavior who says, "I love you"?

During special cultural celebrations, spectacular firework displays light up the night sky, but in the light of day, you see the burned residue and trashed canisters. The fireworks were designed only to thrill for a moment.

Sexual fireworks may bring thrills for a night, but daylight brings emptiness, deeper loneliness, and trashed hearts. *Sexual intimacies do not equal love and acceptance.* But by God's design, sex within a loving marriage meets our deepest needs for closeness, companionship, security, and sincere love. Total, lifelong commitment to a partner in marriage does not hinge on sex, but it is a wonderful part of it.

Sexual activity can lead a husband and wife into a deeper emotional relationship, but for singles, the sense of intimacy will be superficial at best. Sex without marriage will ultimately bring frustration and isolation. God's design is for singles to meet their needs for love and acceptance through close, caring friendships, loving God fervently, and getting significantly involved in other people's lives.

Sure, sex is exciting and fulfilling to some degree. Our normal physical drives crave expression. Fulfilling these strong, natural drives through sexual intimacy is exhilarating.

God built those physical drives into us, and He has designed a way to express them that will bring maximum benefits and lifelong fulfillment. The total intimacy we seek with another person, fueled by our inner drive for physical expression, is available within the sanctity of the marriage commitment.

In for a Surprise

Singles like Christy often feel caught in a tug-of-war. They are pulled in one direction by their desire to experience all of the wonderful benefits that we enjoy when we follow God's design for sexual expression. Pulling the opposite direction is their awareness of the negative consequences of being sexually active outside of marriage.

I remember one night that illustrates this truth vividly. My birthday had passed, but I had no opportunity to do something special because I had been out of town on a speaking trip. When I finally returned home, I decided to celebrate. I took my girlfriend out to an elegant restaurant for a one-time-a-year expensive dinner—a night to remember.

But it ended up being a night of horror. The dinner was delicious and the restaurant had a long French name I couldn't pronounce, but after returning home and going to bed, I woke up at 2:00 AM with severe abdominal pain. I was afraid I was going to die and yet afraid I wouldn't die! I lay there, thinking the pain would subside, but it intensified. With great agony and effort I stumbled into my roommate Tim's room and blurted out, "Take me to the hospital!"

I had just made it to the bathroom when my stomach erupted the expensive meal. Tim hurriedly wrapped some clothes around me and rushed me to the hospital downtown where the doctors calmed both me and my stomach.

The evening had started out so enjoyably and had ended so miserably. The meal had packed a surprise. I loved the food, but afterward it made me miserable. Sex can pack a surprise too.

I was speaking at a conference, and afterward, George asked if we could talk alone. He was concerned about his relationship with his girlfriend.

"Why do I feel depressed?" He asked. "I really like her, but something is disturbing me. I should be happy, but I'm not."

It was an all-too-familiar story. They couldn't be together enough at the beginning. Fun and excitement filled their lives as they spent hours talking about every imaginable subject. Their affection had led to touching, then to hugs, and ultimately to lots more. It seemed to them so natural to express their love in bed. But the thrill started to change to doubts. They began arguing more than usual. Hurt feelings and disappointments came. George told me they were still dating, but now they were acting out of habit rather than enjoying each other.

That was George's story, but he is only one of many. Today thousands of couples are similarly surprised. Sexual activities have brought along unexpected complications and couples are discovering that sexual recreation has unexpected consequences. Yet the media bombards us with its promises. We hear,

"If it feels good, it must be right."

"Sex is the greatest experience."

"Everybody's doing it."

"Hook up with someone tonight and don't worry about tomorrow."

"If you're a virgin, you must not be able to get anyone."

With all the sexual experiences, you would think if those statements were true, that people would be much happier, and misery would give way to joy. But that hasn't happened.

Understanding the Differences

Everywhere I speak at conferences and conventions, people want to talk to me about their needs. And their greatest need is to find real love. Unfortunately, many of these people still have not learned that sex and love are not the same.

Do you know the differences?

Romance is the spark that lights up your relationship. When you want to express love and tenderness, touching seems only natural. But once you begin, the power of sexual urges drives the two of you to go further—maybe beyond what you had intended. But at the time, who cares about tomorrow? If you haven't made a strong moral decision before you get into a compromising situation, it's very difficult to choose wisely when the sexual temptation is right there.

Loneliness is the number one problem that single adults say they face. To have someone to share their life with seems the ideal way to find companionship. But when people are in a hurry and can't wait to develop an in-depth togetherness, sex seems like the easy way.

After counseling hundreds of people, I'm convinced that one of the primary reasons relationships split apart is because of sexual burnout. Both men and women will place the blame for the final goodbyes on arguments, broken promises, incompatibilities, and other legitimate tensions, but many times the underlying sexual involvement is what started the downhill spiral. The negative effects of premature sexual activity are hard to recognize and even more difficult to admit. The myth of the joys of sex without commitment dies hard.

Have you ever spent hours in a long make-out session and then not wanted to see the person in the morning? Everything seemed right the night before—the warmth and thrill of sexual passion. But the next day is a different story.

Your friends or the media may portray the night of passion as normal and expected for a couple. But no one ever talks about the let-down feelings of the morning after. How does sexual involvement destroy dating relationships?

For one thing, it increases loneliness—the very thing that sex is supposed to eliminate. That seems contradictory doesn't it? Someone thinks enough of you to want to be physically close, but that doesn't take away the loneliness. Women say that in the aftermath, they feel lonely again. Men describe the experience as meaningless. However you describe it, you feel empty inside and disillusioned. *Is that all there is?*

Committed love and good sex are built on knowledge, personal understanding, and a shared confidence that you are in a lifelong relationship. They go beyond superficiality.

Lust is never satisfied, but committed love is. Why? Because lust is self-centered and self-directed. People focus the passion of the moment on their own selfish desires. "I will love you if you please me. If you don't please me, I will find someone else who will."

Only committed love satisfies and deepens the relationship. Why? Because love is *other*-centered and giving. The passion of the moment is surrounded by the whole relationship, which sustains both people in good times and difficult times.

Sex is the icing on the cake. What is the cake? It's the commitment bonding a man and a woman together until death parts them. The cake takes a lot of work to create and is fashioned through the heat of pressures and difficulties that mold the couple closer together.

Have you ever swiped your finger through the icing on top of a birthday cake? When you licked it off your finger, it tasted so good that you wanted more. So you scooped up a spoonful. And then another. But the more you ate, the sicker you felt until you put the spoon down and your stomach rebelled. *Ugh! I'll never do that again!*

Sex without commitment is like icing. It feels great at first, but the emptiness and loneliness deep in your heart will eventually make you emotionally sick. Without trust and devotion, passion can produce a kind of superficial caring. It's a false sense of intimacy. Devoid of commitment, the other person can leave you at any moment. The cry of your heart for meaningful connection is smothered. You are alone with memories of degradation and embarrassment. So what will you tell the next lover who comes along?

Sexual involvement between unmarried individuals actually undermines intimacy. The physical closeness ignores the other parts of a person's life. Even when two people consent to make love, they will not achieve true intimacy. A person is much more than a body and sex organs. Sexual intercourse is more than a physical act. It involves the whole being, including the spiritual. To use each other simply for the pursuit of pleasure leaves inevitable emotional scars.

Guilt

"I don't feel guilty," a woman told Paula, my wife. "My boyfriend and I sleep together, and it's okay."

"It doesn't matter whether you feel guilty or not," Paula answered. "According to God's law you are guilty."

If someone is caught stealing, the judge doesn't ask if that person *feels* guilty. That doesn't matter. The perpetrator has broken the law, and the judge determines the sentence according to the act, not how the person feels.

Deep inside each person is a moral code. The Bible says in Romans 2:15 that God's law is written on the heart of each person. Since the beginning of man's existence on this earth, God has implanted His righteous principles into the very fiber of each one of us.

I want to be very clear about this point. God did not give moral laws to hurt us or to make us miserable. In fact, He gave them to protect us and to give us satisfaction.

Governments set up traffic laws to protect us. For example, they dictate on which side of the road a person can drive a car. Suppose no such laws existed. The highways would be utterly chaotic and dangerous. And when we disobey moral or civil laws, the result is deep, nagging guilt.

Dean shared his deeply emotional experience with me. He had met Terri at a big party. They had similar interests and spent many hours together. He just knew that this relationship would be different from his past failures because he was definitely interested in Terri.

They enjoyed touching and hugging. One spring evening as they sat in the apartment, his desire for her was more than he could contain. Their passion seemed to light up the night sky as all his reasoning for minimal sexual contact melted away.

They went further sexually than they had ever gone before. But after his heartbeat returned to normal, the uneasy feelings began.

Sure, it was exciting. He liked having sex. But he began to feel empty and guilty. As he held her in his arms lying on the bed, he began to realize he was doing so more out of a sense of lust than because he genuinely cared.

He couldn't leave her apartment fast enough. He gave her a quick kiss and drove home frustrated and lonely. According to the music blaring in his car, he was supposed to feel elated. But he was both disgusted with himself and disappointed in her. All he could think was, *Here I go again! Same story with another woman. Guilty and sorry.*

The next Saturday night Dean and Terri went back to her place after dinner and experienced the same results. Only this time, the guilt wasn't so overwhelming. But they didn't talk much as their physical desires began to consume them. They both suppressed their guilty feelings, being careful never to discuss what they both knew was wrong.

Dean's heart began to grow cold toward Terri as they communicated less and less and argued more and more. As long as they were having sex, everything seemed okay. But during the rest of the time they got on each other's nerves.

When the end finally came a few months later, they had never admitted to each other the guilt, which had driven a wedge between them. Guilt separates people and can even affect personalities.

Communication

Besides increasing loneliness, undermining intimacy, and producing regret, sexual involvement inhibits open communication.

We've already discussed communication in Blind Spot 1. But it bears repeating. Have you ever noticed that the more you share sexual intimacies, the less you talk? As the physical involvement increases, meaningful conversation decreases. And no strong relationship can exist without regular, healthy, in-depth conversation.

"I tell you the truth," Jesus proclaims, "everyone who sins is a slave to sin" (John 8:34). We actually become enslaved to our passions. We see the results in the frustrations and arguments that split people apart.

But God didn't intend for sex to split people apart. In fact, He created sex to be the superglue that helps bond marriage relationships together. The emotional and mental tie between a man and a woman when they marry is so strong that God says they become one flesh—a unit. "For this reason a man will leave his father and mother and be united to his wife; and they will become one flesh" (Genesis 2:24). The word "united" reflects the basic meaning of joining to one another in loyalty and devotion. The word occurs 60 times in the Hebrew Old Testament and is even used to show how we are to cling to the Lord.* It means "glue." What a beautiful description of love—to be bound to your wife or husband in loyalty and devotion.

Sexual involvement and intercourse are reserved for marriage— not because God doesn't want us to enjoy each other but because He wants to give us the security of a lifelong love relationship. The glue of commitment gives you the security and acceptance to express your sexuality without the fear of rejection.

We are to hold fast to God, and when He unites us with another person in marriage, we are to hold fast to that person like no other.

Relationship with God

Another major consequence of premarital sexual involvement is that it damages our most important relationship of all—our relationship with our Creator.

Let's test this right now: When you are indulging in sexual immorality, do you enjoy praying together?

When Dean was involved with Terri, he didn't want to talk to God. He was afraid that God might convict him of something he

---

* See Deuteronomy 30:20. "United" is translated as "hold fast."

enjoyed doing. Studying the Bible also became harder as his heart grew increasingly colder toward the Lord. Why do we think we can fake people out? We put up a carefree false front until it crumbles into regret and disillusionment. And in the process, we think God is fooled along with everyone else. Think again.

> But there is nothing covered up that will not be revealed, and hidden that will not be known. Accordingly, whatever you have said in the dark shall be heard in the light, and what you have whispered in the inner rooms shall be proclaimed upon the housetops (Luke 12:2-3 NASB).

All the while Dean was dating Terri, he knew that God saw them. He tried to hide. He rationalized. *We love each other. It's okay. Besides, we probably will get married someday.* But they had no deep, lasting commitment toward each other. God is not against sex. He is against the mutual exploitation and defrauding, which robs us of the joy of life.

> Flee from sexual immorality. All other sins a man commits are outside his body, but he who sins sexually sins against his own body. Do you not know that your body is a temple of the Holy Spirit, who is in you, whom you have received from God? You are not your own; you were bought at a price. Therefore honor God with your body (1 Corinthians 6:18-20).

God's holy light exposes our sin. We feel guilty because we *are* guilty—not just of sexual sins, but of self-centeredness. In the same instant, God offers the solution. Jesus never sinned, but He died to cleanse our sins and to clear our consciences. As a result, we can walk in the light and not be fearful of God. The slate is wiped clean. "If we confess our sins," the biblical writer John explains, "He is faithful and just and will forgive us our sins and purify us from all unrighteousness" (1 John 1:9).

Dean shared with me that he finally got tired of hiding and trying to run away from the Lord. The Holy Spirit convicted him of his ungodliness and rationalization. One night he poured out his heart to God about his disobedience in having broken sexual barriers with Terri. He desperately wanted forgiveness and the pleasure of holding fast to the Lord, and God met his need. God's joy flooded Dean's heart as he humbled himself before Him.

Long-Lasting Consequences

People who refuse to open their lives and relationships to God experience inevitable negative emotional consequences. And these are often longlasting. One man I know—I'll call him Ben—ended up destroying his marriage to his second wife.

It all started during his first marriage when he was attracted to Samantha, a female coworker in his office. At first they were just friends, but then they began spending more and more time together on coffee breaks and lunch hours. They shared jokes and stories with subtle sexual innuendos. They became increasingly familiar with each other physically, "innocently" hugging, patting and touching each other. Before long their smoldering passions burst into flame, and they ended up in bed together and involved in a full-fledged affair.

Finally, Ben divorced his wife and married Samantha. However, after the children were born, she became a stay-at-home mother. Samantha began feeling suspicious about Ben. She remembered that their relationship began in the office while his first wife was at home with their children. Now Samantha was at home with *their* children, and Ben was still in the office with other attractive, available women. Her suspicion grew into hostility and anger, and every time he came home 15 minutes late, she was convinced he had been fooling around.

Partners who are sexually active before marriage are often

plagued by jealously and anger for years in their marriage. They know from personal experience that their partners are capable of sexual intimacy outside marriage. They think, *Since he/she was loose with me before we were married, he/she is capable of being loose with someone else now.*

Once I was the guest speaker on a radio show. After interviewing me, the host of the program opened up the phone lines and invited listeners to call in their questions for me to answer. One woman came on the line sounding bitterly depressed.

"My husband is at work right now," she began, "and I have to talk to somebody. We've been married for eight years, but there's no love between us. He comes home drunk and physically abuses me. Our marriage started out to be wonderful; now it's a living hell. I don't know what happened to us."

I've heard similar stories before, so I voiced my suspicions in a probing question. "Were you and your husband involved in premarital sex?"

The woman paused. Then she answered yes. She went on to say that before they were married, she and her husband not only abandoned their Christian values of sexual purity but also rebelled against their parents by choosing to marry each other. She agreed that possibly their rebellion against God and their parents had come back to haunt them in the form of mistrust, disrespect, and abuse.

The long-term emotional cost of premarital and extramarital sex is like exorbitant, compound interest on a loan for something you bought. You continue to pay, and pay, and pay—long after the enjoyment of your new purchase has worn off.

The Battle Rages

In the volatile emotional war between the opposing forces of sexual purity and sexual promiscuity, you may vacillate. On one side you feel the steady pull of Bible-based moral standards urging you to postpone sexual intimacy until marriage.

On the other side you feel yourself being reeled in—sometimes subtly, sometimes abruptly—by sexual temptations fueled by your drives, your old habits, the culture, and the media. If you relax your moral standards in the slightest, you feel pulled even closer to compromise or to being dragged into the mud of sexual regret.

No one felt the tension more than Rob. As a college senior, Rob was deeply involved in the full social scene—athletics, student government, parties, and of course, girls. In his circles, dating included oral sex and intercourse, and he actively participated.

However, confusion and emptiness filled his mind in the mornings. During his senior year Rob discovered the biblical message of Christ's love and forgiveness. He responded by submitting to Him and receiving new life. Rob changed drastically. The standard for his relationships and activities became the Bible and his faith in Christ. Rob got along better with his family, and joy filled his heart. His weekend activities changed, and he severed relationships with his friends who continued to party and get drunk.

"You mean you're not going to have sex again until you're married?" a friend asked him.

"That's right," Rob answered confidently. And he meant it.

In the fall, Rob got a new job in another city. He met a new group of friends, joined a weekly Bible study, and started dating Leslie, who was also a Christian. She was attractive, athletic, and fun. Best of all, she was as committed to leading a godly life as he was. They enjoyed being together, and Rob wished his former friends could see how he and Leslie enjoyed a romantic relationship without sex.

But a month later the bottom fell out. He found himself lying in Leslie's arms—in Leslie's bed—sobbing with inner pain. *God, how could I have gone back to this?* He prayed silently. *Is it possible for me to have a relationship with a woman that will please You?*

Rob thought his passions would never entrap him again, but they pulled him away from his convictions. He was ashamed of his actions. He had gone back on his promises to God. Rob felt alone in his guilt with no one to talk to. Leslie felt the same remorse for her actions, but they never acknowledged their inner heartache. They couldn't help each other because they never discussed their painful feelings, and their silence about their personal guilt only drove them back into bed with each other. By January, Leslie's pain and shame reached the depths as she became pregnant and then had an abortion. Rob was devastated.

The internal emotional war had stretched each of them to the breaking point.

Maybe you have struggled in an emotional war between purity and passion. Maybe you also know the pain of watching your standards crumble in a moment of weakness, or maybe you're now in a relationship where you've compromised your moral courage. Maybe you've been to the depths of despair like Christy or like Rob and Leslie.

Commitment to high moral values and a personal desire for sexual purity can be destroyed easily by moral rebellion and failure. Maybe you only slipped once, or maybe you are trapped in a habitual pattern of moral compromise. Maybe your experience of failure is in the past, but you are still chained to it by bad memories and mental anguish.

You may feel like a moral reject. You may feel worthless and hopeless, with nothing of value to offer God or a potential spouse. You may assume that since you have failed so often, restoration is an impossible dream.

Sex was created by God to be the culmination of the process of bringing two lives together so that they can become a cohesive unit. This oneness develops through growing harmony and companionship, mutual respect and sacrifice. Love is giving the highest and best for the other person even if you must set aside your own desires and needs.

Committed love is like the cake. The ingredients include faithfulness, honesty, kindness, self-control, right choices, honor, patience, and a host of other godly characteristics. Wouldn't you like to possess those qualities? Wouldn't you like to be married to a person who expresses all those qualities toward you? Sex is the God-given means to seal two married hearts together into one. Focus on putting the right ingredients into the cake of your relationship. Enjoy the icing after the wedding.

What hope do you have for obtaining this kind of forgiveness and restoration? Should you expect permanent change without going back to the old ways and habits?

Just keep reading. You'll find out!

Part 2
Putting Life into Your Love Life

We are the instant gratification generation. Everything has to be done right now. If it takes our computer 20 seconds to boot up, we complain that it's too slow. We want a newer, faster one. If we wait three minutes in the drive-through to get our fast food, we look for a quicker restaurant. If developing an enjoyable love relationship takes too much time, we look for a shortcut.

Here is my guarantee for a healthy, enjoyable, lifetime relationship: It will take time and lots of work. Sorry, but no shortcuts will work. Destroying things is always quicker and easier than building them. A tall, strong oak tree takes 50 years to grow, but someone with a chainsaw can cut it down in a minute or so. Workers may take many months to erect a huge building, but someone with explosives could blow it up in seconds.

Draining the life out of a relationship is easy. Just treat each other selfishly, and it will crash and burn. Putting life into a relationship will take time and lots of work. But the benefits far outweigh the effort.

Do you want a relationship that's alive with fun and satisfaction? Do you want to end the day with a sense of accomplishment and peace of mind? Do you want to look back over the history of your relationship and feel fulfilled, knowing that you have built it well?

Do you want to put life into your love life? If that's your desire, the starting point for new life in your relationships is *you*.

The Master Restorer

Remember when I mentioned my love for antiques? I love to

buy an old desk, table, or China closet that the owner no longer wants. Because I can see the value in the antique, I want to restore it to its original condition. I bring it to my friend who is an expert refinisher. He painstakingly strips off the layers of paint or varnish, repairs the broken parts, and refinishes the wood. I gain great personal satisfaction when I see the original luster and glory of a piece of furniture that had been dulled by time and neglect. The "new antique" becomes my prized possession.

I wonder if God experiences a similar sense of satisfaction as He lovingly and patiently works in our lives to bring us back from hurtful, damaging effects of the blind spots in our relationships that we regret.

Before we meet Christ, we are like so many pieces of old furniture locked away and forgotten in a dusty warehouse. Our original beauty and luster are dulled through disobedience and rebellion, but God sees our inherent value underneath the layers of bad choices and sin. When we place our faith and confidence in Him, He brings us out of the back room of the dusty warehouse— He rescues us from the dominion of darkness and brings us into the kingdom of the Son He loves.

In effect, salvation moves us into the workshop of the Master Restorer of human lives. The change of spiritual location is instantaneous—from death to life and from darkness to light. Yet, much like the restoration of antique furniture, stripping away the vestiges of the old life and restoring the beauty of the original creation is a time-consuming process. Little by little, step-by-step, God cleans away the layers of the past and allows His bright spots to shine through.

You may fear that your mistakes and bad choices have permanently stained and damaged your life, but the Master Restorer is ready to go to work. As you let Him restore you, He will strip away the blemishes sin has caused and restore the original beauty of what He created you to be.

Perhaps you have tried to change your behavior time and again (like Rob and Leslie in the previous chapter) only to return to what you were trying to flee. You feel discouraged and defeated by your continued failure. You've confessed your sin many times, but deep inside you wonder if God has already given up on you.

Maybe you've been a Christian for a long time. You thought you didn't have any blind spots and were immune to sexual temptation, but you succumbed, and now you're crushed and embarrassed by your fall. You may be thinking that your life can never be the same again, but the Master Restorer is ready and able to cleanse away the crud of relationship regret and return the God-given beauty to your life.

The Two Options

The road to restoration actually begins with a decision based on Galatians 5:19-25. You really have only two options in life, and those options parallel the two lists in these verses. On one hand, you can choose to follow "the acts of the sinful nature...sexual immorality, impurity and debauchery; idolatry and witchcraft; hatred, discord, jealousy, fits of rage, self ambition, dissensions, factions and envy; drunkenness, orgies and the like" (verses 19-21). But if you choose to dabble in this behavior, you're not choosing the road to restoration, but the sad road to further pain, bondage, and destruction.

On the other hand, the road to restoration begins with a choice for life in the Spirit. The apostle Paul describes the kind of restorative work God seeks to produce in us through His Spirit: "The fruit of the Spirit is love, joy, peace, patience, kindness, goodness, faithfulness, gentleness and self-control" (verses 22-23). In fact, committing yourself to pursue life in the Spirit through Christ is the only way to counteract the power of the sinful passions and desires, which formerly scarred your life (verses 24-25).

If you're ready to choose the fruit of the Spirit for your life instead of the fruit of the flesh, the rest of this book is for you. It will show you how to follow God's principles to experience the forgiveness, the restoration, and the bright life you seek.

Setting out on the road to restoration requires that you establish your alliance with God and declare your allegiance to Him afresh. This is a critical step because your wrong choices and mistakes are direct results of substituting another god for God in your life. That's right: Israel's experience in the Old Testament demonstrates that acts of disobedience are the results of idolatry. Israel was always being drawn away from the Lord to serve the gods of the heathen nations around them. Whenever they embraced the first "I" sin (idolatry) the second "I" sin (immorality) was not far behind.

The root of your regret is pride. The attitude is "I'll do it my way." You set yourself, or someone of the opposite sex, or your passions, on the throne of your life. When you evict God from His rightful place of authority in your life, His standards and will for you usually go with Him. Spiritual death is the result. "For the wages of sin is death" (Romans 6:23). We lack the power to obey and be victorious.

Idolatry was Israel's most frequent temptation and greatest failure. God apparently knew how great the problem would be because the first two of the Ten Commandments deal with the topic of idolatry. Other subjects received only one commandment each, but idolatry was so serious that it alone required the double-barreled treatment.

The road to restoration isn't just a process of changing your behavior or wrong attitudes by correcting old habits and activities, although some changes will need to take place. Restoration must begin with a choice to give Christ His rightful place as Lord of your life. You can't enjoy the fullness of life without Christ and His will at the center of your life.

That's what makes this book so different from many of the current self-help and psychology books on the subject of relationships. Changing your attitudes and behavior is not primarily the result of a formula of sure-fire steps for success. True, you can and should do some practical things to come to terms with your situation (and later in this book I will give you lots of ideas). The transformation in your life, though, must spring from a change of alliance, a wholehearted recommitment of your life to Jesus Christ. Without the foundation of God and His standards at the center of your life, any results you gain will be short-lived.

Furthermore, you don't have the power to heal the hurt or repair the damage you have done to your mind, emotions, and character. Only God can do that. Without His power, you are destined to repeat your mistakes and remain mired in pain and negative memories.

You need the power of God residing within you to heal your relationship regret from the past and change your behavior in the future.

Often people will ask me, "Is there anything I can do about my failure?" The answer is yes and no.

First the bad news: No, you can't go back through time and change the past. What's done is done. You may have to live with the consequences that your blind spots have brought into your life, but God can help you do that productively. In this sense, even the bad news has a positive side.

Now the good news: Yes, you can rid yourself of poor choices and negative thinking so that your past experiences don't rule your present and future behavior. You need not be imprisoned by your past, regardless of how discouraging it may be to you. You can overcome your relationship regret.

Yes, you have hope. For example, I wish you could see Christy and Leslie today. Both of them have been emotionally and mentally restored, and they are free from the pain of their failures. Both of them are married to fine Christian men. Both of them are enjoying fulfilling, godly families. And both of them are presently helping others who have suffered the consequences of sexual immorality. If God can turn their lives around so dramatically, He can do the same for you.

Clean Up
the Inside You

Experiencing God's internal cleansing is the first and most basic of all the steps to putting bright spots into your life. Apart from His forgiving work in our lives, we have no hope. You can try to clean up your act and turn your life around, and you may even succeed to a certain extent. However, without God's forgiveness, you have addressed only surface issues and not the heart of the matter. If you don't deal with your sin and wrong choices before God, all your efforts to change will ultimately fail because your problem is first and foremost a spiritual problem.

As King David revealed in his confession, every sin is actually sin against God (2 Samuel 12:13; Psalm 51:4). Because the first level of offense is against God, the first level of restoration must be forgiveness from God.

In your wrong choices, you may have hurt another person, and you may need to apologize to that person and ask for forgiveness. Important as that step may be, though, it is secondary to seeking and accepting forgiveness from the primary one you have offended—God.

The basis for accepting God's forgiveness is 1 John 1:9: "If we confess our sins, he is faithful and just and will forgive us our sins and purify us from all unrighteousness." Let's look at this verse piece by piece in order to understand and apply its truth.

Accepting Personal Responsibility

In order to receive God's forgiveness, we must recognize and admit our selfishness for what it is: sin. In the New Testament, there are two main Greek words used for the English word "sin." The first word literally means "to miss the mark" as an arrow might miss the bull's-eye on an archery target. The word emphasizes our total inability to hit the bull's-eye of God's demand that we be like Him—righteous and perfect. "All have sinned and fall short of the glory of God"(Romans 3:23). The other Greek word for *sin* means to turn aside from God's expressed will. Our pride chooses to go wrong constantly. We have a fallen nature that is disobedient to God and rebels against His laws. Also, it is translated as "trespass" or "transgression" (see Galatians 3:19 and Hebrews 9:15).

You may say, "But I'm not a bad, degenerate person. I just blew it once or twice in moments of weakness." But missing the mark by an inch is as good as missing it by a mile. Sin is sin, no matter if you missed the mark of perfection or chose to transgress God's Law. And you must confess it for what it is—whether it's having sex outside of marriage, treating a girlfriend or boyfriend unfairly, or lashing out in anger. You must confess in order to receive forgiveness.

First John 1:9 directs us to confess our sins. We are personally responsible for what we have done. Admittedly, many pressures and influences bombard us daily. But the source of sin is our pride, which tempts us to do things our own way. Understanding the causes behind our relationship regret may help us come to terms with it better and be able to build a defense against a repeat of the problem.

God warns us, "Your enemy the devil prowls around like a roaring lion looking for someone to devour"(1 Peter 5:8). Satan hates you and tempts you to speak and act in self-centered ways. He rejoices whenever you give in to temptation.

But the devil can't make us do anything. We are responsible for our choices and attitudes. The Bible admonishes us to "Resist the devil, and he will flee from you"(James 4:7). Give Satan credit for his craftiness and persistence in temptation, but don't blame him for your willful act of rebellion against God's Word. I've heard a lot of ludicrous excuses for all kinds of sins. And that's what they are—excuses. I heard someone say that an excuse is the skin of a real reason stuffed with a lie.

Some people claim, "My friends made me do it." They're referring to the crowd they run around with at work, in school, at the club, or in the neighborhood. They hear their friends talk about sexual exploits as matter-of-factly as if they had gone out to dinner or to a movie. "All my friends are having sex. Everybody does it."

Men and women have been blaming each other ever since the Garden of Eden. When God pointed out Adam's disobedience, Adam put the blame on Eve, and Eve put the blame on the serpent (Genesis 3:8-13).

Passing the buck is simply the fruit of self-centeredness. It is a cover-up, an attempt to escape the embarrassment of being found guilty of sowing wild seeds.

People who blame their misbehavior on someone else teeter on the brink of full-scale self-delusion. They are the first to proclaim innocently, "My friends are all doing it," or "My partner made me do it." They have hardened their hearts and blinded themselves to the personal guilt, shame, and heartache they cause. God is not blind to their real guilt for violating His commandments.

No Excuses

My definition of fun is having a good time with no negative consequences. Going to a party is fun. Going to a party, getting drunk, and waking up with a hangover is not fun. Going on a date is fun. Going on a date and waking up in bed with someone who's not your spouse is not fun, especially when the repercussions include guilt, frustration, and regret. Anyone can come up with his or her own definition of fun, but that person must live with the consequences of their behavior.

Perhaps the most insidious excuse for participating in sin is to claim glibly, "It doesn't matter if I fall. God will forgive me anyway." The apostle Paul asks this individual, "Shall we go on sinning so that grace may increase?"(Romans 6:1). In other words, just because Christ has already forgiven all our sins, do we dare take advantage of His goodness and continue the very sins that sent Him to the cross?

Paul's answer is emphatic: "By no means! We died to sin: how can we live in it any longer?"(verse 2). Forgiveness is not the issue; we already enjoy it. Cheapening God's grace is the issue. Continuing to commit sexual sin (or any other habitual sin) rejects God's call for personal purity.

God's desire for us is that we become like Him—holy (1 Peter 1:14-16). If you center your life and decisions on your own selfish desires, you will fail to experience His joy, peace, and purpose. This is called living "according to the flesh." The Holy Spirit is opposed to the person who lives this way. It may look like he or she is having fun, but God says that mind-set is hostile to Him and ends in death (Romans 8:5-8 NASB).

You Have a Choice

The pressure to conform to the lifestyle of sexually active friends and coworkers and an immoral society is great. You may even underestimate the influence of a romantically aggressive partner on your sexual behavior and responses. Your sexual drives, your emotions, and your passions can sneak up on you and surprise you with their power during a seemingly harmless romantic encounter.

However, when you strip away the superficial veneer on excuses, you expose the basic truth within them all, which is this: You are responsible for your attitudes and actions. You can try to blame other people or the circumstances, but God calls you to repent. (I am not referring to situations where people have been victims of rape or child molestation. Those are issues of an entirely different nature. We are dealing here with moral choices.)

You are an individual with the ability to choose your own behavior. The first step in coming to terms with your past (or present) is to take full responsibility for your wrong choices, regardless of how influential your circumstances may have been.

The most graphic example of moral failure in the Bible is the story of King David and Bathsheba as recorded in 2 Samuel 11–12. Even though the events took place more than 3000 years ago, the story reads like the script of a modern movie.

As David surveyed the homes surrounding the palace from his rooftop one night, he spied beautiful Bathsheba bathing. After learning that she was the wife of Uriah, a leader in Israel's army who was away at war, David sent for Bathsheba and had sex with her.

When David discovered that Bathsheba was pregnant with his child, he initiated an elaborate cover-up that resulted in Uriah's murder. Then he married Bathsheba, who bore the son they conceived illegitimately. Apparently David hoped his immorality was safely buried and that life in the palace would return to normal.

The Bible doesn't tell us what excuses, if any, David may have used to justify his hideous behavior. The rumors of his conspiracy and adultery probably spread throughout the palace, his kingdom, and neighboring nations. Perhaps he blamed Bathsheba or the circumstances. Maybe he felt his actions were okay because he was the king—and kings of other nations did such things. Whatever his reasoning, though, God wasn't about to let David off the hook so easily.

The Lord sent the prophet Nathan to confront David about his sin. To his credit, David didn't try to worm his way out of responsibility by billowing a smoke screen of lame excuses. He owned up to his adultery: "I have sinned against the LORD" (2 Samuel 12:13).

David realized that he was responsible to God for what he had done. Admitting his offense to Nathan was not enough. To be sure, he had violated Bathsheba, conspired to murder Uriah, and lied to the entire nation by covering up his sin, but in his formal confession David pinpoints the crux of his failure: "Against you, you only, have I sinned and done what is evil in your sight" (Psalm 51:4).

Sin is a choice against God. Personal responsibility must begin with accountability to the Lord Himself.

Good News and Bad News

David's sin and his confession of personal responsibility brought bad news and good news. The bad news concerns the negative consequences David experienced, even after he confessed to Nathan and to God. For one thing, the son David and Bathsheba had conceived out of wedlock lived only seven days after birth. For another thing, as Nathan predicted in 2 Samuel 12:10-19, David himself was the victim of family strife and warfare for years. Moral failure often brings with it painful consequences, and they don't necessarily go away just because you own up to what you have done.

The good news is that David's sin didn't disqualify him from being used and blessed by God. Despite the problems in his life after his adultery, God gave him one of the greatest compliments in the entire Bible when He said, "I have found David the son of Jesse, a man after My heart, who will do all My will" (Acts 13:22 NASB).

David was a model worship leader and the composer of many of the greatest hymns ever written. Psalm 78:70-72, a psalm that David did not write, hails him as a man of integrity in his leadership of Israel.

This is good news for you too. As you face up to your wrong choices and sinful activity, and as you take full responsibility for your participation in it, God will totally forgive you and help you move forward to experience all that He wants to do in you and through you.

In order to experience God's forgiveness, you must admit your responsibility for your sin. Other people and circumstances may have influenced your behavior, but ultimately the choice was yours. To confess sin means simply to agree with God's perspective of your behavior and humbly admit to Him, "I'm wrong and You're right." It means sweeping away the excuses and saying to God, "I was disobedient and acted against Your will."

We are not first guilty before God because we have committed wrongful acts but because we are basically self-centered and rebellious against God's law. We have a sinful nature that craves independence from God. This affects our attitudes and actions and cuts us off from God. Apart from God's forgiveness, we are doomed to be punished with everlasting destruction. The consequences include God shutting us off from a relationship with Him and from the majesty of His power on the day He comes to be glorified in His holy people and to be marveled at among all those who have believed (2 Thessalonians 1:9-10).

The good news is that Jesus Christ carried your sin and guilt to the cross (1 Peter 2:24). He has paid the penalty of eternal separation from God the Father, and He has forgiven your sin (Colossians 2:13-14). The Bible says, "When this priest [Jesus] had offered for all time one sacrifice for sins, he sat down at the right hand of God" (Hebrews 10:12). Why did Jesus sit down? Because the work of forgiveness was complete. Some people say that forgiveness wipes the slate clean. I believe the Bible confirms that God has not only wiped the slate clean—He has thrown it away. He offers total forgiveness.

When you come to understand the truth and reality that Christ's death on the cross and resurrection were for you, the way is open for you to enjoy an intimate, eternal relationship with God. His forgiveness cleanses you from all sin—your sin nature as well as specific sins you have committed—and saves you from the horror of condemnation and from eternal separation from Him. The only thing left for you to do is accept the gracious provision God has already made for your sin. Faith is believing God to do what He says He will do.

The First Words Were the Hardest
(Rick, age 35, is an engineer in New Jersey.)

Anna was immensely friendly. Easy to know. Positive. These assets were countered by her blatant immaturity and questionable character and substance, but I must honestly confess, I was too busy staring at her body to see her heart. I was 28, tired of first-date questions, tired of the dating ritual, tired of being single.

As we approached our second anniversary of dating, I was making secret plans to propose to my fair maiden. At the same time, she was making secret plans to dump me. She caught me completely by surprise—which hurt. Part of the surprise was finding her sharing the sheets one weekend with an old boyfriend—which hurt even more. Another part of the surprise was staring into eyes that just days before burned red hot with "I love you," and finding those same thick-lashed eyes filled with indifference—which hurt the most. Two years of relationship were hacked and maimed in just a day.

I knew I had to pray. Still, I debated it. Who was I to ask Holy God for help? How hypocritical! How cheap! My intellect said no. I debated with myself for nearly an hour.

The first words were the hardest. *Dear God...I'm embarrassed to pray to You. I have no right to pray to You.*

At that moment, and for the first time in my life, I saw myself accurately. More importantly, I saw God accurately. His absolute holiness and my absolute dirtiness were as real as my inner pain. I realized that even in my happiest moments with Anna, I had been so miserably distant from Him that life seemed utterly hopeless.

Then I laid out my whole story to Him. It was undoubtedly the most sincere prayer I'd ever prayed. It had no pretense, no formality. I doubt if many of the words I muttered contained more than one syllable.

God's response wasn't a spoken message in my ear or a handwritten message on the wall. But as I waited, something happened in me. Forgiveness. Love. I suddenly knew that this great, pure, holy God loved me and forgave me. I wasn't hoping for forgiveness; I knew I was forgiven—then and there, for everything. I felt vacuumed, freshly painted, spring cleaned.

> My encounter with God that day was only the beginning. The pain didn't evaporate, which was good because the pain kept me on my knees. I never let go of God's hand. I'd wake up in the morning, make a long-distance call to Him, and never hang up. We stayed on the line together all day. The healing was phenomenal. In October I was Lazarus in the tomb, dead and gone, a stinking mess. By mid-January I had "come forth."

Your Response

How do you respond to what Rick said? Have you personally entered a relationship with Jesus Christ by accepting forgiveness for your sin and committing your life to Him? If you haven't, would you like to establish a relationship of oneness with God? It's yours if you put your faith in Him. His promise is, "Whoever hears my word and believes him who sent me has eternal life and will not be condemned; he has crossed over from death to life" (John 5:24).

If you long for this special love relationship with your Creator, I invite you to put your faith in Christ. Take a moment right now to pray and open your heart to Him. Confess your need for Him to cleanse you and give you a new life. He will come into your life and establish a relationship with you for all eternity (Revelation 3:20). You may want to pray a prayer similar to this:

> Lord Jesus, I need You. Thank You for dying on the cross for me. Enter my life and forgive my sins. Because You rose from the grave, I believe You will give me eternal life. I know You have answered my prayer and will make me the kind of person you want me to be.

Once you admit your sin to God, His forgiveness is immediate. At that instant God cleanses you from your sin and its penalty of eternal damnation. The sins God forgives are gone forever. Eternal life is His gift to you.

A Changed Life

Yes, God generously grants us forgiveness, but He also calls us to a change of behavior. At the same time that Jesus refused to condemn the woman caught in adultery, He also challenged her, "Go now and leave your life of sin" (John 8:11).

Furthermore, continuing to sin and then repeatedly claiming God's forgiveness will result in some serious personal problems. I like to illustrate this point with a block of wood, a handful of nails, and a hammer. You can pound nail after nail into the wood and then pull them out and throw them away. Obviously, after the nails are gone, the holes in the wood will remain, and the more nails you drive into the wood and pull out, the more scarred the wood becomes.

As you confess your sins, God forgives you, removes your sins, and throws them away. But each sin leaves an ugly scar, a nail hole, in your life. Physical, mental, emotional, and spiritual consequences will hinder God's building process in your life. Also, each disobedient act, even though it is forgiven, contributes to a habit pattern of negative behavior. The more often you commit an act, the more difficult that pattern is to break.

Though God's grace is great enough to cover a lifetime of sins, we must respectfully receive His forgiveness and seek to rid our lives of those sinful patterns of behavior. When we realize that His kindness has saved us from destruction and torment, our hearts respond with thanksgiving and a deepening desire to live a holy life.

The critical question is this: Do you love Him? Jesus said, "If you love me, you will obey what I command...Whoever has my commands and obeys them, he is the one who loves me. He who loves me will be loved by my Father, and I too will love him and show myself to him" (John 14:15,21).

If a person truly places his faith and trust in Jesus Christ and what He did for him on the cross, the Holy Spirit dwells inside that person. He, the Holy Spirit, is grieved when we sin (Ephesians 4:30). A person who recklessly and consistently goes about sinning shouldn't expect God to forgive and forget. This person really doesn't love Christ, nor does he have a clear picture of what God's love, grace, and forgiveness are all about.

David not only repented and confessed his sin to God, but he also asked God to cleanse him of his sin and renew his purity:

> Cleanse me with hyssop, and I will be clean; wash me, and I will be whiter than snow…Create in me a pure heart, O God, and renew a steadfast spirit within me. Do not cast me from your presence or take your Holy Spirit from me. Restore to me the joy of your salvation and grant me a willing spirit, to sustain me (Psalm 51:7,10-12).

Many people who attend my conferences and hear me talk about God's forgiveness have a hard time believing God can cleanse them. They write messages like this on their response cards: "It's too late for me to be forgiven." "I've been too bad for too long." "I believe God can forgive me for other sins, but I don't think He can forgive me for sins I keep committing."

For some reason, many people think some sins are worse than other sins. They feel that God isn't as willing to forgive the really bad ones as He is to forgive "lesser" sins like cheating, gossiping, or bursting out with angry words.

The Bible gives no indication that big sins are any worse than other sins. However, even if they were, 1 John 1:9 promises that God will purify us from all unrighteousness. The only qualification is faith. Whatever sins we confess, believing in God's promises, He forgives—no exemptions, no exclusions. Some sins may have more social or legal implications than other violations of God's law, but they are as "forgivable" and "cleansable" as any other ones.

No matter how badly you may have fouled up your life, the Lord Himself guarantees that He can clean up your life. Your regret must lead to repentance and confession—changing your mind about your sin and agreeing with God that it is wrong. Repenting means desiring for God to change you, making every effort to turn from past godlessness and choose obedience and purity. You need to develop a new pattern of thinking by letting God renew your mind (see Romans 12:2; Colossians 3:2).

Ask the Lord what He wants you to change in your life. Ask Him if He wants you to break up with someone you are seeing or find new friends who follow Christ. Do you have bad habits that need to be changed? Are you going places you know Christ would not want you to go? Are you looking at Internet sites or photos that are immoral? Pray for strength to turn from wrong decisions and behaviors.

Two Results of Forgiveness

David's confession and cleansing illustrate two attitudes that accompany accepting God's forgiveness. The first is an attitude of joy. Life brings no greater exhilaration than that of knowing that the sin that separated you from God has been cast away forever. David exulted, "My tongue will sing of your righteousness. O Lord, open my lips, and my mouth will declare your praise" (Psalm 51:14). Forgiveness of sin is reason enough to praise God for eternity.

Forgiveness also brings a humble attitude. The prophet Micah recognized the importance of humility in an individual's relationship with God: "What does the LORD require of you? To act justly and to love mercy and to walk humbly with your God" (Micah 6:8).

When you realize you're thinking or acting immorally, you don't need to drown yourself in regret or self-condemnation, but you should experience a genuine, humble sadness. This will accompany the process of confessing sin and accepting God's forgiveness. Paul wrote, "Godly sorrow brings repentance that leads to salvation and leaves no regret" (2 Corinthians 7:10).

Although this emotion may be painful, it is beneficial in order for you to change and to ward off similar temptations in the future.

Believe It!

Do you believe God still loves you despite the wrong choices in your past? Believe it—He does! Do you believe God can forgive you completely for what you have done? Believe it—He can and He will! As you conclude this chapter, put down the book and spend some time talking with God. Ask Him to shine His holy light into your heart. Make a list of the sins the Lord brings to your mind. Confess them in detail to Him. Admit to Him that you are wrong and He is right about what you have thought and done. Write 1 John 1:9 across the entire list and then destroy the list. Remember, the message of the cross of Christ is total forgiveness. Your sins are gone and forgotten. Believe Him. He never lies.

Then praise the Lord for forgiving and forgetting your sin and for placing infinity between you and your specific sins. The issue is now settled forever. You may continue to thank God for your forgiveness, but you never again need to ask God for forgiveness of the specific sins you have confessed to Him.

When we truly experience God's love and forgiveness in our lives, we are free to reconcile with those we may have hurt. Remember the situation I described in Blind Spot 3 when I purchased an antique lamp against Paula's wishes? I confessed to her my self-centeredness and sinful attitudes. She forgave me, and we continued to grow closer in our relationship. Well, some time later, I was really shocked—and excited—when Paula suggested we go to an antique auction. I tried hard not to show my surprise, but I about fell off my chair. She knew I would enjoy going to the auction, and she suggested it for my sake. We agreed, though, that we would discuss thoroughly any purchases before we made them. We had learned a great deal about each other—about giving, sharing personal likes and dislikes, and sacrificing for each other's happiness. We also learned how self-centeredness creates a real strain on a relationship, but humility draws people together.

Set Yourself and Others Free

A young woman lingered nervously at the outer edge of a group of people waiting to speak to me. I guessed that she wanted to talk with me, but she was waiting until all the other conference attendees had left.

When we were finally alone in the large auditorium, she introduced herself and got right to the point. "I've known Christ for several years," she began with a slight quiver in her voice. Small tears leaked from the corners of her eyes. "I'm a respected leader in the Christian organization that sponsored this conference. But I got involved with a man some months ago, and now I have a sexually transmitted disease. Nobody knows except my doctor… and you."

I'll never forget the pain in her voice.

In my efforts to comfort and encourage her, I talked to her about the importance of confessing her failure to God and accepting His forgiveness. She assured me that she had done so, yet obviously something else troubled her deeply. So I kept probing with questions.

Finally, after several minutes, she tearfully blurted out her deepest pain. "I know God has forgiven me, but after what I've done I don't deserve a decent man. And I can't bear the thought of living the rest of my life alone."

My heart hurt for her. She felt her life was in a shambles and no quality man would ever want her. Her heart was broken over the prospect of a lonely future.

Unfortunately, her experience illustrates the inner struggle of countless people who have relationship regrets. Engaging in premarital sex or pushing the limits of your purity has deep consequences that will last for years and will leave you struggling to gain back a sense of purity.

Yes, the grace of God forgives when people truly confess their sins. God forgives those who humble themselves before Him. However, people often struggle to feel liberated from their rebellion. They may understand *God's* ability and willingness to forgive them, but they seem neither able nor willing to forgive *themselves*.

When I speak at conferences about relationship regret, the audience will inevitably include a few who are carrying a heartbreaking load of guilt and want to be free from their past. They are usually so embarrassed about their problems that they feel ashamed and contrite about their wayward decisions. When I listen to these individuals share their stories, I rejoice in the way they have come back to the Lord, but I also empathize with their struggle to free themselves from their mistakes.

This second bright spot in your relationships is often more difficult to accomplish than the first. For some reason we have little problem with God's part in granting forgiveness. God's love for us is so deeply ingrained in our hearts that we believe He is capable of forgiving us. He is sovereign, gracious, and omnipotent.

We're also all too aware that we are imperfect and prone to wander away from the Lord. I often hear people say, "I'm glad God has forgiven me, but I can't forgive myself."

Punishment

You may be unwilling to forgive yourself for sin, especially sexual sin, for several reasons. First, you may feel you still deserve punishment for what you've done. You know your moral failure was a violation of God's law, and even though you have accepted His forgiveness, you still feel guilty. Or you feel obligated to pay for your actions. The woman mentioned earlier was denying herself the possibility of ever marrying a "decent man." The perceived loss of a future "decent man" was her way of dealing with her guilt.

Punishing yourself is a futile attempt to clear your conscience. If you want to earn your standing with God, you must be absolutely perfect—and your rebellious nature has already proved you're not. The punishment for even the slightest deviation from God's standard of perfection is death—complete separation from God. It's a case of all or nothing. No other punishment will do the job.

Now, if you are a Christian, God has already accepted you eternally, and He won't let you go. You can't pay any part of the price for your sin. You need to realize that the entire penalty already has been paid. Christ's death on the cross, in your place, covered all your sins—past, present and future. You can add nothing to His provision, so why not stop trying—and start forgiving yourself? Simply accept His gift.

I Don't Deserve This

A second reason you may have difficulty forgiving yourself is that you don't feel you deserve forgiveness. You may be thinking, *I wasn't tricked into wrong moral choice*s or *I knew I was opening myself up for trouble.* Perhaps you recognized the point at which a romantic evening started becoming more passionate than you had planned, but you didn't do anything to stop it. Now you're having trouble forgiving yourself for an intentional sin.

The solution to this bewilderment is that 1 John 1:9 makes no distinction between intentional and unintentional sins. As we've discussed previously, you are ultimately responsible for what you do. Whether you meant to fall into your sexual sin makes no difference. God has promised to respond to your confession of sin by purifying you from all unrighteousness.

Yes, you must deal with your tendency to put yourself in

compromising positions. That's what the remaining five Bright Spots will help you do. In the meantime, you must accept the fact that sin is sin and that God has forgiven you from all of it. On that basis, you deserve to forgive yourself.

Third, you may not be ready to forgive yourself for your sin because you're convinced you will repeat it. "I know I'm weak in this area," you say, "and I'll probably fall again in the future. How can I forgive myself for something I know I'll do again and again?"

Beware: This argument for not forgiving yourself is often an excuse to continue to sin. You're right—you aren't perfect, and you sin in thought, word, and deed every day. But that's no reason to yield to sin and ignore God's gift of forgiveness. God's grace and power are available every day too. Jeremiah the prophet states, "Because of the LORD's great love we are not consumed, for his compassions never fail. They are new every morning; great is your faithfulness" (Lamentations 3:22-23).

How to Forgive Yourself

1. Remember that forgiving yourself is only a *response* to God's great compassion and faithfulness. He has already made the way for you to accept His forgiveness. Your response helps you embrace the freedom He wants to give you.
2. Confess your sins to Him each day to keep yourself accountable and to keep your mind in check with God's standards for your life. Remind yourself that you cheapen God's grace when you think of Him only as a one-stop shop for forgiveness regardless of what you do.
3. Determine daily to walk in obedience and purity, and ask God for the strength to do so.
4. When you slip, don't wallow in your sin just because you fell again. Instead, take advantage of God's grace. Confess again, immediately pick yourself up, and trust the Holy Spirit to give you the power to keep growing toward maturity.

His Forgiveness Is Enough

If you have experienced God's forgiveness, but you fail to forgive yourself, you are telling God that His forgiveness is not enough. Think about it. By not forgiving yourself you are saying, "Nice try, God, but You don't realize how bad I am. You have forgiven me, but that's not enough to cover my sin." It's a pretty serious charge to accuse God that He doesn't know what He's doing or that the death of His Son—the supreme sacrifice—wasn't enough for your sin. In effect, that's what you do when you refuse to confirm His forgiveness by forgiving yourself.

When you forgive yourself, you simply participate in and affirm what God has already done. God's activity concerning our sin is beautifully summarized in the New Testament book of Hebrews, which quotes from the Old Testament prophecy of Jeremiah: "'Their sins and lawless acts I will remember no more.' And where these have been forgiven, there is no longer any sacrifice for sin" (Hebrews 10:17-18).

At the moment you confess your sin to God, two wonderful things happen simultaneously: He forgives it, and He forgets it. When we human beings talk about forgetting something, we refer to a lapse of memory, but Almighty God is not like that. He doesn't suffer from any lapses of memory. Nothing inadvertently slips His mind. God can only forget something on purpose, not by accident.

That's what He has done with your confessed sin. He has consciously and purposefully willed to forgive it and forget it—and anything God wills to do gets done. So your sin is completely and eternally blotted from His memory. "I, even I, am he who blots out your transgressions, for my own sake, and remembers your sins no more" (Isaiah 43:25). The Old Testament gives several other picturesque descriptions that help us understand why God can never remember what He has forgiven and forgotten:

Job claimed, "My offenses will be sealed up in a bag; you will cover over my sin" (Job 14:17).

Isaiah wrote, "You have put all my sins behind your back" (Isaiah 38:17).

What a mystery! The God who sees everything has purposely placed your sins in a place where He can no longer see them. The Lord also said through Isaiah, "I have swept away your offenses like a cloud, your sins like the morning mist" (Isaiah 44:22). Just as the morning sun burns the fog away, the warmth of God's love and forgiveness have utterly evaporated your sins. Micah closed his prophetic message with these words of encouragement: "You [God] will tread our sins underfoot and hurl all our iniquities into the depths of the sea" (Micah 7:19).

Consider the vast, completed work of God's forgetfulness! It challenges us with beautiful freedom: "Blessed are they whose transgressions are forgiven, whose sins are covered. Blessed is the man whose sin the Lord will never count against him" (Romans 4:7-8). In other words, God has forgiven and purposely forgotten your confessed sins forever. You are truly blessed. Allow the Lord to liberate you!

Remembering God's Goodness
(Luke, age 25, is a U.S. military serviceman.)

Guys aren't supposed to cry. At least that's what I'd been brought up to believe. But when it happens to you, it's a different story.

For weeks I argued with myself, trying to convince myself that breaking up was a mistake. On paper, the two of us were perfect for each other. Strong Christians, similar senses of humor, smart—similarities even down to having the same future goals. For all those reasons, I tried to convince myself that we still belonged together. Maybe a little time and space would be enough to fix things. But I was trying to make it work, and someone else was letting me down. The bitterness began to grow.

Months down the line, God began working on my heart through a series of events. I began to realize my bitterness at the failure of the relationship and just how much of an impact it was having on my life. I was stuck in the past instead of living in the present. I prayed about it and wrote a letter to my former girlfriend, apologizing for my bitterness and for holding the failure of the relationship against her. But deep in the back of my mind, I still felt that now that we had cleared the air, things may be ripe to start again. I was comfortable, we were already very close, and with a little work on my part, maybe this was the best I could hope for in a relationship. How wrong I was.

God has a funny way of showing us the error of our ways. The same time I was dealing with the relationship issues, God began really working on me. Through a couple of Christian authors, I began to realize that God was not a God of the past. He didn't want us stuck there, bound mentally and spiritually by the hurt of lost relationships. God wanted to heal my pain and restore the joy in my heart. I began to realize that the relationship failed because we live in a sinful world.

The business of life, our own sin, and our selfishness (well, mine at least) all were the true factors in the breakup. Not God. This is important: God does not desire for men or women to be hurt. God wants to heal the damage done by our sinful natures and the fallen world around us. He even promises it in Romans 8:28, "And we know that in all things God works for the good of those who love him, who have been called according to his purpose." Not some things, not most things, but *all* things. In my narrow view of the events going on around me, I never stopped to think that this could actually be a good thing. I had forgotten the goodness of God.

As I began taking in all these lessons and learning more and more about the goodness and faithfulness of God, I began to not be as concerned about the breakup or finding the next date. I knew that God had done so much good in my life already that the breakup was for the best. I had learned so much about myself and God through the process that I could finally understand the reason for the breakup. God had turned that painful experience into a valuable lesson and in the process had healed the pain.

The best part now is looking back to when I thought the relationship I was in was as good as it was going to get. And now, seeing where God has brought me in both a relationship with Him and with my new fiancée, I realize I had no idea what I was missing.

Walking in the Freedom of Forgiveness

The theology of God's forgiveness is clear in Scripture, and the importance of affirming God's forgiveness by forging ahead is certainly implied in Scripture. Now, how do we do that? Where is the bridge that leads from the fruitless pall of personal unforgiveness to the freedom of walking out from under that cloud? The key to walking in the freedom of forgiveness is more in what you know than in what you do. When you get a firm grasp on the following two basic truths about yourself as a Christian, you will find your problems with self-forgiveness will begin to disappear.

1. Know That You Are Accepted in Christ

No phrase in Scripture defines who you are as a Christian more completely or concisely than the two words "in Christ." Paul used the phrases "in Christ," "in the Lord," or "in Him" 133 times in his letters. The phrase means that as a believer in the Lord Jesus Christ, you are always intimately one with Him. Nothing about you is outside of Christ. Since you have accepted Christ by faith, He has completely accepted you.

You may be wondering, *How can someone like me, who has a history of moral impurity and still suffers temptation to moral failure, be accepted in Christ?* The answer is that God offers us total forgiveness. It's part of being in Christ.

Paul wrote, "In him we have redemption through his blood, the forgiveness of sins"(Ephesians 1:7). If you weren't forgiven, you couldn't be in Christ. The resounding message of the New Testament, especially Paul's writings, is that your faith in Christ has solved your sin problem once and for all, and you are accepted "in the One he loves" (verse 6).

Study the book of Ephesians carefully and write down all the wonderful things that are true of you because you are in Christ. The more Christ's unconditional love works in you, the easier it will be for you to accept and forgive yourself.

2. Know That You Are Being Transformed by the Holy Spirit

Paul paints a vivid contrast between the individual controlled by sin and the individual who is in Christ:

> Do not be deceived: Neither the sexually immoral nor idolaters nor adulterers nor male prostitutes nor homosexual offenders nor thieves nor the greedy nor drunkards nor slanderers nor swindlers will inherit the kingdom of God. And that is what some of you were. But you were washed, you were sanctified, you were justified in the name of the Lord Jesus Christ and by the Spirit of our God (1 Corinthians 6:9-11).

Your history as a sinner may not be as sordid as Paul's description (or maybe it is), but before you met Christ, God considered you dead in your sin, devoid of any spiritual life. You were a living dead person. When you placed your faith in Christ at salvation, God placed you into Christ, and through the working of the Holy Spirit, He placed Christ in you. Jesus came in to give you spiritual life and to transform you inwardly.

Being placed into Christ was instantaneous and complete. You can't ever be in Christ any more than you were at the moment of salvation. That's why He completely accepts you.

On the other hand, the transforming work of Christ in you through the Holy Spirit is a lifelong process. As you follow Christ day by day, week by week, month by month, and year by year, you are being changed inside (2 Corinthians 3:18). Your old sinful habits are giving way to new patterns of righteous behavior. Your old thoughts are being replaced by thoughts of kindness, love, faith, and hope.

If Only

One of Satan's greatest ploys is to trick you into living in the past instead of enjoying the present and growing into the future. If he can keep you discouraged and dejected about your failures in the past—both before and since becoming a Christian—he can impede the transformation process the Holy Spirit is affecting in you. For example, as you think about the sins you have committed and confessed, Satan can drag you into thinking *if only...*

"If only I had been a stronger Christian."

"If only my parents had been stricter with me."

"If only I had read the Bible and prayed more instead of spending so much time reading all those other books, magazines, and romance novels and going to those Internet sites."

"If only we hadn't gone to that romantic place alone."

"If only I hadn't listened to my friends...I mean my ex-friends."

You can't change or relive your past, so why try? Your past is history. It's beyond the transforming activity of the Holy Spirit. Use the memories as lessons to help you grow today and tomorrow. Allow your failures to reveal blind spots you need to change to Bright Spots with prayer and perhaps professional counseling. Use your unpleasant memories of places you got into trouble as warning signs to keep you away from those places in the future. Let your bad experiences with certain people coach you about the right kind of people you want to hang out with.

And, of course, be thankful for time. Time has a way of erasing the bad memories as you choose not to dwell on them. Your memory is similar to a river. As more water runs into the river from its tributaries, it becomes deeper and wider. So it is with our thoughts and memories. The more you mull over the details of what happened in the past, the deeper you ingrain those events in your memory. You must cut off that river of memory by choosing not to think about those events. Create a new river by thinking about positive events.

Whenever you feel guilty about the failures you have already confessed to God, use that feeling as a way to praise the Lord instead. Rather than cowering under false condemnation, begin to thank God confidently that He has forever forgiven and forgotten those sins. Get alone and praise God aloud for forgiveness. Or meet with a trusted Christian friend and ask him or her to join you in putting guilt to flight through praise and thanksgiving.

Satan not only uses our past to trip us up, but he also uses the temptations of the present to stunt our spiritual growth. Whenever you feel lonely or are being tempted toward evil thoughts or deeds, spend some time affirming your identity in Christ. Say aloud, "I am in Christ and I am completely accepted by God. I am a changed person through Christ's transforming work in me by the Holy Spirit."

Make Changes That Make You Wealthy

A few years ago a front-page story in a Dallas newspaper captivated me. It told about a man who attended an exhibition of beautiful rocks and gems. The man walked up and down the rows of displays until he came to a small box of rocks on a table. A sign advertised that the rocks in the box were $15 apiece. The man rummaged through the box until his eyes fell upon one particular rock. "I'll give you ten dollars for this one," he said to the man behind the table.

"Well, business has been a little slow today," the proprietor replied. "Sure, you can have it for ten bucks."

The man paid for the rock, walked outside the building, and gave a shriek of joy.

He was a gemologist—an expert in precious gems. The rock he had purchased for ten dollars was a star sapphire...the largest star sapphire ever discovered in America, worth 2.5 million dollars!

I've often wondered how the proprietor felt when he read the story in the newspaper. He didn't realize what great value was hiding in his box of rocks. He was a millionaire and didn't even know it! He must have been shocked and heartbroken when he learned that the rock he had sold for ten dollars was worth a fortune.

Our Riches in Christ

A lot of Christians are like that man with the box of rocks. We have the most valuable possessions in the entire world, things that no amount of money can buy: the riches of God He has given those who believe in Him. Yet we often live like spiritual paupers, like people who have very little. We see our weaknesses, our failures, and our sins, and we think, *I'll never be what God wants me to be. I don't have what it takes to live a life of joy and fulfillment. I'll never change.*

Wrong! You are a spiritual billionaire—you just don't know it yet! Your life can change for the better because you have God's riches at your disposal. The secret to success is learning how to get God's wealth at work in you. You can successfully change your blind spots into bright spots when you realize that God has already equipped you with everything you need to do so.

To understand what God has done for us and provided for us, look at these incredible words from the pen of the apostle Paul: "Praise be to the God and Father of our Lord Jesus Christ, who has blessed us…with every spiritual blessing in Christ" (Ephesians 1:3). Paul doesn't say that God *will* bless us, or that He is blessing us *now*, but that He *has* blessed us. It's past tense; it has already happened. God has already blessed you with every spiritual blessing and resource for a successful, pure life.

You may be thinking, *Wait a minute—I don't feel blessed. I have problems. I stumble around. I do the wrong things. And I have trouble doing the things God wants me to do. Maybe I was absent the day God passed out these blessings.*

The key to understanding our spiritual blessings is in the prepositional phrase "in Christ." That's where our spiritual blessings reside. They are reserved for us in heaven in the person of Jesus Christ. If we are in Christ, and God's blessings are in Christ, then God's blessings are available to us because they're all inside that same relationship.

You must understand that everything I'm talking about here is directed to people who are in Christ, those who have committed their lives to Jesus Christ, who have personally put their faith in His death and resurrection. If you are not in Jesus Christ, the wealth of His spiritual blessings is not accessible to you. You need to be *in Him* to receive His blessings.

The secret of the successful Christian life of joy and fulfillment is wrapped up in one word: *faith.* Faith appropriates God's blessings in Christ, which are already reserved and waiting for you, and brings them into your daily walk. God's wealth already belongs to you. If you want to know how wealthy you are in Him, look at what Paul says in Ephesians 1:3-14:

> Praise be to the God and Father of our Lord Jesus Christ, who has blessed us in the heavenly realms with every spiritual blessing in Christ. For he chose us in him before the creation of the world to be holy and blameless in his sight. In love he predestined us to be adopted as his sons through Jesus Christ, in accordance with his pleasure and will—to the praise of his glorious grace, which he has freely given us in the One he loves. In him we have redemption through his blood, the forgiveness of sins, in accordance with the riches of God's grace that he lavished on us with all wisdom and understanding. And he made known to us the mystery of his will according to his good pleasure, which he purposed in Christ, to be put into effect when the times will have reached their fulfillment—to bring all things in heaven and on earth together under one head, even Christ.
>
> In him we were also chosen, having been predestined according to the plan of him who works out everything in conformity with the purpose of his will, in order that we, who were the first to hope in Christ, might be for the praise of his glory. And you also were included in Christ when you heard the word of truth, the gospel of your salvation. Having believed, you were marked in him with a seal, the promised Holy Spirit, who is a deposit guaranteeing our inheritance until the redemption of those who are God's possession—to the praise of his glory.

All these blessings became yours the moment you received Jesus Christ, regardless of how you feel. You just need to reach out and take them.

Paul's prayer for the Ephesians reveals the key to appropriating God's wealth into your daily walk: "I keep asking that the God of our Lord Jesus Christ, the glorious Father, may give you the Spirit of wisdom and revelation, so that you may know him better" (Ephesians 1:17).

Notice the two things Paul prayed for. First, Paul wanted the Ephesians to have a spirit of revelation. That means he wanted their minds opened to things about God they had never seen before.

What did Paul want the Ephesians to see? That which would help them "know Him better." The Greek word translated in English as "know" means "full knowledge." Paul was literally praying, "Lord, fill their minds with everything a human being can possibly know about You." *Wow!* Couldn't you live victoriously if you knew all you could know about God? That's what God's revelation can do.

Second, Paul prayed that God would give the Ephesians a spirit of wisdom. Wisdom is putting into practice all we know about God. Full knowledge of God is useless without the wisdom to know how to act on what we know. Have you seen those cartoon caricatures artists draw of people showing them with huge heads and tiny bodies? God doesn't want us out of proportion like that, our heads filled with knowledge while our actions are selfish and immature. Getting God's wealth into your walk is a balanced combination of revelation and wisdom, growing in your knowledge of God and in your godly actions.

Paul continued his prayer:

"I pray also that the eyes of your heart may be enlightened in order that you may know the hope to which he has called you, the riches of his glorious inheritance in the saints"(Ephesians 1:18).

Paul pinpoints three specific actions you can take to transfer God's wealth into your personal walk. As you make these three positive moves, you will experience power for permanent changes in your life and relationships.

Action 1: Settle Your Future

Paul prays that the Ephesians will "know the hope to which he has called" them. But he isn't using the word *hope* the way we often use it. We say, "I'm planning to play tennis, so I hope it doesn't rain," or "I hope it snows so I can go skiing," or "I hope our team wins the championship." That kind of hope is merely wishful thinking.

The kind of hope Paul prayed for each believer to have is the settled assurance that something you have yet to see is going to happen. For example, we read the words, "In all things God works for the good of those who love him, who have been called according to his purpose" (Romans 8:28). Notice that the verse doesn't say all things are good. It says that all things *work* for your good. That verse requires hope. You may not be able to see any good in a broken love relationship, but hope can see beyond the painful disappointment to the good that God will bring out of it. Nothing is good about a sinful activity that fills you with regret. But the hope to which God calls you sees beyond your failure to the good that He has promised to bring out of it after you have turned it over to Him.

Notice also that this verse doesn't apply to everyone in the world. It only applies to those who love God. God will take all the events and experiences that have taken place in your life and work them out for your good. Even with your blind spots and selfish actions, God can work them out for good in your life if you truly love Him and seek to do His will.

You can exercise hope even in bad situations because God has a purpose for you. Notice the next verse: "For those God foreknew he also predestined to be conformed to the likeness of his Son, that he might be the firstborn among many brothers" (Romans 8:29).

What is God's purpose for those who love Him, those He foreknew? To mold them into the image of Jesus Christ, to produce Christ's character in them—and He aims to keep up the process until it is completed (Philippians 1:6).

John the apostle wrote these words, which are filled with hope: "Dear friends, now we are children of God, and what we will be has not yet been made known. But we know that when he appears, we shall be like him, for we shall see him as he is" (1 John 3:2).

As we follow Christ, we become just like Him. Our attitudes, our actions, our character are conformed to His. That's God's purpose for us, and that's why we can continue to have hope even in the darkest circumstances.

Let me illustrate hope another way. A friend of yours recommends you see a certain movie. "It's an unbelievable thriller," he says. "All I will tell you is that the hero gets the girl at the end of the movie."

So you go to see the movie. It's tense and exciting. The bad guys are shooting at the hero, and the good guy gets hit. Blood is everywhere, and it looks like it's over for him. The audience is tense, but you're relaxed because you know the end of the story. Your friend said that the hero gets the girl, so you know the good guy is going to live.

Then another bunch of the bad guys kidnap the girl and threaten to blow up a city or the world if they don't get the ransom money. The countdown to the potential fateful calamity is quickly approaching the critical point, and the girl is squirming to escape out of her imprisonment. Everybody in the theater is filled with tension—except you. Why? Because you know how it turns out, so you just sit there waiting to see how she's going to survive.

Your life is a lot like that movie. You go through problems, disappointments and tough times, and you experience temptations and regrets. People tell you one thing and do just the opposite. You get confused in the pressure and turmoil—but you know the end of the story. God is working out His purpose by reproducing the image of Jesus Christ in you. That kind of hope can help you settle your future. You can relax—God is in control.

No wonder Paul could write from a Roman prison, "Rejoice in the Lord always. I will say it again: Rejoice!" (Philippians 4:4). We are tempted to say, "Paul, are you crazy? You're in prison. If something doesn't happen soon, you're going to die there."

Paul replies, "You don't understand. Prison is not the issue. God's will for my life is the issue. God is working through my circumstances to make me like Christ."

That's the settled, confident hope you need to face the future. Regardless of what confronts you, God is making you like Jesus. He is fulfilling His purpose in you. You can either help Him in the process or drag your feet by questioning your circumstances and doubting that He can get you through them.

When I was single, I had a problem trusting God for the future. I wanted to get married, but I didn't have any prospects. I also knew that when I found someone I liked, I should wait six months to a year before getting engaged. Then I figured I'd be engaged at least six months before getting married. Occasionally, I would get very discouraged. *It's not fair,* I thought. *I'm getting older by the minute, and I'm still at least a year and a half to two years away from getting married. I don't even have a woman I'm interested in.*

Then I began to think about Christ. He knew what I was going through. He died at age 33 as a single man, but His life was anything but a failure. I experienced tremendous joy in the middle of my struggle as I realized I wasn't alone. God had my future under His control. He had a purpose for my life that far exceeded my temporal concern about marriage. I determined to cooperate with God's purpose of making me like Christ. I would walk in faith and let God do what He wanted in my life to produce the character of Christ in me. I was ready to take on anything because my future was settled. I knew the end of the story.

Action 2: Value Your Worth

Paul also prayed that the Ephesians would know "the riches of His glorious inheritance in the saints." We know from Paul's letter to the Christians at Rome that we have inherited eternal life, heaven, and many other blessings from God by becoming co-heirs with Christ through faith. However, this second part of Paul's prayer in Ephesians 1:18 is not talking about our inheritance; it's talking about God's inheritance.

What is God's inheritance? It's "in the saints." I used to think a saint was a big stone figure of some deeply religious person who lived back in the Middle Ages. According to the Bible, every Christian, past and present, is a saint (a "holy one"). Paul addressed many of his letters to the people in the churches with the words "To the saints…" If you have received Jesus Christ personally, God considers you a saint.

So what is God's inheritance? You and me! Before we were in Jesus Christ, we were lost. God was our Creator, but He was not yet our Father because we were slaves to sin. Because of the death and resurrection of Jesus Christ and our faith in Him, we became the children of God (John 1:12). Thanks to the life and work of Christ, God has inherited everyone who comes to Him through faith in Christ. Don't you feel special knowing that you are God's inheritance?

I was seven years old when I opened my life to Jesus Christ. I often have imagined what the scene in heaven must have been that day. Here is an angel romping around the golden streets in purity and perfection, having a great day as usual. Suddenly, he looks down and sees this seven-year-old kid folding his hands, bowing his head, and asking Christ to come into his life. The angel turns to another angel and says, "Oh, no…look who's coming into God's family now. It's that little Purnell kid. It's going to be a job keeping him on the right path. This means double overtime for all of us."

The angel in my imagination was right. During the years

following my decision, I struggled as a growing Christian. I was always doing the wrong thing at the wrong time for the wrong reasons. I was a hypocrite much of the time. I'd promise God, "I'm going to live for You, God," and I'd do it—for almost 15 minutes.

I often thought, *When I get to heaven I only want to ask God one question: "Why did you ever put up with me?"*

God will simply reply, "Because you're My child, My pride and joy, My inheritance."

Why God feels that way about me is beyond my understanding, but I'm certainly glad He does. If you are in Christ, you are of great value to God. You are His inheritance, His treasure. You have some great prospects for change and growth in your life because you are extremely valuable to God, and God takes care of what belongs to Him. He is even more interested in your development as a person of integrity and purity than you are. What's more, He has what it takes to mold you into the person He wants you to become.

If we are so valuable to God, why do we have so many problems with self-acceptance and self-esteem? I can think of three reasons.

First, we have a misconception of God. We think God is a big ogre in the sky who is against fun and happiness. We picture Him hovering over us with a baseball bat. As soon as we smile or start having fun—*wham!*—He hits us with something bad. "I knew it," we say. "God's out to get me."

We feel God doesn't like us very much and that He's just waiting to punish us, but that's not the scriptural picture of God at all. Jesus showed us the Father's heart when He invited Himself to the home of Zaccheus (a shady businessman) and celebrated with him and his friends. He protected a woman who was caught in adultery and who faced an angry mob of religious accusers. He welcomed children into His arms. He bypassed unnecessary cultural regulations by healing people whenever they came to Him—even on a Sabbath. He even provided the wine for a wedding party! Clearly, God wants us to enjoy life with Him!

Second, we have problems with our self-worth because we compare ourselves with others. We say, *Lord, look at this body of mine. I wish I looked like that attractive person.* We wish we had another person's talents, abilities, personality, money, prestige, or a hundred other things that we envy.

What we're really saying is, *God, You need a little counseling. You messed up when You made me. Let me tell You where You went wrong.* God didn't make a mistake when He made you. You are so absolutely special to God that when He made you, He threw away the mold. God doesn't make clones. No one in the world is like you; never has been, never will be. Don't compare yourself with anyone else—you are incomparable! That's how privileged you are as God's unique creation.

Third, we struggle with our self-worth because of our past sins. You got yourself into trouble. You asked God to forgive you, and He did. Yet every time you try to do something for God, or think about studying your Bible, or think about talking to somebody about Jesus Christ, past failures flood your mind.

Remember what you did two years ago? you think as your feelings taunt you. *You've even repeated it several times since. You'll never amount to anything.* We end up believing the lies of Satan and relegating ourselves to being second-class Christians.

When you feel put down because of your past sins, remember that God's royal blood is flowing through your veins. Jesus Christ spilled His blood to forgive your sins and present you to the Father as His inheritance. Yes, we must walk in humility before Him because we don't deserve His grace. At the same time, though, we can also walk in confidence and strength because God values us as His children, His "glorious inheritance."

Action 3: Believe God for His Power to Change Your Life

Paul's third point in this prayer is in verse 19: that we would know God's "incomparably great power for us who believe. That power is like the working of his mighty strength." This is a power-packed verse—the only verse in the New Testament that contains the three major Greek words for *power*. Paul introduces these words by calling God's power "incomparably great." The Greek for this phrase literally means to "throw an object over a barrier." Paul uses it here to convey that God's power is so great that it goes beyond any limitation or barrier in the universe. God's power is greater than any obstacle in your life.

Paul's first word for *power* in this verse is the Greek *dunamis*, from which we get our English word *dynamite*. God's power is explosive; nothing can stand in its way. "Working" comes from the Greek word from which we get our word *energy*. It means never-ending action. God's incredible, explosive power keeps energizing us day after day to get us past our limitations and change us into the image of Jesus Christ. The other two Greek words, translated as "mighty" and "strength," also describe God's great power.

I think at this point Paul is getting tongue-tied on the subject of God's power. He's exhausted even his vocabulary defining the word power, so he continues by describing how God's power is displayed in the world. God demonstrated His power when...

> He [God] raised him [Christ] from the dead and seated him at his right hand in the heavenly realms, far above all rule and authority, power and dominion, and every title that can be given, not only in the present age but also in the one to come. And God placed all things under his feet and appointed him to be head over everything for the church, which is his body, the fullness of him who fills everything in every way (Ephesians 1:20-23).

First, God's power is so great that it raised Christ from the dead. I think God used more power to raise Christ from the dead than He did to create the universe. When God created everything, He had nothing opposing Him. God just spoke and the universe came into existence (Psalm 33:6-9). When God raised Christ from the grave, He faced a lot of opposition. The Roman Empire and the Jewish religious leaders did everything they could to keep Christ locked in the tomb. Satan and all his cohorts did all they could to make sure Jesus stayed dead. Yet God broke the opposition like you or I snap a toothpick in two.

Second, God's power is so great that it brought Christ back into heaven! That is called the ascension. Think of the thunderous boosters and gallons of fuel needed to lift the space shuttle and its astronauts into orbit. Yet God's power lifted Jesus Christ to the highest heavens in an instant without any earthly assistance.

Third, God's power is so great that it placed everything in the universe under the feet of Jesus Christ. All authority, power, and dominion are under His control. Every person—including you and me—every problem, every nation, and every planet are under His feet. He has authority and rulership over all.

You get the idea from Paul's description that God has a lot of power! And here's the best news of all: God's great, explosive, never-ending, supreme power is available to everyone who believes in Christ. Regardless of who you are or what your background or nationality is, regardless of your limitations, God's power is available to help you overcome your past, your problems, your limitations, and your mistakes. In whatever disadvantages you have experienced or are experiencing, God's power is available to change your life. If you have trusted Jesus Christ with your life, you can rise above your weaknesses, limitations and circumstances. You have the greatest power in the universe within you. Tap into this dynamic resource and expect God's power to do great things in your life.

Depending on God

As you can see from these three guidelines, you have a lot going for you as God's child—but don't let it go to your head. Being proud, self-assured, and overconfident is as counterproductive to growth and change as is failing to come to terms with your future, your worth, or God's power in your life.

This lesson was brought home to me in a frightening way when I was 28 and still single. At the time I was assistant director of Asian ministries for Campus Crusade for Christ, working with leaders who were trying to reach people for Christ. I was near the end of a five-month trip through 27 countries of Asia, Africa, and Europe. I had climbed on a plane an average of once every three days during the five months, and by the time I reached my last stop, Manila, I was exhausted.

One evening at dusk, I was walking back to my hotel room when a gorgeous woman appeared from between two buildings. She walked up to me, grabbed my hand, and said, "Do you want to have a good time tonight?" I had never talked to a prostitute before. I always thought they would be ugly, but this woman was a beauty! I should have pulled away immediately, but I froze.

The woman noticed my hesitancy and took a firmer grip on my arm. "Hey, there's a taxi. Let's go. My husband's not around. We'll have a great time."

You talk about a battle raging inside! I hadn't had a date or an in-depth conversation with a woman for five months. I was tired and lonely, and I wanted a woman to care for me and treat me tenderly. This was the strongest temptation to moral impurity I had ever faced. I knew in my heart that giving in wouldn't be right, but I was unnerved and immobilized. I couldn't say yes, but I hesitated to say no.

When the woman tugged me toward the taxi, I finally snapped back to reality. "No, I can't," I said just above a whisper. She yanked on my arm again, and I blurted out, "I can't go with you because I know Jesus."

Suddenly she dropped my arm and took two steps back. "Are you a priest?" she demanded, her eyes filled with horror.

"No," I answered, my courage rising, "but I'm a Christian, and I know Jesus Christ."

Then, with considerably greater courage, I shouted out, "I know Jesus Christ!" The woman was so shocked that she took off running down the street. When I returned to my hotel room, I got down on my knees beside my bed and cried. I had come so close to giving in. No one ever would have known except me—and God. His power gave me courage to resist the evil confronting me.

We walk in a fallen world. Your world is not interested in building you up or strengthening your moral integrity. It will tear you down every chance it gets. Will you let it? No one else will decide for you.

Will you apply God's wealth to your walk and take advantage of God's power for positive change in your life? Only as you step toward positive changes in these ways will you step away from the negative thoughts and behavior that the world, the flesh, and the devil beckon you to embrace.

Settle your future.

Value your worth.

Believe God for His power in your life.

Because you are in God's family, you have all of His riches as your inheritance. Faith unlocks the treasures of heaven. You are a child of the King of kings. Royal blood is flowing through your veins.

My friend Steve put it this way, "Since my Father is the richest Person in the universe, I want to live like a rich man's son!" How about you?

Wounds with Staying Power

Sometimes, as intent as you are to forget your past, you may still be hurting from emotional and spiritual wounds resulting from your sin. Keeping your wounds in perspective—God's perspective—is important. Being free to love again requires being able to see why those wounds are there. Consider these reasons God may be allowing a wound to remain in your life:

1. *Our wounds drive us to Christ, the Wounded Healer.* God's purpose in our lives is to work everything out for good so that we are conformed to the image of Christ. Sometimes, though, when things are not going too smoothly, we forget God's purpose for us, and we fail to cooperate with His goal of making us like Christ. If we didn't have wounds, we wouldn't need God…and we'd go straight to hell. But when we're hurting, we run back to God. Have you ever noticed that you pray more when things are going wrong? I thank God for the wounds still in my life. Yes, my sins have produced some of those wounds, but the consequences of those wrong choices drove me to God, and all things are working together for His good in my life.

2. *Our wounds drive us to each other.* Wounded people need one other. If we didn't hurt, we wouldn't need each other, and we would be the loneliest creatures on earth. Instead, our wounds drive us to each other for comfort, counseling, encouragement, and help.

3. *Our wounds make us more sensitive to other wounded people.* If you ever have been deeply hurt in a relationship, or have gotten involved in things that were wrong, and God has brought you out of them, you're more sensitive to others in a similar boat. Furthermore, you have learned to accept God's forgiveness, forgive yourself, guard your mind, and dissolve immoral relationships. You're equipped with compassion and experience to help someone who's struggling in this area.

4. *Our wounds glorify God.* Christ and His disciples approached a blind man, and His disciples asked, "Who sinned, this man or his parents, that he was born blind?" (John 9:1). Jesus replied that the man's blindness wasn't his fault or his parents' fault. Instead, it was an occasion through which God would be glorified. Sometimes we don't know why we have wounds. We ask God, *Why this? Why me? Why now?* but we don't seem to get an answer. Our great comfort is to know that God will use our wounds to glorify Himself. I don't fully understand what Jesus meant by His statement, but I can trust that He knows what He's doing even when I don't.

5. *Our wounds help us trust Christ more.* My little daughter, Rachel, came to me once and asked, "Daddy, can we have a horse?" Our backyard at the time was so small that the sprinkler hit all four corners at once. But Rachel, in her childish innocence, wanted to put a horse back there. I could have gotten angry at her for her impractical idea. I could have recited all the logical reasons: The yard is too small; the law doesn't allow horses in our city; we can't afford to board a horse. However, although she was a child and was unable to understand my reasons, I still wanted her to keep coming to me with her desires and questions. So I simply said, "Rachel, I love you, and I would love to give you a horse, but we just can't have one in our yard. You can keep asking me for other things, though."

I think God is the same way. We may not understand the whys of our wounds, but we know that the God who understands the whys loves us and invites us to keep seeking Him and His ways.

I'll close this chapter with six tips to keep in mind as you appropriate your riches in Christ:

1. Don't Allow Fear to Determine How You Communicate

You may cover up negative issues in your life because you don't want to be rejected. But that means you are hiding your true heart, and distrust will eventually ruin a good relationship.

We all want to be loved, but we can only be loved to the extent to which we allow our "real selves" to be known. If you wear a mask or put up walls to protect yourself, and then someone says, "I love you," what do they really love? The extent to which you have hidden yourself from them is the extent to which you can question their love. You will always fear that they love only the part of you that you have let them know. We must learn to be open and vulnerable in relationships.

Yes, opening your heart to someone is risky business. But you can do it in gradual stages. As you are developing a relationship, share minor things at first. Notice people's reactions. Do they hold those things as precious knowledge of you, or do they spread them around to others? Don't open up totally in the first weeks. As you discover that people are trustworthy, share deeper things. The level of your openness should match the level of their trustworthiness.

I was at a critical turning point in my life several years ago. I had decided to leave my job, but I didn't know what my next step should be. Confusion filled my mind as I looked at several options. Should I get a job, go to graduate school, teach, start my speaking ministry across the country, or do something else? What should I do? What direction was best?

I was dating Susan during this questioning period in my life. She was a good friend, and I enjoyed her company a great deal. In the course of our conversation one evening, she asked me what I was planning to do in the future. As I began to explain my difficult situation to her, the frustration and confusion overwhelmed me, and I started to cry.

My immediate thought was, "Oh no, if I continue to cry, I'll probably lose Susan. No woman wants a crybaby for a boyfriend." But I knew that to stop crying, I'd have to suppress my real feelings and frustrations, and I could not be honest with her.

I had to tell someone, so I decided to share with Susan all my thoughts and emotions. When I was finished unloading my heart, I asked, "What do you think about all this?" I expected her to reject everything I had said and to reject me for showing weakness.

Without a moment's hesitation she said, "Seeing you be so real and vulnerable just makes me love and respect you more."

I was both shocked and pleased. She had seen me reveal who I really was on the inside. A woman wants to see a man's heart, not just hear his thoughts. I'm not advocating that men sit around and cry a lot, but I strongly believe that you need to allow a woman to see the real man inside your heart. She'll love you even more.

If you were a parent, you wouldn't leave your child with someone you didn't know and trust, someone you hadn't spent time with or had a chance to observe. The same is true in our relationships.

2. You Can Develop into a Trustworthy Person

Other people can trust you when you keep confidential something they have shared with you, or when they can share how they really feel about something and you don't judge them. Genuine trustworthiness is a cornerstone on which you can build good communication.

Men can tell you what they *think* about something much more easily than how they *feel* about it. Opening up can be very difficult for them, but a woman's encouragement and sincere, gentle questioning can soften a man's hardened exterior. I have found that some women have a real ability to draw a man out of himself, providing they don't do it in a pushy or insensitive manner. This can be a tremendous asset to a relationship.

Women, ask your man how he *feels* about certain things. Listen to what he says, and don't interrupt. When you interrupt with your ideas and challenges, a man feels as if you are nagging him or uninterested in what he is saying. Try not to be disrespectful by turning the conversation to your stuff whenever he says something.

You may enjoy talking all the time, and you may think he is listening. However, he may consider you a motormouth and choose not to open his heart to you. Stop yourself when you start to interject your comments. Count to three and calm down. Listen with a caring attitude.

Probably one of the biggest challenges in dating today is to plan conversation. Most of our activities center on little or no significant interaction. We spend much of our time together going to movies or concerts, watching TV, going to parties, or attending spectator events. One of the easiest dates to go to is a movie. It takes very little effort, and you pay someone else to entertain you for two hours. You hardly have to say a word.

Activities like these are fun, but they don't provide much opportunity for you to interact in depth about who you are, or to share your goals, hopes, hurts, and loves. Set aside time each week to just talk with each other. These conversations can do wonders in building understanding and caring.

Cultivate the habit of concentrating on each other's words and feelings. You probably know the pain of sharing yourself with someone and then realizing the person isn't even listening. That person doesn't seem to be interested in you.

We have a tendency to focus on communicating with our words. Yet that is only 50 percent of interaction. The other 50 percent—just as vital—is listening. It can often be harder work than talking. It not only means hearing every word, but understanding as well. Sensitivity and empathy show you how much you are really interested in the other person's feelings and circumstances.

No one has it all together—not you and not your friend. The "perfect couple" does not exist. We are all in the process of learning and developing. But if you would like to make major changes in your partner's relationship with God, friends, purpose and direction in life, or physical features that disturb you, you probably should not be dating that person now.

3. Make All of Life a Classroom

We each learn, grow, and develop with the help of friends, God, and life experiences. Be patient with yourself and with the person you're dating. God isn't finished with either of you yet. You need to encourage each other to be the very best you can be.

Disappointment is a part of life. God hasn't promised us a

continual Disney World. He offers no contract or guarantee that people will never break their promises and hurt us. In fact, disillusionment can be a tremendous teacher. My experiences with Amy and others taught me valuable lessons that I have applied to my life. My life would be poorer without those tough learning experiences. Many great people have turned their disappointments and failures into stepping-stones of success.

Abraham Lincoln, for example, was defeated five times before winning an election. He suffered a bankruptcy and a mental breakdown. He was also rejected by the woman he loved. But he used the failures to reach for success.

Remember that you were made in God's image, and as the saying goes, "He doesn't make junk." You are special to Him. With all your strengths and weaknesses, you are a valued person. Stop believing lies that would say otherwise. Dave Grant, a speaker and author, talks about the "radiation principle." What we radiate is what we attract. If we radiate confidence and honesty, we attract people with similar attributes. But if we radiate gloom and discouragement, we will also attract like-minded people…if we attract anyone at all.

We must realize that our intrinsic worth comes from our standing with God. If we are self-reliant, we depend on ourselves or other people to give us a sense of worth and importance. But if we are dependent on Him, He fills us with Himself!

Debbie knew very little about sports and could care less. But when she met Ron, a running back for the college football team, her attitude changed. She tried to change her interests to fit his. When they were together she acted as though she had been a big football fan for years. Instead of admitting her lack of knowledge and being honest about her real interests, she tried to fake it. Then came the big Saturday game. Ron played very well and was anxious to see what Debbie's impressions were of the game. When he came out of the locker room to meet her, she said, "It was really exciting, but what was your number?" He left with a deflated ego, and she didn't score any points.

Resist the temptation to try to be something you are not just to please someone. Learning new interests is always good, but pretending is not. Be real. And remember that others do not determine your value and self-worth. Let God help you rise above circumstances and people's attitudes. He has made you worthy and precious.

One of the fastest ways to climb out of low self-esteem is to focus on the needs of others instead of concentrating on your own needs. When you are hurting emotionally, this is hard to do. Yet, that's the best time to reach out to others because many others are hurting also. In fact, as you find strength to deal with your own troubles, God will give you opportunities to share what you have learned with others who are dealing with similar issues.

4. Find Your Common Ground

He gave His life for us, "that they who live should no longer live for themselves, but for Him who died and rose again on their behalf" (2 Corinthians 5:15 NASB).

Sharing together and finding common ground is at the heart of a significant love relationship, creating a partnership bonded for life. Marriage is built on mutual giving to build each other up. But the question for a dating couple is this: Do you have the same desires to build oneness together—for a lifetime? I don't mean a situation where one is giving and the other is taking. The more mutual interests (common ground) you share in your relationship, the more you will complement each other.

You can build on your common ground by overcoming unrealistic expectations. Our culture tells us to be individuals and to go for what we want. But two maturing people who spend lots of time together need to find harmony. Be realistic about each other's strengths and weaknesses, habits, behavior patterns, and attitudes. Seek companionship, not perfection.

Most importantly, put your hope in something that will last. Jesus is the same yesterday, today, and forever. He is always true to His promises. He will never build you up just to let you down. He will never deceive you or paint an unrealistic picture of His love for you.

Keeping your spiritual life in balance is one of the best ways to guard against unrealistic expectations and self-centered thinking.

5. Build Your Friendship into a Healthy Love Relationship

Here are some excellent questions to ask and discuss with your dating partner. Learn about each other's interests, hopes, and dreams. Build mutual respect and desire to mold your lives together.

1. What are our common interests?
2. What expectations do we have of each other?
3. How do we react when these clash? What is a good way to resolve this?
4. Which of our expectations are unrealistic, and why?
5. What steps can we take this week to work at establishing better harmony in our relationship?

In my book *Finding a Lasting Love*[2] you will find lots of other ideas about building a friendship that may lead to a love relationship.

If you are currently and consistently doing something that you think might be wrong, find a close Christian friend, pastor or counselor to share it with. Get it off your chest. If they recommend that you stop doing it, then make every effort to do so. But don't get down on yourself when you stumble. Instead, focus on doing and being that which would please God. Continue to share your struggles with your friend or counselor. Ask that person to pray for you, and commit yourself to doing those things that are right and pure. As a result, you will begin to feel the very best about yourself.

6. Please God Above Pleasing People

In Jesus' Sermon on the Mount, He said some pretty profound things that can genuinely help one find the inner sense of peace and contentment that comes from doing right.

Here are some of the characteristics of people who please God according to Jesus in Matthew 5:3-10:

- They are *poor in spirit,* humble before all-powerful God, constantly searching for wisdom, confident, but not conceited.

- They are *mournful.* That means when they are down they are not knocked out because they are dependent on a loving heavenly Father. They are also sensitive to hurt and pain—others' as well as their own.

- They are *gentle,* with a servant attitude toward others, understanding other people's sensitivities, and easy-going under pressure.

- They *long for righteousness* and seek God's guidance. They are intolerant of wickedness and injustice, steadfast in personal morality.

- They are *merciful,* forgiving wrongs done to them, compassionate toward people who have needs, and responsive to requests for help.

- They are *pure in heart,* truthful, sincere in their love for others, trustworthy, refusing to play games.

- They are *peacemakers,* persistent in building harmony, friendly and cooperative even to disagreeable people.

- They are *persecuted for righteousness*, resistant to harm-
ful peer pressure, faithful to Jesus Christ regardless of
the opposition, and courageous when receiving abuse
and mockery.

Sounds tough, doesn't it? These qualities seem impossible to possess. Well, they are—apart from God's transforming power.

Someone said that the Christian life was hard. It isn't hard to live at all. It's impossible! The only way to please God is to have Him living in you. Then trust Him to produce these qualities in you.

Guard Your Mind

The human mind is like a wild bull. Before you gave your life to Christ, your mind roamed freely, thinking what it wanted to think. You may have allowed your mind to entertain unbridled, impure thoughts by feeding it material that promoted immorality, jealousy, envy, lust, and a host of other sinful activities. Your lifestyle tantalized the raging bull of your mind to dictate your attitudes and behavior.

After you became a Christian, you discovered that the wild bull of your mind wasn't instantly transformed into a harmless calf. The old thought patterns, ideas, memories, and temptations were still there. The wild bull charged recklessly through your nice Christian thoughts and made shambles of your attempts at purity and obedience to God.

Here's a fact of life—you cannot turn a wild bull into a house pet. However, you can put a ring in its nose and lead it out of the house and into a secure pasture where it will do the least harm. Similarly, you will never be able to rid your mind totally of all sinful thoughts and temptations.

Your mind is also like a computer with unlimited memory capacity. Every wrong thought, word, and deed you have experienced is filed there. A lifetime of spiritual growth, prayer, and discipline are required to rewrite all that negative input.

In the meantime, the wild bull of your mind snorts and paws the earth, threatening you with thoughts and temptations you wish were gone forever. Thanks to the resurrection power of Christ and the indwelling Holy Spirit, you have the authority to jerk that bull of your mind around by the nose and make it behave. Nobody else is going to do it for you. You are the sole guardian of your mind.

Many people think a holy life would be boring. "You want to be *pure? Don't you want to have any fun?*" What they don't realize is that the greatest adventure is living in close relationship with God. And talk about fun! Nevertheless, there is a catch. We have to live God's way. He didn't ask us for advice when He set up the rules, and He's not asking us now. Following God's will brings satisfaction, peace of mind, and purpose in life. Getting there is sometimes a difficult story.

Jeremy had his first sexual experience when he was in high school. That was the beginning. From then on he had one goal in mind for every woman he dated—sex.

In the following months and years, Jeremy's life revolved around his sexual conquests. He fed his fantasies by visiting pornographic websites and poring over articles and pictures in sex magazines. Sex was constantly on his mind.

After a couple of years in college, Jeremy trusted Christ as his personal Savior. At the time of his conversion, Jeremy didn't realize all the changes he needed to make in his thought life and his relationships with women. He continued to stock his mind with sexually stimulating materials, and he still planned ways to get the women he dated into bed.

He soon discovered that his sexual exploits as a Christian were followed by a hangover of guilt the next day. He tried to rein in his urges and desires, but his mind was permeated morning, noon, and night with thoughts of sex. He knew deep in his heart that God was against his plans to get his dates into bed with him and that he would feel guilty if he carried out those schemes. So Jeremy decided to change his ways.

Sometimes, though, his resolve faltered. After each failure, he suffered waves of guilt and wondered if he was even a Christian at all. His vacillating lifestyle made him doubt the validity of his relationship with Christ. *Will I ever wake up in the morning with a clean mind, a mind that isn't cluttered with sexual desires? Will I ever date a woman without wanting to have sex with her? Is the Christian life always going to be a losing battle with the impure contents of my mind? Will I ever experience the victory that other Christians talk about?*

The Battle for Your Mind

Jeremy's struggle illustrates the huge conflict many Christians experience on the road to freedom from sexual and relationship regret. The center of the conflict is the mind, and your ability to live with a clear conscience depends on the outcome of the battle for your mind.

The world isn't interested in your desire for a clean mind. Indeed, most of the world will try to invade your mind and manipulate your thoughts. Sexy ads try to induce you to buy products to enhance your attractiveness or your ability to relate better.

Toothpaste and whitening agents promise to take years off your yellowing smile. Fad diets try to help you to whittle down your waistline. Many beer or liquor ads subtly portray that people who drink their products win new friends and get the attention of the popular, beautiful people. Some of these invitations require you to compromise your standards as a Christian. Somebody must stand at the gate of your mind, regulate what it receives, and control its behavior. That somebody is you.

Guarding your mind is a difficult, full-time job, but it's the only way to move past your regrets and move into the freedom of righteousness. I want to share with you several guidelines that will help you guard your mind.

Anyone who has worked with computers knows the term GIGO. It's an acronym that stands for "garbage in, garbage out." The phrase reminds the computer user that if an error is put into the memory, that error will show up in the computer's output.

Good or bad, whatever you put into a computer is what you get out of it.

Just like with the computer, whatever you program into your mind will come out in your behavior. A man came to me once complaining that he couldn't control his sexual urges. "I can't help myself," he concluded. "I'm just oversexed." As I talked with him he admitted that he regularly visited internet porn sites and thoroughly investigated each month's issue of a sexually stimulating magazine.

"You're not oversexed," I said. "Your activities are trashed up because your mind is trashed up. As long as you keep filling your mind with mental garbage, your behavior will be worldly garbage."

Think About This

Let GIGO stand for "God in, God out." If you want the truth, beauty, and purity of God's Word to show up in your behavior, you need to program the truth, beauty, and purity of God's Word into your mind. Paul gave Philippian Christians this instruction: "Whatever is true, whatever is noble, whatever is right, whatever is pure, whatever is lovely, whatever is admirable—if anything is excellent or praiseworthy—think about such things" (Philippians 4:8).

Paul invited believers to flood their minds with positive, enjoyable, uplifting, and scriptural qualities. Only with this kind of input would his readers be able to produce the kind of output he called for in the next verse: "Whatever you have learned or received or heard from me, or seen in me—put it into practice." Godly thoughts always precede righteous behavior.

The primary reservoir for the positive qualities Paul listed is the Bible. If you want to drown your impure thoughts, you must immerse your mind in God's Word by reading it, studying it, memorizing it, and meditating on it. David said, "How can a young man keep his way pure? By living according to your word...I have hidden your word in my heart that I might not sin against you" (Psalm 119:9,11).

John's story illustrates that positive effect of God's Word on the wild bull of an impure mind. John grew up attending church every Sunday. At age 12 he responded to the gospel by receiving Christ as his Savior.

Not long after his conversion, some of John's neighborhood friends introduced him to pornographic magazines. The pictures he saw in those magazines fanned the flames of boyhood lust. Through his junior high and senior high school days, John bought his own magazines and perpetuated his fascination with pornography. During college he frequented topless bars in an attempt to quench his thirst for tantalizing sights. But everything he saw never seemed to be enough.

During this time John was also involved in masturbation. He knew his thoughts and lustful desires were wrong, but he felt trapped by his own uncontrollable sexual passions. Shortly after graduating from college he began to realize how miserable he really was. He could see that the path he was traveling was a one-way journey to emotional and spiritual destruction. He desperately wanted inner peace and victory over his obsession with pornography. Finally, he turned back to God, repented of his sins, and recommitted his life to Christ.

Unfortunately, John's fierce battle with his impure thought life was far from over. He continued to struggle with lust and the sordid memories from his past involvement with pornography. He found it difficult to resist the temptation to undress in his mind every attractive woman he met. He knew God had forgiven him, but he cried out to God for relief from the dark oppression of his evil thoughts.

The answer came though a new hobby. John joined a Christian band in his hometown. The other members of the band were committed believers who desired to help John mature in his relationship with Christ. One of John's coworkers introduced him to a topical Bible memory system. John began memorizing Bible verses aggressively. Almost immediately the Scriptures that filled John's mind began to transform his thinking about himself, about God, and about others.

One of the first verses John committed to memory was 1 Corinthians 6:19-20: "Do you not know that your body is a temple of the Holy Spirit, who is in you, whom you have received from God? You are not your own; you were bought at a price. Therefore honor God with your body."

John kept this verse card and others lying on top of his desk at work. Whenever an impure thought tempted him, he read or quoted the passage and thought about its meaning in his life. By consciously meditating on Scripture, John diverted his mind from lustful thoughts and focused on positive qualities.

John still struggles with lust and impure thoughts about women, but by saturating his mind with God's Word, he is learning to keep the wild bull in its pen. The Scripture verses John has stored away are gradually helping him overcome the emotional and psychological scars of the past.

Jeremy, whose story opened this chapter, had a similar experience. Despite the impurity which seemed to dominate his thinking, Jeremy determined to obey God in his behavior. He disciplined himself to read his Bible and pray every day. Soon he realized the importance of memorizing Scripture verses, so he began to do that too.

After a few weeks of memorizing verses, Jeremy noticed that he wasn't waking up each morning with thoughts of sex on his mind. Sexual fantasies were occupying less and less of his waking thoughts.

He was able to spend time with a woman on a date and not feel driven to seduce her. The influx of God's Word through memorization and meditation was cleansing his mind. He began to enjoy the Christian life as the burden of his discouragement over impure thoughts lifted.

As John and Jeremy each discovered, victory in the battle for the mind comes through filling your mind with God's truth. The Holy Spirit will use the Bible verses you internalize to transform your mind and your character into the likeness of Jesus Christ. Also, the card file of Scripture verses that you program into your mind will help you replace lustful thoughts with godly thoughts.

Instead of yielding to the temptation of an impure thought, focus your mind on a section of Scripture that answers the temptation. That's how Jesus responded successfully to Satan's temptation (Matthew 4:1-11).

Temptation vs. Sin

Another critical guideline for guarding your mind against future moral failure is to realize that you're never impervious to temptation. Just because you have yielded to the temptation to sin in the past and have received forgiveness doesn't mean you are rendered immune to it in the future. If anything, you are even more vulnerable. You've been down that road before. Your graphic memories of the past experiences can amplify the intensity of a current temptation. The key to resisting temptation is to be ever alert to its presence and its potential danger.

Temptation can come in many forms. You can be tempted to impure thoughts or behavior by an old flame that calls unexpectedly. You can be tempted by a new acquaintance who is attractive to you. Suddenly you're wondering what it would be like to be intimate with him or her. You can be tempted by the comments of other friends as they discuss their romantic exploits in front of you. You can be tempted to dwell on illicit relationships promoted in books, magazines, spam e-mails, music, TV shows, and movies. Even without any outside stimuli, your thoughts and memories can flash tempting scenes on the screen of your mind for you to dwell on.

Remember, temptation is not the same thing as sin. Temptation is an invitation to commit evil. Sin is accepting the invitation. The

Bible tells us that Jesus had a perfect record for declining the invitation to sin. He was "tempted in every way, just as we are—yet was without sin" (Hebrews 4:15). You don't need to feel guilty about being tempted. It happens to everyone. Sorrow, confession, and forgiveness are only necessary when you yield to temptation.

The first target of temptation and the first area to fall to temptation is your mind. That's why you must be alert to temptation in order to guard your mind. A sinful act is always preceded by a sinful thought. Jesus declared that mental adultery is as bad as physical adultery (Matthew 5:27-28). Sin occurs first when your mind accepts temptation's invitation and you commit the act in your imagination. For example, if the memory of a past sexual experience comes to mind, temptation invites you to dwell on that experience, recreate the setting in your mind, and willfully relive the encounter. If you can train yourself to expect temptation, you can quickly refuse the invitation to mentally commit adultery. When temptation takes your unguarded mind by surprise, you may find yourself well into the mental act before you realize you've fallen.

Temptation comes from three main sources. The first source is the world with all its alluring temptations. The second is your own evil desires. James wrote, "Each one is tempted when, by his own evil desire, he is dragged away and enticed" (James 1:14).

The third source is Satan, who "prowls around like a roaring lion looking for someone to devour" (1 Peter 5:8).

Satan is actively involved in trying to trip you up. He will bring to mind a romantic experience of the past and tempt you to feel lonely or desperate. He will tell you that nothing is wrong with sexual encounters outside of marriage as long as you love your partner. He will insinuate that God doesn't really care, and he will suggest that you fulfill your needs for love and intimacy in physical relationships. Satan always lurks in the shadows, hoping to catch you off guard with his invitations to sin. You can guard your mind against him by being alert to his tricks and refusing his temptations (James 4:7).

Your Equipment for Battle

Since this is warfare for your mind and soul, learn as much as you can about the equipment God has given for you to fight temptation and win the battle. Take full advantage of the resources at your disposal for opposing evil and sin.

First, you have Christ's resurrection power. Thanks to the victory Jesus Christ won for us in His death and resurrection, neither your evil desires nor Satan can force you to sin. As a Christian, you have the authority in Christ boldly to crucify your old self and its evil ways. The Bible says that sin has no more power over you (Romans 6:1-7).

Jesus broke sin's power when He paid its penalty on the cross and defeated death forever in His resurrection. His resurrection showed His power over sin and death. Because you are His follower, you are no longer a slave to sin. The choice is yours to refuse the invitations to sin that come from your evil desires and from Satan. Seize the victory over temptation that Christ has provided for you.

Second, you have Christ's authority to say no to sin. He also has equipped you with the power to defeat sin. The indwelling Holy Spirit is present within you to empower you for obedience and righteousness. You cannot resist temptation alone. You need the power of the Holy Spirit flowing through you to guard your mind against sin.

If you find yourself giving in to evil desires or letting your mind entertain impure thoughts that come along, you need to take spiritual inventory to find out what is short-circuiting the Holy Spirit's power in your life. His power is ineffective when you harbor known sin or when you are living for your own desires instead of His. You must confess your sin to God and accept His forgiveness and cleansing. Thank Him that Jesus has already paid the penalty for your sin. Give the Holy Spirit the steering wheel of your life in that area. Let Him guide you out of the danger zones and into His victory.

Through the victory of Christ and the power of the Holy Spirit you have everything you need. Rely on those resources.

Third, you have the Bible as your sword to battle evil and press on to conquer temptations. Just as Jeremy and John did, saturate your mind and soul with God's Word. This is like putting bullets in your gun to shoot down the enemy forces of wickedness.

Plan Ahead

Prepare your defensive strategies. Plan how you will resist temptation well in advance—before it confronts you. If you wait to plan your defense until you and your partner are snuggled together on the couch in your dimly lit living room, the battle is already lost. Inflamed passions will always be able to subdue an unguarded mind.

You need to decide long before the event what you will do, how you will respond, and where you will draw the line. If you have a date at 8:00 PM, plan your defense against sexual temptation during your morning quiet time with God or at noon while you're eating lunch. That's when you can decide clearly what you will and will not do based on your weaknesses and the temptations you can expect.

For example, let's say that you and your date are planning to go out to dinner and then return to your date's apartment to watch a movie. You know that everything will be fine…unless the two of you lie down on the carpet together to watch the movie. That's when your sexual urges start to run wild. Knowing this, don't wait until you get back to the apartment to decide if you will lie down on the carpet. Decide ahead of time that, no matter what happens, you will not lie down to watch the movie.

You can expect the logical decisions you made before the fact to be tested in the heat of battle. Your date may switch on the movie and then sprawl on the carpet saying, "Wouldn't you be more comfortable lying here on the floor beside me?" Your date may turn down the lights and turn up the charm. But if you stick by the decision you made while thinking logically earlier, you will be able to resist the temptation.

If you know that stepping inside that apartment will expose you to more temptation than you can resist, make other plans. Your evening doesn't have to include watching a video in a dimly lit living room. If you know that having drinks at a party for two hours and then heading to the bedroom with your date will lead to problems, decide to skip the party and do your talking at a restaurant.

Anticipate every possibility for failure and mentally lock in a plan of defense or escape.

Your passions may be stronger than your mind. That's why your mind must outfox your passions by telling them ahead of time what you are going to do. Even when you have made your thoughtful advance decisions, your passions can voice a strong argument at the moment of temptation to alter your plans for purity. Be especially aware of rationalizations, such as *What harm can lying on the floor do?* Prepare yourself for this eventuality by telling a trusted friend of the same sex what you have decided. Ask him or her to pray for you and to call you the next day to ask you pointed questions about your activities with you date.

Here's a good verse for guarding your mind against temptations: "Clothe yourselves with the Lord Jesus Christ, and do not think about how to gratify the desires of the sinful nature" (Romans 13:14).

Your prayerful, logical preparation for temptation will save you countless numbers of problems when the heat is on.

Putting the Ring in the Bull's Nose

Keeping your mind pure is a battle, but God will honor your commitment to fight the good fight. Here's a recap of some of the steps that can help you along the way:

1. *Remember GIGO.* What you put in your mind is what you are going to get out of it. If you are filling it with garbage, then garbage will flood your thoughts and often affect your actions. Fight to put God in your mind, using Scripture, Christian friends and movies, and music and TV shows that are uplifting. Form a GIGO Group ("God In, God Out" accountability group) with other Christians of your same gender.

2. *Saturate your mind with Scripture.* Write "fighting" verses on index cards. Pick Scriptures such as 1 Corinthians 6:19-20 and 10:13, which challenge us to God's higher standard. When temptation hits you, pull out the cards and read the verses. Pray the Scriptures into your life and memorize them. Say them aloud if you have to. Do whatever is necessary to ground yourself in God's bondage-breaking words.

3. *Stay alert.* You already know what you are tempted by, but sometimes it can hit you unexpectedly. If you are, for instance, a man tempted by Internet pornography, then a pop-up ad of a naked woman can catch you off guard. Try to think ahead. Get a really good spam blocker. Do the same with other tempting situations. If you are tempted to cheat on a girlfriend, then don't put yourself in compromising situations with other women. Deciding not to spend alone time with another woman who has a crush on you when you have a girlfriend is probably a wise decision.

4. *Target what is short-circuiting the Holy Spirit.* Confess your secret sins. Get them out there in the open before God. He already knows them, but He wants you to live your life in the light and not in the darkness. God's power won't be effective in your life if you don't confess your sin and accept His great forgiveness and trust Him to change you.

Say Goodbye to the Wrong People

Christi was hurting, and her pain showed on her face. She confided to me that her boyfriend, Michael, was acting strangely. He stopped calling or emailing as regularly and wasn't getting on his instant messaging. She tried to contact him many times, but he rarely returned her emails and phone messages. He seemed to be pulling away from their relationship, and she didn't know why.

"Christi, tell me about your relationship with Michael," I probed. "Does he show interest in developing a friendship with you?"

"I think we have a pretty good relationship," Christi beamed proudly. "I'm in love with him and really want to please him."

"What does that mean?" I asked.

"Well, by showing my affection. We spend intimate time together in his apartment a couple of times a week when his roommates are not around. If I didn't do that, I am afraid that he would leave me and find someone else."

"Christi, he's obviously feeling guilty and frustrated," I said. "He's trying to pull away from you. Besides, how can you as a Christian justify having sex with Michael when you two are not married?"

"Well, I admit I feel bad about what we're doing. But I love him and don't want to lose him. Doesn't that make it okay? When you love someone, you should show it."

Avoid Rationalizations

I hear these kinds of rationalizations all the time. Some people go to ridiculous lengths to excuse their sinful behavior. Often, they don't want to learn what God's viewpoint is about male/female relationships. From cover to cover in the Bible, the Lord speaks on that topic, and He has a lot to say about it. The Scriptures clearly forbid sex before marriage, and marriage in the Bible always includes the formal elements of compliance with civil law as well as public acknowledgment.

Furthermore, the Bible doesn't condone sexual activity between a man and a woman just because they're engaged. The truth is, almost half of all engaged couples break up anyway.

You have no absolute guarantee that you're going to marry the person you become engaged to. The only valid occasion for sexual activity is within the bounds of legal matrimony.

People today need to accept the truth of God's Word on the issue of sexual relationships. This may sound simple, but it's nonetheless accurate: *God knows best.* Evaluate your behavior in the light of what the Bible says about healthy relationships, and discipline your mind by aligning it with what He says. If you need to review the facts, earlier chapters in this book spell out in detail God's standards for morality. Part 4 of this book contains specific Scripture quotations on the qualities of a healthy relationship.

Tessa and Nick were engaged to be married when they came to talk to me. In the course of our discussion about their relationship, they rather happily admitted that they had been sleeping together since they became engaged.

"You're both Christians, and you know what the Bible says about premarital sex," I said. "What caused you to start sleeping together before the wedding?"

"We committed ourselves to each other under God when we got engaged," Tessa answered confidently. "The closer we got emotionally, the easier it became to get closer physically. Sure, we know it might be wrong, but we're already married in God's sight."

Lots of couples sleep together before marriage, but that doesn't make in right in God's eyes. Sex may attract you to each other, but it will never hold you together. It's not the "glue" many couples suppose. Rather, it's the explosive that blows apart many serious relationships.

Bottom line: If you want to grow closer to God, you need to deal with those relationships that tear you down. He has a much better plan for you than the world does. Remove all hindrances to a loving relationship with the Lord. Get serious about Christ. Do you want to remove a major barrier to loving Him unreservedly? Dissolve all relationships, both present and past, that are pulling your heart and behavior away from the Bible's direction for your life.

A Pure Mind

One of the greatest gifts you can bring to your eventual marriage is a mind that's disciplined by God's truth and righteousness. Everything you say and do is controlled by your mind. Whatever you allow to fill your mind will eventually come out in your behavior. As you endeavor to cleanse your mind with God's Word, the Holy Spirit will transform your life into a pleasing fragrance of life (2 Corinthians 2:14-16).

Once you allow God's truth to discipline your mind, you may feel guilty about impure relationships in your past. When the Lord convicts you about having premarital sex with your former girlfriend or boyfriend, or perhaps even casual "hook-ups," deal with the problem immediately, clear up your conscience, and be set free. Let me first comfort you and then caution you about dissolving unhealthy relationships.

First, allow your guilt to prompt you to evaluate whether or not you have confessed that past sin to God. If you have not, do so now and receive God's forgiveness. Take advantage of God's promise: "'Come now, let us reason together,' says the LORD. 'Though your sins are like scarlet, they shall be as white as snow; though they are red as crimson, they shall be like wool'" (Isaiah 1:18).

God's forgiveness can completely purge your heart of the stains of sin and guilt, and that can give you great comfort!

Now for the caution: Don't feel you must go back to an old flame to apologize or ask forgiveness. You may just be sticking your head back into the lion's cage by allowing the confrontation to open old, painful wounds. You may be exposing yourself unnecessarily to a weak spot that could cause you to fall again. I know several people who went to former illicit lovers to apologize, only to fall back into immorality.

The risks of a personal meeting with a former lover are great. The embers of old emotions may unexpectedly flare up, and you could get burned. Memories of the "good times" can subtly overpower your good intentions, and you may become vulnerable to the former romantic atmosphere—a familiar song, a favorite restaurant, the old friends. You need to know your weak spots and guard against them.

If you do need to apologize or seek forgiveness, call the person on the phone instead of visiting him or her in person. If the telephone conversation becomes a temptation to relive former behavior, hang up as soon as you can! Or write him or her a letter or email instead. Don't put yourself in a position where your desire to dissolve an immoral relationship becomes a temptation to resurrect it. It's not worth it.

This step to overcoming relationship regret may involve even the difficulty of breaking off a present serious relationship that has become immoral.

Let's say that you have recently come to terms with your relationship regret, confessed your sin to God, and accepted His forgiveness. You are rejoicing that the sins of your past are forgiven and forgotten. However, the man you have been sleeping with still wants to continue. Or the woman you met, fell in love with, and have been going to bed with is still the woman you want to marry despite your previous failures. The temptations you're fighting now are the same ones you yielded to in the past—and they're just as strong. In addition, this present relationship tends to bring out the worst instead of the best in you. What should you do?

Your first tendency is probably to continue the relationship. After all, you were attracted to the person in the first place, and that attraction may still be strong. You may want to cling to this person because he or she is a tremendous boost to your ego or meets a deep need in your life. Your "friend" claims to love you and wants to continue being intimate with you. Here is someone who makes you feel very special and important. This may be the only person you have ever met who has loved you so deeply. You're remorseful about your past, but you don't want to repeat it. You're struggling with your decision because the thought of this special person walking out of your life is almost too painful to consider.

What you need is objectivity and discernment. Evaluate your present relationship prayerfully and clearly. The following questions will help you assess the level of true friendship you have with this person. You will find these revealing questions and many more in the "Friends and More" quiz in my book *Finding a Lasting Love*.

- Do you really try to understand each other?
- Do you listen attentively to each other as you share your fears, joys, ambitions, failures, and hopes?
- Is each of you humble when you are right and teachable when you are wrong?
- Can you support and encourage each other's spiritual gifts?
- Do you agree on the nature of romance?
- Are you comfortable with the way you each react (both positively and negatively) to significant circumstances?
- Do you adjust to and compromise with each other when you have differences?

- Do you respect each other's sexual boundaries?[1]

If you want to rid yourself of regret and be free to love again, you have only two choices concerning your present relationships. Both are difficult, but you will never purify your present relationship if you don't make a choice and act upon it. As King Solomon wrote, "Can a man scoop fire into his lap without his clothes being burned? Can a man walk on hot coals without his feet being scorched?" (Proverbs 6:27-28). Trying to live in God's power while retaining the relationship of an old flame is playing with fire.

Option Number One

Your first choice is to go back to zero in sharing physical intimacies.

If you want to institute a morally righteous relationship, you must reverse the progress of your physical involvement. The only way you can do so is to suspend all physical contact with that person—cold turkey—for a minimum of three months. I'm not just talking abstaining from sex. I'm talking about no more skin-on-skin contact whatsoever: holding hands, snuggling in the car or on the couch, kissing...anything.

"Wow, that's pretty radical!" I can hear you saying. "Why must we do something so drastic? Why can't we just back off a little by going part of the way but not all the way to zero?"

Your habit patterns for physical involvement are already established. You not only know how to get to first base with this individual, but you know what it means to get to second base, to third base, and to score. You may say, "We won't go beyond kissing," but once your lips touch, your thoughts and emotions are already programmed from experience to keep going.

Trying to stop the momentum of lovemaking between two people who have already experienced oral sex or intercourse is like trying to stop a runaway freight train. You need to make a complete break with those patterns by deciding not to be physically involved with that person. You won't run the bases if you stay in the dugout and refuse to go up to bat.

You will find that suspending all physical activity will help you evaluate the strength of your relationship apart from sex. For example, many couples consider dinner out, a concert, or a movie as the preliminaries for the "main event," which happens later on the couch or in the bed. When you decide to eliminate the main event and that which leads up to it, you're left with the preliminaries—conversation over dinner, watching a movie together, participating in a sport, and the like. Do you still enjoy being with your partner when the prospect of physical intimacy is out of the picture? Does he or she still enjoy your company? Do you find anything in common beyond a sexual interest in each other? Is there any emotional, intellectual, or spiritual depth to your relationship? Do you both desire to put Christ at the center of your relationship?

Suspending physical activity will also clarify your partner's motives in the relationship. For example, when you were sexually active, your partner may have smothered you with "I'll love you forever," "I can't live without you," and, "You're the only one for me." When you tell that person you intend to adopt a lifestyle of moral righteousness and you aren't even going to hold his/her hand for three months, she/he may change the tune to "If I can't make love with you, I'm out of here." You may even discover that what you thought was love was really merely physical lust.

Kicking the physical touching habit cold turkey is an extremely difficult step. It requires a complete shift from the physical to the spiritual and relational. Determine together to keep each other pure before the Lord and not violate each other's trust. If you think your relationship cannot stand the zero contact test, you have one other choice to consider.

Option Number Two

Your second choice is to terminate the relationship.

If you cannot establish moral purity before the Lord, you must break it off and dissolve it. Your commitment to Christ and moral integrity must supersede your commitment to anyone who is a perpetual temptation to moral failure.

Whenever I recommend this serious step to individuals, I try to do so with a measure of hope. I tell them that the separation may not be permanent. God may restore the relationship after a period of separation. That's why I suggest that individuals who separate not destroy the mementos of their relationship: photos, scrapbooks, souvenirs, or records or tapes containing "our songs." Instead, box them up and store them out of sight until you level off emotionally and discover God's ultimate plan for your relationship.

Craig and Sarah are an encouraging example of what God can do when individuals value personal righteousness in their romantic relationships. Craig was the top football player in our state university when I met him and led him to Christ. He had been sleeping with his girlfriend Sarah off and on for about a year.

As he began studying the Scriptures, he realized that premarital sex was contrary to God's plan for his life. One day he went to Sarah and said, "Sarah, I love you, and I want to be with you, but I have recently become a Christian, and I don't want to go to bed with you anymore."

"You're a Christian?" Sarah responded excitedly. "That's wonderful! I'm a Christian too!"

"If you're a Christian, why have you gone to bed with me all these months?" Craig demanded angrily.

"Because I loved you, and I wanted you to love me," Sarah answered defensively. "I was afraid that if I didn't give in to you, I would lose you."

When I saw Craig after his confrontation with Sarah, he was steamed. He was so deeply repulsed by Sarah's loose behavior as a

Christian that he was angry and hostile toward her. I suggested that he break off the relationship and let God heal his wounds. He agreed. Craig wanted nothing to do with Sarah whatsoever. Because the college they attended was so huge, they were able to avoid each other. They went their separate ways, rarely saw each other, and never spoke.

As the months passed, Craig became a devoted Bible student, and his faith in Christ grew remarkably. Unknown to him, Sarah was experiencing a similar growth. The breakup had devastated her, and she responded to her pain by renewing her faith in Christ and committing herself to live a righteous life.

Nearly two years after their separation, Craig and Sarah bumped into each other at a party hosted by mutual friends. They hesitantly shared what God had been doing in their individual lives. Soon they began seeing each other again. They developed an enjoyable friendship based on their mutual commitment to Christ and His guidelines for developing a relationship that will last a lifetime. Two years after their unplanned reunion, Craig and Sarah were married. Today they have three children and a terrific marriage.

Craig and Sarah's story illustrates what God can do when you put Him and His Word above your sexual desires. God used Craig and Sarah's separation in a wonderful way to mature them, purify them, and prepare them for a Christ-centered marriage. They will never forget how God picked up the pieces of their shattered relationship, healed and purified their hearts, and brought them back together.

God may or may not restore a relationship you dissolve to pursue moral integrity. That's His business. Don't try to determine for God what the future of your relationships should be. You take care of the present decisions by following Christ with your whole heart. Let God take care of the future for both of you.

For practical suggestions on terminating a relationship, look at the chapter entitled "How To Break Up with the Wrong One."

If and when He chooses to bring you back together, your renewed relationship will be wonderful. When God puts people together, He does it the right way.

BRIGHT SPOT 6:

Purify Your Passions

In the months before they were married, Allison and Jacob experienced all the natural romantic, passionate feelings you would expect in two people who were engaged and deeply in love. At that time, Allison was living in Illinois, and Jacob was living in Colorado. They carried on their courtship mainly through long telephone calls, emails and instant message chats that were filled with loving words and dreams for the future.

On those sporadic occasions when they did get together, though, their passions were strong and demanding. After being apart for weeks at a time, the tender kisses and embraces were thrilling. They battled against the surging tide of temptations that beckoned them to become sexually involved before reciting their marriage vows. Jacob knew he had to keep his sexual urges in check.

He wanted to honor God and show his respect for Allison, but she was so lovable and touchable…He didn't know how to handle his passions during the last weeks before the wedding.

Finally Jacob settled on a plan for guiding his behavior when he was alone with Allison. He called it the bikini barrier. Jacob told Allison that until they were married, he would not touch the parts of her body that a bikini would cover. During those long, romantic encounters, when Jacob was tempted to explore, he remembered his commitment to observe the bikini barrier. As a result, Allison's respect for Jacob shot sky-high, and his decision to keep a tight rein on his passions before the wedding made the honeymoon even more exciting for both of them.

Jesus' Passion

Like other emotions, passions are amoral. They are neither good nor bad in themselves. Nothing is wrong with passionate feelings. Your emotional response to your thoughts and circumstances is what makes them either an asset or a liability in your relationships with the opposite sex. You may be a romantic, emotional, and passionate creature. That's the way God made you. He doesn't want you to ignore or deny the existence of your passions. They are a part of your total makeup. But you must learn to bridle your passions and express them in a positive, godly manner.

We often talk about our passions originating in our hearts, but when the Bible talks about passions, it locates them in the area of the solar plexus. The King James Version of the Bible often referred to inner passions with terms like "bowels of mercies" (Colossians 3:12) or "bowels of compassion" (1 John 3:17). Today we say, "I have a strong gut feeling," or "My stomach is in knots." Our deepest passions affect us physically. Sometimes our feelings are so strong that we actually get sick—we can't eat, or our stomach aches. Our passions affect us physically and seem to demand some kind of physical release.

Gut-level human passions are not restricted to romantic feelings. The New Testament describes Jesus Christ as a passionate person, one who felt deeply for the people around Him in a nonsexual way. His feelings moved Him to positive responsive action. He channeled His passions to meet the needs of those who stirred His emotions.

He felt compassion for the multitudes, so He prayed for them (Matthew 9:35-38), taught them (Mark 6:34), healed their sick (Matthew 14:14), and fed them (Matthew 15:32-38). He was moved to compassion when He met a couple of blind men, and He healed them (Matthew 20:29-30). Jesus' love touched a leper, and He cured him (Mark 1:40-42). He felt compassion toward the widow of Nain, and He raised her son from the dead (Luke 7:11-17). Jesus always turned feelings of compassion into pure, constructive, positive deeds that served others.

Jesus' emphasis on the greatest commandment reflects His concern that we express our passions in purity in all our relationships: "'Love the Lord your God with all your heart and with all your soul and with all your mind.' This is the first and greatest commandment. And the second is like it: 'Love your neighbor as yourself'" (Matthew 22:37-39).

More than anything else He taught, Jesus wanted His followers to be totally consumed with love for God and for people. By His example, we know that this all-consuming love was to issue forth in positive, caring deeds. If that's not passion, I don't know what is!

Your Deepest Longings

You can express your passion by wholeheartedly living for your longings. Deep down inside of us reside deep longings for certain things. These needs crave fulfillment, but satisfying them requires that we understand their true nature.

What are some of our deep longings? The first is a longing for intimate companionship and friendship. We desire to deeply love someone, to pour into that person all of the pent-up compassion and caring that fills our heart. We also want that person to love us with equal intensity and honesty. It's a two-way street, giving and receiving.

I have often said, "What we deeply desire is to be loved by someone for who we really are and to return love toward that person for who they really are. We crave acceptance. No one wants to love a person who is a fake, a superficial pretender. We want to genuinely love and be committed to one person for a lifetime." Thousands have heard that statement, and no one has ever told me that this was not their deep longing.

The second longing we have is for peace of mind. The turmoil and stress of daily life hound us. Sure, we are sometimes thrilled by the adventure and activities of life. But we crave a sense of calm—peace in the midst of the storms. Experiencing tranquility in the midst of the pressures of everyday living is a characteristic of strength.

Third, we want security. We fear being lonely for the rest of our lives. A fear of failure or losing at love sometimes stops us from developing a relationship because we don't want to experience rejection or a host of other difficult human emotions. No wonder people will do almost anything to be assured of stability.

Last, we long for significance. We want to be valuable to somebody and to know that our life is worthwhile. Regardless of whether we have someone or not, the thought that our life here on this earth counts for nothing is a disheartening one indeed.

The satisfaction of these longings takes time and a set of personal standards that are based on the Word of God. While I was single for 42 years of my life, I was able to see how God could satisfy my deep longings. He took away the sting in my life that demanded, "I've got to have a wife to be happy," and He taught me to build good friendships. The process was long and sometimes confusing, but God helped me see what my real longings were and kept me from falling for the momentary pleasures.

We all need to become aware of our true, deep longings. We also need to expose the things in our life that would detour us from the path of living for those longings. All through life we can expect other cravings and desires to distract us and entice us to get off track. When these times come, we must say emphatically, *No! I'm living for Christ, who will fulfill my longings, not for the satisfaction of superficial passions.* You'll be amazed at the freedom you will enjoy when you can say no to anything that could distract you from your longings. The mixed-up person is the one who can't distinguish his longings from the distractions.

Our society says, "Act responsibly." What does that mean? Our nature is to do what benefits us the most. Our self-centeredness is very strong and can cause us to do things we will eventually regret. That's why you must start with your mind. Your mind says to your passions, *I have decided to do what pleases God regardless of the pressures I face along the way.* You must decide how you're going to behave long before you get to the place where your passions can steer you off course.

The temptations are always present to short-circuit your deep longings. The reason is simple. You can satisfy those momentary passions in just that amount of time—a moment. Without determination, instant gratification often wins out over your deepest desires, which you can only fulfill over time and with discipline.

Remember the definition of fun we saw in an earlier chapter? Real fun is "having a good time with no negative consequences." In each situation you face, you will have a decision to make. *What kind of consequences do I want for my life?* Robert Louis Stevenson once said, "Everybody, sooner or later, will sit down to a banquet of consequences." God loves with an everlasting love that doesn't diminish with the ups and downs of living. He is the only one who is capable of satisfying the deepest longings of your heart. Remember this saying: Accept short-term pain to realize long-term gain.

Perhaps the most volatile of all human passions are those connected with romantic feelings and sexual urges. We need to discipline ourselves to express our drives related to the opposite sex, and all our passions, in positive, God-honoring ways. Yet we are tempted to let these strong emotions run away with us and dictate our behavior. Sometimes our passion-driven responses toward the opposite sex get us into trouble. In the heat of the moment we are liable to make hasty, selfish decisions we will later regret.

Sexual passions are not wrong, but they do need to be channeled and purified. Learn to recognize the power of the drives within you, direct them away from expressions that are immoral and ungodly, and direct them toward expressions that are positive and uplifting.

The Scriptures offer several ways for you to purify your passions.

1. Run from Compromising Situations

When you are tempted to push toward moral compromise, you need to purify your passions by getting yourself out of those situations as quickly as possible. Paul instructed the Corinthian Christians, "Flee from sexual immorality" (1 Corinthians 6:18). He gave a similar order to Timothy when he wrote, "Flee the evil desires of youth" (2 Timothy 2:22). To flee literally means to run for your life. Sometimes you need to purify your passions by running for your moral life away from a tempting situation or person.

You can't find a better biblical example of purified passions than in Joseph. Genesis 39:1-12 records his story. As a slave in Egypt, Joseph became the faithful, trustworthy servant of Potiphar, the captain of the king's guard. Joseph was so conscientious in his work that Potiphar gave him authority over his entire household. Before long, Potiphar's wife began having designs on Joseph's handsome body and probably tried to seduce him many times—but he refused. When Potiphar was away, she worked her wily ways to coax Joseph to come to bed with her. Joseph's response to her sexual seductions reveals his resolve to subject his passions to God's authority: "How then could I do such a wicked thing and sin against God?" (verse 9). Aware of the temptation, Joseph kept as much distance as possible between himself and his master's wife.

One day the woman found Joseph alone in the house. She grabbed Joseph by the cloak and demanded that he come to bed with her. Joseph didn't stop to argue. He yanked himself out of her grasp and ran out of the house, leaving his cloak in her hand. The evil woman was so upset at Joseph's refusal that she falsely accused him of assaulting her, using the cloak as evidence against him. Since Joseph was only a servant, Potiphar believed his wife's lies and punished Joseph by throwing him into prison. That seemed like a bad ending for a good man. However, God eventually honored Joseph's integrity and used him to save Egypt, and his own family, from famine.

Joseph's example of moral purity reveals two ways you can flee immorality and purify your passions. First, just as Joseph kept his distance from the tempting seductress, you need to keep as much space as possible between you and those things that entice you to fall. For example, if you realize that your sexual desires are aroused by certain books or magazines, don't buy them. If certain websites enflame your mind with wicked thoughts, get some applications or an internet service that will block those sites from appearing on your monitor. If you find yourself wanting to act out with your girlfriend or boyfriend some of the steamy scenes in movies, don't go see them or rent them. If you can't go into the video store without renting the wrong kinds of movies, don't go into those stores. Become aware of the temptations that pollute your mind and purposely stay away from them.

Second, when you find yourself unexpectedly cornered in a potentially compromising situation, get yourself out of there fast. Like Joseph, you may become the intended victim of someone else's immoral designs. What do you do when, during a good-night embrace, your girlfriend urges you toward more intimate sexual contact or your boyfriend tries to violate the bikini barrier? Your aroused passions want your date to continue, but you know that in 30 seconds your defenses will crumble, and you will be sorry tomorrow. You need to run for your moral life. Don't delay to explain. Just say good night and leave immediately. You can talk about it later on the phone, but in the moment of strong temptation your first order of business is to run.

2. Stand Strong and Resist

Another method for purifying your passions is to take a biblically defensive stance against temptations to impurity. Paul instructed the Ephesians, "Be strong in the Lord and in his mighty power. Put on the full armor of God so that you can take your stand against the devil's schemes" (Ephesians 6:10-11).

Sometimes you need to run from temptation, and sometimes you need to stand and fight. If you wanted to escape all human temptation, you might have to move to a mountaintop to live all by yourself. Even there you would not be outside the realm of temptation because you can't run away from your natural desires, thoughts, and memories. You must learn to stand your ground and to defend yourself with the spiritual armor God has provided.

Take a look at Ephesians 6:10-18:

> Finally, be strong in the Lord and in his mighty power. Put on the full armor of God so that you can take your stand against the devil's schemes. For our struggle is not against flesh and blood, but against the rulers, against the authorities, against the powers of this dark world and against the spiritual forces of evil in the heavenly realms. Therefore put on the full armor of God, so that when the day of evil comes, you may be able to stand your ground, and after you have done everything, to stand. Stand firm then, with the belt of truth buckled around your waist, with the breastplate of righteousness in place, and with your feet fitted with the readiness that comes from the gospel of peace. In addition to all this, take up the shield of faith, with which you can extinguish all the flaming arrows of the evil one. Take the helmet of salvation and the sword of the Spirit, which is the word of God. And pray in the Spirit on all occasions with all kinds of prayers and requests. With this in mind, be alert and always keep on praying for all the saints.

Notice that the first piece of armor God has provided for our protection in the midst of spiritual warfare is for the stomach, intestines, and sex organs—the physical counterparts to our inner passions. For the Roman soldier, the belt was more like a girdle that cinched his free-flowing tunic around his midsection, allowing freedom of movement in battle. Soldiers often attached other pieces of armor and weaponry to the belt, making it an indispensable foundation garment for warfare.

The belt of truth suggests that you must defend your passions against moral compromise with the truth of God's Word. Regardless of how broadly contemporary society may promote premarital and extramarital sex, the Bible is clear and definite about reserving sex for marriage. You will be ill-prepared to fend off the world's loose moral standards unless you are firmly grounded in what the Bible says about sex, love, and marriage. More personally, you need to "gird up your loins" daily with God's Word in order to make the right decisions when your passions are being tested in relationships with the opposite sex.

3. Pursue Godly Values

Someone in sports probably coined the phrase "The best defense is a good offense." That principle applies to the discipline of purifying your passions. You must not only defend against sin's encroachment on your passions by fleeing immorality and wearing the armor of truth, but you also must launch an offensive by pursuing positive, godly values.

In the same verse that Paul wrote, "Flee the evil desires of youth," he added, "and pursue righteousness, faith, love and peace" (2 Timothy 2:22). The word "pursue" in this verse means "to run swiftly in order to catch."

It was sometimes used of a bow hunter who had only wounded his prey with his first arrow. As the animal tried frantically to escape its fate, the hopeful hunter relentlessly tracked it, knowing he would eventually outlast his prey and realize his prize.

Paul wrote almost the same instruction to Timothy in his first letter: "Pursue righteousness, godliness, faith, love, endurance and gentleness" (1 Timothy 6:11). In each case, the apostle challenged the young, single pastor to be relentless in pursuing those positive qualities that would fill his life with the goodness God promises.

Purifying your passions is not just a matter of fending off sin but also of pursuing righteousness in your whole life. You're not just trying to purge your passions of pollution; you're also trying to infuse your passions with godliness, faith, love, peace, and other positive characteristics. Moral purity is not a list of don'ts; it's a discipline of do's.

Pursuing godly values is a difficult process. It just doesn't happen overnight; it takes time. You must discipline yourself to pursue righteousness through prayer, Bible study, making right choices, and saying no to activities of lesser value.

It's not an easy life, but Christ never promised you an easy life. He promised you the best life, and you attain the best life only through the discipline of pursuing goodness. One of the major differences between an Olympic champion runner and the casual neighborhood jogger is persistent hard work and discipline. Christ is calling you to be a champion of purified passions.

Get Off Your Emotional Roller Coaster

Do you enjoy going to amusement parks? I do. I enjoy all kinds of rides, but my all-time favorites are the roller coaster and other high-speed thrill rides. I don't mind waiting in line to ride one, especially when I can ride either in the front seat or the backseat. I love the front seat. When I crest that first huge hill and look straight down the steep decline, my heart feels as if it were going through the top of my head. When I ride in the backseat, I get tossed around so much that it makes my head spin. For me, that's fun!

The roller coasters are full of excitement and fun. An interesting thing about riding these modern roller coasters, though, is that you go up and down and you get bounced around, but you always end up where you started. You never actually *go* anywhere. You get lots of thrills, but you make no progress.

The Christian life is not supposed to be a roller-coaster ride. Sure, you will always have ups and downs, and sometimes you may get bounced around, but at least you're going somewhere. You're making progress. If your Christian life is a bumpy ride with no progress, you will experience discouragement and eventually want to give up the faith.

Similarly, if you're committed to coming to terms with relationship regret and living a life of healthy choices, you will hit some bumps in the road. Sometimes you won't seem to be making any progress. My advice? Don't give up. Keep going and stay on the right road. No one wants to get stuck on an endless bumpy ride that goes nowhere. In this Bright Spot we will smooth out some of the hills and fill in some of the valleys of your experience to produce some discernible progress in your life. When you learn to refocus your future, you can step off the roller coaster of life and really go somewhere with God.

Letting Go

Daryl had a tough time getting off the roller coaster of his past sins and bad habits. He tried repeatedly to get his walk with God going again, but all he did was make the same mistakes over and over. Daryl wondered if he could ever be free to love again in God's way. Here's how he put it:

> I couldn't see how God was going to fulfill Romans 8:28 in my life: "In all things God works for the good of those who love him, who have been called according to his purpose." How could He use my past and my sexual involvements with women for good? All I knew was that I had a lot of memories to deal with that were not easy to erase. I was not beyond being tempted again—not by any means. Often I would sit and struggle with my regrets and wish I could relive the past and make better choices.
>
> As I committed myself totally to Jesus Christ and His lordship in my life, though, I began to study the Scriptures daily. God's instructions and promises began to come alive for me. When I read Paul's words, a new vigor and hope began to surge through me. He wrote, "One thing I do: Forgetting what is behind and straining toward what is ahead, I press on toward the goal to win the prize for which God has called me heavenward in Christ Jesus" (Philippians 3:13-14).
>
> I knew I needed to lay my past failures at the cross and leave them there. I needed to press on, to look forward, and to concentrate on all that God wanted me to become.
>
> Now, ten years later, I look back. Incredibly God has fulfilled His promise to me to work all things together for good. Through the years, as I have truly sought to know

Him, love Him, and of course, obey Him, He has taken my
past and fulfilled His promise. I have a deeper understanding of people, their needs, and why they choose the
course of action they do. God took my past and used it to
help others. He made everything work together for good
in my life, something that, in the beginning of my walk
with Him, I never thought He would be able to do.

Daryl learned a principle that we all need to learn in order to
move ahead with Christ: If you want to go forward, you can't dwell
in the past. As Paul said, we must forget what is behind and strain
toward what is ahead.

Here's another way to look at it. Trapeze acrobats swing back
and forth on one bar until another trapeze bar swings into view.
In order to grab onto the new bar and continue their act, they must
let go of the one they're holding onto. They'll never move on to
the next phase of their act until they let go—and they'll never let
go of that bar until they decide to let go.

Like Daryl, you must let go of your past if you want to move
into God's future for your life. The choice is yours. You can
continue to allow your past to hinder you, or you can accept its
lessons and let go of it. You can either wallow in self-pity and regret
over the past or you can reach for and grasp the magnitude of who
you are in Christ. You can either remain the pawn of your passions
and demanding emotions or you can begin living for your deep
longings, which will eventually fulfill your heartfelt desires. You
can't do both, just as a trapeze artist can't ride two bars at once. You
must decide to let go of the past, focus your future, and go for it.

A Confident Faith

Deciding to focus your future requires another trait that trapeze
artists display: faith. When the acrobat lets go of his trapeze, he
does so believing that when he spins around in midair, another

swinging trapeze bar will be within his grasp. He confidently releases what he can see to reach for something he cannot see, knowing it will be there when he needs it.

The Bible is crystal clear about the importance of faith in following Christ: "Without faith it is impossible to please God, because anyone who comes to him must believe that he exists and that he rewards those who earnestly seek him" (Hebrews 11:6). Faith focuses on God, who is above the circumstances of life. It sees His invisible characteristics flowing in and through the person who trusts the Lord. If all you ever do is deal with the things and circumstances you can see, you will be like everyone else—depending solely on self to get by. That's just a long, bumpy roller-coaster ride going nowhere. On the other hand, faith unlocks the mystery of God's presence, the movement of the Lord in your everyday events. When you learn to tap into the unseen godly dimension by faith, you will experience a unique power to face the future, and you'll never be the same.

Jesus Christ summarized the essence of our focus in life when He declared that the greatest of all commandments is to love God intimately (Matthew 22:37). Christ's statement is a direct quote from the Old Testament. Loving God is not just a New Testament idea; God has always wanted us to love Him intimately. He doesn't choose favorites, but He does desire that we all become His close disciples. If you focus your life and your future on developing a loving, intimate relationship with God, you are in the jet stream of the Holy Spirit. To know God intimately is the greatest goal in life. As you focus on that goal, everything that detracts from it will become unimportant by comparison.

Developing an intimate relationship with God doesn't happen overnight. It's a never-ending, lifelong adventure that involves persistent study of the Scriptures and prayer. Becoming intimate with God also means inviting Him into every area of your life and making Him the focus of everything you do. Loving God is a daily commitment that requires discipline, perseverance, and determination. Yet the joy of the journey is fantastic, especially when you take advantage of God's promise of strength: "The LORD…gives strength to the weary and increases the power of the weak. Even youths grow tired and weary, and young men stumble and fall; but those who hope in the LORD will renew their strength. They will soar on wings like eagles; they will run and not grow weary, they will walk and not be faint" (Isaiah 40:28-31).

Saying No to Lesser Things

Another way to focus your future is by learning to say no to anything that would sidetrack you from your goals. Our culture urges us to satisfy our cravings and do what feels good. If you follow that advice, pretty soon you're going every which way but not getting anywhere, doing everything but accomplishing nothing.

We need to say no to some things. In fact, you ought to stand in front of the mirror every day and practice saying, "No, no, no, no, no." Then, when a questionable activity or relationship begs you to say yes, you will have already practiced declining it. Here are a few examples:

Say no to people who tear you down. Bright Spot 5 encouraged you to say no to any relationship eroding your moral integrity. "But," you may object, "if I break up with him, he'll be hurt."

That may be true, but by continuing the relationship, you are being decimated. Don't try to protect the other person at the expense of your own future. Also, don't try to play God in that person's life. Do what you must do to honor Christ, and leave the other person in God's hands.

Others resist saying no to a damaging relationship by rationalizing, "If I break off with her, she'll never come to Christ because I'm the only Christian she knows."

That's like telling the Holy Spirit He can't reach your friend without your help. You not only have a relationship problem, you have a faith problem. You don't believe in the power of God. You need to trust the Holy Spirit to reach your friend even if you leave the relationship.

Saying no to a relationship isn't the end of the world, although it may feel like it for a while. During my years as a single adult, I was involved in several broken romantic relationships. Some of them were casual dating relationships and others were more serious. Even though none of them were immoral, three of those breakups were heartbreaking. Still, through those hard times I learned some great lessons about myself, love, friendship, and trusting God. If you let God teach you to say no to the relationships He says no to, you will be richer for it.

Also, say no to lesser things. For example, I love to read the newspaper. Some days I'll spend a long time reading a paper and put off talking to God and reading the Bible. When I get to the end of the day I say, "Sorry, God, I didn't have time to meet with You today." Then as I look back on my day, I realize I would have been better off meeting with God for an hour and skipping some of the newspaper. I said no to the greater thing and yes to the lesser thing.

Nothing is wrong with reading newspapers or good books, watching TV, or going shopping, but if these things detract from the things that really help you keep your life on track, you must say no to them. An old saying goes something like this: "The good is the enemy of the best." Sometimes our lives are missing the best because we have not learned to say no to the good.

Say no to time pressures as well. Sometimes we can make too much time for the activities we love. Other times, we don't allow any time for anything. Don't let yourself get frazzled by pressures in your daily time schedule. We all seem to be caught up in a whirlwind of activities. Somebody says, "Let's go for pizza," or, "Let's play basketball," or, "Let's go to a movie." You don't want to turn your friends down or miss out on a good time, but your calendar is overloaded. You're missing out on needed rest. You're not doing a good job at work. You're lagging in your personal time with God. Learn to bring coordination to your life and say no to things that tend to knock your life out of balance.

God's Promises as You Focus Your Future

Focusing your future means choosing righteousness above all other choices and leaving the results to God. Serving God with moral integrity may cost you some fleshly pleasure and desirable relationships, but ultimately, you won't be sorry for choosing God's ways over the desires of your flesh. The pleasures of sin look good, but the results are always negative in the long run. In contrast, when you focus your future on God's righteousness, God promises some tremendous blessings and benefits. Here's a small sampling from Psalms:

- The Lord watches over your way (Psalm 1:6).
- The Lord surrounds you with His favor (Psalm 5:12).
- The Lord is present with you (Psalm 14:5).
- The Lord sees you and hears your prayers (Psalm 34:15).
- The Lord delivers you out of your troubles (Psalm 34:19).
- The Lord condemns your foes (Psalm 34:21).
- The Lord upholds you (Psalm 37:17).
- The Lord refuses to forsake you (Psalm 37:25).
- The Lord becomes your stronghold in troubled times (Psalm 37:39).
- The Lord sustains your life (Psalm 55:22).
- The Lord shines His light on you (Psalm 97:11).
- The Lord loves you (Psalm 146:8).

Saying Yes to Righteousness

Choosing righteousness is the only smart choice. God's rewards are worth enduring any momentary discomfort you may suffer from the world, your flesh, or the devil.

Moses grew up with the privileges and prestige of Egyptian royalty. Opulence and wealth surrounded him. Egypt was the foremost military and political power in the world, and Moses was the adopted son of the king's daughter. He could have had it all: fame, fortune, women, power. Instead, Moses chose to serve God.

God asked Moses to leave the security of his Egyptian family and accept a new identity, a new role, and a new mission. Moses responded obediently. "He chose to be mistreated along with the people of God rather than to enjoy the pleasures of sin for a short time. He regarded disgrace for the sake of Christ as of greater value than the treasures of Egypt, because he was looking ahead to his reward" (Hebrews 11:25-26).

Moses lost his security, his wealth, his prestige, his power—everything. He was probably ridiculed, laughed at, called derogatory names, rejected, and humiliated for his choice. Yet he paid the price because of his commitment to obey God; "By faith he left Egypt, not fearing the king's anger; he persevered because he saw him who is invisible" (Hebrews 11:27).

Did Moses have a choice? Of course he did. God never forces us to obey Him. He invites us to choose obedience to Him and promises His presence and provision as we do so. Focusing your future means committing yourself unreservedly to obeying God in your life.

Did he make a dumb choice? History tells us the story. He is considered one of the greatest leaders of all time. And, although we don't fully know what God's reward to Moses was, God did select Moses to appear with Elijah on the Mount of Transfiguration when Jesus was on earth (Mark 9:2-4).

Moses focused on his future and the unseen God who would guide him through it. God calls us to make the same choice.

I don't know a better illustration of a couple committing their lives and futures to God than the story of Tom and Sharon. They fell in love while working in the same city during summer vacation. They both returned to college in the fall; Tom to Dallas and Sharon to St. Louis. During the school year they wrote romantic letters to each other. Being apart was hard on both of them. They wanted very much to be together.

At the same time Sharon was being tormented by a growing dilemma. She sensed God was guiding her to become a missionary to Indonesia. The more she prayed and the more she read the Bible, the more her heart went out to the people there who needed Christ. Whenever she read anything about Southeast Asia, she was thrilled at the possibility of taking God's message of love there.

Sharon hadn't talked to Tom about Indonesia. They had discussed some of their plans for after graduation, but she kept quiet about what God was saying to her about missionary service.

Thanksgiving weekend was approaching. Tom was coming to visit, and Sharon was confused. She loved him deeply, but she didn't know if he would want to serve Christ with her in Indonesia. What if she decided to follow Christ's leading and Tom didn't want to go? She wondered if he had become more important to her than God.

When Tom arrived, Sharon was excited to see him, but she was so upset inside she couldn't bear to tell him about her dilemma. That first night they attended a lecture by a missionary from Asia. The room was so crowded when they arrived that they could not sit together. So Sharon sat in the chair directly in front of Tom.

As the missionary spoke, she prayed, "Lord, speak to Tom. Show him Your purpose for his life—and show me Your purpose for mine."

Sharon could not mistake the moving of the Lord in her heart. When the missionary spoke about Indonesia, her mind was filled with possibilities of going there—but what about Tom? What was he thinking? What was God saying to his heart? Sharon knew that she must choose to follow God's leading regardless of God's plan for Tom. In the stillness of her heart, she affirmed her commitment to serve God in Indonesia—with or without Tom.

After the meeting, Sharon turned her chair around. "Well, what do you think about everything you heard?" she asked cautiously.

He was silent for only a moment, but it seemed like ten years to her. "I really haven't said much to you about the specific direction of my future," he began, "but tonight confirmed it in my heart.

"I really love you, Sharon. You are very important to me—but the Lord is directing me to become a missionary to Indonesia." Sharon almost fell off her chair with shock and excitement.

Tom and Sharon have been married for more than 40 years. They have served the Lord together with their four children in various parts of the world, including 13 years in Indonesia.

These two wonderful people demonstrate to me and countless others the rewards of focusing your future on Christ and His plan for our lives. He knows you, and He knows your future. If you are to get married someday, He knows all about your future spouse and his or her future. When you give everything you are and have to Him, your future will be in clear focus.

Have you gotten off your emotional roller coaster?

Melt the Wall of Ice That Separates You

In the gorgeous, clear morning in the Colorado Rocky Mountains, the rushing stream cascaded over huge boulders and birds sang in the aspen trees. The scene was delightful.

But I was miserable! My friend Glenn and I had pitched our tent next to that stream the previous night so we could be far from the tent where our dates slept. Things just were not going too well, especially between me and my date.

We had come up to the mountains during a break. I had just finished teaching at the Institute of Biblical Studies held each summer at Colorado State University. So before the next sessions, the four of us, along with a carload of others, had headed for the beautiful Rocky Mountains.

Although my date and I had been friends for a year, we had been dating for only about a month. But on this short trip, our relationship started to deteriorate.

Have you ever watched a wall of ice form between you and your date? Everything you say is taken wrong. Conversation is strained and the heart is cold. Everything you try to do goes over like a lead balloon. Eventually, you just give up trying. You dread the time left to spend together, so you constantly look at your watch, hoping for the end to come soon. That's the way I felt.

I don't usually pick up hints very well, but I was getting her message loud and clear. Her shoulder was colder than the snow on the mountaintops. Oh, we talked, but it was to fill up the silence rather than to share the breathtaking beauty we saw all around us.

One evening we had fun—Joan, Glenn, and me. We had pitched our tents, and the three of us stretched out on a blanket looking up at the stars. They were so clear that you could almost reach up and touch one. My date sat alone over by the fire even though she wasn't cold. What a boring time for her—and for me.

Three long days of this ice wall. I was miserable. When I woke up the last morning of our trip, I decided to go downstream. Sitting on a large rock in the stream bed, I thought about our relationship. As far as I was concerned, it was finished. I was writing her off my list. The pain of rejection was too much to bear. I had had it!

I had carried a small New Testament with me, and I chose a passage from Luke 6 to read. I needed something to get my mind off the situation.

"But I say to you who hear," Jesus proclaimed, "love your enemies" (Luke 6:27 NASB). To me it was obvious: He was talking about my date. Look at what she had done to me—pain!

"Do good to those who hate you." Jesus really understood my date and her attitude toward me.

"Bless those who curse you," He went on. "Pray for those who mistreat you." My date definitely had mistreated me.

My attention, as I read the rest of the passage, was on my pain and hurt. I had felt rejected, so I was going to reject her!

But then I came to the eye opener—Luke 6:38: "Give and it will be given to you," Jesus promised. "For with the measure you use, it will be measured to you."

I was startled! My focus had been on myself and not on her needs. I had only wanted out of the relationship. I was hurt, and I wanted to hurt back.

Christ's emphasis was on love—my attention was on "your enemies." His command was to "do good"—I saw only "those who hate you." I did not want to give to her, I wanted to reject her. My self-centeredness and sin became hideous to me. I could not fathom how rotten my attitude had become. I had allowed myself to wallow in self-pity and pain.

Christ said, "Love." How? I was weak and hurt. In my mind, she deserved to be rejected and hurt in return. But Jesus had given Himself on the cross for people who were a lot worse than she was. He loved His enemies. Could I give to my date?

My heart broke, and I sobbed, "O Lord, I need You! Change my hardness and forgive my selfishness. Fill me with Your love and power."

I was scared, but now I wanted to give to my date. We had to melt the ice wall—even if we never went out again.

The camp was empty. Over an hour had elapsed since my departure. I looked all over for her. And then I saw her. Way upstream she was sitting on some boulders with her back toward me. She didn't notice me as I approached her. My legs felt like rubber. All my courage drained away and I wanted to hide. *Give, and it will be given to you* kept filling my mind. I called on Jesus for strength and wisdom to know what to say.

"Hi...mind if I join you for a few minutes?" I timidly asked.

"No, I don't mind," she replied with a surprised look on her face.

"What are you doing?" I felt like I had just swallowed my tongue.

"Oh, just thinking and reading. What have you been doing?"

"Oh, reading. Can I show what I read?" My heart was pounding.

"Sure."

I fumbled through the pages. "Love your enemies." (I did not add, "That means you.")

I read the whole passage and finally got to "Give and it will be given to you." I stopped and looked up at her. The moment had come! But I knew that somehow Christ would help me through this torture.

"Uh...these last four days have been difficult ones for me.

Something is wrong with our relationship. I have tried to be friendly and help you have a good time, but things have not worked out very well between us." I paused and got my breath. *This is the hardest conversation I've had in years,* I thought.

"When I read this passage this morning, God opened my mind toward you. With all honesty, I want to be your friend. However, your desire may be to stop dating me. That's okay. I just want to let you know, my heart is open to build our friendship. I don't want any walls or any bad feelings between us."

She looked down at the rocks and slowly asked, "Would you like me to tell you what's been on my mind?"

"Yes…I'd like to know."

"Well, I started to like you," she blurted out. "But to protect myself from possibly getting hurt, I became overly critical of you. That's why I acted so distant. I didn't know how to handle my feelings."

I was speechless! In my wildest imagination I never guessed that would be her response. As we talked further about the situation and cleared up the misconceptions, joy and excitement flooded my heart.

I gave her a big hug and said, "It is so much better to be vulnerable and honest. The Lord Jesus gets the credit for breaking down the wall between us. Would you like to thank Him with me for this guidance?"

"I'd love to."

There on the rocks we poured out our hearts to God in thanksgiving and joy.

Seven months later I was speaking at a large meeting at West Virginia University. During my talk on "How to Know When You Are in Love," I used this incident in Colorado as an illustration of giving in a relationship.

At the end of the meeting, we had an open forum time.

After I answered several questions, one student spoke up, "What ever happened to that girl you were on the rocks with?"

"What day is it today?" I asked.

"It's Thursday, January 28," somebody else replied.

"Well, in two days I plan to ask her to marry me!"

The whole auditorium erupted in cheers and applause.

Two days later, in a quiet romantic restaurant in Atlanta, I asked Paula, "Will you marry me?" She was speechless. She had not expected it. The next day, she said yes.

On May 30, 1982, we exchanged rings during our wedding ceremony. Inscribed on the inside of each ring is Luke 6:38: "Give, and it will be given to you."

Part 3
Dealing with a Breakup

How to Heal
Your Broken Heart

So Serious Girlfriend or Boyfriend has become Serious Ex-girlfriend or Ex-boyfriend. Nothing is easy about a breakup. If you've been through one recently or are in the process of The Big Breakup right now, then you know they are painful. Sometimes very painful.

Hey, that's why Neil Sedaka wrote a song about it. His words are still as true today as they were before he even penned the catchy chorus back in the 1960s. ("They say that breaking up is hard to do. Now I know, I know that it's true...") No other words could explain it more accurately. It's just *hard*. But sometimes a true heartbreak helps us understand just how challenging love is in this world—but how effortless God's great love is.

Nevertheless, your post-breakup time won't always be pretty. Regardless of who decided to say goodbye, coming to terms with the loss will hurt, and it will release all kinds of emotions and mind-sets. Grief. Sadness. Anger. Denial. Blame. They're all in there just as if someone had died.

Be Alert

But remember that when you're at your lowest, you will be especially vulnerable to Satan and his cunning ways. Remember that Satan only came to "steal and kill and destroy" (John 10:10) and that he is "roaming through the earth and going back and forth in it" (Job 1:7) looking for someone to prey upon. If you were disappointed in your behavior during your relationship, Satan may try to convince you that the breakup was totally your fault. While you go through the grieving process of letting go, you may feel like you always will be sad and that God will not grant you happiness in a relationship ever again. If you become angry at your ex-significant-other, Satan may tempt you to withhold forgiveness.

In his book on spiritual warfare called *Waking the Dead,* author John Eldredge writes that Satan is hoping to make us agree to his plan:

> When we make those agreements with the demonic forces suggesting things to us, we come under their influence. It becomes kind of permission we give the Enemy, sort of like a contract...Some foul spirit whispers, I'm such a stupid idiot, and they agree with it; then they spend months and years trying to sort through feelings of insignificance...If you are having trouble taking in all of this, let me ask you: Have you had this experience? Something bad happens, and you start telling yourself what a jerk you are. Do you really think the source of that is just you? Or God?[1]

Be aware of what Satan wants to do and the reality of the work he is hoping to accomplish on this earth. But even more importantly, remember that God is the giver of hope. He promises to work good in all things—not just some things, but all things—for those who love Him and are called according to his will (Romans 8:28).

Remember as you go through the breakup process that God always overcomes (John 16:33). If you have trusted Jesus as your Savior, then you can overcome temptations because Christ is working in you to help you fight (1 John 5:4). Even though a breakup is painful and Satan may try to destroy your hope, nothing can separate you from God's endless love—not even the demons! (See Romans 8:38-39.)

Sometimes only through a breakup do we learn certain life-changing lessons and learn to trust and love God in a way that can come from a broken heart alone.

Healing takes time. If you've had an especially bad breakup, the wounds may require many months to heal. Sometimes, in this fast-paced world, I wonder whether people take time to heal and prioritize the post-breakup time as a unique opportunity to prepare themselves better for the next person they meet.

But not all is gloom and doom from here. Have hope. God hasn't left you. David says "I sought the LORD, and he answered me; he delivered me from all my fears. Those who look to him are radiant; their faces are never covered with shame...The angel of the LORD encamps around those who fear him, and he delivers them" (Psalm 34:4-5,7). Day by day, God will make the way for you to love again. He is the great counselor and healer of wounds. So as you move ahead in the next days and months, cling to Him. And as you do that, consider these tips to help you move up to the next part of the good plan He has in store for you.

Accepting the Decision

First things first. If you're going to move on, you must accept the reality of the split. This sounds pretty obvious, but dealing with the hard truth before you is one of the most difficult. Nights usually reserved for date nights now are free, and even the less obvious parts of the relationship—like nightly phone calls—will become blaringly noticeable in their absence. During this time, you will naturally want to return to what is familiar. You're going to want to call your ex when you've had a bad day at work. Around the holidays, you're going to wish your ex were by your side at all the family gatherings.

In moments of weakness or loneliness, going back to the

relationship would be very easy, even if your reasons for breaking up were very clear and definite. You may remember only the good times together and overlook the bad times. Feelings are complicated in that way. You usually only remember the positives, and that's why breaking up and getting back together must never be an emotional decision. Our emotions don't give us a true perspective of the situation. Sometimes reconciliation is possible—we'll discuss that later. But most of the time, when you call it quits, you should mean it.

Take Nick and Leigh as an example. The two twentysomethings from California had been dating seriously for about seven months when they decided to spend some time apart because of difficulties in their relationship. Although this wasn't an official breakup, it felt like one, and it was hard for both of them. But there's nothing like a natural disaster to get you saying "I love you" again. A wildfire burst across the state, and as the flames raged outside, the pair fell back into the old patterns of a happy couple.

This is understandable. A colossal fire was threatening to turn the state into ashes, and life always seems shorter when a big disaster is coming. But they really were playing with fire. Before long, Nick and Leigh officially broke up. In the ensuing months, letting go was painful for both of them.

Nick hadn't given Leigh a clear reason for the initial breakup, and Leigh blamed the split on a silly fight they had. But in the end, it turned out Nick had cheated on Leigh by kissing another woman.

Nick felt terrible and launched a campaign to win Leigh back. And for the most part, it worked. Nick pledged to meet with Leigh's family to set things straight. He promised to do everything he could to prove Leigh could trust him again. He wrote a letter asking for another chance, and he showered her with expensive gifts.

Leigh wanted to trust Nick again, but she had difficulty letting go of his deception and believing Nick still loved her after the deep rejection she felt when he broke up with her. Leigh didn't trust Nick anymore, and she became a fighter and an interrogator. Leigh wanted to believe Nick was going to fight for her, and his efforts to win her back gave her some hope. But because the situation was emotional and Leigh was hesitant to get involved again, she asked that Nick not call her for a month so they could pray about their relationship. Nick agreed, promising his heart was with Leigh and that he would be there for her when they talked again.

But a month passed and Nick changed his mind. Nick was interested in another woman. Of course, nothing is wrong with a single man or woman choosing to begin a relationship with someone who may be a better match. But something was very wrong with the way Nick stretched out his breakup with Leigh. He put her on an emotional roller coaster that finally ran off the tracks.

More than five months had elapsed since the pair had broken up the first time, but by continuing to pursue Leigh after the breakup, Nick caused more pain once he finally decided he was ready to move on.

"I feel like we've broken up ten times," Leigh said.

All this heartache is the result of refusing to accept the reality of a breakup. Pain, pain, and more pain. God can take any circumstance and use it for good, but Jesus said "Let your 'Yes' be 'Yes' and your 'No' be 'No'" (Matthew 5:37). Anything in between a yes and a no is confusing and hurtful and ultimately will delay the healing process.

So don't do this. If you break up, make it a clean break with the person. That means no talking. No writing. No communicating. (The only exception to that rule is if you need to apologize for a wrong you have committed against that person. If you didn't reconcile during The Big Breakup, then write your ex-girlfriend or ex-boyfriend a letter. But put it behind you just as soon as you drop the letter in the mailbox.)

I know that's difficult. And at the time, even thinking about walking away for good hurts—especially when you are the person who is on the receiving end of the break-up.

But both of you need room to heal. Some distance is very good. Time really can help heal wounds.

Men, don't pursue her again. Ladies, don't grill his friends for information on what he has been up to. Both of you, *just let it go*.

The Paper Shredder:
The Best Post-breakup Investment a Woman Can Make
(Leigh, age 25, is a researcher in Los Angeles)

Women, do yourselves a favor. After you and your man have said your goodbyes, go buy yourself a paper shredder. I'm not kidding. During my breakup with my first serious boyfriend, I wished I had one. For the future, I'm making the investment.

I'm the kind of person who did everything short of bronzing the cards and letters and tokens of affection my boyfriend gave me while we were dating. I loved them, and long after he sent them, I would open them and read them over and over again. Yes, it's great when you are with him. Those words make you remember all the great things about him and how lucky you are to have him.

But after the breakup? Not so good. So trust me on this one. It's hard to do at first, but resolve to immediately throw everything away. When my boyfriend Nick and I broke up, I sent the photographs, the cards, and the framed poem penned in his very own handwriting (sniff, sniff) straight into the trash can. When we broke up the second time, I did one better. I sent all the gifts he gave to me—including a beautiful suit—to my best friend. Nick also gave me gift certificates to my favorite fast-food restaurant. We were living in different states at the time, and I was supposed to use them for a "long-distance lunch date" where I would eat at the restaurant and call him. At the time, I thought the idea was sweet and sentimental. After we broke up, I gave the gift certificates to a homeless man in a park near my work.

It wasn't bitterness that drove me to throw away the items or give away the gifts reminding me of Nick. It was just better for my heart. We women love the words, we love the gifts, and we love the sentiment. Sometimes the memories were just too much for me. But knowing I was helping someone else—like the homeless man who probably had not had a decent meal recently—helped my heartache a little.

So ladies, along with that paper shredder, add something else to your post-breakup shopping list. Also buy a really large trash can, or a dumpster if you have the budget. Rid your life of anything that makes you rush for a box of Kleenex and a tub of Häagen-Dazs. Your heartache may take a while to wane, but you'll feel a little better with every drone of the shredder or thump of those trash bags full of memories.

And finally, don't be bitter about it. Fight to keep your heart soft about the situation, regardless of how badly it ends. And please, ladies, don't hold his sweatshirt for ransom. Do something good for your ex and just start praying he treats correctly the next woman he gives it to wear.

Process Your Emotions

Okay, I don't need to tell you. There's a reason it's called a breakup. You're going to feel broken. And in the midst of that, you need to express your hurt and pain and grief. Emotions often well up within us, and if we try to smother them, eventually they will return in a more destructive manner. Our bodies will take the toll of these emotions if we don't process them correctly. So don't be phony after you and your ex part ways. Don't pretend you're happy or even in a good mood when you're not. Don't smile when deep down inside you are ready to explode. Nobody likes to be rejected (and remember, the heartbreaker hurts too). So whether you are the heartbreaker or the heartbroken, don't be ashamed or embarrassed about expressing your hurt.

My wife, Paula, told me about a time she broke up with a boyfriend she really liked. She felt so down that she decided to go to a movie she knew would be a tearjerker. The movie made her cry even more. But in expressing her grief and letting it out, she was able to reach down inside her heart and understand what she was going through. Who knew a movie could be so therapeutic? But it was.

Women usually express their emotions more easily than men do. When a woman suffers a breakup, she goes on a shopping spree, gets her hair highlighted, and spends hours rehashing the same story with every single one of her closest 50 girlfriends.

Men are usually the opposite. They may go spend a little money on a new golf club or buy a new shirt, but they usually don't talk about the breakup immediately. Instead, they pile their buddies in a car and get out of town to watch a basketball game. They go to the movies, to the sports bar, or to the tennis court, and they play hard and tell jokes. But they don't talk. But men, if you don't process your feelings, you are only going to slow down your healing process. Once you have accepted the reality of the breakup, you need to treat it like a permanent split. Break out of the "men don't cry" stereotype and cry. Turn over your emotions to the Lord. Talk with your close friends, family members, or mentors about how you feel. Do whatever you need to do to let everything out. That way, you won't drag out the process between the breakup and your next date.

You'll also be healthier as you enter your next relationship. A conversation about your most recent ex-girlfriend or ex-boyfriend is sure to kill your first date with a new person. No one wants to live in the past while trying to pursue the future. So do yourself and your next date a great favor and process those emotions.

Yes, healing takes time, so don't rush the process. You may find yourself despondent for two or three months after a break with your ex of a year or more, but don't let that get you down. Grief has no time limit. Depending on the relationship, the memory of some wounds always hurt just a little bit. The best thing you can do is allow yourself the time to heal and trust God to move you forward.

The process is difficult because you feel defeated and shattered. But don't think that if one person rejects you, the next person will as well. And of course, don't think that you're some sort of reject yourself. You were made for healthy, happy relationships.

Trusting God with Your Emotions
(Lisa, age 24, is a graduate student in Columbus, Ohio.)

Want to hear my forgiveness story? Brian was interested in me, but he wasn't ready for a relationship. So when he called us "purposeful friends," I had hope that we would turn into something more. But then he stopped talking to me, and I later found out he was interested in dating another girl. So goes "purposeful friendship." I was really wrapped up in how I thought he treated me disrespectfully. This wasn't the way a friend should be treated (especially by another Christian).

I went over and over in my head what I'd say to him about how I thought he was wrong, and I seriously considered talking to him about it. I told one of my Christian friends what I was thinking of doing. But instead of agreeing with me, she told me I shouldn't say anything to him and instead I should just forgive him. She (gently) reminded me that he was at a point where he definitely was not going to see my side of things and probably wouldn't honestly care that much about my side of the story.

She said I was just hurting myself by building up this bitterness. She was definitely right, and I went home that night and just prayed to God to give me the strength and obedience to forgive him.

God is just so amazing because I can say now without a doubt that I've forgiven him, and I've totally just given that situation over to God. So much of me wanted the "fair" thing to be done, but I found this verse and just clung to it: "Yet the LORD longs to be gracious to you; he rises to show you compassion. For the Lord is a God of justice. Blessed are all who wait for him!" (Isaiah 30:18). What a great reminder that God is the one who will take care of everything in His perfect timing. I just need to wait on Him!

By the way, I ran into Brian a few weeks ago at church, and by the grace of God, I could talk with him and not feel anything—not anger, not frustration, not attraction, but only friendship. God knows best, and I just need to obey Him. I am honestly so happy now!

Turn to the Lord for Comfort

He is the one who is always there, even when you feel lonely and depressed, even when you don't think your situation could get much worse. You may feel alone, but God hasn't left you. He has said, "I have loved you with an everlasting love; therefore I have drawn you with lovingkindness" (Jeremiah 31:3 NASB). That love is constant and consistent even in your pain.

During my senior year of college, my girlfriend, Amy, broke up with me for another guy. I had a hard time dealing with it because I really cared for her, and her decision hardly seemed fair. I was so angry and upset that I began to hate her for all the pain and confusion she had caused me.

Loving others is difficult when they don't love us in return or reject us or cause us pain. We're tempted to turn away from them because they turned away from us, but can you imagine what would have happened if Jesus had responded to His hurt by withdrawing? He might have said, "Nobody appreciates Me. Everybody has rejected Me. Do you think I'm going to get hurt again by going to the cross? Forget it." Thank God, He didn't do that! Instead, He kept reaching out to people until His death on the cross touched the whole world with God's love. When people cause us pain, we need to forgive them the same way Jesus did: "Father, forgive them, for they do not know what they are doing" (Luke 23:34).

One day shortly after Amy and I had parted, I was sitting in the library trying to study. My mind was filled with self-pity, and my heart was filled with hatred. But in my hostility, Christ began to remind me of Scriptures I had read years previously.

Dick, God said in my mind, *I want you to love her.*

Love her? I thought. *Impossible! How could You ask me to love her after what she has done to me?* For the first time in my life, I could not control my mind. I hated her even though I knew I was wrong. I felt overwhelmed by my emotions.

Then the Lord reminded me that Paul had a "thorn in the flesh" (2 Corinthians 12:7). Some scholars think Paul had an incurable, painful eye disease. Others believe he was plagued with epilepsy or bothered by all the problems that the churches he founded were experiencing. Whatever the problem was, it was excruciatingly difficult for him. He couldn't handle it, so he begged God three times to take it away. But the Lord didn't want to take it away, and Paul wrote:

> "But he said to me, My grace is sufficient for you, for power is perfected in weakness." Most gladly, therefore, I will rather boast about my weaknesses, that the power of Christ may dwell in me. Therefore I am well content with weaknesses, with insults, with distresses, with persecutions, with difficulties, [with breakups], for Christ's sake; for when I am weak, then I am strong (2 Corinthians 12:9-10 NASB).

In my time of weakness and helplessness, Christ promised to give me His comfort and strength. Because Christ is in my life, I can find a way through my deepest problems.

I memorized and meditated on those verses. Even though the tension, pain, and hurt lasted for months, Christ gradually took away the bitterness and hostility. Every time I was tempted to indulge in self-pity and anger, I read those verses out loud. I clung to Christ, and His strength overshadowed my weaknesses. And the Lord did something in my heart that I never could have done on my own: He brought kindness and compassion into my heart for Amy.

By turning to the Lord to find comfort, I grew in my confidence of God's provision. Like Paul, I grew in my assurance of God's good plan for me. My life was not shattered. God was in control! He would lead me to the woman of His choice in His time. I was secure in His eternal purpose and plan for me!

So don't put off turning to the Lord. Give Him everything you're feeling and ask Him to comfort you. Open up that Bible you've been putting off reading, and read God's promises. They will help you overcome your doubts and fears in your post-breakup time. I can guarantee just reading a Psalm every morning will help you to see your life not as a failure but as something worth living in hope and anticipation of seeing God fulfill His promises. The more you exercise your spirit by seeking God and studying His Word, the stronger you are going to get.

Giving Everything to God
(Cynthia, age 24, is a public relations account executive in Los Angeles, California.)

I met John in Nebraska when my company sent me there for an 8-month stint. I have always had a personal commitment to avoid romantic relationships with coworkers, but after a couple of stressful and lonely months I began to feel down, and John started asking me out.

A few weeks passed, and I really enjoyed his company and the feelings I was developing for him. But almost as soon as the relationship began to mean something to me, he suddenly became less available. When I broke it off, he didn't take it well at all. So a week after I broke up with John, I agreed to go out with him on a date to "talk things out." We had a great time, and the date ended with a kiss. I regret having gotten involved in the first place, but I really regret having gone out with him again after I made the decision to end the relationship. The *very* next day he became a monster in the office. I believe he only went out with me to make sure he still had some control over me. Once he knew he did, he found every way possible to put me in my place.

I never confronted John. I knew I had to just get away from him and cut him out of my life. I decided after all he had put me through, he did not even deserve to see me upset. As far as I was concerned there was nothing to talk about—I just needed to get out of that town ASAP. I left town and never said goodbye.

After I left, I kept up on the office gossip. But every time I would hear a story, the bad feelings would come back. I had a hard time for a while and couldn't stop beating myself up over what had happened. I finally realized I had to forgive myself to really move on. The first thing I did was stop making myself available to hear the stories. I made a conscious decision to leave the past in the past and focus on my future.

> At so many points I remember feeling hopeless and low. I remember one day in particular when John had yelled at me in the office. I was so upset—as soon as I had a few moments alone, I pulled out a small Bible and began reading. I realized God didn't want me to come out of my bad experience bitter and cold. He wanted me to come out of it stronger, wiser and closer to Him. Somehow, going through the ordeal pushed my faith to a new level.
>
> I have come so far since that day. Going through this ordeal has taught me to trust God like I've never done before. I never would have learned to do this over the course of the past several months had it not been for the trial I experienced. Learning to trust God has brought me true peace.

Look for the Lessons

At first no one wants to look for the lessons in a breakup. It's just easier to dwell on what your ex-girlfriend or ex-boyfriend did to mess things up. But once you've processed your emotions and turned to the Lord for comfort and healing, you're ready to look at your relationship with a new perspective. During this time you can better gauge the missteps of the relationship and identify the ways you want to improve your next relationship.

Many people go from relationship to relationship and remain blind to certain problems in their lives. Take a close look at those things that you don't like about yourself and ask the Lord to make any necessary changes. He will tell you if your character or your communication skills or the way you handle conflict needs to be improved. And if it does, He will help you.

But don't be too hard on yourself. All of life is a growing process, and God loves you just the way you are because He created you with your unique personality. He loves all of you. He wants us to rely on Him to grow in our likeness of Him. And here's the greatest part about looking for the lessons in your past relationships. You have no risk because God has assured us that He fully accepts us. Our relationship with Christ makes that possible (1 Corinthians 12:12-13). We are secure in God's hands, and though He may point out some character traits that need improvement, He is developing us into mature people for His purposes (Ephesians 4:11-13).

So don't be afraid to ask yourself the hard questions. *Am I a peacemaker, or do I drag out fights? Do I hold grudges? Am I too selfish? Do I show kindness and compassion and respect?* Think about the difficult areas of your relationship and determine your role in the difficulty.

Honor Your Ex

Whether you are the heartbroken or the heartbreaker, the time between when you say goodbye and when you go on your next date is going to be difficult. Remember that a split is going to make both people suffer in some way—at least for a little while.

But if you were the person to make the decision to end the relationship, then the post-breakup time includes an added responsibility for you. It's called honoring your ex.

That may be difficult, especially if your ex-girlfriend or ex-boyfriend mistreated you or made the split difficult. But God never put limits on love, and for that great gift, we can't either. Jesus' command to us makes no way around it: "Love each other as I have loved you" (John 15:12).

Honoring your ex doesn't necessarily mean you will have a relationship with him or her anymore. In most cases, having a friendship at first is not healthy because the two of you are trying to move on, and watching life continue outside of the relationship you shared is going to breed sadness, jealousy, and resentment.

Honoring your ex takes a more subtle, disciplined approach. It's basically treating him or her the way you would want to be treated (Luke 6:31) and making yourself sensitive to the situation. That doesn't mean putting your life on hold. If you have spent time healing and identifying the blind spots of your past relationship, you may be ready to move on to a new relationship. But it's not advisable to jump into a brand-new relationship immediately.

Our tendency is to move forward too quickly. We live in a culture where we begin the 24-hour rush just as soon as we get out of bed in the morning. But I'm encouraging you to take some time to evaluate where you are before moving on. By doing that, you will be able to more clearly see what you want, and you also will honor your ex.

Just give it some time and work to humble yourself. Guys, don't turn into playboys—flirting with other women in front of your ex-girlfriend and planning trips to exotic places with them. Getting another woman's attention may help you feel better, but in the process you are hurting a woman you once cared about very much. And even if you think you are ready to pursue a new, healthy relationship, don't do it immediately. Nothing is worse than when your ex-girlfriend finds out her boyfriend of a week ago is dating the next cute thing. If your new love interest is really worth it, she'll wait for the right time to move forward.

Women, you love to talk. We know you do. But don't run around to all your friends, telling them just how much your ex-boyfriend did you wrong. You're looking for support and encouragement, but in the process you are presenting one side of a story that could potentially defame your ex-boyfriend's name. Of course, we all need to talk about some things, so talk to God. Tell your closest friend or a mentor what's on your heart, but do it in confidence. Don't try to win your mutual friends to your side.

And while you are at it, make a point to hang out with guy friends if you are a guy and girl friends if you are a girl. Making plans with your ex-boyfriend's guy friends is a big no-no. You may be okay with it, but I can guarantee that he won't be. During this time, guys can easily turn to women for encouragement and empathy. But you're doing your ex a service when you free up his guy friends to be there for him. In the process, you won't force friends who care about both of you to choose the person to whom they will be loyal.

Finally, don't feed the gossip circles surrounding the big breakup. You will honor your ex and earn his or her respect if you make an effort to silence the rumors. When someone asks the reason for the split, please don't give the details. "We didn't have chemistry" or "He was too controlling" or "She was too emotional" may all be truthful, but you don't need to say that. Instead try this: "You know, (fill in the blank) is a really great person, but it just didn't work out." End of story. It lets people know in a nice way that you aren't open to talking about the details. And people get the hint. They won't ask again.

Sometimes breakups are especially painful, and finding a place in your heart for honoring your ex is difficult. I know that feeling because I've been let down in big ways by the women I dated before I married Paula. But I also know that God can change hearts. He changed my heart so I could honor the people I've dated. But think of the other person because Christ thought of you first. Becoming Miss Party Girl or Mr. Playboy after the breakup is selfish. Christ has forgiven you and honored His creation, despite the missteps you make over and over again. You can do that for your ex.

Form New Relationships but Don't Rebound

So what do you do in the time between your breakup and your next date? Don't drop your friends, and don't vow to never talk to a man or woman again. On the other hand, don't go crazy either.

People are ready for the emotions of a new relationship at different times. Right now you may not be able to envision the next Serious Girlfriend or Boyfriend, but God already knows who that person is. And if He has allowed a breakup in your life, he or she still is out there until God tells you otherwise.

But before you jump back into the dating scene, do a heart check. Make sure God has healed your heart and you have processed the breakup.

Often when people are hurt, they don't immediately process the pain. Instead they run from it and right into the arms of another person. But I'm telling you right now, don't rebound. Just don't do it. The only time it works is if you are playing a basketball game, so just don't leave the opportunity for it in your post-breakup relationships. Flirting with the cute guy at a party or asking another woman on a weekend excursion may make you feel like the cool playboy or girl, but those actions will only end in disaster.

While we are talking about trips, just rule them out all together. When Nicole and James broke up, James planned a trip to Las Vegas with his friend, Anna. James and Anna were just friends, and James was hurting, so a trip away with another woman seemed like a good way to forget about his pain and have a little fun.

But what seems like a good idea at the time can turn into the perfect set up for Satan to make you stumble. Two Christians of the opposite sex on a trip alone together—in Las Vegas of all places? Yep, you get the idea.

Thankfully, James ended up deciding to cancel the trip. But, trips alone with people of the opposite sex form emotional attachments with the other person. And then before you know it, you have a rebound on your hands. You'll cause pain not just for yourself, but also for the person you are hoping will get you over your ex. And when you finally process the pain, you'll have the pain of your breakup and of your rebound.

So before you start investing in other relationships, decide that you are not going to rebound. But do start getting to know other people. You don't have to date them. In fact, you shouldn't start dating immediately. Try to take it slowly.

David, age 25, a mortgage broker from Texas, knew he still needed some time after a serious relationship ended with a woman he loved. He knew the relationship was over, and he wanted to move ahead, but doing so was difficult. David found that waiting on God and giving himself time was key. *I'm in no rush,* he decided.

Several months after his breakup, David started getting more involved in his church. There he met Laura, a strong Christian woman whom he thought he would like to date. But one of Laura's friends was interested in David, and he wasn't sure he could ask Laura out immediately. He knew that most women won't go on a date with someone their friend likes.

But David didn't get frustrated. The complicated situation just showed him that God has His own version of perfect timing. And it gave David more time to heal and to get to know Laura better as a friend before asking her out.

How can you get to know others without rebounding? Take the initiative and invite a group of people to dinner. If you aren't an organizer, ask one of your social-director friends to plan a night out with friends. Sit by new people at Bible study or at church, join a singles group, or start playing a coed sport. Start investing in people who share similar interests, and you will find friends who can support you as you heal and maybe even a few potential future dates!

Get to know people of the opposite sex—especially ones you don't think you would ever date. The least you will have is the opportunity to develop good friendships.

Finally, believe in yourself and work to develop your self-confidence. Remember that God is not through with you yet. Even if every person in the world were to reject you, the Lord never will. In fact, you can endure the pain of rejection and broken dreams easier because He is the only one who determines your value. When you trust your life to Jesus, you will never lose. You are worth the whole world (Mark 8:34). You can have a good view of yourself because God is upholding you, developing you, and giving you perspective.

The Top Three Ways a Guy Can Honor a Woman on a First Date

1. *Be chivalrous.* That old saying that chivalry is dead is a lie. Guys, be gentlemen, and you will win the respect of your gal. Open the door for her. Bring her flowers. Pay for dinner.
2. *Be a listener.* Really listen to what she has to say. Too often, guys talk about themselves because they are trying to impress women. But women like to be heard and understood. As the relational gender, women tend to warm up when they know someone is truly listening and has a sincere desire to know their hearts.
3. *Be intentional.* If you are interested, then let her know. You can communicate this in a variety of ways, whatever your style is. For example, if you really like a women, don't take her to Starbucks (unless her favorite restaurant is Starbucks). Step it up a bit. You don't have to blow all your extra money, but showing her that you are a man with a plan will help her trust you and will impress her.

Invest in Others

Whenever I was hurt because of a broken relationship, I was tempted to withdraw from people to wallow in my loneliness and self-pity. But God showed me I was responding to my pain in the wrong way. Christ said the second greatest commandment is to love people (Matthew 22:39). A breakup is a great time to focus on reaching out to others in love despite our feelings of pain, depression, or discouragement.

Sure, you may not feel like it at first, but you will find healing for your pain in making others happy. This is an interesting phenomenon. The more I reached out to others, the less time and energy I had to feel sorry for myself. The more I saw the real need and pain of others in situations worse than mine, the better I felt.

In the midst of your hurt, you still have something to offer another person, even if it's just a listening ear. As you listen, you will discover you are not alone in your pain. Others are suffering too, and you can minister to them from what you have learned. Paul instructs us to comfort others with the comfort we have received from God. God heals us so that we can help others to heal (2 Corinthians 1:3-7). Listen to them and share with them what God has done for you. This will bring healing to your soul as you reach out and comfort others.

But this doesn't have to be the typical "helping little old ladies cross the street" kind of gesture. Helping little old ladies cross the street is, of course, just fine. But you also can get creative and organize fun projects that can be whatever you want them to be.

Offer to paint a nursing home residents' fingernails, go help build a house with Habitat for Humanity, or organize a food drive or a Christmas shopping spree for a less fortunate family. Adopt a military unit serving abroad and send the soldiers care packages, gather formal dresses from your friends (the ones usually only worn once!) and donate them to a program for high school girls who can't afford prom dresses, or send an anonymous donation to a charity, to your church, or to a neighbor.

Pick out a few activities you have an interest in and take charge of the details. Investing your time will not only make your heart feel better but will also take your mind off the breakup.

Also, pray for opportunities to invest in those ministries while you are single. Katie, a 30-year-old teacher in Florida, always knew her single years were a preparation period for a future time in her life when God would use her as a wife and a mom. But she didn't just sit during her preparation period. She prayed that God would help her to see the years as a special time for her and God alone. And she prayed for opportunities to invest in others and for fun friends.

God responded in big ways, sending her both friends and opportunities that not only helped her pass the time but also helped her live her life in significant ways.

Try New Things but Don't Go Overboard

Breaking up brings a few good things, and an open schedule is one of them. You can start enjoying all kinds of activities you didn't have a lot of time to do when you were with your Serious Girlfriend or Boyfriend.

You wanted to take Italian cooking lessons, but you always found yourself spending your evenings talking to Serious Boyfriend. You had planned to take up a basketball league, but your weekends were spent planning dates with Serious Girlfriend. You really wanted a dog, but all your money went to presents for your girlfriend or boyfriend and suddenly you had no extra money for dog food. Now instead of lamenting your new-found freedom, start looking for the opportunities to do the activities you've always wanted to try but didn't have the time or money to do.

But be careful. The key is not to go overboard. Nothing is wrong with a few new clothes or a new look, but just don't go overboard with your retail therapy. Don't buy with the mind-set you will get your ex back with your new clothes and look, and whatever you do, don't go into debt. Your ex-girlfriend or ex-boyfriend just isn't worth the wounds to your credit card.

When to Reconsider

Just when you thought you were getting over your ex-girlfriend or ex-boyfriend, you get a call or an email asking how you are and what you've been up to and adding the words you wanted to hear when the two of you split six months ago: "I've made a terrible mistake. You are the only one for me, and I want you back."

Ladies, I know this is an extremely vulnerable situation for you because as women, you love to hear compliments and to feel special. It's just an added bonus to have your ex-guy expound on his foolishness and how miserable he has been without you. Actually, men can be vulnerable in this scenario too. Everyone wants to be needed and loved, and if your past relationship was with a person you really cared about or even loved, then reconsidering can be especially trying.

But deciding to go back to a relationship that has ended is dangerous without a lot of prayer and a lot of direction from God. Give this question up to God and ask Him to show you the changes your ex-girlfriend or ex-boyfriend has made that will prove he or she has dealt with their blindspots and is ready to make the relationship work.

You've got a part in this too. If your ex-girlfriend or ex-boyfriend promises to prove to you that they have made changes and you can trust him or her again, then I'm challenging you to really hold up that standard and make him or her prove it before you consider another try at the relationship.

Going back is too easy if you still are sad or lonely or missing your ex. And without careful thought, the relationship could send you on an emotional roller coaster all over again. You might remember the great times the two of you shared, when in reality, the two of you as a pair were a disaster waiting to happen. Often we remember only the romantic day trip to the beach, the boat ride where you two spotted dolphins jumping through the surf, and the sunset kisses...etc.

Rarely will you dwell on the ten fights spread out over the four times you broke up, but you must face reality. Remember Leigh, the woman whose boyfriend, Nick, cheated on her while a California wildfire blazed outside? Leigh struggled during the post-breakup months to remember the reasons why the two had gone their separate ways. So she made a list and hung it on her wall. But this wasn't just any list. It was a poster-size version that she couldn't miss every morning when she woke up. It read something like this:

Top Ten Reasons Why I'm Glad I'm Not with Nick Anymore

10. He doesn't want to be with me.

9. He ran from our problems.

8. He won't talk to me.
7. He said he loved me and wanted to marry me, but he didn't know what he wanted.
6. He couldn't make his mind up about me.
5. He flirts in front of me.
4. He wouldn't tell me the truth.
3. He planned a trip with another woman.
2. He told our friends we broke up because we didn't have chemistry.
1. He forgot my birthday.

The list wasn't intended to help Leigh hold on to bitterness, and, in fact, it didn't. Often she would have dreams in which Nick was playing the part of the perfect boyfriend. Waking up to the list was difficult, but it grounded Leigh in the reality of the situation.

Sometimes remembering the negative helps us to move on because it is truth. When we fall in love, we don't always see the whole picture immediately. As Leigh's dad told her after Nick broke up with her the second time, "Now it's time to get mad." I'm not suggesting you go on an all-out angry rage against your ex-girlfriend or ex-boyfriend. What I'm saying is that we have to look at the situation realistically. That means being honest about your feelings when someone has wronged us and calling the situation what it is. Of course, Jesus commands us to forgive. But in evaluating the aftermath, the problems of the relationship, and the character of your ex, all of which are very real, you're going to be thankful you're not reconsidering a relationship with the same lovestruck eyes and heart you had in the beginning.

I almost never recommend getting back together with an ex. Usually it doesn't work out. But for those of you reconsidering, make sure you can answer yes to what I call the Big Three checklist for relationships the second time around.

1. Have You Both Consulted God?

God has your life, and He can work good through anything for those who love Him. But He has a reason for closing doors and saying no to the relationship you may have desperately wanted. The only way you're going to know if you should reconsider a relationship is by hearing from God first. That takes prayer. In your conversations with God, ask Him to reveal the character of the man or woman you should date, to point out the warnings, to show you a man or woman who is repentant and is willing to work on the blind spots that gave the two of you trouble in the past. He is going to give you an answer sooner or later. He's just not on our time schedule! Hold onto the Lord's promise: "Do not be anxious about anything, but in everything, by prayer and petition, with thanksgiving, present your requests to God. And the peace, which transcends all understanding, will guard your hearts and your minds in Christ Jesus" (Philippians 4:6-7).

2. Does Your Ex Have a Repentant Heart?

Surely he or she is sorry for cheating on you. But is their heart truly repentant? Repentance has everything to do with turning away from the sin. We may mess up again, but we will have what Paul called a "godly sorrow" (2 Corinthians 7:10). It's a condition of the heart that has been touched by the consequences of the sin and the gravity of God's forgiveness. It's a heart that strives not to selfishly and recklessly make the same mistakes again. If your ex still is comfortable with the sin in his or her life, then he or she isn't going to think of you or God first.

3. Has Your Ex's Character Withstood the Test of Time?

While you are waiting on God's answer, evaluate how your ex has changed. Keep praying that God will reveal to you the changes. Sometimes only time will tell if the old patterns will trump the new or vice versa. If your ex-girlfriend was one to drag out fights, then has she put more effort into being a peacemaker? If your ex-boyfriend said he was going to earn your trust back, then does he follow through with even the small things, like calling when he says he will? Change requires great effort, and it can't be done without God's help. Unless your ex is committed to relying on God and following through with the changes that will help make your relationship better the next time around, he or she isn't really serious about you or the relationship. You don't have to turn into a private investigator or watch your ex with an eagle eye. You'll be able to tell by paying attention to how he or she relates to you in daily situations.

Learning What Real Love Is
(Chris, age 30, is a newspaper reporter, Naples, Florida.)

I knew I wanted her from the moment I saw her. She's beautiful, smarter than she thinks, sweet, and funny. She and I were close friends. We confided. I was the one she called in tears when her latest boyfriend had hurt her. I was the one who protected her name when people badmouthed her. I fell in love with her, but she didn't feel the same. Never did. And we never talked about it. But in the end, I felt exploited.

There's an easy way to prevent someone from hurting you. Say no. Take your life back. Be honest when she hurts you. Explain how you respect her and like her but also how her actions have hurt you. The measure of how she truly feels about you will come in her response to that. If she feels about you the same fondness you feel for her, she'll try to fix what's wrong for the sake of the friendship.

And recently I've learned something even more important. As I've discovered the promises the Holy Spirit has made to us, I've found that my own feelings of self-worth shouldn't be wrapped up in the whims of a female. I can get over her and let her go. I can trust God, and even though His direction for me may not be according to my timing, He'll provide.

Remember that we need to say no to some things. We've got to learn to say no to anything that will sidetrack us from what we know is godly and right. In our culture, saying no to any kind of pleasure is nearly unheard of because it means holding back on your fun. Our culture urges us to satisfy our cravings and do what feels good. But if you follow that advice, pretty soon you're going to get caught up in the glitz and glitter of the world that leads to wrong choices, pain, and sorrow.

Say no to people who don't respect your standards. If you are involved in a relationship that is eroding your moral integrity, you need to say no to that relationship. "But," you may object, "she'll be hurt." Perhaps, but by continuing the relationship you are being damaged. Don't try to play God in that person's life. Do what you must do to honor Christ, and leave the other person in God's hands.

Say no to people who aren't faithful. In today's married world, it's estimated that more than 40 percent of all marriages have had a spouse cheat. Don't put yourself through a relationship as a single with a man or woman who can't commit to you. If you have been cheated on, and your ex has shown a repentant, undivided heart to the Lord, then giving him or her a second chance may be appropriate. But remember, you aren't married yet. You have an out, and you can say no to someone who has questionable character or someone who isn't ready to be faithful to you. Dating prepares people for marriage, and if he or she isn't practicing fidelity now, he or she won't after the two of you exchange vows. God can change people's lives, but you need to remember that you may not be part of the equation right now or ever. Don't stay with someone who isn't going to honor you.

Say no to people who tear you down. Relationships are emotional, no doubt, and the intensity of those emotions is sometimes overwhelming. But relationships that are emotionally abusive are the ones you want to get out of quickly. Does your ex-girlfriend or ex-boyfriend verbally or physically abuse you because he or she gets wrapped up in emotion? Does he or she criticize you harshly, blame you for everything, and later apologize with crying and presents? Does he or she drag out fights by talking about the same problems over and over again without trying to work on a solution? I can't say for sure (except in the case of physical abuse) because you need to evaluate the situation and the person you know, but I would wonder if your ex-girlfriend or ex-boyfriend is being manipulative. If so, then he or she is making the relationship very unhealthy, and you need to say a permanent goodbye.

Saying no to a relationship is not the end of the world, although it may feel like it for a while. It was during the hard times when I went through a breakup that I learned some great lessons about myself, love, friendship, and trusting God. If you let God teach you to say no to wrong relationships, you will gain more than you ever expected. If you follow Christ diligently, you will never be sorry.

How to Break Up with the Wrong One

Several relationships may come and go before you find the person who is going to be the best match for you. Breakups hurt, but one of the biggest mistakes you can make is staying with the wrong person. Anyone who has gone through a breakup doesn't wish again for the pain that comes along with it. But ultimately, it can be the best decision for both people, even though it will require tremendous courage and honesty. But there is a right way and wrong way to say goodbye, a way that can cause unneeded pain to the other person and a way that can build them up and leave them at peace.

Seek God's Wisdom and Guidance

God will give you wisdom in what to do and how to do it (James 1:2-8). When going through the difficult and painful task of severing a relationship, knowing God's hand is guiding you can give you confidence. He promises to go before you and give you courage and strength.

In the struggle of trying to determine His will, I have often turned to this wonderful promise: "Trust in the LORD with all your heart, and do not lean on your own understanding. In all your ways acknowledge Him, and He will make your paths straight" (Proverbs 3:5-6 NASB). The Lord is interested in everything about you and desires to show you the steps to take so that your decisions and actions will be the best for you and for others.

God gives you not only guidance but also strength to do what is right. The apostle Paul expressed his thanks to God for His power to do the impossible: "Now to Him who is able to do exceeding abundantly beyond all that we ask or think, according to the power that works within us, to Him *be* the glory in the church and in Christ Jesus to all generations forever and ever" (Ephesians 3:20-21 NASB). His power works to overcome our weakness and fear. Saying goodbye to someone you have been dating is not easy. Emotions and nervousness can make the situation tense and awkward. God's courage and guidance are available to you when you trust Him (see Philippians 4:19).

Seek His wisdom. Ask Him for help. He understands what you are feeling and the difficult place in which you find yourself. And remember, He definitely wants you to know the happiness and joy of a relationship that builds you up and fulfills you instead of one that tears you down and frustrates you.

He is the God of all peace and comfort. You can always come to Him, knowing He is there to help you. Trust Him. He knows what is best for you, and He wants to help you find it.

Prepare Yourself

Think through as clearly as possible your reasons and motives for breaking up. What are the contributing factors that have brought you to this decision? Are your motives honest, kind, and sincere? Are they consistent with God's Word?

Never break up merely to get attention or sympathy or to elicit a *deeper* commitment from your partner. That is playing a deceitful game. Never break up just to express anger or hostility or to put someone in his or her place. Strong emotions may be involved, but express your thoughts decisively and firmly—and kindly.

If the other person doesn't want to break up, you may have to deal with defensive feelings and attempts to hold on to the relationship. When you clearly understand the things that are causing you to break up, and when you express them honestly, clearly, and calmly, you will be able to handle the pleas from the other person more effectively. Have your conclusions and reasons well thought out *ahead* of time. (Writing them down can be helpful.)

Ask Close Friends for Advice

Go to some strong Christians you can trust. Your pastor or an older couple may be able to help you. Share with them your situation. In sharing, do not spread lies or half-truths to gain support for your side. Simply tell them your honest thoughts and feelings. Ask for their advice and prayer support. What would they do in your situation? Do they *agree* with your approach? Can they support you in your action? Proverbs 12:15 (NASB) says, "The way of a fool is right in his own eyes, But a wise man is he who listens to counsel."

Get Together

If at all possible, find a time and a place where you and your dating partner can meet alone. Never try to break up in public or in front of friends. That would be very embarrassing for both of you and could easily cause resentment. If you are geographically separated, if the situation is too threatening or if you are afraid of physical abuse, write to the person. "Dear John letters" are infamous, but in reality, you often can express your feelings more clearly in a letter. Writing can be a very practical and mature way of ending a relationship. Follow up with a phone call to make sure you were understood, and talk it over with a positive attitude.

If possible, however, meet face-to-face. Because you have shared your life in a special way, closing the relationship in a personal conversation together is the gracious thing to do. When you look for a place, choose a non-romantic setting. Backing down on your intentions is easy in this emotional time, but later you would regret it.

Remember to allow time for talking and sharing feelings. Don't just drop the bomb and leave. Discuss the situation. Endeavor not to be hurried or just to blurt out your decision without being sensitive to the other person's reactions. Be firm, but treat the person as you would want to be treated in the same situation.

Tell the Truth in Love

Ephesians says, "But speaking the truth in love, we are to grow up in all aspects into Him, who is the head, even Christ" (Ephesians 4:15). To speak the truth in love means that truth without love is harsh, just as love without truth is hollow. We need both truthful love and loving truth. Don't play games. Avoid making double-meaning statements and telling half-truths or "little white lies." Be honest; try to express your reasons and your feelings as tactfully and positively as possible. Transparency may be very difficult with your emotions so involved, but you can rely on Christ to give you wisdom and peace of mind. Express very openly that you appreciate and value your friendship but that you do not desire your relationship to continue on a romantic basis. And if you feel the best arrangement would be not to see the person for a while because of deep hurt or a potentially uncomfortable situation, be open with your feelings and expectations. Tell the truth, but do it in love.

If the individual has bad habits or attitudes that are definitely wrong, express these in a gentle but positive manner. The book of Matthew tells us we are to confront a person who has sinned and done something wrong (Matthew 18:15-17). Help the person realize that although your relationship is no longer the same, you want to build him up. Don't act like a boss or a judge or make personal attacks. Rather, point out in love the things that concern you. Don't hurt the other person on purpose even if you have been hurt yourself. The way you say things can mean the difference between devastation and development.

Might you be the one who has acted improperly at times? Have you wrongfully hurt your dating partner? If so, you need to seek forgiveness for your unloving actions or attitudes. We should seek forgiveness and cleansing first from God. If we humbly come to Him with our sins and disobedience, He removes all barriers that prevent us from having close fellowship with Him (see Colossians 2:13-14).

However, Christ has added a new dimension. "If therefore you are presenting your offering [gifts] at the altar, and there remember that your brother has something against you, leave your offering there before the altar, and go your way; first be reconciled to your brother, and then come and present your offering" (Matthew 5:23-24 NASB). Having a clear conscience before God and before a person you have wronged is a wonderful thing. Take that difficult step of forgiveness. Even if the person is obstinate and refuses to forgive you because of the pain he or she feels, you can walk away free. You have taken the proper approach. Your acceptance is in God. He has cleansed you and does not condemn (Romans 8:1). The memory of your behavior may linger, but you have received God's forgiveness. Learn from the experience so that in a future relationship you will act differently.

When I was dating a woman named Gail, I did several very selfish things. I didn't show deep concern for the problems she faced with her parents and with her job. My lack of thoughtfulness bothered her. She became frustrated with me and eventually broke off our relationship. I was blind to my self-centeredness. Several weeks later I finally realized I had acted selfishly and asked her to forgive me. Although we never had another date, my conscience was cleared. Through it all, God taught me some significant lessons, and I learned to be more sensitive and kind to the women I dated.

Paula has been very thankful for my past relationships because I learned things from them, things that have helped develop my present attitudes and behavior. She learned many significant things about men from her previous dating relationships. Therefore, when Paula and I got married, we both benefited from many of the painful lessons we had learned in the past.

Be Definite

The person may try to dissuade you or may become angry and defensive. Your emotions may be in an upheaval. However, the Bible says to "let your yes be yes, and your no, no" (James 5:12 NASB). If you vacillate, the person may take advantage of your indecisiveness and play on your emotions to make you feel guilty or unsure. However, if you have thought through your reasons clearly and have sensed God's guidance, then in a gentle and kind manner, you can be clear and firm.

Reconsideration does have its place, however. If you openly discuss the things that really bother you and sincerely plan steps to change unwanted behavior, you might choose to continue the relationship. But if in your heart and mind you believe you definitely should not continue, then you should express that. Make a clean break. Sever the relationship, but do not destroy the person in the process. Give time for a response, but stick to your guns.

Remember, you can love a person without wanting to be married to that person. Not all love is marriage love.

The Oreo Cookie Approach: How to Break Up in the Best Way Possible

Once you've decided it's time to break-up (or that you just don't want to go out on another date with a girl or guy), that dreaded conversation when you have to end things looms. It won't be easy, but follow this three-step process to get on with the breakup and still leave your date with a sincere and encouraging ending.

1. *The top cookie:* Start with something encouraging and specific. ("I've really enjoyed getting to know you. You are such an interesting person and obviously have a heart for God.")

2. *The cookie filling:* This is the breakup part. Try to be succinct. Practice beforehand what you will say so you sound confident. ("But you know, I don't think this is going to work. I just want to be honest up front

because I don't want either one of us to get hurt more than we have to at this point.")

3. *The bottom cookie:* End with something encouraging and specific. ("I want you to know that I really appreciated you spending time with me and getting to know me. I have really valued our time together and although this is hard, I know God is going to do great things in both our lives.")

Part 4:
God's Instructions for a Healthy Love Relationship

Do you want to know exactly what God thinks about the topics covered in this book? He has given us His ideas and thoughts in the Bible.

In order to have a truly satisfying life—and enjoy successful relationships—it's vitally important that you make sure your thoughts and behavior are in line with His will for you. When you think and live according to His will, you will experience His rewards and His blessings.

The following "Quotes by God" give you passages on the four topics covered in this book. Study the verses often and meditate on their meaning. Ask God to apply them to your life. Memorize several passages in each category so you will have them in your mind when temptations hit you or when doubts come.

When I was a young boy, I learned a little saying that has carried me through many rough waters:

"God said it; I believe it; and that settles it."

Fill your mind and your life with the Word of God. Thank Him for His promises. They are yours to rely upon.

Singles and Sex

Exodus 20:14

You shall not commit adultery.

Proverbs 2:16-22

[Wisdom] will save you also from the adulteress, from the wayward wife with her seductive words, who has left the partner of her youth and ignored the covenant she made before God. For her house leads down to death and her paths to the spirits of the dead. None who go to her return or attain the paths of life. Thus you will walk in the ways of good men and keep to the paths of the righteous. For the upright will live in the land, and the blameless will remain in it; but the wicked will be cut off from the land, and the unfaithful will be torn from it.

Proverbs 5:1-23

My son, pay attention to my wisdom, listen well to my words of insight, that you may maintain discretion and your lips may preserve knowledge. For the lips of an adulteress drip honey, and her speech is smoother than oil; but in the end she is bitter as gall, sharp as a double-edged sword. Her feet go down to death; her steps lead straight to the grave. She gives no thought to the way of life; her paths are crooked, but she knows it not.

Now then, my sons, listen to me; do not turn aside from what I say. Keep to a path far from her; do not go near the door of her house, lest you give your best strength to others and your years to one who is cruel, lest strangers feast on your wealth and your toil enrich another man's house. At the end of your life you will groan, when your flesh and body are spent. You will say, "How I hated discipline! How my heart spurned correction! I would not obey my teachers or listen to my instructors. I have come to the brink of utter ruin in the midst of the whole assembly."

Drink water from your own cistern, running water from your own well. Should your springs overflow in the streets, your streams of water in the public squares? Let them be yours alone, never to be shared with strangers. May your fountain be blessed, and may you rejoice in the wife of your youth. A loving doe, a graceful deer—may her breasts satisfy you always, may you ever be captivated by her love. Why be captivated, my son, by an adulteress? Why embrace the bosom of another man's wife?

For a man's ways are in full view of the LORD, and he examines all his paths. The evil deeds of a wicked man ensnare him; the cords of his sin hold him fast. He will die for lack of discipline, led astray by his own great folly.

Proverbs 6:23-35

These commands are a lamp, this teaching is a light, and the corrections of discipline are the way to life, keeping you from the immoral woman, from the smooth tongue of the wayward wife. Do not lust in your heart after her beauty or let her captivate you with her eyes, for the prostitute reduces you to a loaf of bread, and the adulteress preys upon your very life. Can a man scoop fire into his lap without his clothes being burned? Can a man walk on hot coals without his feet being scorched? So is he who sleeps with another man's wife; no one who touches her will go unpunished.

Men do not despise a thief if he steals to satisfy his hunger when he is starving. Yet if he is caught, he must pay sevenfold, though it costs him all the wealth of his house. But a man who commits adultery lacks judgment; whoever does so destroys himself. Blows and disgrace are his lot, and his shame will never be wiped away; for jealousy arouses a husband's fury, and he will show no mercy when he takes revenge. He will not accept any compensation; he will refuse the bribe, however great it is.

Matthew 5:27-30

You have heard that it was said, "Do not commit adultery." But I tell you that anyone who looks at a woman lustfully has already committed adultery with her in his heart. If your right eye causes you to sin, gouge it out and throw it away. It is better for you to lose one part of your body than for your whole body to be thrown into hell. And if your right hand causes you to sin, cut it off and throw it away. It is better for you to lose one part of your body than for your whole body to go into hell.

Romans 13:12-14

The night is nearly over; the day is almost here. So let us put aside the deeds of darkness and put on the armor of light. Let us behave decently, as in the daytime, not in orgies and drunkenness, not in sexual immorality and debauchery, not in dissension and jealousy. Rather, clothe yourselves with the Lord Jesus Christ, and do not think about how to gratify the desires of the sinful nature.

1 Corinthians 5:9-11

I have written you in my letter not to associate with sexually immoral people—not at all meaning the people of this world who are immoral, or the greedy and swindlers, or idolaters. In that case you would have to leave this world. But now I am writing you that you must not associate with anyone who calls himself a brother but is sexually immoral or greedy, an idolater or a slanderer, a drunkard or a swindler. With such a man do not even eat.

1 Corinthians 6:13-20

"Food for the stomach and the stomach for food"—but God will destroy them both. The body is not meant for sexual immorality, but for the Lord, and the Lord for the body. By his power God raised the Lord from the dead, and he will raise us also. Do you not know that your bodies are members of Christ himself? Shall I then take the members of Christ and unite them with a prostitute? Never! Do you not know that he who unites himself with a prostitute is one with her in body? For it is said, "The two will become one flesh." But he who unites himself with the Lord is one with him in spirit.

Flee from sexual immorality. All other sins a man commits are outside his body, but he who sins sexually sins against his own body. Do you not know that your body is a temple of the Holy Spirit, who is in you, whom you have received from God? You are not your own; you were bought at a price. Therefore honor God with your body.

Ephesians 5:3-7

Among you there must not be even a hint of sexual immorality, or of any kind of impurity, or of greed, because these are improper for God's holy people. Nor should there be obscenity, foolish talk or coarse joking, which are out of place, but rather thanksgiving. For of this you can be sure: No immoral, impure or greedy person—such a man is an idolater—has any inheritance in the kingdom of Christ and of God. Let no one deceive you with empty words, for because of such things God's wrath comes on those who are disobedient. Therefore do not be partners with them.

1 Thessalonians 4:3-8

It is God's will that you should be sanctified: that you should avoid sexual immorality; that each of you should learn to control his own body in a way that is holy and honorable, not in passionate lust like the heathen, who do not know God; and that in this matter no one should wrong his brother or take advantage of him. The Lord will punish men for all such sins, as we have already told you and warned you. For God did not call us to be impure, but to live a holy life. Therefore, he who rejects this instruction does not reject man but God, who gives you his Holy Spirit.

Revelation 21:6-8

He said to me: "It is done. I am the Alpha and the Omega, the Beginning and the End. To him who is thirsty I will give to drink without cost from the spring of the water of life. He who overcomes will inherit all this, and I will be his God and he will be my son. But the cowardly, the unbelieving, the vile, the murderers, the sexually immoral, those who practice magic arts, the idolaters and all liars—their place will be in the fiery lake of burning sulfur. This is the second death."

Revelation 22:13-16

I am the Alpha and the Omega, the First and the Last, the Beginning and the End. Blessed are those who wash their robes, that they may have the right to the tree of life and may go through the gates into the city. Outside are the dogs, those who practice magic arts, the sexually immoral, the murderers, the idolaters and everyone who loves and practices falsehood. I, Jesus, have sent my angel to give you this testimony for the churches. I am the Root and the Offspring of David, and the bright Morning Star.

Forgiveness and Restoration

Psalm 51:1-12

Have mercy on me, O God, according to your unfailing love; according to your great compassion blot out my transgressions. Wash away all my iniquity and cleanse me from my sin. For I know my transgressions, and my sin is always before me. Against you, you only, have I sinned and done what is evil in your sight, so that you are proved right when you speak and justified when you judge. Surely I was sinful at birth, sinful from the time my mother conceived me. Surely you desire truth in the inner parts; you teach me wisdom in the inmost place. Cleanse me with hyssop, and I will be clean; wash me, and I will be whiter than snow. Let me hear joy and gladness; let the bones you have crushed rejoice. Hide your face from my sins and blot out all my iniquity. Create in me a pure heart, O God, and renew a steadfast spirit within me. Do not cast me from your presence or take your Holy Spirit from me. Restore to me the joy of your salvation and grant me a willing spirit, to sustain me.

Psalm 103:12

As far as the east is from the west, so far has he removed our transgressions from us.

Isaiah 1:18

"Come now, let us reason together," says the LORD. "Though your sins are like scarlet, they shall be as white as snow; though they are red as crimson, they shall be like wool."

Romans 6:22-23

Now that you have been set free from sin and have become slaves to God, the benefit you reap leads to holiness, and the result is eternal life. For the wages of sin is death, but the gift of God is eternal life in Christ Jesus our Lord.

1 Corinthians 6:9-11

Do you not know that the wicked will not inherit the kingdom of God? Do not be deceived: neither the sexually immoral nor idolaters nor adulterers nor male prostitutes nor homosexual offenders nor thieves nor the greedy nor drunkards nor slanderers nor swindlers will inherit the kingdom of God. And that is what some of you were. But you were washed, you were sanctified, you were justified in the name of the Lord Jesus Christ and by the Spirit of our God.

2 Corinthians 5:17

Therefore, if anyone is in Christ, he is a new creation; the old has gone, the new has come!

Ephesians 1:3-4

Praise be to the God and Father of our Lord Jesus Christ, who has blessed us in the heavenly realms with every spiritual blessing in Christ. For he chose us in him before the creation of the world to be holy and blameless in his sight.

Ephesians 2:1-10

As for you, you were dead in your transgressions and sins, in which you used to live when you followed the ways of this world and of the ruler of the kingdom of the air, the spirit who is now at work in those who are disobedient. All of us also lived among them at one time, gratifying the cravings of our sinful nature and following its desires and thoughts. Like the rest, we were by nature objects of wrath. But because of his great love for us, God, who is rich in mercy, made us alive with Christ even when we were dead in transgressions—it is by grace you have been saved. And God raised us up with Christ and seated us with him in the heavenly realms in Christ Jesus, in order that in the coming ages he might show the incomparable riches of his grace, expressed in his kindness to us in Christ Jesus. For it is by grace you have been saved, through faith—and this not from yourselves, it is the gift of God—not by works, so that no one can boast. For we are God's workmanship, created in Christ Jesus to do good works, which God prepared in advance for us to do.

Colossians 2:13-14

When you were dead in your sins and in the uncircumcision of your sinful nature, God made you alive with Christ. He forgave us all our sins, having canceled the written code, with its regulations, that was against us and that stood opposed to us; he took it away, nailing it to the cross.

Hebrews 10:15-17

The Holy Spirit also testifies to us about this [one sacrifice]. First he says: "This is the covenant I will make with them after that time, says the Lord. I will put my laws in their hearts, and I will write them on their minds." Then he adds: "Their sins and lawless acts I will remember no more."

1 John 1:7-9

If we walk in the light, as he is in the light, we have fellowship with one another, and the blood of Jesus, his Son, purifies us from all sin. If we claim to be without sin, we deceive ourselves and the truth is not in us. If we confess our sins, he is faithful and just and will forgive us our sins and purify us from all unrighteousness.

Benefits of Right Living

Psalm 1:1-3

Blessed is the man who does not walk in the counsel of the wicked or stand in the way of sinners or sit in the seat of mockers. But his delight is in the law of the LORD, and on his law he meditates day and night. He is like a tree planted by streams of water, which yields its fruit in season and whose leaf does not wither. Whatever he does prospers.

Psalm 37:27-31

Turn from evil and do good; then you will dwell in the land forever. For the LORD loves the just and will not forsake his faithful ones. They will be protected forever, but the offspring of the wicked will be cut off; the righteous will inherit the land and dwell in it forever. The mouth of the righteous man utters wisdom, and his tongue speaks what is just. The law of his God is in his heart; his feet do not slip.

Psalm 92:12-15

The righteous will flourish like a palm tree, they will grow like a cedar of Lebanon; planted in the house of the LORD, they will flourish in the courts of our God. They will still bear fruit in old age, they will stay fresh and green, proclaiming, "The LORD is upright; he is my Rock, and there is no wickedness in him."

Psalm 112:1-9

Praise the LORD. Blessed is the man who fears the LORD, who finds great delight in his commands. His children will be mighty in the land; the generation of the upright will be blessed. Wealth and riches are in his house, and his righteousness endures forever. Even in darkness light dawns for the upright, for the gracious and compassionate and righteous man. Good will come to him who is generous and lends freely, who conducts his affairs with justice. Surely he will never be shaken; a righteous man will be remembered forever. He will have no fear of bad news; his heart is steadfast, trusting in the LORD. His heart is secure, he will have no fear; in the end he will look in triumph on his foes. He has scattered abroad his gifts to the poor, his righteousness endures forever; his horn will be lifted high in honor.

Proverbs 11:30

The fruit of the righteous is a tree of life, and he who wins souls is wise.

Proverbs 14:34

Righteousness exalts a nation, but sin is a disgrace to any people.

Jeremiah 17:7-10

"Blessed is the man who trusts in the LORD, whose confidence is in him. He will be like a tree planted by the water that sends out its roots by the stream. It does not fear when heat comes; its leaves are always green. It has no worries in a year of drought and never fails to bear fruit." The heart is deceitful above all things and beyond cure. Who can understand it? "I the LORD search the heart and examine the mind, to reward a man according to his conduct, according to what his deeds deserve."

Matthew 5:3-12

Blessed are the poor in spirit, for theirs is the kingdom of heaven. Blessed are those who mourn, for they will be comforted. Blessed are the meek, for they will inherit the earth. Blessed are those who hunger and thirst for righteousness, for they will be filled. Blessed are the merciful, for they will be shown mercy. Blessed are the pure in heart, for they will see God. Blessed are the peacemakers, for they will be called sons of God. Blessed are those who are persecuted because of righteousness, for theirs is the kingdom of heaven. Blessed are you when people insult you, persecute you and falsely say all kinds of evil against you because of me. Rejoice and be glad, because great is your reward in heaven, for in the same way they persecuted the prophets who were before you.

Romans 8:12-17

Brothers, we have an obligation—but it is not to the sinful nature, to live according to it. For if you live according to the sinful nature, you will die; but if by the Spirit you put to death the misdeeds of the body, you will live, because those who are led by the Spirit of God are sons of God. For you did not receive a spirit that makes you a slave again to fear, but you received the Spirit of sonship. And by him we cry, "*Abba, Father*." The Spirit himself testifies with our spirit that we are God's children. Now if we are children, then we are heirs—heirs of God and co-heirs with Christ, if indeed we share in his sufferings in order that we may also share in his glory.

2 Corinthians 4:16-18

Therefore we do not lose heart. Though outwardly we are wasting away, yet inwardly we are being renewed day by day. For our light and momentary troubles are achieving for us an eternal glory that far outweighs them all. So we fix our eyes not on what is seen, but on what is unseen. For what is seen is temporary, but what is unseen is eternal.

Galatians 5:16-25

So I say, live by the Spirit, and you will not gratify the desires of the sinful nature. For the sinful nature desires what is contrary to the Spirit, and the Spirit what is contrary to the sinful nature. They are in conflict with each other, so that you do not do what you want. But if you are led by the Spirit, you are not under law. The acts of the sinful nature are obvious: sexual immorality, impurity and debauchery; idolatry and witchcraft; hatred, discord, jealousy, fits of rage, selfish ambition, dissensions, factions and envy; drunkenness, orgies, and the like. I warn you, as I did before, that those who live like this will not inherit the kingdom of God. But the fruit of the Spirit is love, joy, peace, patience, kindness, goodness, faithfulness, gentleness and self-control. Against such things there is no law. Those who belong to Christ Jesus have crucified the sinful nature with its passions and desires. Since we live by the Spirit, let us keep in step with the Spirit.

Revelation 2:7

He who has an ear, let him hear what the Spirit says to the churches. To him who overcomes, I will give the right to eat from the tree of life, which is in the paradise of God.

Temptation Busters

Psalm 139:23-24

Search me, O God, and know my heart; test me and know my anxious thoughts. See if there is any offensive way in me, and lead me in the way everlasting.

1 Corinthians 10:12-13

So, if you think you are standing firm, be careful that you don't fall! No temptation has seized you except what is common to man. And God is faithful; he will not let you be tempted beyond what you can bear. But when you are tempted, he will also provide a way out so that you can stand up under it.

Ephesians 6:10-18

Be strong in the Lord and in his mighty power. Put on the full armor of God so that you can take your stand against the devil's schemes. For our struggle is not against flesh and blood, but against the rulers, against the authorities, against the powers of this dark world and against the spiritual forces of evil in the heavenly realms. Therefore put on the full armor of God, so that when the day of evil comes, you may be able to stand your ground, and after you have done everything, to stand. Stand firm then, with the belt of truth buckled around your waist, with the breast-plate of righteousness in place, and with your feet fitted with the readiness that comes from the gospel of peace. In addition to all this, take up the shield of faith, with which you can extinguish all the flaming arrows of the evil one. Take the helmet of salvation and the sword of the Spirit, which is the word of God. And pray in the Spirit on all occasions with all kinds of prayers and requests. With this in mind, be alert and always keep on praying for all the saints.

Philippians 4:8-9

Finally, brothers, whatever is true, whatever is noble, whatever is right, whatever is pure, whatever is lovely, whatever is admirable—if anything is excellent or praise-worthy—think about such things. Whatever you have learned or received or heard from me, or seen in me—put it into practice. And the God of peace will be with you.

Colossians 3:1-10

Since, then, you have been raised with Christ, set your hearts on things above, where Christ is seated at the right hand of God. Set your minds on things above, not on earthly things. For you died, and your life is now hidden with Christ in God. When Christ, who is your life, appears, then you also will appear with him in glory. Put to death, therefore, whatever belongs to your earthly nature; sexual immorality, impurity, lust, evil desires and greed, which is idolatry. Because of these, the wrath of God is coming. You used to walk in these ways, in the life you once lived. But now you must rid yourselves of all such things as these: anger, rage, malice, slander and filthy language from your lips. Do not lie to each other, since you have taken off your old self with its practices and have put on the new self, which is being renewed in knowledge in the image of its Creator.

Titus 2:11-14

The grace of God that brings salvation has appeared to all men. It teaches us to say "No" to ungodliness and worldly passions, and to live self-controlled, upright and godly lives in this present age, while we wait for the blessed hope—the glorious appearing of our great God and Savior, Jesus Christ, who gave himself for us to redeem us from all wickedness and to purify for himself a people that are his very own, eager to do what is good.

James 4:7-8

Submit yourselves, then, to God. Resist the devil, and he will flee from you. Come near to God and he will come near to you. Wash your hands, you sinners, and purify your hearts, you double-minded.

1 Peter 5:6-9

Humble yourselves, therefore, under God's mighty hand, that he may lift you up in due time. Cast all your anxiety on him because he cares for you. Be self-controlled and alert. Your enemy the devil prowls around like a roaring lion looking for someone to devour. Resist him, standing firm in the faith, because you know that your brothers throughout the world are undergoing the same kind of sufferings.

2 Peter 1:3-9

His divine power has given us everything we need for life and godliness through our knowledge of him who called us by his own glory and goodness. Through these he has given us his very great and precious promises, so that through them you may participate in the divine nature and escape the corruption in the world caused by evil desires. For this very reason, make every effort to add to your faith goodness; and to goodness, knowledge; and to knowledge, self-control; and to self-control, perseverance; and to perseverance, godliness; and to godliness, brotherly kindness; and to brotherly kindness, love. For if you possess these qualities in increasing measure, they will keep you from being ineffective and unproductive in your knowledge of our Lord Jesus Christ. But if anyone does not have them, he is nearsighted and blind, and has forgotten that he has been cleansed from his past sins.

1 John 2:15-17

Do not love the world or anything in the world. If anyone loves the world, the love of the Father is not in him. For everything in the world—the cravings of sinful man, the lust of his eyes and the boasting of what he has and does—comes not from the Father but from the world. The world and its desires pass away, but the man who does the will of God lives forever.

1 John 4:4

You, dear children, are from God and have overcome them, because the one who is in you is greater than the one who is in the world.

Hebrews 12:1-3

Since we are surrounded by such a great cloud of witnesses, let us throw off everything that hinders and the sin that so easily entangles, and let us run with perseverance the race marked out for us. Let us fix our eyes on Jesus, the author and perfecter of our faith, who for the joy set before him endured the cross, scorning its shame, and sat down at the right hand of the throne of God. Consider him who endured such opposition from sinful men, so that you will not grow weary and lose heart.

Notes

Blind Spot 1—Talking Without Communicating

1. Laura Carrel, quoted in *The News & Observer,* March 17, 2005 (page A1) about a study reported in the journal *Nature,* March, 2005.
2. *Psychology Today,* 2003.

Blind Spot 2—"Poor Me" Attitude

1. *Washington Post,* July 20, 1977.
2. James Dobson, *Hide or Seek* (Grand Rapids, MI: Revell, 1974), p. 136.
3. Dick Purnell, *Discovering God's Unique Purpose for You* (Eugene, OR: Harvest House Publishers, 2005).

Blind Spot 3—Struggle for Control

1. Don Meredith, Sally Meredith, *Two Becoming One* (Chicago, IL: Moody Press, 1999), p. 38.
2. Dick Purnell, *Finding a Lasting Love* (Eugene, OR: Harvest House Publishers, 2003), pp. 41-160.

Blind Spot 4—Desires That Become Demands

1. "Janet Daily, Queen of Hearts," *Redbook* (June 1983), p. 66.

Bright Spot 5—Say Goodbye to the Wrong People

1. Dick Purnell, *Finding a Lasting Love* (Eugene, OR: Harvest House Publishers, 2003), pp. 45-49.

How to Heal Your Broken Heart

1. John Eldredge, *Waking the Dead* (Nashville, TN: Thomas Nelson, 2003).

Other Excellent Harvest House Books
by Dick Purnell

FINDING A LASTING LOVE

Singles make up 40 percent of the American adult population, and most of them want to find their lifelong mate. Dick Purnell reveals the questions, answers, and insights on dating he shares through conferences, interviews, and articles. Going straight to the heart of the matter, he discusses:

- insights for understanding the opposite sex
- how to avoid short-circuiting a good relationship
- suggestions for finding a potential partner and
- what God's Word says about relationship

Finding a Lasting Love is beyond a "how to" for the dating reader. It's a biblical exploration of relationships and an invitation to approach dating and life with a healthy, growing faith. Formerly *Becoming a Friend & Lover.*

31-DAY EXPERIMENT BIBLE STUDIES

Knowing God By His Names

Growing Closer to God

Discovering God's Unique Purpose for You

Singles and Relationships (with Kris Swiatocho)